SHADOW
PLANET

Books by William Shatner

QUEST FOR TOMORROW

Delta Search
In Alien Hands
Step into Chaos
Beyond the Stars
Shadow Planet

SHADOW PLANET

QUEST FOR TOMORROW

———

WILLIAM SHATNER

An Imprint of HarperCollins*Publishers*

EOS

An Imprint of HarperCollins*Publishers*
10 East 53rd Street
New York, New York 10022-5299

Copyright © 2002 by William Shatner

ISBN: 0-06-105119-5

Library of Congress Cataloging-in-Publication Data

Shatner, William.
  Shadow planet / William Shatner.
    p.   cm.—(Quest for tomorrow)
  ISBN 0-06-105119-5
  1. Life on other planets—Fiction.   I. Title.

PS3569.H347 S53   2002
813'.54—dc21

                                   2002025383

First Eos hardcover printing: November 2002

Eos Trademark Reg. U.S. Pat. Off. and in Other Countries,
Marca Registrada, Hecho en U.S.A.
HarperCollins® is a trademark of HarperCollins Publishers Inc.

Printed in the U.S.A.

FIRST EDITION

10 9 8 7 6 5 4 3 2 1

www.eosbooks.com

DEDICATION AND ACKNOWLEDGMENTS

The inspiration for many of these books has come from my own life.

I have gone through my passages and so does the redoubtable Jim Endicott.

Each memory, for both of us, colors the perception of our lives.

I was able to invest in Jim the grief and sorrow that I felt by the passing of my wife.

And so, too, I hope to shower on our Captain the good fortune that also comes in living a full life. Out of the ashes of a terrible experience comes the ability to regenerate and keep on growing. Jim Endicott finds new life and so do I. Once again, I look around me with hope and expectation, and so will our hero.

A new marriage, and a new granddaughter. Life continues its upward spiral. The grapes of life on the arbor of experience. I dedicate this book to my wife and granddaughter.

L'chaim.

SHADOW
PLANET

PROLOGUE

Death approached in the shape of a glittering child's game.

The *Outward Bound* seemed to hang motionless in deep space, nearly lost amid the greater glare of the billion stars that made up the Milky Way.

Inside its flimsy skin, ten million inhabitants continued with their lives. Most of them were not even aware of the drama that had recently played out in one of the main cargo bays, when the Stone Cowboys, led by Kerry Korrigan and Jim Endicott, had stood off a siege by the *Outward Bound*'s security forces from inside the Kolumban ship they'd hijacked.

Nor were they aware when a strangely shaped vessel popped out of subspace very close to the onrushing Terran colony ship.

Aboard the *Outward Bound*, no alarms sounded as this vessel appeared. First, nobody was watching for it. Second, even if someone had been watching, he wouldn't have seen it. The stealth technology used by those who flew it was far beyond the ability of Terran science to crack.

And even if the *Outward Bound* had been able to penetrate this ship's cloaking devices, Terran observers might not have recognized the ship for what it was. It certainly didn't look like anything a Terran would have called a space vessel, nor did it resemble the ships used by the Hunzza or the Albagens, either.

The Terrans might have recognized it for something else, though: The *I Ching* was still thrown, and the resulting jumble of sticks still interpreted. This ship resembled nothing so much as a handful of such thrown sticks, a mystical scattering yet to be interpreted by human minds.

From a distance, it was three dozen glowing green rods, a pretty thing, almost a toy. From a distance, it looked tiny. From a distance, it was impossible to see its true size, nearly three miles long and half a mile across its central axis, a shifting agglomeration bound together by titanic forces that operated on principles human science had not yet puzzled out.

Inside those sticklike cylinders, things *hummed*. The universe is full of surprises, and one of the greatest of these is the multitude of shapes, structures, and chemical arrangements that are capable of supporting not only life, but intelligent life.

Eons before apes scratched themselves and took their first tentative steps down from the trees on Terra, on a single planet much deeper into the galactic core, the light from the sun that warmed that planet began to shift.

The tiny, insectlike creatures there began to change in response to the higher measure of hard radiation that pierced their chlorine-laden atmosphere. At first they died by the trillions, but some survived, a version better equipped to thrive in the deadly rays that bathed their world.

These alien founding fathers were not intelligent; intelligence was a survival trait yet far in their future. But, washed constantly by radiation that dictated far too high a level of ruinous mutation, some found a way to control the changes that threatened them. They became partly radiant beings themselves. Rather than genes, they encoded their data in the most minuscule of vibrations, energies harnessed and bounded by their physical structures.

Intelligence came later, in response to different imperatives that bound them into shifting masses of light and matter. In time (and by a process best described as "ordered accident"), some of these amorphous blobs learned how to join in temporary union, thereby gaining enough complexity to support the transfer of information that we call intelligence.

Meanwhile, on Terra, the monkeys had stopped scratching themselves and throwing feces at one another long enough to turn their sticks into clubs and begin the long climb up the new tree called civilization.

Different time lines, different life-forms, different worlds, and those worlds in different places. Sharing between them only the one primeval and eternal command: *Survive!*

By the time humanity finally loosed itself from the gravity well of its own planet, these strange creatures, half flesh made of organic compounds seen only in Terran test tubes, and half energy spawned by the deadly radiations of their original sun, had expanded to a million worlds.

They learned to tinker with the hearts of stars and the skins of planets, learned how to create the utterly alien environments they needed to thrive.

By human standards, they moved slowly, a world at a time, but they had a lot longer to do what they needed to do, and when the monkey-humans finally boiled onto the universal stage, their own empire was vast.

Then the humans came, with all the shocking speed and ferocity of their expansion as they gobbled world after world. Humans in their great copulating masses, eating and swallowing with insatiable appetite and uncaring hunger as much of the galaxy as they could reach.

Like a cancer.

Something had to be done. In the councils of the world-minds, cautious as flickering match lights in a storm wind, it was determined that stealth would be best. Any revelation was potentially dangerous; by nature, the beings of flesh and energy practiced all the arts of concealment. Their entire genetic history had been a perfection of the art of hiding from the death that rained on them from their own star. It had made them more cautious than other races, and now caution ruled the plans they made. What could be done by indirection and deception would be done. Naked, direct force would remain only as a last resort, although in extremity that would be used, too.

So when the ship that looked like a game of pickup sticks, full of clicking flesh and flickering energy, slipped from the subquantum basements beneath the fat, thick atomic world, this ship was called *Last Resort* in the language of those who crewed it.

They were a literal people.

The *Last Resort* edged closer and closer to the lumbering *Outward Bound*, every electronic sensor probing, skittish as a moonbeam on a wind-tossed lake.

It wasn't so bad that the deception had failed, and that somehow the humans had discovered the deadly nature of Heat. That might have been dealt with. But what could not be tolerated was the possibility that the humans had penetrated beyond the living mask of the Kolumbans to the shadowy and hidden figures behind that mask. To themselves, in other words.

So the *Last Resort* came to do whatever was necessary, awaiting only the orders of the world-minds hidden deep within the shimmering heart of their empire.

Finally, a point of agreement, of consensus within the communion (that was what they called themselves, the Communers) was reached, and a message dispatched to the *Last Resort*. It was a difficult decision, and not without risks, but the Communers deemed the risk acceptable.

Various machines and strategies were activated aboard the *Last Resort*, energies shaped and channeled and finally loosed. The principle was arcane in the extreme, but the result simple. The *Last Resort* manipulated the warp and woof of space itself, shaking it like a rug, sending invisible but certainly not intangible ripples coursing in a vast arc toward the unsuspecting Terran colony ship . . .

The *Outward Bound* vibrated, then burst apart like a rotten fruit, ten million souls vaporized in a millisecond, and in another millisecond nothing was left but a slowly expanding ring of dusty white light, already fading.

The *Last Resort* stayed to collect confirmatory samples for the world-minds to analyze, but this didn't take long. When it was done, the Communer ship slipped back into subspace as quietly as it had come, leaving silence in its wake.

Survival is the only universal imperative.

CHAPTER ONE

1

The kid who was a killer stood just outside the room and listened to the conversation beyond the cracked-open door.

"You think we just finished the hard part, capturing this ship and escaping from the *Outward Bound*?" Kerry Korrigan was saying. "That was the easy part. *Now* we get to the hard part."

Korrigan smiled. It wasn't a pleasant expression. Jim Endicott knew it wasn't meant to be. There was a striking contrast between the two boys sprawled comfortably on the puffy, oversized furniture designed for alien shapes twice their own size. Endicott, his whip-slender frame corded with a compact layer of muscle, was dark-haired, green-eyed, thoughtful and sober, the sharp planes of his features muted and shadowy in the odd, orange-tinged alien light.

Korrigan, equally thin, was three inches taller, with fast-twitch reflexes that made him look as if he might leap at the ceiling on an instant's notice. With his sharp, high blond crew cut and eyes as blue as fresh-poured glass, he presented an impression of lazy elegance that belied the nervous undercurrents of his physical presence.

The killer, poised beyond the door, had known Korrigan for several years. Known him well enough to fear him. But it wasn't Korrigan he was thinking about killing.

Inside the room, Jim stretched, his movements slow and precise as a cat's. "You don't think breaking up the Stone Cowboys, a gang you started and led for three years, then hijacking a ship filled with huge, hostile aliens and resisting an armed attack by all the security forces of the *Outward Bound*, and *then* managing to keep those aliens from freeze-drying us in space vacuum was all that big a problem?"

"At the time, maybe it was." Korrigan flashed his switchblade grin again. "But that was yesterday. What have you done for me today?"

"You don't cut a guy any slack, do you? Maybe it should be you running the deal. You know that's what I wanted in the first place."

"And you know why I wouldn't take it. The reasons were good then, and they still are. I'm not bad shakes at running a street gang and organizing the dope trade, But this adventure-in-a-hijacked spaceship is a whole new thing. You've got the skills to run it. I don't. Maybe, in a few years, I'll pick up enough so I won't get us all killed if I'm in charge. But for now, Jimbo, you the man."

"And that makes you . . . ?"

"That makes me the number two man. I get to give my thug tendencies full sway. You give the orders. Somebody doesn't like them, I slap them around till they do like them."

"You don't look like you could slap around a week-old cream puff."

"So I gave a little blood for the cause in that fight with Darnell."

"And a few bruises, and some sprains, and some skin."

Korrigan shrugged. "Oh, you know. Can't dance without breaking a few eggs. Or bones. It'll heal."

"I've never had my own thug before."

"You never had a lot of things before, growing up in that nice, sheltered, middle-class hick environment of yours."

"Hey!"

"Not that I don't envy you for it. I never had it, and there were a lot of times I'd have given anything to get up in the morning and think I had my future all spread out in front of me."

"But you do. We do. The future's always in front of us. What do they say? Today is the first day of the rest of your life?"

"Huh. Is that so? It may be true, but if the rest of your life can be counted in days, what good is that?"

"I don't think it's that bad. Do you?"

Korrigan stared at him. "Like I've been trying to tell you, it ain't that good, either. You worry me sometimes, Jim."

"I do? How?"

"That underneath that soft, mushy exterior beats a heart of soft mush. If I didn't know better, I'd think you were a nice guy."

"What a terrible thing that would be."

"You don't get it, do you?" Korrigan said. "I mean, it's okay if you *are* a nice guy. But there are gonna be times you can't act like one."

"Well, sure. I know that."

"Do you? Really? What if you had to kill one of the kids. Not for consciously doing something bad, just for making a mistake."

"I can't imagine that happening."

"Which is what worries me. I can imagine it. I had to do it once. It wasn't easy, but it had to be done, and I did it. If I had to, I'd do it again."

"You killed one of the Cowboys?"

Korrigan looked away. "You sound like you're judging me. You shouldn't do that. Not till you understand the world you live in now. And especially not until you understand that the world you live in now is different from the world you grew up in."

"I didn't mean . . ."

"Sure you did. What I said horrified you. Come on, admit it."

"Well . . . maybe."

"Well, yes, is what you mean."

"What happened?"

"Something complicated."

"You don't want to tell me?"

"It's not something I'm proud of. But you do things you're not proud of because they have to be done, and somebody has to do them."

"All right, if you're not going to tell me . . ."

"Maybe I will. Someday. But right now, I'm afraid it would only get in the way."

Jim shifted. His left leg was starting to go to sleep. He wished the rest of him could follow suit. The last two weeks had been hectic. Even his sixteen-year-old resiliency had been sorely tested. The best thing he could imagine was twenty-four hours in a bed with clean sheets. Well, not quite the best. The absolute best would be in a bed with clean sheets and Samantha.

He doubted that either desire would be gratified any time soon.

"If you don't trust me, why did you back me up on everything? Even risk your own life?" he asked Kerry.

"Who said I don't trust you? I do trust you. But I trust you to be yourself. You can't help it, you *are* who and what you are."

"You don't seem to think much of what that is, then. Whatever I am."

"Jim, listen to me carefully. You don't have a clue about your own strengths. Or your own limitations. That's not unusual, most people don't. It takes somebody looking in from the outside to see the truth. As far as you're concerned, I'm that somebody."

"Does that work both ways?"

"Sure."

"Okay. Then I can live with it. I guess. You know what?"

"What?"

"You're an arrogant sonofabitch, aren't you?"

Kerry grinned. "Is that some of that outside-looking-in stuff?"

"Yeah, I guess."

"Well, I am an arrogant sonofabitch. But I'm not the most arrogant sonofabitch *in this room.*"

"You think?"

Kerry lurched to his feet with a soft groan and slapped Jim on the shoulder. "I *know.* Come on, let's see if Samantha has figured out how to use that alien galley to make something besides rancid pink paste. Remember when I warned you not to eat the brown food? Back in the cafeteria on the *Outward Bound*?"

"Sure."

"Know what? I miss the brown food."

"So do I. We didn't know when we had it good."

"Do we ever?"

Jim laughed. They moved toward the door.

In the hall beyond, the killer slipped away in silence, considering what he'd heard.

It was worse than he'd thought. He might have to kill Korrigan first. He wasn't sure if he could get that job done. But he thought he might try anyway.

2

Elwood Grieger, hands in pockets, leaned his eerily tall, frighteningly emaciated body against one wall of the corridor and stared blank-eyed at the featureless gray expanse on the other side.

Ferrick Autrey said, "Hey, Elwood, how you doing?"

Elwood jerked at the sound of Ferrick's voice, a spidery, startled convulsion.

"Whoa," Ferrick said. "What are you so jumpy about?"

Elwood looked like a kid trying to grow into his own body, and not succeeding well. He had big, knobby hands, a small, neat head, and feet like gunboats, all connected by a frame that seemed constructed of baling wire overlaid with a thin, tight-stretched layer of almond-colored skin. His gray eyes peered out at the world beneath epicanthic folds and a frenzied shock of reddish-blond hair that looked as if it had been spun from copper pennies.

If somebody had asked him about his ancestry, though nobody ever did, he would have grinned bitterly and said, "Mongrel."

Ferrick Autrey was a chocolate fireplug, as squat and broad as Elwood was lean and tall. His raisin-colored eyes twinkled above a nose like the prow of a battleship. He was so thickly muscled he looked as if he'd been inflated. The one thing the two boys shared was the quality of their gaze, a certain cold, remote steadiness that belied their youth. They had both seen and done things no kid should ever experience—and they had enjoyed it. Killer's eyes.

Elwood shrugged. "You know. This is a spooky ship. Makes you edgy."

"Stinks, too. Kolumbans smell like cinnamon-flavored dog food. You seen Kerry around?"

"Kerry?"

"Yeah, you know. Our former beloved leader."

A shadow flickered in Elwood's eyes. "Former leader. I want to talk to you some more about that."

Ferrick shook his head. "We already talked, Elwood. What's done is done. The Stone Cowboys are gone. And Kerry ain't the leader no more."

"I don't know . . ."

"You better know. Just deal with it, okay? It ain't gonna change. Might as well get used to it."

Elwood stared at him. "I could change it . . ."

"How you gonna do that?"

"Fight Endicott. Kill him, maybe."

"Man, you crazy. I mean, I know you're bad, but Endicott ain't no easy bite to chew. Not that Kerry would ever let you try anyway."

"Why would he stop me? I mean, it was him Endicott pushed out."

"You just don't get it, do you?"

"Get what?"

Ferrick sighed. "Sorry. I keep forgetting, you weren't there. When things were getting decided. Jim didn't push Kerry out. In fact, he didn't even want the top slot. It was Kerry that pushed *him* to take it. Told him he wouldn't go along if Jim wouldn't run the show."

"Why would he do that?"

"Kerry's deep, man. He had his reasons, though I ain't sure he ever told anybody *all* his reasons."

"And you go along with this?"

"Well. . . . Look, whatever reservations I got, I keep them to myself. Safer that way. Besides, what choice do I have? Any of us have? We all had our chance to stay on the *Outward Bound*. When we decided to stick with Kerry and Endicott, that was our decision. So now we deal with it. Okay? End of story."

Elwood eyed him in speculation. "You really aren't okay with everything, are you?"

"Don't get the wrong idea, Elwood. You make some kind of bullshit play, don't come to me for backup."

"But you wouldn't try to stop me, either."

Ferrick looked away. "I don't wanna talk about this anymore. Did you see Kerry?"

"Yeah. Him and Endicott went that way"—he tipped his head toward the end of the corridor—"about ten minutes ago."

"They say where they were going?"

"I didn't ask."

Ferrick lumbered past him, then paused. "What are you doing, anyway, standing around like a zombie? You got nothing to do?"

Elwood grinned, shrugged.

"Get your scrawny ass down to the engine room. I'll be there in a few. I bet I can find something for you to do."

"Cool, Ferrick."

"Yeah," Ferrick replied. "Cool it is."

3

Hunky Pittfield, short and chunky, his hair a spiked topknot, looked like an overdressed pineapple in his makeshift apron as he sniffed at a pan filled with a thick layer of dark green, bubbling mush.

"I dunno," he said, his expression dubious. "It still doesn't smell like food. Not any food I ever ate, anyway."

"Taste it," Samantha Hamilton said.

"Sam . . . come on. How come I always have to be the guinea pig?"

" 'Cause you're a guy. It's your job to be brave."

Hunky looked down at his apron, which was a swath of cloth torn from one of the puffy cushions in the Kolumban crew's quarters. "Right. Super chowdog."

"It's a dirty job . . ."

"And I'm always somebody. Gimme a spoon."

Sam handed him a copper-colored utensil with a triangle-shaped bowl far too large for a human mouth.

Hunk dipped, lifted, took a deep breath. Closed his eyes. Tasted, chewed. Swallowed.

"Well?" Sam said.

Hunky opened his eyes. "It won't kill me. I guess."

Sam grinned. "High praise, then."

"At least I didn't puke this time," Hunky said.

"A definite improvement."

"I guess."

Sam contemplated Hunky's sour expression. The galley of the newly renamed *Endeavor* was huge by her standards. Maybe for the oversized Kolumbans it was as small and efficient as the cooking cubicles she'd used on Terra as a little girl, but it seemed a dark and cavernous space to her now.

She and Hunky were the two best cooks in the group of forty former Stone Cowboys who'd hijacked the ship from the Kolumbans and used it to escape the *Outward Bound*. In the firefight, siege, and eventual risky dose of vacuum breathing that had followed, she supposed that Jim, Kerry, Ferrick, and Elwood had been heroes. But that was done with, and now a different kind of heroism was needed. Circumstances had dictated they had come aboard with little more than weapons and the clothes on their backs. She'd already demonstrated the value of a good cook in the trick Jim Endicott had devised to get them into the barricaded bridge and dislodge the aliens holed up there. Now more was needed, because forty hungry kids had to eat. She and Hunky were in charge of discovering the secrets of the alien galley, so the new crew wouldn't starve to death.

She didn't think she was getting enough respect from the would-be warriors, either. She and Hunky had been working their tails off in the galley, figuring out the computer programs, learning how to operate the alien cooking equipment, analyzing the contents of the ship's stores for combinations of vitamins, proteins, and minerals that would nourish the ravenous metabolisms of forty active teenagers.

So far, they'd managed to come up with recipes that would keep humans alive, but the results looked and tasted horrible. Only Jim Endicott seemed to understand and appreciate her problems. Everybody else just bitched.

Jim was unlike any boy she'd ever known. He was smart, handsome, kind, and had not been brutalized in childhood the way she and every other Pleb she'd ever known had been. Even her old flame, Kerry Korrigan, by far the best of the boys she'd known before, bore the scars of his upbringing, and was capable of a cold, unfeeling cruelty she doubted Jim would ever understand. However, she still hadn't made up her mind whether this was entirely a good thing. She knew that some of the Stone Cowboys thought that because Jim was kind, he was weak. She knew that wasn't true. In some ways, Endicott was the strongest kid she'd ever known. But she worried that his kindness, which was a part of his strength, might also blind him to certain realities.

It was a puzzle, complicated by the knowledge that she was falling in love with him.

"Hey," Hunky said. "You there? You with me?"

Sam blinked. "Sorry. Just thinking."

He shoved the pan under her nose. "Think about this, girlfriend. Would *you* want to scarf this crap down?"

"It's not crap, Hunky. It will keep you alive."

"If you can stand to swallow it. I'm not sure it wouldn't be better to starve."

She felt a sudden urge to cry. Even Hunky was deserting her. Couldn't anybody understand how *hard* . . . ?

"Gimme that damned thing," she said, and yanked the pan out of his hand. She turned and slammed it upside down into one of the big steel sinks, sending globs of sticky black goo flying everywhere. Slam, bang, bam!

"Hey," Hunky said. "I didn't mean—"

"Shut up. Just *shut up!*"

She leaned over the sink, shoulders shaking silently. Hunky hesitantly touched her shoulders. "Sam?"

"I'm okay. Just give me a minute to . . . to . . ." To do what? She didn't know.

"What's going on?" Jim Endicott stood in the doorway, Kerry Korrigan behind him, both staring at the tableau by the sink. Jim crossed the room.

"Sam? You okay? What's the matter?"

She gestured at the mess splattered in the sink, swiped at a couple of dark, viscous spots on her cheek. Tried a smile.

"Dinner," she said.

He stuck one finger into a large blob, lifted it to his mouth, licked. "Not bad," he said. "Tastes like chicken."

She blinked at him through tears. "You're a terrible liar," she said. "But I love you for it."

4

Elwood Grieger might look like he was dying of malnutrition, but he normally ate like a starving grizzly. Not so now, as he sat on the floor of the giant engine room, back against the wall, a pan the size of a small dish tub on his lap, a pointed spoon as big as a sandbox shovel in his right hand. Dubiously, he stirred the inch-thick layer of glop on the bottom of the tub.

"I've seen stuff that looks more like food fall out of the south end of a northbound donkey," he remarked to Ferrick Autrey, who sat next to him. "Smelled better, too."

"You ain't never seen a donkey," Ferrick replied.

"Saw one in a zoo once. When I was a little kid."

Ferrick eyed his own meal and sighed. "Sam says it won't kill us."

"This is horseshit," Elwood muttered.

"No, I don't think that's what it is. Just looks like it."

Elwood lifted his spoon, brought it slowly to his lips, then tossed it back into the guck, disgusted.

"They expect us to eat this stuff?"

Ferrick shrugged, eyeing his own meal. "What choice do we have? It's all we got—unless we want to start eating each other."

Elwood stared at him. "Don't tempt me. You got some meat on you, boy."

"Huh. And you wouldn't even make a short snack. Too stringy."

They both laughed. "But seriously, Ferrick, this really does suck. Everybody's getting teed off."

"Yeah, I know."

"So what are we gonna do about it?"

Ferrick set down his bowl, shifted, stared at him. "We ain't gonna do nothing. What do you think we gonna do?"

"Ferrick, that just don't seem right. If Endicott wasn't—"

"Don't start with Endicott again, okay?"

"Who else, then? It was his idea."

"I already explained that it wasn't. Not all, at least."

Elwood stared off into the hazy distance of the huge engine room. The air smelled faintly of ozone, and was filled with a subliminal hum, the barely perceptible backwash of the great engines that twisted space into nanosecond-wide doorways that let them slip through in no time from *here* to *there*.

He knew next to nothing about the forces that powered those drives. Ferrick knew considerably more, and had promised to teach him, but so far as he was concerned right now, those hulking, silent white housings wrapped in multicolored tubes could have been as easily powered by magic as by science.

Ferrick watched the blank, mildly unfocused expression slowly settle across Elwood's parched features and thought: *Oh, shit. He's getting that* interested *look again.*

The last time he'd seen that look on Elwood's face was when Elwood was doing his best to kill everybody he could reach with the shatterblaster he had aimed through the main hatch of the *Endeavor*. Some people have a natural talent for things. Elwood's natural talent was murder.

Ferrick didn't stop to wonder what had happened to Elwood to make him that way. Or maybe that nothing had happened, that he'd hadn't been born with the talent, some kind of genetic thing. Ferrick's own life had taught him not to muse much on how things got the way they were, especially how people got the way they were. In his world, one spent energy coping with what *was*. It was all well and good to spare a moment's thought to how a fifteen-year-old kid got hardened enough to ram a knife into your belly, but not while the kid was actually trying to do the ramming. Most of Ferrick's life had been spent avoiding the reality of knives, particularly those aimed at his gut. As a consequence, he tended to be pragmatic about the larger questions.

But Elwood was a special case. That dreamy, *interested* expression wasn't aimed at him, wasn't aimed at anything or anybody, but as soon as Ferrick saw it, he understood that it was a problem, maybe the kind of problem that could catch him in a nasty backwash. Because that look meant Elwood was dreaming about killing something. Ferrick was pretty sure the something was Jim Endicott. And while Ferrick was nowhere near as certain about Jim's value as Kerry Korrigan was, he had done okay for a long time by trusting Kerry's decisions. Besides, if anything fatal happened to Jim, Kerry would ruthlessly return the favor. And Ferrick sure as hell didn't want to be on that shit list, even by accident. Which could happen, if Elwood was involved. Elwood was supposed to be under his authority. Kerry had specifically told him to keep Elwood busy in the engine room when Elwood wasn't undergoing training on the ship's bridge. "Make the evil little bastard learn something useful," was what Korrigan had said.

Ferrick doubted that an advanced seminar in assassination was what Kerry had in mind, and if he let Elwood get away with practicing his natural talents on Jim Endicott, Kerry might not stop with just Elwood when it came time to pay the piper.

Elwood had never seen Kerry in full-tilt-boogie mode, but Ferrick had, back when they were carving a place for the Stone Cowboys in the steel corridors of the *Outward Bound*, using nothing much more than their fingernails and Kerry's ruthless, deadly determination.

Elwood was a killer. But Ferrick knew that Kerry, if the mood was on him, could be a slaughterer. He didn't know much about Terran history, but he'd learned a little. The closest comparison he could come up with was between Jack the Ripper and Attila the Hun. One laid waste to people. The other destroyed entire cultures. Kerry Korrigan frightened Ferrick Autrey in a way that Elwood Grieger never could—because Elwood didn't have the imagination to become what Kerry was. Nor did he have the imagination to see the difference between Kerry and himself and understand why Kerry should *scare* him.

Too dumb to be scared, that was Elwood. It gave him an advantage in some situations: Elwood would be shooting when others were still thinking. But in other situations that was a great way to get dead, and take a lot of others along with you.

"Elwood," Ferrick said, "whatever you're thinking about, stop. Okay? Just stop."

"Lotta people don't like what's going on now."

"So? All that tells me is there's a lot of dumb people around."

"You calling me dumb?"

"Not exactly. More like ignorant."

"What's the difference?"

Ferrick shrugged. "Dumb is dumb. You're born with it. Ignorant means you don't know something, but if you ain't dumb, maybe you can learn."

"What you're saying is there's something I don't know?"

"Yeah."

"Like what?"

Ferrick waved one hand. "Think about where we are."

Elwood looked out at the engine room. "On this friggin' ship."

"Right. In the middle of nowhere. Can't go back, either. There's like maybe forty of us, kids, on our own. In other words, we're stuck with what we got. So we make the best of it."

"And eat this crap? You call that making the best of it?"

"Elwood, listen to me. At least we're eating, and it ain't killing us. It's not like if you don't like it, you can move on down the street. Down the street is nothing but vacuum."

Elwood didn't answer.

"Maybe you think you got a better way to handle things?"

"Couldn't be any worse."

"Yeah, it could. And you should think about that."

"How?"

"We could be dead. Look, Kerry took good care of us for a long time. So cut him some slack, why not?"

"If Kerry was the one in charge."

Ferrick sighed, spooned up some glop, swallowed, grimaced. "You are one stubborn mofo, aren't you?"

Elwood watched him eat. He grinned. "I guess so."

"You want to get yourself killed, I won't stop you. But you get the rest of us killed, I'm gonna kill you myself. Personally."

"That don't make any sense."

"You get my meaning, though."

After a moment Elwood nodded. Then he spit into his tub of goo, got up, and walked away.

Gonna be trouble, Ferrick thought.

5

The ship was as long as a hundred-story building was tall. It was an ungainly-looking creature, designed for deep space, never intended to know the atmosphere, let alone the gravity of a planetary surface. If the ship tried to land on any planet larger than a bowling ball, the gravity well would crush it like a ball of tinfoil.

That being said, it was still, in the element it had been designed for, sturdy, competent, and deadly. As Jim stood on the bridge, much larger than the command rooms on human vessels he'd visited in virtual reality, he reflected on the history of the cruiser they had renamed the *Endeavor*.

From its lines, he knew it had been originally built in one of the vast Hunzzan ringyards that circled a number of their planets, gigantic orbital industrial complexes that, over a period of many years, sucked whole systems dry of raw materials and spewed out millions of ships.

It would be nearly impossible for one person, even an avid student, to remember the nearly limitless number, type, class, and manufacturing date of all those ships, especially since the Hunzza built not only for themselves, but for many of the smaller hegemonies, federations, and single systems in the Greater Galactic Region. The Hunzza had been shipbuilders for thousands of years, and were famed for the quality of their work.

The Hunzza also built the ships for their own navies, and kept the features and specifications of these vessels top secret. But the *Endeavor* was a standard cruiser they built in bulk for general sale—a sort of space-going military workhorse. They'd been building it, with minor variations and improvements, for almost a hundred years, and as it happened, it was a ship that Jim had thoroughly studied in his military strategies classes back on Wolfbane. He had even virtually "fought" the ship in virtual-reality battles, sometimes as weapons officer, sometimes as the commander.

The *Endeavor* had undergone some cosmetic modifications to its interior to make it suitable for Kolumban use, but in all other aspects it was a ship whose systems Jim knew from the ground up. The problem was he was the only one who did. All of the Kolumban crew had been killed in the Cowboy takeover of their ship.

Luckily, if one knew how to program the operating systems—and Jim did—you could pretty much set the vessel to autopilot for routine travel. Jim had done so, programming in a slow, conservative series of jumps. He needed time to train as many of the Cowboys as he could in ship-handling operations before they arrived at Kolumba.

Ferrick Autrey was his star pupil, with his natural affinity for the theoretical and practical aspects of the *Endeavor*'s drives and internal operations. But Kerry wasn't far behind in picking up the high-level strategies involved in conning the ship from the bridge. Eventually, Jim was sure, Kerry would make a superb executive officer and backup pilot, just as Ferrick showed signs of becoming a crackerjack chief engineer. Finally, a kid named Elwood turned out to be an absolute genius at picking up the nuances of the *Endeavor*'s weapons systems.

Elwood made Jim nervous. He could sense the younger boy didn't like him, but Elwood was the best he had, so he had no choice but to use him. Besides, Ferrick vouched for him, and was also training him in the esoterics of engine room operations. In effect, Elwood was becoming a sort of all-purpose backup, a valuable asset—but one Jim wished he could trust more than he did.

"What about Elwood?" he said, as he and Kerry walked down a corridor that still bore scorch marks from the pitched battle the Cowboys had waged to capture the ship. "Do you trust him?"

"You kidding? I don't trust anybody. Not even you, not all the way, at least."

"Don't be slippery."

"Me?"

"Asshole," Jim said. "Come on, tell me."

They reached the main hatch for the bridge. Kerry peered inside, stopped. "Hold up."

"What?" Jim said.

"He's inside. At the weapons console."

"Elwood?"

"Uh-huh."

"He likes his guns, I got to give him that." Jim checked his nailtale, a tiny digital watchscreen embedded in one of his fingernails. "He's not even scheduled for training duty. This is on his own time."

"Elwood's dedicated, all right. If he gets interested in something."

"That's good, right?"

"There's only one thing that really interests Elwood, though."

"Yeah?"

"Killing things. People, mostly, but he isn't totally rigid about that. Pretty much anything will do."

"So you're saying he's psycho, and you *don't* trust him?"

"Jimbo, if not being a psycho was a qualification for my trust, I'd have come on this little jaunt by myself."

"And me, of course."

"Don't bet on it. You're as nuts as old Elwood, but in your own way."

"What? You're saying I'm like him? A psycho killer?"

"Not like him. Elwood don't have much imagination."

"I don't get it."

Kerry grinned. "If you told Elwood to kill somebody, he'd reach for a club or a gun or a knife. But that's about it."

"And . . . ?"

"He'd never dream, for instance, of boiling out the lungs of a whole ship full of humans and aliens in deep-space vacuum."

Jim closed his eyes. Sighed. "All right, you made your point."

"But to answer your questions, I trust him the same way I do you. To do what comes naturally. Which means, for your purposes, that Elwood worries me just a little bit."

"You're my exec officer, Kerry. I depend on you to tell me things I need to know. Without the mysterious bullshit, okay?"

"Okay. That's fair. Takes some getting used to, but it's fair. Which is part of what I'm talking about."

"Note I said without the mysterious bullshit."

"Right. If I'm having trouble getting used to a new role in life, think what it's like for a guy like Elwood. A smart kid, a dangerous kid, but not very imaginative."

"What's imagination got to do with it?"

"If all you've got is a hammer, every problem looks like a nail."

"And what is Elwood's hammer?"

"I already told you."

"He kills things."

"Exactly."

"So if Elwood starts to think I'm a problem . . ."

Kerry winked at him. "Very quick. That's why you're the captain, and I'm only the lowly exec officer."

Jim eyed him sourly. "I'm the captain because you made me do it. You sure that wasn't because you know it's the captain who gets to wear the big sign marked *problem* around his neck?"

"Wow. Very, very quick."

Jim edged past Kerry to the hatchway and checked out Elwood. Elwood was hunched in a huge Kolumban chair in front of the weapons station, looking like a toothpick in a teakettle as he peered with blind concentration at the array of screens before him. Precariously balanced on his neat, tidy skull was a pair of virtual-reality inductance pads, like earmuffs for titans. It made Elwood look faintly ridiculous, like those antique collector's Disney cartoons from the twentieth century, the ones about a mouse . . .

"He looks harmless," he said, as he stepped back into the hallway.

"He's not," Kerry said. "But it's not just him by himself that worries me. It's the politics."

"Huh? What are you talking about, politics?"

"Jeez, *mon capitan*, are you that dumb?"

"Ignorant, maybe. Enlighten me, oh brilliant exec of mine."

"It's the food."

"Okay, now you *have* lost me. What about the food? Except that it's awful?"

"That's it. It's awful. Look, Jim. We got forty kids aboard. Almost all of them are, by Terran standards, scum of the earth. Like me. But we found a way to make things work. We were doing okay aboard the *Outward Bound*. At least till you came along. Then everything changed."

"Hey, wait a minute. You *know* it wasn't like that."

"Sure I do. And in fact, the kids that came with us were sort of like the cream of the crop. The real stoneheads, which was almost everybody, stayed behind with Darnell. Even so, we don't exactly have a crew of scientists or doctors or other geniuses. People who appreciate the big picture. What they mostly think about is little stuff. They'll take on a ship full of big hairy aliens if you or I tell them to do it. But if you force them to eat shit—or stuff that looks like a reasonable facsimile—day after day, they start to get pissed."

"What's that got to do with Elwood? Or politics?"

"I told you. Elwood's strongest suit ain't imagination. But if Elwood gets the feeling that a lot of other people think the same way he does, then maybe he'll take it into his head to do something about it. That something being you, if you get what I'm saying."

"I don't like the sound of this. I think what I'm hearing you say is that you already know Elwood thinks I'm a problem. And that some other people agree with him."

A troubled expression flickered across Kerry's clear features. "I'm not totally sure, actually."

"How about a guess, then? Maybe a name or two?"

"That's the politics, Jim. Elwood is kinda tight with Ferrick."

"You aren't saying Ferrick would back some kind of play against me from Elwood?"

"Back it? No, Ferrick isn't that stupid. He knows if he pulled something like that, in the end he'd have to deal with me, too."

"And Elwood doesn't know that?"

"Oh, Elwood knows."

"Well?"

Kerry shrugged. "He just doesn't give a shit." He started to turn away, but Jim touched his shoulder.

"Kerry, have we got a mutiny brewing?"

"I don't think so. Not yet."

"What about Elwood, then. If what you say is right, he's the real problem."

"No," Kerry replied. "Elwood's a symptom. The problem is the food. We got to fix the food, Jim. You do that, and I'll fix Elwood."

The way Kerry said it made Jim feel a sudden chill. "Fix him? You mean what we talked about before? What you said about doing the necessary stuff?"

Kerry's eyes looked the color of river ice. "If I have to," he said. "I told you, if I had to, I'd do it again."

CHAPTER TWO

1

———

You could stay with me," Jim said. "I took the captain's quarters. It's huge. Plenty of room. And, uh, kind of lonely."

Samantha eyed him wearily. "Thanks, but no thanks."

"Hey. I didn't mean—"

"Sure you did. And I'm flattered. In fact, if things were different, I'd jump on it in a second. Jenny snores, you know? Like a damned machine or something. Drives me nuts." She smiled. "But you're not thinking, Jim."

"What do you mean?"

She dropped her gaze, flapped one hand vaguely. "Oh, you know . . ."

They were standing just inside the main entry to the galley. Like every other chamber on the *Endeavor*, it was oversized by human standards: steel sinks as big as whirlpool tubs, metal counters that reached neck-height on Hunky and Jenny, who were arguing quietly next to a computer screen displaying the nutrient information about a recipe they were concocting. The place had the dim, echoing feel of a cathedral, where even the quietest sounds possessed a sharp, lonely discreetness—like water dripping slowly into an empty pail. In fact, the whole ship felt like that. Like they were all mice, crawling around in a land of giants, squeaking as loud as they could to keep the shadows away.

"No," Jim said. "I don't know. Tell me."

Sam turned away from him. "The others . . ."

"What? I couldn't hear you?"

"What will everybody else think? If I moved into your room?"

He stared at her. "Who cares what they think?"

"I do. And you should."

He raised his hands, let them fall. "Sam, I'm sorry. You've lost me."

She took his arm, tugged him out into the corridor. When she spoke, she pitched her voice in a low, intense whisper. "Swear to God," she said. "Sometimes you're the dumbest smart guy I've ever known. What's it gonna look like if I'm in your room every night. There's almost forty guys aboard, only three girls. And you take one of them for yourself like some kind of . . . jeez . . . selfish pig."

"Hey, *wait* a minute!"

"Look, I know that sounded terrible. I didn't mean it to, but it's the truth. You've got enough problems without buying yourself one you don't have to."

Jim glanced up and down the corridor. Empty. Thank God for small favors. He knew his cheeks were burning bright red.

"Sam, what the *hell* are you raving about? I know Kerry thinks I'm an idiot about half the time, and it looks like you do, too. I'm starting to think so myself. Honest to God, I don't have a clue what you're trying to tell me."

She stared up into his eyes. "I really don't think you do." Clicked her tongue against her teeth, sighed. "I keep forgetting . . ."

"What? That I'm a hick from the sticks? That I didn't have the luxury of growing up in some outcast poverty subculture with a gang for my family?"

"Now you're mad."

"Yeah, I am. Look, I know there's lots I don't know. I'm trying to learn just as fast as I can, just like everybody else on this tub. But damn it, Sam, you have to help me. So does Kerry. Just assume I'm an idiot, and spell it out in words of one syllable." He tried a grin, knowing it probably didn't look very friendly, but it seemed to calm her a little.

"Jim, I don't know what you hear. About how everybody feels about you."

"I hear from Kerry. He says I won't win any popularity contests right now. Evidently everybody holds me responsible because they can't get their usual recycled soymeal cornflakes for breakfast."

She nodded. "Which is really my fault, not yours. Those darned Kolumbans. Why couldn't they eat normal food like normal people?"

That did strike him as funny. Maybe they all were living in a dream world.

" 'Cause they're Kolumbans. And they do eat normal food. From their point of view, at least. We're Goldilocks. They're the three bears."

She stared at him as if he'd lost his mind. "Goldilocks?"

"Forget it. Look. I don't know what you *think* you're telling me, but here's what I'm hearing. If you move in with me, the rest of the guys on the ship—most of them, at least—will think I'm hogging you for myself, and I'll get even more unpopular than I already am. Is that about right?"

She nodded.

"Okay. Now do you see the implications of all that, at least from my point of view?"

She didn't get it. He could see it in her eyes. The kids on the ship thought it was tough getting used to an alien environment. Sometimes, talking to them, trying to understand the way they thought, he felt like he was an alien, too.

"Implications?" she said.

"Yeah. The only way that forty guys can get pissed at me for hogging you is if they think they've got a claim on you, too. But there's no way, right?"

"A claim?"

"I mean, you haven't balled all forty of them, have you?"

Two hard, red spots appeared on her face, as if some magic, invisible brush dipped in blood had gouged at her cheekbones. Her black gaze seemed to *buzz*. It startled him so much he stepped back reflexively, and for one ridiculous moment wished he were armed.

His involuntary backward move gave her enough room to launch a full-armed, looping right hook that caught him at the base of his jaw and snapped his head to the side.

"*You . . . bastard!*"

And she was gone, leaving what felt like a steaming hole in the atmosphere where she'd been standing. Hunky stepped through the doorway and grinned at him.

"You do have a way with the girls, Endicott."

Jim glared at him. "So tell everybody."

"Tell everybody what?"

"That I'm not *hogging* her." He turned and stalked away, his heels making harsh chugging sounds on the naked metal floor.

Hunky shook his head. "Pressure must be getting to him," he muttered. He turned and reentered the kitchen.

"Sam? You wanna taste this latest batch? Hey, are you crying?"

2

The three of them waited nervously in the small sector control room, one of many nondescript cubicles crammed with alien equipment adjoining the main engine chamber. Timmy, a short, muscular blond kid, gnawed on a cuticle as he watched Beaver and Frank pitch small bolts against the wall, a version of the arcane "pitch-penny" none of them had ever heard of.

"Gotcha," Beaver said, flashing protruding top teeth in the grin that had given him his nickname as he picked up his bolt. "Now you owe me *ten* million creds."

Frank, dark, beefy, phlegmatic, said, "Double or nothing."

"Again?"

"Double or nothing, sure."

"Ssstt!" Timmy said. "Somebody outside."

They froze, staring at the door. Timmy, without looking, groped until his fingers found a loose pipe. The door slipped open. He raised the pipe.

"Don't go hitting on me with that thing," Elwood said. "I'd have to hurt you."

"Elwood!" Timmy lowered the pipe, then glanced at it as if he were surprised to find it in his fist. "Uh, sorry."

"No, no, that's good," Elwood said. "First thing to remember, you gotta keep your guard up. Keep alert, be prepared for anything. Right?"

"I guess so."

"Truth, man. Believe it." Elwood nodded at the other two. "Frank, Beaver."

"Elwood," Beaver said. Frank didn't say anything, just glowered.

"Something up your butt, Frankie?" Elwood said, his voice mild.

"Dunno."

"Come on."

"Huh. Okay, what's going on? Why are we here?"

"You enjoy your breakfast this morning, Frank?"

Frank spit on the floor. "That shit? What do you think?"

"I think you wish you'd never come on board this tin can. Never listened to Kerry. Never let this Endicott guy take charge."

Frank nibbled at his pendulous lower lip, shrugged. "Maybe."

"No maybe about it. And you two. Beaver. Timmy. What do you think? You happy with everything?"

Beaver wasn't a talker, but Timmy was. Elwood thought that Timmy might have the makings of a leader. That was okay with him.

Timmy said, "You know why we're here, Elwood. You can trust us." He glanced at Frank. "All of us."

Elwood eased further into the dimly lit room, slouched against an oversized control console. The others unconsciously turned to follow his movements, as unthinking as sunflowers moving to face the sun. "Never said I couldn't, did I?"

They all stared at one another. The others sensed a shadowy whisper of danger, but for all of them except Frank, the taste was exciting.

Frank was perpetually angry, about what even he couldn't have said. This whole scene was starting to piss him off.

"Elwood, you scrawny bastard," he grumbled, "you eat the same crap we do. So what's all this mystery stuff about? We gonna wipe this Endicott guy or what?"

"Jeez, shut *up!*" Elwood said. "Don't ever say something like that." He looked around nervously. "I don't know how this ship is wired. Maybe there's microphones and shit." He blinked, turned, stared at the console behind him. "There probably *are* microphones." He batted at a few switches, muttering to himself. "Wish I knew more . . ."

Timmy's face had gone suddenly pale, his freckles standing out like splatters of brown ink. "You think anybody heard?"

"Shit, I don't know . . ." Then Elwood caught himself. "Wait a minute. This is crazy."

"Sure is," Frank mumbled.

"No, worrying about speakers. Look, this ship is huge. Kerry and Endicott, and Ferrick, too, they're working like twenty hours a day, trying to hold it together and train enough of us to keep the basic services operating and get us up to speed on how to fly and fight the ship. Even the girls, spending all their time in the galley or working with Ferrick on ship's maintenance. You think anybody's got time to sit around listening to speakers in every room on this crate? Besides, if they were doing anything like that, I'd know. I'd have to know. I'd be one of the ones doing it."

"I dunno what you're unhappy about anyway," Frank grunted. "You're already one of the high mucky-mucks, hanging out on the bridge, sucking up to Endicott. What kind of problems you got? We're the ones eating warmed-over crap and pushing heavy stuff around. Like we're donkeys or something. At least you can talk to them. Ferrick just tells me to shut up whenever I say anything, like if I even have to scratch my butt or something. 'Shut up, Frankie,' that's all he ever says to *me.*"

I'd tell you the same thing, you moron, Elwood thought.

He'd been playing things by ear. This was his first effort at real conspiracy, the first meeting. He'd planned just to feel things out, see what these guys thought, see what he had to work with. But he was starting to take a serious dislike to Frankie, and from that was beginning to emerge the ghostly filaments of a plan . . .

So he said, "I get you, Frank. They treat me like shit, too, just in a different way. It's not like it used to be with the Cowboys, when we were all equal. All for one and one for all."

Frank wasn't quite *that* stupid. "It wasn't never like that. There was always bosses. Kerry, mostly. And Ferrick, Darnell."

Things were settling down. Good. Elwood glanced at the big console, trying to figure out which of the oddly shaped protuberances might be microphones, then decided to hell with it. If they couldn't talk anywhere on the ship, then nothing was going to happen anyway. It was a risk, but one they'd have to live with. Besides, unless they somehow got his number entirely, he *would* know if they started monitoring the comm system. *Have to remember to be careful, though . . .*

"Yeah, Kerry was always in charge. And you didn't mind that, did you? None of us did. He took care of us. But not anymore. Now it's Endicott, and he doesn't give a shit about us at all. He ain't even a Cowboy."

Beaver spoke for the first time. "Sure he is. Kerry said so."

"Nothing against Kerry, but he's wrong. Endicott ain't even been initiated. Never beat in, nothing. I mean, do we know anything about this guy at all?"

Nobody said anything. "Look at it. Does he care if we starve? No, he makes us eat this alien garbage like we were dogs or something."

"Kerry backs him," Beaver said.

"Well, I don't understand that, either. Kerry made the Cowboys. Why would he give them up like he did?" Elwood paused. "Unless Endicott's got something on him . . ."

"That's crazy. We know Kerry longer than he does. Fact is, I heard Kerry saved Endicott from a beating, maybe worse, when he got arrested right after he came aboard the *Outward Bound*."

"Yeah, I heard that story, too," Elwood said. "Hey, I'm not saying he *does*, just that Kerry's acted weird about the whole thing and there's gotta be a reason. We were doing real good, then Endicott shows up and everything falls apart. Now look at us."

"We didn't have to leave the *Outward Bound*," Beaver pointed out. "Nobody made us."

Elwood hadn't expected so much argument. Maybe this conspiracy stuff wasn't as easy as it looked on the surface. Still, these guys were morons . . .

"Did anybody tell you what we was getting ourselves into? I don't remember anybody telling us we were gonna end up eating nothing but tubs of rotten goop."

"Yeah," Timmy said. "That's right. If I'da known that, maybe . . ."

"And the rest of it. You know where we're going? To this Kolumba planet, right? Any of you know anything about it?"

Headshakes all around.

"Well, I hear stuff. Up there on the bridge. Kerry and Endicott, that's about all they talk about. What they're gonna do when they we get there, how they're gonna do it."

Elwood could feel the interest level ratchet up. Everybody knew they were headed to Kolumba, but nobody really knew the details.

"Yeah?" Frank said. "What do you hear, then?"

"I hear bullshit."

"What's that mean?"

"They're gonna take on a whole friggin' planet. Endicott, he says we gotta make Kolumba stop sending out dope. They grow it there or something, I guess, the Heat we used to deal."

That got everybody's full attention. Aboard the huge Terran colony ship *Outward Bound*, they'd all belonged to the Stone Cowboys, the largest and most powerful gang on the gigantic vessel. The business of the Cowboys had been dope, a drug called Heat that turned out to have some nasty side effects. It drove a large percentage of its users into murderous psychosis. They all knew this. But the rest of it had been confined to the higher reaches of Stone Cowboy management, people like Kerry, Jim, Ferrick, and Samantha. Elwood couldn't claim to know the whole story even now, but he rubbed the right elbows these days, knew how to keep his mouth shut, knew how to listen and read between the lines . . .

"See, when Endicott found out it was the Heat that was making everybody go crazy, he went to Kerry and told him it had to stop."

"Wait a minute. It was Endicott that figured it out?" Timmy said. "I heard it was Kerry."

"You hear what they want you to hear," Elwood said. "Kerry almost killed him over it. They joke about it now, when they think nobody's paying attention, but I don't think it was a joke at the time."

"Whoa," Beaver said softly. "They talk about it?"

"Just with each other," Elwood said. "Like I told ya. They'll never tell *you* the truth. After Endicott took over, everything's different."

He knew he was repeating himself, but these weren't the brightest ion flares in the propulsion tubes. You had to take an idea and pound it like a nail into their thick skulls, until the point reached some blob of brain matter that—maybe—could handle it.

"So how come Kerry didn't kill him? It woulda been better if he had." Timmy gestured at the shadows in the corners of the room. "We wouldn't be here, for one thing. I was almost a sector supervisor back on the *O.B* . . ."

"I don't know," Elwood said softly. "I think Kerry forgot where he came from. Forgot what he is."

His voice trailed off.

"Well, what are we gonna do about it?" Frank grated.

"We're gonna do what we should have done in the first place," Elwood told him. "We're gonna bring back the Cowboys. What do we care about some planet full of orange gorillas? We got us a ship. There's a whole galaxy out there. If Endicott wants a crusade, let him find some other suckers."

Timmy glanced at Beaver. "What about Kerry? Kerry won't be easy. He's a bad dude."

"Once it's done with, Kerry will go along," Elwood said confidently.

"And if he doesn't?"

"I'm a bad dude, too."

3

Cold. And dark. And the stinks.

She lay on her bunk and stared blankly at the ceiling. It would have been better if she'd died with all the rest, but she hadn't. She wasn't sure why. She could have let it go right at the beginning, in the fire and the death screams.

Now she was alone, surrounded by enemies. Little pale hairless things, but what killers they were. The bug people were right to fear them. She hadn't really understood that at first, when it had all begun. But now she did.

Unlike all but a few of her own kind, she was almost cosmopolitan. She'd been out in the galaxy, had seen the vast Hunzzan ringyards spread against the dark of space like necklaces of diamond fireflies. She had dealt with the wolf people, furry ones like herself but smaller, though still understandable. All of them were powerful, the snake Hunzza, the wolf Albagens, the insectile Communers. But the pale vole people, the humans, they frightened her the most.

The other races were old, long-established. The humans had exploded out of nowhere to colonize hundreds of worlds in barely an eye blink of galactic time.

Her people were only one world and had no friends. Unless you called the bug people, the Communers, friends, and she didn't.

She clenched her thick, ropy fingers into huge fists and bit back a soft howl. She wouldn't show them fear. She wouldn't show them anything.

Until she had a chance to show them something they wouldn't like. Then she'd show them something.

4

Elwood waited until his trio of coconspirators slunk out the door, then slumped back against the control console and let out a long, slow breath. Plotting was harder work than he'd bargained for. But it was interesting, trying to figure out how to balance the various personalities, as well as manipulate them without their knowledge toward his own ends. Like a big freaking puzzle, one that changed even as you slid the pieces into place.

That was the way to think about it. As a game. Not something personal, just a game played against another gamer. Was Endicott a game player? Elwood thought he might be. He had to have something, some skill in that direction. Otherwise, how could he have taken over the Cowboys and moved Kerry out of the leadership? Kerry was no mean gamer, either. He was a politician, and politics was really nothing more than a game of convincing people to give you power over them.

Elwood stared at the shadows, his fishing-pole frame relaxed, his expression dreamy, except for his eyes. He didn't know that this was all too familiar to Ferrick, that Ferrick called it his "interested" look, and that Ferrick had warned Jim Endicott about it. Ferrick's thesis was that the only thing Elwood was truly interested in was killing things, and there was some truth to that analysis. But not even Ferrick knew Elwood's whole story.

When Elwood was eleven years old he'd started to get the beginnings of his growth and had shot up almost overnight. He and his mother and her boyfriend were all living in a Pleb housing development in SoCal Greater Sector on Terra. Until then, Elwood had been painfully short and skinny. Now he became painfully tall and skinny. Some of the kids began to whisper the word *freak* whenever he slouched past. It took him a while before he realized it was him they were talking about.

He'd always been a shy boy, preferring the silence of his own company to the raucous camaraderie of other boys. As for girls, they hadn't even begun to rise above his personal social or sexual horizons. To find himself no longer merely ignored, which he didn't really mind, but actively mocked, a target for the sort of general cruelty only young boys are capable of, was an unpleasant shock, and one he was not well equipped to cope with.

He lacked the inborn capabilities of either humor or self-deprecation, and so was unable to deflect the general cruelty into the less corrosive paths of shared jokes. His own lack of self-esteem (a Pleb at the bottom of even the pathetic Pleb pecking order) prevented him from taking the jibes as anything other than confirmation of his own lack of worth—a destructive self-hatred that was reinforced at home as much as elsewhere.

Nor was he the kind of athletic, physically outgoing child who could turn natural gifts into easy popularity. Finally, his own intellectual strength became so tattered by circumstances that he began to *believe* the cruel jibes aimed at him. He was just learning how to think of himself in adult terms. The world told him he was a freak. Elwood started to believe it.

But he wasn't suicidal. Miserable, depressed, uncertain, in pain, yes, but not suicidal. He had the notion that all people were divided into two camps: the suicidal or the homicidal. When pushed far enough, the suicidal collapsed, gave in and gave up. The homicidal, on the other hand, snapped into paroxysms of outer-directed rage, and dealt damage to their tormentors in psychotic misproportion to the offenses offered. Or would like to.

He didn't have this understanding fully codified at that point, but he did notice that there were boys nobody made fun of, even when those boys (and a few girls) were eminently mockable. From this, it was a short step to understanding why. That was easy. Everybody was afraid of those kids. Even people who, on the surface, should have no reason to fear them. But feared they were.

It took Elwood a little longer to understand why that was. It took watching a fight for him to finally figure it out.

Adolescence is an ongoing tapestry, woven not just by oneself, but by the whole world, and things change from day to day. The unpopular become popular, the weak become strong, the uncertain become sure. To an eleven-year-old boy, the world can look completely different from one day to the next.

Harry Friedlund had always been a worm. Elwood had never paid him much attention. He was a short guy, and all puberty had done for him was broaden his chest a little and give him faint patches of unattractive, greasy-looking curly hairs on his chin and under his ears. He was wracked by acne, and his mother, lost in a fog of wireheading and strange designer drugs, never bothered to have his eyes examined, so that his genetic tendency to nearsightedness left him groping through the world like a half-blind mole. On top of it, he smelled funny, an acrid mixture of unwashed clothes and skin, and a copious sweat that smelled of onions and vinegar.

Elwood's only concern with Harry Friedlund was the secret pleasure that there was somebody around even more despicable than he was. Given a choice of targets, the worst of the bullies and mockers would choose Harry over Elwood every time. Which offered the added pleasure of providing Elwood somebody that his own society certified as being on a lower rung than Elwood himself, and therefore suitable for even him to look down on.

Most education was done at home, via WorldNet specialized education subsidiaries, but current thinking decreed that the socialization process, even for Plebs, dictated a certain amount of time each day should be devoted to group learning, and so the idea of the schoolroom had never entirely disappeared.

Five days a week at one in the afternoon, his stomach queasy, Elwood would leave his small apartment, take the vators sixty flights down, cross a broad stretch of concrete, board a float train, and ride for three minutes to a tree-filled greensward dotted with brightly colored cottages, the SubSector 7–B–1 Education and Socialization Center.

After the most recent years of his shape-changing agony, Elwood had developed an active dislike for green, open spaces, one that would stay with him the rest of his life. But on this day he wasn't the target. When he entered the Structured Play Activities Area (SPAA–6), he saw a small group of boys clustered at the fence on the far side. His first instinct was to ignore them: any gathered bunch of kids boded ill for him. And he recognized in their stances a certain predatory tension, what he imagined sharks must look like as they closed in on helpless prey.

But as he moved on past as inconspicuously as he could manage, a skin-scratching screech from the center of the pile froze him, involuntarily turned him. It sounded like somebody was being killed in there.

The cluster shifted, heaved, and opened a lane wide enough for Elwood to make out Harry's contorted features, a bruise under his left eye, a strand of bright blood trailing from his right nostril. And his pants down around his knees, heavy belt buckle dangling loose, pasty shanks lined with ancient whip marks exposed to the merciless afternoon light. Harry felt a sickening twinge at the sight of those scars. At least his own feckless family didn't beat him . . .

Teeth gleaming in the sun, Harry made a sound like broken glass scraped across a blackboard as he tried to cover himself. One of his tormentors darted at him, grabbed the belt buckle and tried to pull the belt free. Harry's pitiful wails migrated up into the bat level, nearly silent, a painful emptiness in the atmosphere.

He grabbed at the buckle himself, ripped it away from the other kid, jerked it from the belt loops. His pants tumbled to his ankles. He stepped out of them, kicked them away. Looked totally ridiculous, Elwood thought, though his thought was merely interest, and held no pity.

What Harry did next astounded him.

He lifted the glittering buckle and slashed at *his own face*. A sharp red punctuation mark suddenly stretched from brow to cheek. Again! Again!

Elwood's mouth fell open. It was too horrifying to watch, but he couldn't turn away.

The cluster of boys began to back off. And Harry, spit, blood, and elbows flying, launched himself at the nearest attacker, belt whirling like a razor-tipped bullwhip.

It took three stunned teachers to finally pull him off. His tormentor went into three days of nanotech reconstruction, and Harry went into three months of psy-tech. When Harry returned, he seemed unchanged, perhaps a bit more silent and reclusive than before. He never offered violence again, but it didn't matter. Everybody walked wide around him.

Elwood finally put it together. He'd been wrong. It wasn't just the suicidal and the homicidal. There was a third category, a malign blending of the two. Those who were willing to die in order to kill.

The next time a kid called him a freak, Elwood simply launched himself on the much bigger boy, fastened his teeth on the boy's nose, and bit down. He absorbed a horrible beating before they finally pried him off, but his attacker had to get what was left of his nose rebuilt, and his face never looked quite right again.

The difference between Elwood and Harry was simple. Elwood hadn't snapped. In fact, even as his jaw was being broken, he'd found the entire process . . . interesting. Especially the part where a large chunk of the other kid's nose had come loose in his teeth, and he'd spat it right into the kid's eye.

Like Harry, Elwood underwent enforced counseling and psy-tech readjustment and various other indignities. When asked if he was sorry for what he'd done, he said he was. But he wasn't.

As far as any feelings for his victim went, he had none. He'd learned the hard way, with the taste of blood and flesh in his teeth, that other people were meat.

Elwood shook himself, woke from his reverie, found himself staring at the muted blinking lights on the control console. He licked his lips, remembering the taste of the blood.

He smiled to himself as he slouched from the room, careful to close the door behind him. Jim Endicott had messed with his life. That was Jim's mistake, but Elwood's natural objectivity told him Endicott hadn't *known* it was a mistake. That was okay. He'd learn soon enough.

Elwood planned to show him.

5

Jim woke out of a nightmare, a dark, shapeless, fireshot thing full of shadowy horrors he couldn't remember. He lay sweating beneath an oversized, hairy spread whose weave was so wide and rough it was like sleeping beneath a doormat. They still hadn't gotten the atmosphere system fully adjusted for human preferences. The room was hot as the inside of a rubber boot on a desert hike, and smelled about the same.

He stared into the darkness and felt a stab of despair so sharp it took his breath away. It had been two days since Sam had slugged him. He'd tried to avoid her afterward, but that wasn't possible. And now she was freezing him out. His jaw still ached when he tried to chew. She packed a hell of a punch for a girl . . .

The interior of the captain's quarters was big, stifling, uncomfortable in the extreme, and in a weird way it seemed to symbolize his current condition: trapped in unpleasant darkness with no way out. But that was stretching it. His problems might seem impenetrable, but the room had a door. He groaned, checked his nailtale—three in the morning, *Outward Bound* time—and climbed down off the puffy cushions. He pulled on pants and a shirt, combed his rumpled hair with his fingers, and stepped out into the corridor.

To his left, about thirty feet away, was the entry to the bridge. Bright pink light spilled from the opening. He could hear the soft murmur of voices, the skeleton night crew still at work. Kerry was probably in there, riding herd, making sure everybody kept up with the training schedule.

He yawned, then turned the other way and padded silently along, no destination in mind, just a vague unease, an itch that needed scratching.

The ship was silent, with most of its ominous red lights dimmed, so that shadows leaped and bloomed in every corner, puddled at every turning. Even barefoot, he was aware of the faint whisper of the soles of his feet along the steel passages, contrapuntal to the steady in-and-out of his own breathing.

He wandered along, immersed in his own thoughts, until a bright puddle of light appeared in the corridor ahead and he realized with a start how far he must have walked. He was deep in the bowels of the ship, down in the warren of cubicles devoted to the lesser Kolumban crew members who were now all dead.

In the gleam of the single light a husky figure, squatting on her haunches, rose to greet him. Jim fumbled for a name to put on the stocky, short-haired blond girl facing him with a quizzical expression on her face. And something else in the look, too, but Jim couldn't figure out what it was.

"Hi . . . Magda," he said.

She nodded. "Jim."

"Everything quiet?"

"As a tomb."

Magda stood in front of a closed door, cradling a shatterblaster in her muscular arms. She eyed Jim with curiosity. "What brings you around this time of night? Couldn't sleep?"

"Something like that."

"Well, things are cool here. The gorilla hasn't stirred except to open up at feeding time." She clicked her eyes at a huge, empty bowl sitting on the other side of the doorframe. "Good to the last lousy drop," she said.

"Is it that bad? I mean, I know it's awful, but it won't kill you."

Magda grinned. "Just makes you wish you were dead. That's what Hunky says, and he's one of the cooks. Anyway, the gorilla likes it."

"Her name's Ur-Barrba."

"Is that so?" Magda picked at a pimple beside her nose.

"Her Kolumban name."

"What other kind of name would she have?"

"Uh . . . yeah." Jim felt suddenly ridiculous. He was becoming disconcertingly used to the feeling. "Keep up the good work," he said.

She stared at him. "Nothing to it. I can sit on my ass with the best of them."

Was she laughing at him? He didn't know. It sort of felt like it. And what was with this "keep up the good work" bullhookey? He realized he sounded like a pompous schoolteacher. He couldn't believe it had fallen out of his own mouth.

He felt himself blush. *What an asshole she must think I am.*

"Okay. Take care."

She nodded, slid back down. He was glad to get away. Why did everything he did, said, even thought, feel like it was wrong?

Up ahead, another pool of shadows where the corridor made a sudden turn. He could feel her gaze on his back. But it seemed as if everybody was watching his back lately.

Was that paranoia? Or just reality?

He heard the soft murmur of whispered voices farther down the hall, coming from around the corner. He looked down at his bare feet and wished he'd worn shoes.

6

They could see the dim glow from the light over the door where Magda stood guard reflecting off the wall beyond the turn in the corridor. They were clumped together, Frank reluctantly in the lead, Elwood and Timmy behind, all of them jumpy from seeing Endicott finally make a visit to the Alien's secluded jail cell—an ideal spot for an ambush. Beaver had opted out at the last moment, and Elwood was trying to decide what to do about that.

Later, he thought. *Get this done first.*

He put his hand at the small of Frank's back and pushed. Frank turned and glared at him, started to speak, but Elwood raised one finger to his lips, then nodded toward the turn in the corridor.

"*Go on,*" he whispered.

Frank hesitated. "You sure Magda's in on it?" he hissed.

"I'm sure. She lets us know when he usually comes around. Shut up and go."

After a moment of locked eyeballs Frank nodded, turned, went on. Jim Endicott came around the corner like an apparition, unexpected, seeming bigger than life. Frank grunted in shock, then swung hard at the other boy. Endicott dodged back, ducked, then came in with some kind of fancy martial arts bullshit. Elwood didn't know what it was, but it was effective. Frank doubled over, belching and farting simultaneously as Endicott's strike knocked all the wind out of him.

Elwood shoved Timmy forward into the tangle. Timmy let out a yowl and windmilled his fists wildly. One blow caught Endicott as he was moving in and stood him up. Endicott turned toward Timmy, and Frank, getting his breath back, lunged at him. Something bright gleamed in his fist.

Elwood, caught in the frenzy of battle, felt time slow down for him. The sliver of metal in Frank's hand set off a lightning train of thought. Just let Frank do it?

But that wouldn't work. Later, Kerry would look at the facts: three guys had jumped Endicott unawares, and knifed him to death. He'd have to do something, because even under the old Cowboys system of justice, unprovoked murder merited the death penalty.

The calculations stormed through Elwood's brain in the space of a single flickering heartbeat. He shoved Timmy again, as Endicott fought for balance. Elwood dropped his long arms, fingers clawed, and reached out . . .

7

The sound of muffled voices, a bare instant of warning, and then Jim turned the corner and the melee exploded around him.

All he saw were shadows. Somebody large swung on him. Knuckles grazed his chin and then his reflexes jerked him out of range, as he twisted to the side, ducked, and launched a wheel kick at the onrushing shape.

Felt his bare heel sink deep into muscle and fat, heard the explosion of air from his target as the shape suddenly doubled over. Then another one, smaller, fists flying out of the murk, high-pitched shrieks. Somebody going berserk.

He thought there might be another one, but he had all he could handle with the first two. The little one was like a human buzz saw, and now the big one was coming up, moving forward, and he saw the glint of light on metal . . .

Knife!

His reflexes were doing all the work. His mind watched with a kind of disconnected wonder as his body waged its war for survival. He slipped to the side, sucked in his gut as the blade went sliding past.

The smaller guy was coming at him again, a rain of blows, none dangerous, but distracting. The big guy turned, grunting with effort, blade held low and flat, an experienced knife fighter.

The little guy stumbled, fell forward, arms flailing, wrapping around Jim's knees, tangling him. More motion, hard to make out, no faces, just staccato movements in the gloom, the sense of onrushing threats, too many . . .

His mind, still sitting in the back of his skull, droning on with a play-by-play of the action, like some kind of deranged announcer. A split-second of knowledge: *I've screwed up. Now I'm going to die.*

And the knife, sweeping up in a long, slow, disemboweling arc.

"No!"

He tried to counter with a cross-hand trap, but felt steel slice into the skin of his left arm, a stripe that felt hot and ice-cold at the same time. He pivoted, the sudden smell of wet copper in his nostrils.

Blood! the play-by-play announcer in the back of his mind noted.

Tangled, bleeding, more frightened than he'd ever been, even during the firefight at the cabin on the mountain, Jim fought to save himself, knowing he'd already lost. Saw something quick, snakelike coming in. Another one? The tangle of grunting, wheezing bodies of which he was a part had become a single organism to him, an organism with netlike arms and steel teeth. Now another one, another moving body in the murk . . .

A gasp! Then a groan, and the big one, the one with the knife, sank away. The little one, the buzz saw, wrapped around his knees . . . gone.

Something rattled on the metal floor. Without thinking he squatted, his hand going to the shiny object next to the body. Picked it up, stood.

Another shape, at his rear, running. Magda.

"What the hell?" she shouted.

He turned to face her, dizzy, fighting a sudden wave of nausea. The ugly snout of her shatterblaster was aimed right at his chest. "Hey, don't point that thing . . ."

"You're bleeding!"

"Yeah, I—" He staggered, put out one hand to steady himself on the wall. Looked down. A figure lay at his feet, twisted, groaning.

In the light from the distant doorway, the blood on the blade looked black. Magda stared at the knife in his hand, popeyed, then went around him. Knelt.

"It's Frank," she said.

Jim looked down the gloomy corridor. Empty as his own thoughts.

"There were more. Two, I think . . ."

She looked at him. "Who were they?"

"I don't know. I couldn't see. It happened so fast."

Frank moaned. "Stabbed me . . ." he whispered.

Magda put her hand on his chest, brought it away covered with sticky black blotches.

"Damned straight . . ." she muttered. Glanced at Jim. "That your blade?"

He lifted the crimson knife. "No. I mean, I didn't . . ."

"I think he's dying," she told him.

CHAPTER THREE

1

Magda and Jim carried Frank to the bridge, where they were most likely to find immediate help. Frank, in the red light, was as pale as a virgin's wedding gown. The black splotches on his front were growing, melting together, as blood leaked out of him. Jim's own wound left a trail of splatters behind them as they horsed Frank along. Frank tried to speak, but nothing issued from his lips except a foam of bloody bubbles.

"Got a lung, looks like," Magda observed bleakly.

Jim's own blood loss was making him weak, dizzy. He didn't know how much longer he could carry Frank's weight. His vision began to go black at the edges, narrow down into a thin circular tunnel focused straight ahead. His mind was focusing, too, concentrating on only one thing, *Get this kid some help, don't let him die*!

They staggered onto the bridge in a bloody, weaving tangle of arms and legs.

Kerry turned. "What? Jesus, what happened?" And was up, out of the captain's chair, moving toward them.

"Here," Kerry said, "lay him on the floor."

Others were coming, too. Jim stared at them, at their faces, trying to figure out what had happened. Was happening. He raised one hand, half warning, half begging.

"I didn't . . ." he whispered.

Everybody seemed far away, faces distorted, voices echoing, fading. Then the tunnel closed completely, and he spun slowly down into darkness.

There were times Kerry Korrigan was grateful for his rough upbringing. To survive and, later, thrive, he had to become tough and smart. One alone wouldn't have been enough. After many years of practice, these two essential traits had become second nature to him. They served him in good stead now, as he barked out quick, soft orders.

"Get his shirt off," he said, gesturing at Frank. At that moment, Jim Endicott uttered a quiet sigh and collapsed.

Kerry worked the equation in his mind instantly. Frank was a low-level soldier, not even a soldier now that the Cowboys were history. If he died it would be a minor loss. But Jim was the only one who really understood the *Endeavor*, the only one who'd had any formal training in running a starship and its crew. Without him, they were a bunch of kids in a hijacked tin can they didn't know how to fly or fight. He was indispensable.

Kerry ignored Frank and immediately turned to Jim. He knelt next to him, gently fingered the pulse at his neck, then lifted his arm and examined the deep slash. Blood still throbbed turgidly in the wound.

"Pressure bandage," Kerry said crisply. "Gimme a shirt, somebody."

Magda was on her knees next to Frank, staring at his bleached face. The only spots of color were his lips, which were slowly turning blue, and a few bubbles of fresh blood at the corners of his mouth. "Kerry, Frank's really bad . . ."

Kerry ignored her. He pointed at a blocky redheaded boy. "You. Strip off your shirt. Tear it up. Quick!"

He took several of the strips and formed them into a pad, then used the rest to tie the pad tightly against Jim's arm. Only when he was finished did he finally turn to look at Frank.

He bent down, put his ear to Frank's mouth, then gently sought the pulse beneath the wounded boy's jaw. It was there, but faint, fluttering.

"Anybody got a knife?"

Silence. Then Magda said, "He does," and tipped her head at Jim.

Jim had dropped the blade when he passed out. They found it underneath him. Kerry stared hard at Jim, then turned back to Frank and cut his shirt off.

The wound didn't look like much, a slit only an inch or so long beneath his rib cage, surrounded by a swelling purplish bruise the size of a fist. Kerry brushed the bruise lightly with his fingertips. Frank let out a groan and tried to twist away, but didn't wake.

Magda said, "The bleeding's slowing down."

Kerry's eyes found her. "I think it's internal. See the bruise?"

She chewed her lip and looked away. "He needs an autodoc."

"Even if I knew how to work an autodoc, what kind of doc you think you're gonna find on a Kolumban ship? A doc for Kolumbans, that's what."

"Jeez. What are we gonna do?"

Without looking up, Kerry said, "Somebody find Ferrick. Tell him to bring an autodoc if he can find one. Maybe we can figure something out."

"They better hurry," Magda said.

2

Elwood entered the engine control room in a studied half slouch, hands in pockets, gray eyes clear, a blank expression on his face.

Ferrick, huddled with another kid over a complicated-looking piece of equipment that floated six inches above the deck, glanced up, saw him, and snapped, "Where the hell have you been?"

Elwood shrugged. "Not that it's any of your biz, but grabbing a snooze. Why? What's up your nose?"

"Get over here. I need some help."

Elwood moved slowly toward him, his demeanor making it plain he wasn't the kind of guy who jumped just because somebody said *jump*.

"What is that thing?"

"Kolumban version of an autodoc, if I'm reading the spec translations right."

"Yeah? You sick or something?"

Ferrick shook his head. "We gotta get it up to the bridge. Endicott got into a fight with somebody, got cut up pretty bad. And the other guy's about to croak. Endicott knifed him in the gut."

"Is that so?" Elwood said mildly. He pushed his hands deeper into his pockets.

"Come on, butthole, give me a hand."

Elwood said, his tone still mild, "Is Endicott hurt bad too?" He paused. "What's your hurry?"

It took Ferrick a moment to get it, but when he did, his eyebrows crawled together in an angry vee. "You asshole, what do you think, I'd let Endicott die to make you happy? Besides, it ain't Endicott."

"Hey, man, did I say that I wanted Endicott to die?"

"Not out loud." Ferrick stared at him. "The other guy, Frank. The one that's in bad shape. Ain't he a buddy of yours?"

"Frank? Big Frank? Nope, he's no friend of mine. Know him to say hi to, but that's it."

"Funny, I thought it was different," Ferrick said, still scowling at him.

Elwood moved toward the autodoc. "Let's get this thing moving. What's the problem with it?"

Ferrick stepped back, brushing his blunt-fingered hands against his heavy thighs. "I don't know. We got it turned on okay, and it floats like it's supposed to, but it doesn't want to move. Just sits there like it's glued to the deck or something. Probably some kind of automatic steadying mechanism. We could move it a little, but only a couple of inches a shove."

"You said you looked at the specs for it?"

"Some. What I could find real fast, which wasn't much. And I can't understand most of it. I got a little bit by reading it out loud into the translator machines, enough to turn it on. But I guess my accent is screwed, 'cause the rest of it came out all gobbled up."

Elwood squatted next to the machine and stared at what appeared to be a control panel. A touchpad, oversized by human standards, was positioned beneath three small screens, all glowing with light. Two were blank; the third was filled with alien characters as incomprehensible as worm trails.

Elwood peered at this screen, his eyes squinted.

"Make any sense to you?" Ferrick asked.

Elwood shook his head. "Looks kinda familiar. You sure it's Kolumban?"

"What else could it be? This is a Kolumban ship."

"Yeah, but Endicott . . . he says the Hunzza made it for them. And this looks more like Hunzza writing."

"How the hell would you know?"

"I'm not a total dummy, Ferrick. I've seen it before. Their kind of writing. I'm pretty sure this is it."

"So okay, then. Can you get this thing moving?"

"Huh? I said what it looks like to me. Doesn't mean I can read it."

"*Sonofabitch!* What the hell am I standing here listening to *you* for, then?"

Elwood shrugged again. "Dunno. You're the one who asked me."

Ferrick closed his eyes. The muscles in his jaw worked silently. He opened his eyes. "We'll push it."

"Hey, that thing's as big as a small tank."

"So? It's floating, ain't it? No friction. Let's get going."

"You really are in a hurry," Elwood said.

"That's right. I am. 'Cause if anybody bites the big one because we didn't get this thing up there in time, I'm gonna explain to Kerry exactly what the holdup was. Get it?"

"I'm pushing," Elwood said, as he bent his bony shoulder to it.

The contraption moved slowly, but it did move. A few inches, each time all three of them shoved.

"This is gonna take a while," Elwood grunted.

"Shut up," Ferrick said. "Push."

3

Jim was coming around, his eyelids flickering, his lips moving silently, as if he were dreaming badly. Frank lay motionless on the deck; they'd brought one of the scratchy Kolumban blankets to cover him with, and now he resembled a brown, fuzzy cocoon. Magda sat cross-legged, pale and watchful, cradling his head in her lap. Blood still simmered softly at the corners of his mouth. Every few moments, she wiped it away with a leftover strip from the torn-up shirt.

"Where the hell is that autodoc?" she muttered.

Kerry pulled another fuzzy blanket up around Jim's neck and patted it down. He looked like a worried daddy soothing a sick child into sleep. He glanced at her across Jim's body.

"All right. Tell me what happened."

"I don't know. Jim came by, we talked a little, then he headed on down the corridor. I wasn't really watching. Then I heard some noises, sounded like a fight, and then Jim—or somebody—yelled. I didn't want to leave my guard post, but something was going on down there, though I couldn't see anything. You know how dark and shadowy those corridors are, especially when the lights are set on low."

"So what did you do?"

She shrugged. "I left the door and headed down there to see what was going on. I was a little nervous . . ."

"You had your blaster?"

"Sure."

"Okay. Then what?"

"I heard some more yelling as I came up, and when I turned the corner, there they were."

"There who were?"

"Jim and Frank. Jim's arm was all bloody, and Frank was down on the deck, groaning and thrashing around. Jim was standing over him with a knife in his hand."

Kerry's gaze flicked to Jim, then back again. "Jim was holding the knife?"

"Yeah."

"So you figure Jim stabbed Frank?"

"Well, sure. What else?"

Kerry pursed his lips but didn't answer for a moment. Then: "But Jim helped you get him up here. Did he say he stabbed him?"

Magda's gaze wavered. "No, he said he didn't. Listen, what does it matter? We got to do something about . . ." She placed her palm on Frank's forehead. Cold, sweating . . .

The sounds of a muted scuffle at the door, hushed, angry voices. Samantha burst onto the bridge, eyes wild, hair streaming.

"I heard—where is he—oh, God!"

She leaped across Frank's prone body as if it were a speed bump and landed next to Jim. "What *happened*?"

"Leave him alone," Kerry said. "He got cut, but I think he's okay."

"He's unconscious."

"Shock, some blood loss. I got the bleeding stopped."

The pressure bandage on Jim's arm was a sticky, solid red, but Kerry was right. The bleeding seemed to have subsided. Sam smoothed Jim's hair away from his brow. "Jim," she whispered. "Jimmy . . ."

"Screw Jimmy," Magda said, her voice as flat and brutal as a chisel in the face. "What about Frank?"

Sam glanced at Frank, but it was as if she didn't see him. Her eyes immediately turned back to Jim. Magda's lip curled. "Oh, sure," she muttered. "Frank's dying, but oh my God, your boyfriend's got a little scratch, and we know what's *really* important on this damned tub . . ."

Sam paid this no attention, but Kerry did. Kids were drifting onto the bridge, wide-eyed, some silent, some whispering to one another. He knew they'd heard what Magda said.

"Shut up, Magda. You ain't helping anything, not even Frank."

"What the hell do you care?" she spat back at him. "You're as bad as she is. As *he* is. All you care about is your precious buddy boy, and he's screwed *everything*!" Then, amazingly, tough Magda burst into tears.

Things were getting out of hand. Kerry knew it, but he didn't know what to do about it. He wished he could wave one hand and make Frank disappear, but Frank wasn't going anywhere. He lay there, a silent, dying lump, like an bad omen. A real bad omen.

"Somebody go find Ferrick, find out what the hell's going on with the autodoc!" Kerry snapped.

Nobody moved. They were all staring at Frank, and at Magda weeping over him like some bereaved goddess mourning a fallen hero.

At which moment, like an answer to a prayer Kerry didn't know he'd made, Ferrick Autrey backed through the door onto the bridge, followed immediately by the large, awkward shape of an autodoc being pushed along by half a dozen boys under the direction of Elwood Grieger.

Thank God, Kerry thought, rising quickly to his feet. "Over here," he said, and pointed at Frank.

The small mob wrestled the unwieldy thing down the main bridge ramp and then fell away, all of them except Ferrick now also staring at the dying boy.

Something about the way that Elwood looked at Frank snagged Kerry's attention, but Ferrick spoke in a low, taut whisper before he could pursue the thought further: "You figure out what the hell happened with all this yet?"

Kerry shook his head, then moved over to the machine and looked at it. It floated silently half a foot above the deck, intricate and enigmatic, like a squatting idol.

"Shit," Kerry said. "I don't have a clue." He glanced at Ferrick. "You get it figured out?"

Ferrick said, "Elwood says the writing on the screen is Hunzzan, but he can't read it."

"Great. That's a big help. Hey, Elwood. You know anything else about it?"

Elwood shrugged.

Kerry felt a sudden wave of frustration; the autodoc could fix Frank, if only they knew how to use it. But they didn't, and so Frank was going to die, and the entire rickety structure he was trying to build aboard the *Endeavor* would suddenly be exposed for the shaky, jerry-built mess it was.

Kerry could not, *would not* let that happen. He closed his eyes, took a breath. When in doubt, try anything. Try everything. What did he have to lose?

He leaned over and peered at the touchpad, at the blank, mysterious buttons and switches. Reached out, touched one switch, hesitated, pushed it.

The second screen, in the middle next to the one with writing on it, flashed bright red. A harsh buzzing sound erupted from some hidden speaker. The autodoc rose slightly higher in the air, hovered, then settled back down.

"Don't do that," Jim Endicott said.

"Hey . . . don't try to get up."

But Jim was struggling to his feet despite Sam's efforts to keep him down. "Jim," she said, "you shouldn't be—" She tried to take his arm, but he lurched away from her toward the autodoc.

When he reached it, he grabbed hold with both hands to steady himself, took a deep breath, glanced at Frank.

"How long was I out?" he asked Kerry.

"Several minutes. You know how to run this thing?" Kerry pointed at the screen with the script on it. "Elwood says that's Hunzza writing."

"Yeah, it is."

"Can you read it?"

"Barely. But I don't have to. This is a standard Hunzza autodoc. They send 'em out by the millions with the ships they build."

"So you *can* run it?"

Jim straightened, wavered, caught himself again. Beads of sweat stood out on his forehead. "I could get it going, probably. But it wouldn't help. It'll be programmed with a template for Kolumbans. That won't do him any good."

"Then we're screwed. He's screwed."

Magda glared up at them. *"You can't just let him die!"*

Jim staggered. Kerry caught him. "You're in no shape to—"

"Help me. Hold me up," Jim said.

"You're nuts."

"Maybe . . ." Jim slowly crouched down, Kerry supporting him from behind. He leaned forward, his eyes slitted, staring hard at the screens on the autodoc. His lips moved silently. He traced the characters on the left-hand screen with one fingertip, then said, "Okay."

"What?"

"I don't read much Hunzzan, but I think this is a standard model."

"What's that mean?"

"The Hunzzan build a ton of 'em, all alike, then program them individually for whoever buys their ships. If this one is like that, then it can be reprogrammed. And I think it is."

"You mean reprogrammed for humans?"

"Yeah."

"So how do we do that?"

"There might be a template already in the machine database, but I doubt it. If this is one of the standard models, though, there's another way."

Something in Jim's voice made Kerry squint at him. "I'm not gonna like the answer, am I?"

Jim shrugged weakly. "In some versions, the machine can develop a new template by scanning a model."

"A model?"

"Yeah. A sample of the species."

"You mean like scan me or you?"

Jim was looking over the screens again. He tapped tentatively on the touchpad. The third screen lit up, showing a different set of characters. He tried again, and once more the screens changed. Now all three were blue, filled with lines of Hunzzan characters. He touched the pad a final time. Instantly six flexible metal arms extended from the top of the machine, like tentacles. They wavered, questing for a moment, then began to drift toward Jim's body.

"Hey! What are you doing?"

"Giving it a template," Jim said.

"Naw, man, wait a minute. Is this dangerous?"

"It's a deep scan. There'll be some physical probes as well. If I'm wrong, there could be some . . . damage."

The tentacles were close to Jim now, four clustered at his chest, the other two reaching for his skull. One of them sprouted a ring of needle-fine teeth.

"I'm not gonna let you do this. If it has to be done, I'll do it," Kerry said.

Jim stared at him. "No. It's the captain's responsibility. My ship, my crew. I take care of them."

"Jim, you can't—"

"Hold me up."

Kerry put his fingers on either side of Jim's chin and forced his head around until they were staring into each other's eyes. "Look at me," he said grimly. "Do you know what you're risking?"

Jim didn't flinch. "Yes," he said. "Frank's life, if you don't stop screwing around. Now *hold me up*."

A moment of strained silence. Jim peered blearily around, saw all eyes focused on their tense tableau, saw faces filled with the same glazed, blankly expectant expression people wore when they watched the aftermath of a bad accident. Then he felt Kerry's big hands grip him tighter, lift him.

"What do I do?" Kerry whispered in his ear.

"Just hold me up. A little closer . . . okay, that's good."

The waving metal tentacles moved closer. The autodoc emitted a sharp click and everybody jumped. Then whatever guided the tentacles seemed to find a focus and the amorphous, shifting pads on the ends of the twisty arms settled as one on Jim's body.

Another *click*! A beam of light lanced from the machine and crawled slowly over Jim's face. He closed his eyes. The tentacle with the needle teeth had come to rest above his right ear, like an earmuff. Or a brain sucker.

This protrusion also began to click, not once, but a continuous series. Jim sighed, his eyes still closed, and began to topple backward. Kerry shifted his stance to get a better grip on him and snapped at Ferrick: "Help me hold him."

Ferrick had been watching with the same slack-jawed, slow-motion interest as the rest, but at the whiplike tone in Kerry's voice, he leaped nimbly across Frank's prone form and joined in. Together they held Jim steady, supporting his entire dead weight in their arms.

Jim's head suddenly lolled bonelessly forward. The tentacle-sucker thing stayed with him, clicking faster and faster. What little color remained on Jim's face drained away. In the harsh light, his bones seemed to rise through his flesh like razors through milk.

The light beam continued to crawl over his face, its focus boiling with thousands of tiny, multicolored dots, as if a horde of minuscule insects were heaving up from the pores of his skin.

He raised his head, gasped, began to shiver. Ferrick looked at Kerry. "What's happening to him?"

Kerry shook his head.

"I don't like this," Ferrick said. "He don't look good."

"His choice, man," Kerry replied.

Ferrick lowered his voice even further. "But we gotta live with the results. What if he croaks? Over that piece of crap lying on the floor there, you kidding me?" Ferrick tilted his head in Frank's direction. Magda, still sobbing, caught the movement and looked up at him.

Jim began to convulse. Kerry and Ferrick struggled to hold him. Sam screamed.

"Shit. I think he's dying," Kerry said.

Jim's knees unlocked. He went limp, dropped like a sack of flour. Kerry and Ferrick, unbalanced, fell down with him, arms and legs tangled. Jim landed hard. His head bounced off the deck, came to rest on Kerry's stomach. Kerry propped himself on his elbows.

The autodoc made a soft ratcheting sound. The light beam went out. The big machine settled fully onto the deck as its metal tentacles retracted seamlessly into its body. All three screens went dark, then flashed back on, white and blank.

Jim opened his eyes. "Tap the touchpad three times," he whispered. Twin lines of blood leaked slowly from his nostrils. There was an oval, abraded patch on the side of his face where the sucker had been.

Kerry reached up, found the touchpad, tapped it.

The screens went blue. Lines of Terran script began to scroll down. The autodoc rose back off the deck and hovered six inches up.

"*Waiting for instructions,*" the autodoc said in perfect Terran.

Jim smiled softly and passed out again.

4

When he woke, Jim found himself in a filmy, dreamlike haze full of fuzzy, thunderous voices, as if giants were booming at him from miles away. He'd gotten sick once as a little kid and run a high fever on a camping trip, far away from medical help. This was sort of like that time, with the world gone malleable and strange. He felt disconnected from reality, an oddly pleasant feeling, as if he were outside himself, yet still somehow watching himself with detached interest. It was comforting. For an instant he thought about how nice it would be to stay here in his private dream space, never go back to the real world and the problems waiting for him there.

But gradually the fog cleared. He let it drift away with regret as the voices around him sharpened into a mutter of discreet whispers. Sam's voice, tense and angry, rode above the rest, like a wasp rasping above bumblebees.

"*You see what happened, Kerry? Two people almost got killed. You've got to take over again till we get this straightened out. It's too dangerous to let it go on.*"

Then Kerry's voice, lower, soothing, but with an undercurrent of tension: "Calm down, Sam. It's too late for that. It would only look like weakness—on Jim's part, on my part. The cards were dealt a long time ago. Now we have to play the game out the way it is."

"Don't give me that macho crap," she said. "This isn't a game, and Frank and Jim aren't cards. Do cards bleed? Kerry, we've got to stop this. Jim isn't right for it. Damn it, I . . . Jim, I . . ."

Love him? Jim thought. Go on, say it . . .

But she didn't. She paused, then said, "He's a target now. I don't know who's stirring it up, but somebody's out to get him."

"Sam, I'll take care of it. Okay? Just let me deal with it."

"I don't know . . ."

Jim opened his eyes. He found himself lying on the oversized Kolumban bed in the captain's quarters, covered to his waist with one of the scratchy rug blankets. As far as he could tell, he was naked beneath the blanket.

"How's Frank?" he said. His mouth felt as if he'd been chewing a wad of dust. He blinked and licked his lips. The chapped skin scraped dryly against the underside of his tongue. He blinked again, and his vision unblurred with an almost audible click inside his skull, like a monitor screen abruptly snapping on.

Sam's face was hard-edged with strain as she whirled. "You're awake."

He lifted his arm, stared at the long pink scar where the knife wound had been. "I guess we got the autodoc working?"

Sam brushed aside his question as if it were an annoying gnat buzzing in her ear and landed on the edge of his bed, bouncing him hard enough to send a queasy roll through his stomach. The kiss she planted full on his lips mitigated the effect quickly. Her lips were soft and warm and the kiss was thorough.

Over her shoulder, Jim could see Kerry grinning at them. "Whoa," Kerry said. "Would closing my eyes be enough, or should I just leave you two alone for a while?"

Sam unlatched herself, turned, and said, "Bastard!" But she was grinning, too.

"Hey, forget about him," Jim said. "Let's go back to what you were doing with me. I'm the sick guy, I need tender, loving care."

She placed her hand on his stomach, then moved it down, onto the blanket. "You don't feel sick to me."

"Jeez," Kerry said. "Maybe I *should* leave."

Jim blushed. "Cut it out."

She turned her grin on him as she tightened her fingers on the blanket. "You don't really mean that, do you?"

"Uh . . ." He felt the flush in his cheeks growing hotter. That part of him beneath the blanket and her hand was responding to her touch. Responding fiercely, in fact.

Kerry let him roast in his own overactive juices a few moments more, then suddenly clapped his hands together. "Okay, kids, that's enough. Sam, take a hike. Jim and I need some man talk."

She was still grinning, but there was a shade of something less happy in her voice when she replied: "Maybe you need a little girl talk with all the man talk."

"What's that supposed to mean?"

"That it seems to me there's been a little too much getting decided based on guys and their *cojones*, if you get what I mean."

Now Kerry's grin slipped. "Sure, I get it. You're saying that guys let their balls do their thinking."

"You put it that way. But I wouldn't argue it too much."

Jim thought Kerry might explode. As the leader of the Cowboys, he hadn't been used to having his orders questioned, not even by Sam. But Kerry surprised him. "Look, Sam, I know you've got some problems with the way things have been going lately, and real quick now all three of us are going to sit down and discuss what you want to talk about. What I want to talk to Jim about now, though, doesn't have anything to do with that. I just need a few minutes, okay? Then, if you want, come on back in and we'll talk about the rest of it."

Evidently Sam had been waiting for an eruption, too, because Jim felt the tension drain out of her as Kerry spoke. When he finished, she nodded. "Okay, that's fair enough."

She slid off the bed, stood, headed for the door. "I'll be outside. Call me when you're ready."

"I will," Kerry said. He closed the door behind her, turned to Jim, let his breath out. "I thought she might slug me."

Jim looked down at the mound beneath his blanket, now slowly subsiding. "I might slug you myself."

"Yeah, yeah. Leave old one-eye alone. There's more where that came from, it's a renewable resource. Listen, pal, we've got big trouble, and we need to talk about it. So we're both on the same page."

Jim shrugged. "So talk." He paused. "You don't trust Sam?"

"How many times have I told you I don't trust anybody?"

Jim sighed. "And I shouldn't, either. I know. Okay, what's this big trouble?"

Kerry pursed his lips. "Remember when I said things hadn't quite got to the mutiny stage yet?"

"Yeah, I remember."

"Well, I've changed my mind. Now I think they have."

Jim was pulling his clothes back on as Kerry filled him in. "Which gets us to the most important part. What the hell happened between you and Frank? Why'd you stick him?"

"What? I didn't stick him." Jim pulled his pants on, snapped the buckle shut, and stared at Kerry. "Where'd you get that idea?"

Kerry spread his hands. "Well, Magda found you standing over him with a knife. And he sure had a deep enough hole in him."

Jim pulled his shirt on. "Did you find a knife on him?"

"Huh? Nope."

Jim raised his arm. The scar had faded a bit even in the short time they'd been talking, but it was still visible. "Where do you think I got this?"

"Uh . . . from the knife you took away from him and rammed into his worthless gut?"

"Not quite," Jim said. "I dunno who did the ramming, but it wasn't me."

"Wait a minute. You saying there was more than Frank involved?"

"Yep. That's exactly what I'm saying."

"Holy shit. Then it's worse than I thought. Okay, tell me the rest."

Jim walked him through it, describing the chaotic events as well as he could, though Kerry didn't seem happy with the tale when he was finished with it.

"So you think two, maybe three of them? But you didn't recognize any of the other guys?"

Jim shook his head. "Not even to know for sure if they were all guys. Man, you had to have been there. It was so quick, and with the lousy light and all . . . I was too busy to worry about taking a census."

"Okay, okay," Kerry said. He began to gnaw on one knuckle, his gaze going unfocused as he thought about it. He looked up. "Could one of the others have been Ferrick?"

"*What?*"

"Think about it."

"Uh . . . I don't think so. Ferrick's a horse. I didn't get the feeling there were any real big ones except for Frank, and he was right there in my face. You know how you can sense the way people take up space? It seemed to me the other guy—or guys—weren't real big." Jim considered. "You know, now that I think about it, they *weren't* big. But they were fast. Real, real fast. Like snakes."

Kerry nodded. "Mmm . . . like snakes. How about Elwood?"

"Who? Elwood Grieger, the tall, skinny guy?"

"That's Elwood."

Jim returned to the bed, sat on the edge, pulled on his boots. "Kerry, what's going on? Hell, Ferrick's one of *us*, the leadership. You've mentioned him and Elwood before, that they might be a political problem or something, but not involved in anything like this. Ferrick or Elwood trying to kill me? What do you know you haven't been telling me? And *why* haven't you been telling me?"

Kerry shook his head. "I dunno. Maybe because I thought I could handle it before it got to you. Maybe because I'm still more of an old Cowboy than I like to admit, even to myself. Or maybe just because I'm an idiot . . ."

This was so unlike Kerry that Jim just stared at him. "Hey," he said finally, "I didn't mean to judge. Whether you trust me, I do trust *you*. Don't forget that."

Kerry shook his head, his expression unhappy. "And don't forget what I keep telling *you*. You might do better not to trust even me. 'Cause the more I think about it, the more sure I am that I've screwed up big time. And if I have, it won't be up to me to fix it. It'll be you."

He moved over, sat beside Jim, suddenly raised his hand and slammed a fist into the soft mattress. "*Damn* it!"

"So tell me," Jim said. "Tell me all of it."

"You sure?"

"I'm the captain," Jim said. "That's the way you wanted it. So you have to tell me."

"Why?"

"It's my ship," Jim said simply. "I have to know."

So Kerry told him.

5

—————

The knock on the door of the small control room off the main engine chamber startled them. Elwood's spider frame was tense as an overwound clock spring as he went to the door and whispered, "Who?"

The reply was muffled. "It's me, Frank. Open up."

Elwood opened the door just wide enough to admit Frank's large bulk. Which for some reason didn't look quite so large. There was a hunched, punctured feeling about the way Frank walked, the way he held himself.

Elwood closed the door behind him. "Frank," he said.

Leaning against one of the control consoles on the far side of the room, his face in shadow, Timmy said, "Hey."

Frank didn't say anything, just shuffled to a chair and sat heavily.

He looks like somebody whipped him, Elwood thought. *Well, somebody did.*

"What was it like, Frank?" he said softly. In the dim red-orange glow, in the air that smelled of cinnamon and dust and ozone, his gray eyes had a sheen on them, as if they might glow if the lights suddenly went out.

Frank stared at him uneasily. "The autodoc? I don't remember."

"No, not that. I been under an autodoc before. But I never been stabbed. What was that like?"

Frank shuddered. "It was like somebody punched me real hard. All the air went out of me. I couldn't get my breath, no matter how hard I tried. I felt so . . . helpless." He glanced up. "That fuggin' Endicott . . ."

He doesn't know, Elwood thought. *He thinks it was Endicott that did him.*

Elwood felt himself relax. He hadn't realized how keyed up he'd been. Worried that if Frank understood what had happened, knew who had *really* stabbed him, he might have to do it all over again. But this time make sure nobody got Frank to an autodoc quick enough . . .

"That sounds rough," he told Frank.

"It was. I'm gonna get that sonofabitch for it, too."

Elwood smiled. "That's right, Frank. You are. With my help, you are."

"Oh yeah? How's that gonna work?"

"You hear anything about what's been going on since you ate that blade?"

Frank shook his head. "I just got out of bed a couple of hours ago. Ain't hardly talked to nobody. Timmy told me you guys was meeting here, so I came."

"Endicott's back on the bridge like nothing happened. Been there all day, giving orders, smacky as you please. You can't even see anything on his arm, maybe a faint scar, but that's all."

"Arm?"

"Where you *cut* him, dumbass. Don't you remember nothing?"

Frank shook his head, bewildered. "No, I don't. Not really. Everything happened so quick. And then he stabbed me."

"Well, you did. I saw it, it was a pretty good one. Too bad you didn't do a better job. All our problems would be over."

Frank grunted sullenly.

"You were lucky, you know," Elwood told him.

"Lucky? I got stabbed, you nimrod. Damned near died. You call that luck?"

"Yeah, considering what happened after, or we wouldn't be talking about it now."

"What do you mean?"

"Everybody thinks Endicott did it to you for no good reason, just because you were against him. They don't know it was your knife. I been helping the idea along a little, of course." Elwood offered him a purse-lipped smile. "Which is probably what the big meeting tonight's gonna be about."

"What big meeting?"

"The one where you accuse Endicott of trying to kill you, and demand a Cowboy trial by fire."

Frank stared up at the taller boy, his mouth slowly dropping open. "That's good, Elwood," he said finally. "That's real good."

"It wasn't your knife," Elwood told him. "It was his knife."

Frank, slow though he was, was finally getting into the swing of things. He grinned nastily. "That's right. It was just a knife out of the galley. Could have belonged to anybody. It was his, all right."

"The knife he tried to kill you with, just because you weren't going along with his program. Just because you were acting like a real Stone Cowboy, not some pansy-ass little wimp Kerry set up to lord it over us."

"That's right, Elwood, just like that."

Elwood's grin grew wider. "Make sure you remember it that way." He moved closer, put out one hand, paused.

"Let me see it," he said softly.

"See what?"

"The hole where he stabbed you."

Elwood's gray eyes gleamed with a sheen of cold liquid fire. For him, there was nothing like death, wounds, carnage, blood. Nothing in the galaxy he found more *interesting* . . .

6

The Kolumban cruiser might have seemed crowded when it was full of hulking, furry Kolumban bodies, but with one exception they were all dead now, and the forty humans who remained rattled in the dim, vast confines like bees in an oil drum.

Kerry discussed the timing of what they planned with Jim, though not with Sam, and when they were agreed, Jim sent out a ship-wide summons to the first all-crew meeting. There was a pair of good-sized cargo holds aboard the *Endeavor*, though the ship's usual cargo to the *Outward Bound* could have been carried in a large suitcase. It was Jim's opinion the ship had also been used for purposes other than ferrying dope to the Terran colony ship, though he had no idea what they might have been. The idea that the Kolumbans might have been ferrying lots of dope to lots of Terran colony ships had not yet crossed his mind. And Ur-Barrba, the one Kolumban still alive, wasn't talking, not about the ship, or about anything else, either.

Kerry had sent people to scour the ship for loose chairs. As the rest of the crew filtered into the cargo hold, they found a motley arrangement of oversized Kolumban seats arranged in a broad semicircle enclosing a sort of stage about a meter high. People climbed into the chairs, most of them feeling the unsettling ghosts of childhood memory, a time when everything in the world was huge. Now they sat like children, kicking their legs over the edges of their seats, their feet dangling well above the deck, trying to mask their discomfort with mocking laughter and bad jokes.

The chairs had been Jim's idea. "If we let them sit on the deck or stand, they'll feel more at ease. I don't want them feeling that way."

Kerry understood right away. He would have made a fine psy-war commander, Jim thought. The kind of deviousness involved in manipulating people against themselves without their knowledge came naturally to him. In a way, it was a little frightening. He was glad Kerry was on his side. But it was sort of like having a loaded nuclear weapon in the bedstand. If it blew up, it wouldn't matter who it was aimed at. It would take everybody within range.

He was still musing on this as the last of the stragglers drifted in and settled into their oversized chairs. Idle conversation buzzed up and down, but Jim could sense the tension-filled undercurrents. At least some of these kids were aware that something major was up. And with their names still burning at the forefront of his concerns, Jim picked their faces out in the crowd: Ferrick, on the platform with Kerry, his expression stolid and watchful. Kerry had insisted their *de facto* chief engineer be kept in the dark.

"If he's with us, it won't matter," Kerry had said. "And if he's not, I want to know about it now, not later."

Reluctantly, Jim had agreed.

Other names . . . Timmy, a little guy Jim barely knew even to speak to, sitting cross-legged on his chair, face animated with laughter at somebody's whispered joke. Kerry had mentioned *him*, too, in their private planning session, and Jim had remembered the small attacker who had come windmilling at him in the fight, knuckles like hard walnuts. Frank, silent and scowling, one of the few who looked almost normal in his oversized seat. And Elwood Grieger, disdaining a chair entirely, leaning his spidery length against the farthest wall in splendid isolation. Jim let his own gaze pass quickly over Elwood, but not before he got the full effect of Elwood's steady gray eyes focused on him, and the faint smile flickering at the corners of his wide mouth.

Elwood thinks I'm interesting, Jim realized. And something about the way Elwood stood, half-slouched, half-alert, triggered a previously buried memory: a spidery shadow, quick as a rattlesnake, and the sudden snapping movement just before Frank had gone down. He leaned in Kerry's direction. Kerry lowered his head as Jim raised one hand to conceal his whisper.

"It was Elwood. He was the third guy. He's the one who stabbed Frank."

Kerry nodded, but said nothing, just straightened up and watched the crowd. Finally he glanced at his watch and clapped his hands. "All right, everybody. Shut up now, come to order." He waited until the scattered conversations had trailed off and he had everybody's attention. "Good, thanks. Okay, welcome to the first all-crew meeting of the starship *Endeavor*."

A muttered rumble of agreement followed, along with a few catcalls and one sharp, rising whistle.

"Smartass," Kerry said, but his grin took the edge off the word. He waited until he had silence again, then said, "It's been a long, strange trip, huh? But you can say one thing. At least the chow's been good."

The chorus of boos that greeted this was deafening. Kerry cocked one eyebrow. "What did I say? You don't like mushy green dog food?"

More boos, interspersed with a few good-natured hoots. It was obvious Kerry knew how to handle his audience. It was also obvious, Jim thought, that they still liked and trusted him, despite all the hardships they'd undergone. He felt a troubled pang. Why couldn't he get that kind of respect and admiration? He had their best interests at heart as strongly as Kerry did. He was sure of it. Kerry wouldn't be backing him if he didn't. Why couldn't the rest of them see it, too?

That was the hardest thing to understand. That some of them even wanted to *kill* him, and he had no idea what he'd done to cause such hate. It really *was* like trying to deal with aliens.

As he mused on this, he watched Ferrick, who was watching Kerry. Ferrick was a hard one to read. He had never actually done anything to openly oppose Kerry or Jim's plans, but Jim still couldn't shake the notion that Ferrick would never wholeheartedly support his leadership. Kerry certainly didn't trust Ferrick. But then, how much weight to put on that? Kerry would be the first to admit he didn't really trust *anybody*.

Kerry was winding up his informal intro now, cracking a couple of jokes, waving casually at faces in the back of the crowd. Finally he raised his hands and said, "All right, here's the main course. Our captain—you know, the one *you* guys elected—has a few things to say.

Let's hear it for Jim Endicott—no, make that *Captain* Jim Endicott!"

Jim stood, and found himself moving toward the front of the stage in utter silence.

Kerry suddenly brought his hands together. A moment later, a couple of others followed suit, and then more, so that by the time Jim stood beside Kerry the welcoming applause seemed genuine.

But it wasn't. There was a drilled, grudging feel to the clapping. Ferrick had only clapped a couple of times, and then stopped. And neither Elwood Grieger nor Frank had applauded at all. They just stared at him, watchful, expectant, as if they were waiting for something only they knew about.

"*Here we go,*" Jim murmured to Kerry as he moved in beside him.

"It's all yours," Kerry replied. He waved a final time and stepped away, leaving Jim alone to face his crew.

He swallowed hard, then opened his mouth to speak, but before he could say anything, big Frank slid out of his chair, stood, and marched toward the stage.

For a moment the two boys stared at each other, Frank glowering, Jim trying to keep his own expression pleasant, though he couldn't control the tension that suddenly tightened his muscles. When Frank said nothing, just kept on staring menacingly at him, Jim finally spoke.

"The first thing I want to say is," he got out, but then Frank interrupted him.

"We don't want to hear none of your bullshit, Endicott," he roared. "You fuggin' tried to kill me. What do you got to say about *that*?"

The room exploded in pandemonium. Suddenly everybody was on his feet, yelling, waving his arms, moving forward. Except, Jim noted, for Sam, who stayed in her chair and watched the festivities with a worried expression on her face.

Had she applauded for him or not? He didn't remember noticing one way or the other.

Frank stood, arms crossed over his bull chest, staring truculently up at Jim. "What do you say, Endicott? I'm waiting."

Jim wanted to back away from him more than anything he could think of, but some part of him understood that if he showed any weakness at all, they'd be on him like a pack of wolves. Not *all* of them; some were holding back, faces suddenly still and fearful as the full import of what was happening sank in. But others knew, oh, yes, they knew all right, he could see it in their faces, in the predatory glints in their eyes.

And for one panicked moment he wondered if it had *all* been a setup. Kerry had warned him, over and over again, to trust nobody, not even Kerry. Could Kerry have betrayed him, too?

A flash of memory cracked through his mind like a bolt of lightning: the gunfight on the mountain, his mother screaming, the madwoman in body armor coming toward him . . .

He stepped forward, then jumped down from the stage, faced Frank head on, and shoved forward until they stood chest-to-chest.

A look of startlement appeared on Frank's face. He hadn't expected this. Good.

"What do you want me to say, Frank? What do you think you want to say to me? Or didn't you get it all out the other night"— Jim let his voice rise to an accusing, full-throated yell—"*when you tried to kill me with a knife in the dark like a sneaking little coward?*"

It was the worst insult anybody could offer to a Stone Cowboy. Frank's face turned a dark, congested red, as if somebody had stuck a hose into his ear and pumped blood into his skull under high pressure. "*You calling me a coward?*"

Jim kept pushing forward, bumping his chest against the stockier boy, forcing him back. "*What do you call somebody who tries to stab another guy in the back?*"

Out of the corner of his eye, Jim saw that the chaos in the room was getting worse. A couple of shoving matches, one full-blown fistfight, grunts, wild swings, and everybody else yelling at the top of his lungs.

Sam was still sitting, chin on fists, watching silently.

"*I didn't do nothing to you! You tried to kill me, 'cause you ain't no real Stone Cowboy, Endicott!*"

Frank drew back one fist the size of a hamhock, a food item he'd never seen but would doubtless eat in an instant, given the choice between it and another tub of green gook. Jim felt himself automatically relax into a defensive position. His mind might be churning furiously, but his body knew what to do.

But Frank never launched his blow. Elwood stepped up behind him, grabbed his wrist, and said, "Wait."

At the same time Jim felt Kerry moving up to stand next to his right shoulder. Kerry said, "Ice it, Frank."

Out near the chairs and the milling crew members, Ferrick Autrey put his head down and bulled straight through the would-be brawlers, scattering them like a bomb in a flock of startled pigeons.

It was Ferrick's physical presence, and his willingness to use it, that more than anything brought a sudden calm to the proceedings. Everybody knew Ferrick. Nobody wanted to screw with him.

The shouting faded away. People blinked as if surprised to find themselves where they were, then looked around blankly, wondering what to do next.

Ferrick told them.

"Sit your stupid asses down!" he bellowed. "You're actin' like nursery babies. What you think this is?"

A few shamefaced mutters followed this, then a couple of shrugs. And a moment after that, Ferrick stood alone on the floor, fists balled, glaring at them as they shuffled to their seats. When all was orderly again, he turned and looked at the group by the stage.

"You guys better get this settled," he said. "This is bullshit."

Kerry took Jim's elbow and tugged him back toward the stage. "Your place is up there," he whispered.

"I can handle it," Jim said, stung.

"You forget everything we talked about?"

Yeah, Jim thought. *I did. Shit.*

He nodded, shook Kerry's hand away, and climbed back up on the stage. Kerry and Elwood stood below, Frank, still steaming like a kettle on the boil, sandwiched between them.

Elwood said, "Ferrick's right. We gotta get this settled."

Kerry moved away from the other two, then faced them, his blue eyes flashing dangerously. "Ain't nothing to settle. Your boy here started up with the captain of this ship. Only thing to settle is how much time his lard ass spends in the brig."

"He isn't my boy," Elwood said. "He's a Stone Cowboy. And that's how we settle it. The Cowboy way."

Jim, standing alone on the stage, had a full view of the rest of them, and he saw the way the invocation of the magical name changed the looks on many faces, replacing anger and tension with wistfulness. It hit him hard, then, how much they missed what they'd had, what they'd willingly—and now he also understood, unknowingly—given up to follow him and Kerry into the *Endeavor* and the unknown future that went with it.

He might have nodded knowingly when Kerry told him he didn't really understand the rest of them, but inside he'd been brushing off those warnings, much as he'd swat away a film of inconsequential spiderwebs. He'd been a Stone Cowboy, hadn't he? He'd sold dope and slept with the Cowgirls—well, one of them—and didn't that make him as much a Cowboy as anybody?

Now he knew. It was those faces that taught him, the longing in them. He hadn't walked a mile in their shoes, not the real ones, the ones they'd worn all their young lives. He'd merely tried them on, wiggled his toes a bit, and then threw them away. Not just for himself, but for all of them.

No wonder they hated him. Not all, maybe, but some of them did. Oh, yes, they'd taken a vote, elected him their captain, but he knew how hard Kerry had worked to manipulate that vote, make sure it went the way *he* wanted it to. Had manipulated *them*, in fact. Maybe some of them had sensed that manipulation as well, and in their own minds made their vote conditional: *We'll give you a try, okay, see how you do. But if you screw up* . . .

And now he'd screwed up. He looked at their faces and despaired, because everything he'd done, everything he'd tried to do, was built on a lie. The lie of free consent. They hadn't consented freely; how could they? They couldn't *know* what plans he had, how he, in his monstrous arrogance, had envisioned their future for them. He had decided for them all, based on his own morals, ethics, the things he considered true and good. And his worst sin was the unconscious assumption that his own beliefs trumped theirs, that by virtue of birth, upbringing, education—all the advantages they had *not* had—his beliefs were somehow better than theirs, his truth more true, his morals and ethics partaking more of the good.

But they sensed it. Even those who couldn't articulate, even to themselves, what exactly was wrong, they knew *something* was. And instinctively, they knew who was at fault. The interloper, the outsider. The phony Stone Cowboy.

Jim Endicott.

Now he knew it, too. And he saw the plans he and Kerry had made for this meeting . . . no, be honest, the *scheming* they had done, as just more of the same old, same old. Deception and manipulation, tricks that denied the basic humanity and intelligence of the crew he had sworn to respect, honor, and protect.

Had sworn to lead.

Was this leadership? If it was, it made him sick to his stomach. This all rushed through his skull like a summer storm, flashing over the horizon of his awareness, booming on through with thunder and lightning, smashing trees and ripping off roofs, leaving him spent and shaken at the utter ferocious speed of it.

He felt as if he'd been mugged. By himself.

Some of this must have been on his face as he forced himself to take a couple of shuffling steps toward the edge of the stage, raise one hand, and try to speak. Kerry looked up at him and shook his head.

Let me handle it was what the gesture meant. But Jim wasn't going to let him do that. There'd been too much handling already. Now it was time to—

"Kerry, I want to say something . . ."

But Kerry flapped one hand at him—shut the fug *up*—and turned back to Elwood and Frank. Jim stood, openmouthed, as the import of what Kerry was saying, like a distant radio suddenly tuned sharp and loud—finally penetrated his own funk.

"You fat pile of crap," Kerry said, and poked Frank in the chest. "You think you're gonna challenge the captain? This *ain't* some frickin' street gang anymore. This is a starship. I told you a million times, Stone Cowboys are gone. Dead. Over with. You got it? You can't just—"

Elwood moved closer. "It ain't gonna work, Kerry. Look around you."

There was something in the complete, final knowingness of his calm statement that brought Kerry's head up, almost involuntarily. He did look, and saw the same thing on too many faces that Jim had already seen. That wistful longing, the golden memories of how things once had been, before fear and loneliness and bowls of green goop. Even if it hadn't been that way, that was how they remembered it now.

Jim could see the realization on his face. The best laid plans . . . with a big, hobnailed boot rammed sideways up their ass.

Jim nodded at the understanding that suddenly flowed like clear liquid across Kerry's face. "He wants to fight me," Jim said. "Okay, I will. I'll fight him."

Kerry took a deep breath. "Stone Cowboy trial, huh?"

As he spoke, a susurrus of outdrawn breath whispered over the rest of the crew. Stone Cowboy trial. Settle it the old way. They understood that. They approved.

But Kerry still had an ace up the tattered sleeve of his scheming. "He's still the captain. But even under Cowboy law, he can designate a champ. That's me. You don't fight him, fat boy. You fight me. And since the charge is attempted murder, a life-or-death charge, then that's how we'll fight." Kerry grinned. "To the death. How does that suit you, you tub of rancid guts?"

Frank's face looked as if somebody had taken an axe to his chin, let everything above his eyeteeth drain out. He raised his hands—Jim saw they were shaking—and stepped back.

"Hey, wait a minute. I didn't mean—"

But before he could finish, Elwood was in front of him, staring at Kerry with intense interest.

"He can have a champ, too," Elwood said. "That would be me. I'll fight you, Kerry. Just like you want. To the death."

"You have to stay out of it, Jim. No matter what happens. Even if he kills me."

Kerry was stripping off his shirt, revealing the barely healed cuts, the bruises that looked like rotten spots on the skin of a tomato, the lumps that still remained from his epic battle with Darnell, back on the *Outward Bound*, what now seemed like a million years ago.

He was huddled with Jim on the far side of the stage. Frank, Timmy, and Elwood were on the opposite side, heads bent, conversing in whispers, every once in a while glancing at Jim and Kerry.

"At least one thing went fuggin' right," Kerry said. "Now we know Ferrick wasn't involved." He slid his gaze to where Ferrick was sitting beside Sam, both of them stone-faced, silent.

"Kerry, I can't let you do this. Look at you. You're in no shape to take on Elwood. He *will* kill you. This isn't a game anymore. I don't have to designate you my champ. I can call it off. I'm the captain."

"You call this off," Kerry said, "and you won't be captain for long."

"How long will I be captain if he kills you?"

Kerry wiped his big, knobby hands on his thighs. "You might be surprised, Jim. If you don't do anything insanely stupid, I can guarantee that if Elwood kills me, he won't outlast me by more than two days."

"What? Why? He'd be the winner. He'd be in charge. Maybe not in title, but that's what it would be."

Kerry shook his head. "Nope, trust me. He wouldn't be anything. He'd be dead. All you'd need to do would be to lock yourself in your quarters and wait for a knock on the door."

"A knock? Yeah, my execution squad."

"No. It would be Ferrick. If not Ferrick, somebody he sends."

"Ferrick?"

"Uh-huh. That's the good thing that came out of this. Now I know for sure Ferrick ain't involved with Elwood and the rest of them. So he'd be the one. He'd kill Elwood."

"Why would he do that?"

" 'Cause him and Elwood are too much alike. Elwood's counting on that, the stupid fug."

"That makes no sense. If they're alike . . ."

"Ferrick knows he can't run the ship. He knows more about it than anybody but you, and he knows he can't. If he thought he could, he'd be standing over there with spider boy right now. But he ain't. And if he don't want it, he sure as hell won't let Elwood have it. You watch. Elwood croaks me, Ferrick will croak him, and then hand the whole thing back to you. And this time it'll stick, because there won't be any mutiny left." Kerry paused, rubbing the side of his nose. "There's another reason Ferrick'll scrag him."

"What?"

"Ferrick doesn't have anything to do with this, so Ferrick's still my friend. He'll do it out of revenge. Elwood thinks he's tough, and maybe he is. But he ain't butt-paper wipe on Ferrick."

Kerry chuckled softly. "So even though this whole thing blew up in our faces, one way or another you'll win. I'd rather you win by me stomping that stringy mofo into deck paste, but if it has to be the other way . . ."

Kerry shrugged. Jim stared at him.

"You'd let him kill you to—"

"Won't *let* him do nothing. But if it happens, it's okay. Remember, I told you I'd do anything, even kill one of the kids if I had to? Well, that includes me. Did you think it didn't?"

It took him a couple of seconds, and then the import of what Kerry was telling him hammered fully into his mind. "Do you know what you're *saying*?"

Kerry's soft smile was almost kind. "I'm one of the kids, too," he said.

Then he made two fists, rapped his knuckles lightly together, and turned toward Elwood. "Wish me luck," he said over his shoulder, as he bounced away.

"Jesus Christ," Jim said. He didn't know if he meant the words as a prayer or a curse. He guessed it didn't matter. Kerry hadn't heard.

He wondered what Kerry *did* hear as he moved toward Elwood, who stood shaking his shoulders, his long arms whipping weirdly, limp as spaghetti. Some kind of death march, he thought. He's listening to trumpets only he can hear. What a frigging *waste.*

And then, out of the blue, the oddest thought: *It's a test. But I've taken it before. I can pass it.*

Buried in the most hidden part of his mind, clawing slowly up as if shoving away the dusty clods of a long-concealed grave, an *unmarked* grave, something raised its head and looked at him, looked at him from the inside of himself.

And smiled.

This impression—memory, daydream, nightmare, whatever it was— faded almost as soon as it appeared, leaving behind the feeling that something *important* had just happened, but Jim couldn't quite figure out what.

It was the sound that chased the thread of revelation away, the chunky, meatbone slap of flesh meeting flesh. The vision vanished in the familiar assault on his ears of the sounds of violence; it was in front of him, this old grunting ballet of blood, the dance he'd spent much of his childhood and early youth learning, on mats, in dojos, under the tutelage of robots and masters and his own opponents.

From a distance, a ballet is all grace and levitation, a split-second dream, a measured fantasy. But sit up close, in the first rows, just beneath the stage, and the mask of beauty is stripped away. The dancers gasp and heave and strain, they sweat and fart with effort, and the stench of their overheated bodies would gag a stoat. Beauty parsed too finely becomes less than the sum of its parts, and fearsome in its destructive reality.

Kerry's first punch slid gratingly off the top of Elwood's jawbone and scraped away the lower lobe of his left ear. Jim could see scraps of pale, blood-smeared flesh clinging to the knucklebones on Kerry's right hand. It was a sucker punch, one that should have ended the fight before it even got started, delivered while Elwood was still grinning and nodding at some lugubrious bit of encouragement from Frank. It should have left Elwood dazed and head-rung, easy meat for a kick to the balls, a whirling elbow to the bridge of the nose, or any of another dozen blows Jim could run through without even thinking about them.

So could Kerry, evidently, because, flowing out of his punch at Elwood's head came a whirling, twisting kick that should have ruined Elwood's right kneecap as surely as the first punch should have cracked his skull.

Neither thing happened. Elwood slipped his head to the side, *just enough*, losing a piece of ear meat but saving his skull in the process. And he was already pedaling backward, so that the kick that ought to have crippled him fell two inches short, catching nothing but air, leaving Kerry unbalanced and half falling. Jim saw the look of sudden pain that flickered on Kerry's pale features, as if the effort of the kick had stretched something in his leg, a tendon, a bruised muscle, *something* that didn't like being stretched.

That whisper of ghostly agony bothered Jim more than either of Kerry's two ineffective blows. It was like a small red waving flag that cried *danger*! Or worse, a white flag. But Jim knew Kerry wouldn't surrender. He'd go down fighting. He'd *die* fighting if he had to. Hell, for all Jim knew, that might be Kerry's real plan anyway, and all the other stuff just soothing bullshit to keep Jim from stopping him from doing what he intended to do anyway.

For one dizzy instant Jim's mind whirled crazily around that circular thought . . . *stop me from stopping him from* . . . and then, with a little lurch, his brain righted itself, just as Kerry had managed to right himself and recover from his missed kick, though he barely dodged Elwood's answering kick, a vicious strike aimed right at his unprotected balls, in the process.

Now the two of them were squared off, eyes tensely focused on each other's bellies. *Don't watch the hands or the head,* Jim thought. *Watch the body. You can't fake with your gut . . .*

Good advice. He'd learned it years before in a classical martial arts class, learned it the hard way, in fact, probably the same way Elwood and Kerry had also learned it—by getting his head half knocked off.

He'd also learned how to *watch* a fight, interpret the small signs like the wash of pain that had marred Kerry's face as he launched his first blows. To the uninitiated, it might look at this instant as if Kerry was winning; blood was smeared from Elwood's ear down his neck and across his chest in a splattery fan. But the blood was leaking from a minor wound. It looked far worse than it was.

And now Elwood was coming back in, his long, weirdly limber arms snaking toward Kerry like cobras. Striking and landing in sharp, crisp combinations: pock, pock, *pock*!

Kerry was blocking most of these, but Jim could see he'd lost a bit of his naturally reflexive speed. Some of the blows were getting through, landing on his jaw, his forehead, rattling his brain inside his skull.

Worse, almost none of Kerry's return punches was landing at all. Elwood was simply dodging them, slipping easily from side to side, catching almost everything on his forearms or skinny, hunched shoulders.

Kerry had Elwood by at least fifty pounds, and under normal circumstance his reflexes were as fast, even faster. If he'd been healthy, Jim thought, the fight would be over now, with Kerry grinning triumphantly over his fallen victim. But Kerry wasn't healthy. The damage he'd sustained in his earlier battle with Darnell was slowing him down. Worse, it threw his timing off, so that he looked jerky, stuttering, and what should have flowed without effort now seemed painfully awkward and disjointed.

Elwood had been peppering him with those deceptively light combinations, concentrating on Kerry's eyes and the ridge of his eyebrows. Going for his vision. If he could close Kerry's eyes, or cut his brows enough to get blood flowing into his eye sockets, he'd be able to do pretty much whatever he wanted to.

Jim could see the lumps beginning to rise at the corners of Kerry's eyes, see the red blotches that would turn purple and yellow. Except, the way things were going, those bruises would never appear, because Kerry would be dead.

But Kerry wasn't going down easily. He was covering up, hunching behind his raised arms and fists like a turtle pulling back into its shell, and he was still firing his own blows, long, looping rights and lefts, and if they weren't doing much damage, they were at least holding Elwood at bay.

It wouldn't last, though. With growing dismay, Jim could see that Kerry was tiring. He wasn't blocking as many of Elwood's punches as before, was covering up less quickly, and was throwing fewer of his own blows. Worse, Elwood seemed to be gaining strength. His ear was still bleeding, but there wasn't enough blood loss to slow him any, and his combinations still hit with sharp, biting power, snapping Kerry's head back, stirring his brains like pudding in a pot.

Unconsciously, Jim moved closer to the edge of the stage, his own fists clenched at his sides, gritting his teeth as he watched the battle now almost directly below him.

Elwood glanced up at him, saw him watching and, amazingly, winked at him. It was a momentary lapse that betrayed who the real target was, but it was still a lapse. To challenge Jim, Elwood had taken his eyes off Kerry, and that should have been enough. With the old Kerry, it would have been, and a spark of this still remained. But not enough. Kerry lunged forward, going for a leg whip, but not fast enough. His ankle hooked nothing but the empty space where Elwood's calf had been, and then Kerry was down, sprawling and wide open.

Elwood leaped and twisted in midair like a coiling serpent. He came down with all his weight poised over his right leg, arms windmilling for balance as he crashed the sole of his boot into the middle of Kerry's face.

The sound of bones snapping and cartilage tearing was clearly audible, as was Kerry's grunt of agony. Blood exploded from his crushed nose. He groaned and spat out a wad of teeth filmed with blood. He shook his head, got an elbow under himself, tried to rise. Elwood measured him carefully, and kicked him again, this time in the side.

Kerry's ribs went with a horrible crackling sound, like cellophane crumpled in a fist.

Elwood kicked him again. And again. And again.

Kerry looked up at Jim, the light going out of his eyes. His lips moved, but nothing came out. Jim knew what he was saying, though.

I'm one of the kids, too . . .

Jim leaped down from the stage and landed next to Kerry in a martial arts stance.

"Stop! It's me you want!"

Elwood smiled and kicked Kerry again. Jim moved forward, dimly aware of other shapes approaching.

Elwood backed away, suddenly watchful.

Ferrick said, "You have to let it end, Endicott. You and Kerry called it this way. You can't interfere now."

"The hell I can't! If you think I'm going to let him stomp Kerry to death, you've—"

"Do you want to fight both of us?" Ferrick said softly. He looked around. "This is Cowboy business. Do you want to fight *all* of us?"

Jim looked around. Many of the other kids were out of their seats now, watching him with tense, expectant expressions. Like a pack of wolves, and just as dangerous.

And he didn't care. In that instant, he knew he would kill every single one of them, if that was what it took to save Kerry. He took a deep breath, raised his hands.

Elwood said, "Forget it, Endicott. You can't take us all. It's over. You lost."

A stir at the door as Magda, who'd been left on the bridge standing watch, rushed into the room. Her face was pale, her eyes wide with fear.

"You'd better come!" she yelled. "There's a big ship out there and it's coming fast."

Jim glanced at Ferrick, then down at Kerry, who was squirming blindly on the deck, trying to curl up into a ball around his shattered ribs and blown guts. When he moved, he left squirmy smears of blood on the metal plates.

Elwood said, "Fug this," and raise his foot to stomp again.

Without so much as looking at him, Ferrick hit Elwood so hard it knocked him ten feet through the air, and when he crashed to the floor, he was out cold as a chunk of frozen sirloin.

"Let's go," Ferrick said. He looked down at Kerry, then back at Jim. "Captain."

"Hurry *up*!" Magda shrieked.

"Do you mean it?" Jim said softly to Ferrick.

"Yeah," Ferrick said.

"Then help me carry him."

Ferrick nodded. "Okay."

So the two of them carried Kerry to Jim's cabin and hooked him up to the autodoc. It took almost half an hour, with Magda yelling in the background increasingly frantic reports of the mysterious ship and its approach. But Jim ignored her. In the back of his mind he thought of it as a lesson, not just for Ferrick, but for all of them.

They'd been ready to kill him. But now they needed him. Well, they could have him. But no longer on their terms, only on his. He was captain. If the alien vessel blew them all to hell while he tended to Kerry, then so be it.

He wasn't really one of them; he hadn't walked a true mile in their shoes. But they hadn't walked in his, either. And in the end, was either necessary? Their need was mutual. It could transcend the barriers of their differences.

Or they could all die. As far as Jim was concerned, it was up to them. As he stared down at Kerry's ruined face, he really didn't give a damn how it turned out.

Ferrick did, though. He watched Jim as Jim watched Kerry. And as Jim smoothed Kerry's battered, bleeding brow, Ferrick turned to Sam and whispered, "Get some of the guys you trust and drag that fugger Elwood into the smallest room you can find, lock him up, and throw away the key. Toss Timmy and Frank in with him for good measure."

Sam said softly, "Is that the way it is?"

"Yeah. From now on, that's the way it is."

She nodded, turned, and headed out.

By the time Jim finally reached the bridge, the Communer ship was almost in striking distance.

CHAPTER FOUR

1

Jim was still struggling with his own conflicting emotions: he wanted to protect the crew of his ship, but at the same time was angry enough at them, at the treachery of some of them, to blast them all straight to hell without a second thought.

He wrestled with it as he and Ferrick entered the bridge at the top level and made their way down to their respective stations: Jim to the oversized Kolumban seat—almost a throne—where the captain presided over the entirety of the ship's controls, able to monitor or override any other sector or control system if he so desired. Ferrick moved down to the next level, where he could watch over the complexities of the engineering systems that made the ship a ship, and not an inert hunk of lifeless metal.

Jim watched him, then said, "Wait."

"What?"

Jim pointed to a large complex of screens and control pads on his own level, a few feet to his left. "Sit there."

"But that's Kerry's . . . oh."

Jim nodded.

"You can run engineering from there, but I need an exec, too. With Kerry out of it, except for me, nobody knows more about this tub than you do."

Ferrick nodded, climbed back up the ramp, and took his seat. Jim surveyed the rest of the bridge: almost all the kids had crowded in and were standing along the outer walls, silent as a flock of watching crows. All of the major control complex stations were filled except for one.

"Where's Elwood?"

"What?" Ferrick said.

"What did you do with Elwood?"

Ferrick stared at him. "I had him locked up."

"You better unlock him. He's the best gunnery officer we've got."

"He tried to kill you."

"Well, he's not gonna try that again, right? You won't let him."

"That's right. I won't."

"So get him up here."

"Man," Ferrick said, shaking his head. "You're nuts."

"No," Jim replied. "I'm the captain."

Ferrick pointed at one of the kids along the wall. "You! Go find that craphead and drag his scrawny ass up here. Wait a second, a couple more of you go with him. I want Elwood Grieger up here, no arguments. Got it?"

The three of them nodded and hurried out. Jim watched them go, then turned and faced forward. "Bridge shields open," he said.

A soft whirring, more felt than heard, whispered through the levels of the bridge as the entire front end of the large room seemed suddenly to vanish. Even Jim, who had seen this before in virtual-reality simulations, felt a twinge of vertigo. Some of the others gasped; although they'd been living aboard ships of one kind or another for years, none of them had ever gazed on naked space from such a close, personal viewpoint.

The universe seemed to explode from behind the retracting shields like a vast, glittering sea of cat's eyes gleaming up from beneath the smooth black skin of eternity. The VR Sims on which he'd trained were supposed to be indistinguishable from the real thing; after all, the stimeos were hooked directly into his brain. But, though he couldn't explain how, he could tell the difference.

Something weirdly familiar nagged at him as he thought about that, but he couldn't grab it, and it was gone almost as soon as it appeared.

His heart was beating a little faster, but after a few seconds his cautionary reflexes kicked in and he forced himself to ignore the show. Instead, automatically, he scanned the quadrants in front of him, looking for the mystery ship. Of course he couldn't find it. Even if it was right on top of them, there was no way the naked human eye could pick it out a single vessel against the vastness of the starfields.

"Magda, throw the realtime scans up on the main screen," he said.

From two levels down, Magda said, "Initiating main view screen . . . now."

An opaque holoscreen abruptly appeared against the glimmering stars, a dark rectangle twenty feet square, its surface swirling with colors like an oil slick on a windy day. It flickered, then focused again on a different scape of suns. In the center a single star gleamed much brighter than the rest.

"Enlarge," Jim said.

Click by silent click the holoscreen expanded the prismatic shape until its true form became visible: it looked like nothing so much as a scattering of glowing blue-green pickup sticks.

"What the hell is it?" somebody muttered.

I don't have the vaguest clue, Jim thought, dismayed.

But he didn't say this aloud, relying on the first rule of captaining: When you don't know, pretend that you do. Or shut up.

He chose *shut up,* and leaned forward in his big chair. A touchpad obediently extended itself from his main console, rising to meet him. He ran his fingers across it, watched the identification database appear on one of his monitors, flickering from one shape to another as it offered him several visual pattern correlations.

None of the pictures he examined looked much like the glittering handful of needles in the main holoscreen, but he checked each possibility carefully before finally rejecting it.

In the end, he knew no more than he'd known before; whatever it was out there, it wasn't in the identification database the Hunzza had supplied to the Kolumbans when they sold them this ship.

"Ferrick, anything hitting our shields?"

Ferrick was watching his own screens intently. "Not as far as I can see."

Jim leaned back in his seat and gnawed on a knuckle as he stared at the stars, and the screen of stars in the middle of the stars.

Stars . . .

Then it hit him, what had whispered to him before too low for him to understand: *stars*!

They shouldn't have been there. He'd programmed the ship's autopilots to take them to Kolumba in a series of short, slow jumps—but the time spent in realspace between those jumps should have been only a few seconds. Yet here they were, hanging around in realspace long enough for another ship not only to find them, but to come creeping-sneaking right up on them.

"Hey, Magda, how long have we been in realspace?"

The stocky girl checked her screens. "Almost four hours."

"But that's imposs—" He didn't finish because even as he spoke, he realized what must have happened.

"Are we in a solar system?" he said.

"Sure," Magda said. "I thought you knew."

"What system?" Jim said.

She turned and stared at him as if he'd lost his mind. "According to the autopilot, it's the Kolumban system. Where we've been heading all along."

Jim closed his eyes and sighed. He'd done the best he could to jury-rig the ship's controls for Terran use, but evidently he hadn't been as smart or thorough as he'd thought. He must have misprogrammed the autopilot, and as a result of his mistake they'd arrived in the Kolumban system a week early.

Which brought up some new questions: had the mystery ship been waiting for them? Or had it somehow tracked them through hyperspace to their destination?

Was this a Kolumban vessel? Or did it belong to the Kolumban's patrons, the enigmatic Communers? Or was it something else entirely?

"Jim . . . uh, Captain . . ." Ferrick said abruptly.

"Yes?"

"The intruder ship has stopped. It's no longer on a closing course with us."

Jim checked his own screens again. Ferrick was right. The odd scattering of luminous stick shapes, which had been inexorably closing the distance between itself and the *Endeavor*, was now maintaining itself relative to Jim's vessel and the Kolumban sun in a stable trajectory, neither approaching nor retreating.

He pummeled his tired brain, trying to recall long-past military strategy classes. Was this development ominous? A lot depended on the strange ship's weapons systems. If he had some idea what those might be, then he could draw logical conclusions about the vessel's maneuvering. But he didn't know.

He stared blankly at the big room spread out below him. He sat on the top level; descending like a giant, tan-carpeted staircase were five more levels, each shelf a rough semicircular curve in shape, the inner part of the curve facing the huge pseudo-view screen at the front. Many of the stations were empty; he had a major staffing problem, and had been able to train only a few of the kids to operate what he thought were the most critical systems; engineering, ship's ops, weapons . . .

"Where's Elwood?" he said, without looking at Ferrick.

"Dunno," the other boy grunted. "Hang on." He spoke softly into a throat mike, then looked up. "Gotta problem."

"What?"

"Elwood says he don't want to come. Says you can go fug yourself."

Jim shook his head. "God, he's got a hard-on for me. What did I ever do to him?"

"Well, I guess it's me, too."

"You?"

"Uh-huh. I sort of broke his jaw a little, is what they're saying he's unhappy about." Ferrick raised his right fist and examined it dubiously, as if he had no idea where it had come from. His knuckles were abraded, and one was turning blue and swelling up.

"Hurt my hand," he mumbled.

Jim stifled a sudden urge to burst out laughing. Ferrick, who had proven himself not to be an enemy, yet who was still not a friend and perhaps never would be, worrying about a scabby knuckle when the ship out there might blow them all to kingdom come.

Then he understood. Ferrick was as aware of that ship and the dire possibilities it bore and he himself was, but he knew his own limits and limitations. The ship was the *captain's* problem. If the captain wanted him to do something, then he would try to do it as well as he could. In the meantime, his skinned knuckles were familiar. He knew what to do about those.

I'm in his shoes, Jim thought. *I don't know how or why, but I am.* And in the shock flare of that understanding, he knew why Ferrick had intervened. Kerry had been right after all. Ferrick would have let Elwood kill Kerry, but he *would* have killed Elwood in his own turn. Partly out of revenge, yes, but mostly because Ferrick was incapable of trusting, let alone serving, one he regarded as less capable than himself.

Keep it in mind, Jim warned himself. *He'll serve the captain, the one who earns that title in his* own *mind, but no one lesser.*

"Damn him," Jim said. "I need a gunner. I could do it myself, but I've got the rest of the ship, too."

Ferrick nodded. "I can do what I can, but I'm not Kerry. You trained him to run this thing, not me." He gestured at the console in front of him. There was no shame in his admission. He spoke as if he were describing the color of the metal in front of him. Ferrick, Jim realized, wasn't terribly imaginative. It was one of the things that made him so frightening. And so dangerous.

"I can go talk to him," Ferrick said.

"No," Jim replied. "Just bring him up here. I'll talk to him. If he still refuses to come, drag him."

Ferrick nodded, a faint smile flickering on his heavy lips. "That'll put him in a good mood, all right."

"Nothing's gonna put Elwood in a good mood," Jim said grimly. "But maybe I can put him in the right mood."

"You're the captain," Ferrick replied.

"That's right. I am."

Ferrick spoke into his throat mike. From down below, panic thrumming in her voice like acid bubbles rising through dark water, Magda said, "What's it doing now? Look at it. What's it *doing*?"

As she spoke, in a voice rough and burred with terror, a knot of struggling, cursing boys caromed onto the bridge, Elwood entangled in the midst of their web of struggling, heaving flesh.

Jim cast a quick glance at the holoscreen: the shape of the alien ship was indeed changing. The arrangement of its thin filaments had been, at least to his own eyes, random. But now the sticks were slowly moving away from each other, falling into a long and regular parallel line, with the tips of each light shaft pointing directly at the *Endeavor*. Like a line of spears, Jim thought.

He felt his own fear and hid it reflexively; if he allowed terror to grip him, it would eat the rest of them alive. Never before had he really understood what it was to have so many others utterly dependent on him. Even Ferrick, with his iron-fashioned soul and his stolid, unimaginative acceptance of his own mortality, was watching him with a wall-eyed, questioning expression.

They dragged Elwood Grieger down the ramp to the captain's chair and dumped his carcass at Jim's feet as if it were a sacrificial offering.

Elwood ended up on his hands and knees, lank hair hanging in a sweaty curtain across his face. But when he raised his head and stared up at Jim, his gray eyes sunken in rings of lumpy bruises, his lips split, his dusk-golden skin scraped and marred, there was no fear in him.

From the arrogance in Elwood's haughty gaze, Jim thought, it was impossible to tell that he was on his hands and knees. He might have been observing his own humiliation from some distant high place where all things and all concerns were reduced to the doings of the most insignificant insects.

They stared at each other.

After a moment that seemed much longer than it really was (in the background Magda was still muttering about the alien ship), Jim nodded and said, "Okay, if you won't help us for yourself, then what about the rest of them? All the ones you call your friends?"

Elwood's lips moved in a cracked sneer: "If they were really my friends, I'd be sitting in that chair instead of you. And you'd be looking up at me. You'd be the one begging."

"Are you begging?" Jim asked.

"You know what I mean."

"Jim, that ship—" Ferrick said. Jim lifted one hand for silence without looking at him. He concentrated on Elwood. There was more at stake between the two of them than the question of whether the alien vessel was hostile or not, or what its strange maneuvering meant. Ferrick didn't possess the imagination to see the larger issue, and even if he had, he would have dismissed it as trivial. Jim knew that Ferrick's methods were more directly brutal than his own. They solved immediate problems; breaking Elwood's jaw had been such a solution. Of the implications of such outcomes—their ramifications, their effects on bigger problems—Ferrick was as innocent as a fish is innocent of the water in which it swims.

He stared down at the top of Elwood's head—the skin beneath that rank, tangled hair was pink, not golden, he noted crazily—and missed Kerry terribly. Missed his blue killer's eyes, missed his blazing killer's imagination, missed *him*. But this was his own thing to do, perhaps the first such trial he'd had to face since that long-ago decision to apply to the Solaris Space Academy against his father's orders.

And that one had turned out to be a disaster, hadn't it? His family shattered, his true future ruined, his dreams reshaped into nightmares that even now woke him weeping in the darkest part of the night? Oh, yes, *captain*, he thought bitterly. What a mockery this all is!

I'm playing a game, he thought with a sudden dismay that was as wearying as it was disheartening. *I call myself captain, and scheme with others to make the rest of them call me that, too. But we're* all *children playing at a game none of us really understand. This lumbering Kolumban vessel, bought but not made, by a people who could ride it but not build it, is no great white ship of Earth. It's a stolen car, a joyride, a toy, and more fools all of us for pretending anything else.* And that was the best description he could think of. They played a game of *let's pretend*, except somehow, horribly, the stakes of the game had become life and death.

He looked down at Elwood, seeing from his vantage point the way the spidery boy's jaw bulged awkwardly beneath its paint of purpling bruises—still broken. *It must pain him,* Jim thought, *but he shows no sign. His eyes are clear.*

He hates me.

"You think you should be up here, and me down there? Fine. It's done."

He rose from the captain's seat, stepped down, put his arms around Elwood Grieger's chest, and gently lifted him to his feet. He was astonished at how little the other boy weighed—it was as if Elwood were half bird, his long bones filled with air. But the thin layers of muscle over those empty bones went suddenly as hard as sheets of malleable steel.

"Here," he said gently. "The captain's seat. It's yours. Take it. And take everything that goes with it."

"Jim—" Ferrick said, but Jim ignored him. He sat Elwood down, patted him once on the shoulder, then stepped away. He stiffened his body to full attention and snapped off a crisp, military salute.

"What are your orders, Captain?" he said.

Elwood gaped at him.

"I won't let you," Ferrick said. "He ain't no captain. We didn't elect—"

"If he'd killed me, he would have been. The Cowboy way, remember? So now he is," Jim said. "And I'm his champ. You'll have to fight *me* first. That's your Cowboy way, too."

Ferrick's blocky features gaped dumbfounded at him. Kerry would have seen through it, but it was beyond Ferrick's turgid, pragmatic understanding. His dark eyes reflected the pain of an animal trapped in dumb steel teeth with no idea how it had managed to become entangled. Jim felt a moment's worth of pity for him, but only a moment. Ferrick didn't really like him, either.

Not that *liking* had anything to do with it.

He saluted Elwood again. "What are your orders, sir?" he repeated.

Elwood sat in the captain's seat looking uncomfortably aware of how small he was within the confines of the huge alien throne. His almond eye sockets, bruised and puffy, cupped his skittering eyes like crooked fists holding rolling, white-rimmed marbles.

"You . . ." he said. "I order. My orders are. You . . ."

Behind him, Ferrick growled softly.

"You don't mean this shit!" Elwood burst out. "It's a trick, isn't it?"

Jim said nothing. He stood and waited, dumbly patient, exhausted. He had taken the last dice he had, and tossed them to the winds of fate. Now he awaited whatever storm those winds might bring.

A blank, bull-like anger began to twist and pull at Ferrick's features. His mahogany skin glowed with heat. He stepped forward and dropped one heavy hand on Elwood's thin shoulder, turning him.

"Get your ass outta that—"

Jim moved without thought, glorying in the ease and release of thoughtless reflex. He had already decided. His body knew how to achieve the rest. He let it do what it wanted, what it had been trained for most of the years of his life to do.

His hands moved with breathless, precise speed: slap *whack*! Ferrick should have remembered. He'd seen this before, in a fight shortly after Jim had appeared aboard the *Outward Bound*. But Ferrick had been busy then, and maybe he hadn't seen enough of it—or all of it.

The others gasped. To them it looked like a magic trick, those blurring hands, the sound of blows like sorcerer's handclaps. And Ferrick fell away, blood pumping from his nostrils, his eyes dazed and suddenly vacant. He sat down hard in his own chair. After a moment he shook his head and tried to rise.

"Don't," Jim said. "Elwood's the captain, and I'm his champ. I won't let you touch him."

Ferrick stared up at him, full awareness slowly leaking back into his eyes. Along with a film of crazed, fatalistic hopelessness.

"Why are you doing this?" he whispered.

"Because I have to," Jim told him.

Then he turned back to face Elwood, who stood, swaying just the tiniest bit with the shock of his changed circumstances. His young face was creased with thought, and for the first time, his gaze fully *interested*.

Jim stiffened and saluted again. "What are your orders, Captain?"

He was aware of all the others now, the ones lined along the walls, their faces straining toward him as blank and stunned as sunflowers. Even tough Magda stared, mouth open, with the strange parallelogram of sticks hanging suspended in midair behind her, forgotten but now growing, growing . . .

But this was all on the periphery, not just of his vision, but of his consciousness. Only the sun of Elwood's face, now fully ablaze with *interest*, held sway on his full attention.

Elwood shook his right arm like a man shaking out a bullwhip and then, with his trademark serpentine suddenness, launched a thunderous blow to Jim's jaw. The blow landed like a cudgel, with an audible crack, the crunching of bones made even louder in Jim's ears by the echo chamber of his skull.

He staggered backward but caught himself on the edge of the captain's console with one hand. He took a deep breath. His lip was badly split, and blood coursed like a new spring from the corner of his mouth.

He straightened, forced himself to attention, and saluted. "What are your orders, Captain?"

Sss*whap*!

This blow caught him high on the side of his skull, at the edge of his ridged eye socket, and closed his eye instantly with a swollen, bruise-colored bag of gore. It sent him to his knees, his brain spinning wildly, consciousness slipping away from him like the edge of a black bedsheet.

He fought it, breath trickling slowly back into his heaving chest like water into a parched and empty well. He slobbered in great, shuddering gouts of air and waited until the storm of vertigo had drawn away. Then he stood again. Saluted.

"What are your orders, Captain?"

Elwood's face seemed to be receding from him as he watched it through the bloodshot lens of his single remaining eye. His head throbbed with high, silvery pain, a shriek of agony only bats or rabid dogs might hear. But the bedrock of *interest* in Elwood's eyes had begun to shift, as tectonic murmurs of uncertainty cracked the hidden fault lines that had always been there.

The third blow came out of nowhere like a dark comet crashing into the cratered backside of an empty moon. Jim's knees went jelly-soft as his legs floated out from under him. He landed hard on the carpeted deck, his one good eye still open, staring blandly at the brown fuzz of the carpet, the smell of dust suffocating his nostrils.

He lay paralyzed, unable to move nor wanting to move. It was better to lie there in the pounding moment and the throbbing silence, an empty cipher, a code not even he had any further interest in unraveling.

Why did I do this? he wondered, and could find no answer. It didn't matter. The time for answers was long past, intellect less than a faded rag, and only instinct remained.

Later he would not remember how he'd pulled himself up, muscle on flaccid muscle, bone on creaking bone, will on blind, dumb will, to his feet again, but he did it. As he stood, swaying like a drunk, his face a crushed wasteland of peeping bone and weeping bruise, he heard them—he couldn't really *see* anymore—gasping and grunting in horror and shock. But he paid them no more attention than he did Ferrick, whose dark features looked as if somebody had spilled clotted cream into them, bleaching his skin to the color of the bones that lay hidden— or perhaps not so hidden now—beneath.

He tried to raise his right arm, but it wouldn't move, and when he concentrated, he could feel nothing there. So he lifted his left hand instead, brought trembling fingers to his forehead (where he felt a sticky, clotted expanse that reminded him more of crusted raw hamburger than human flesh) and said, "What are your orders, Captain?" as teeth sputtered like popcorn from his shattered jaw.

One more, he thought. *One more will kill me.*

Elwood stared at him as if he'd never seen anything like this. Elwood who killed coldly and with clinical interest, now revealed something on his paste-pale features that none of the onlookers had ever seen before. It might have been disbelief. Or it might have been terror. Whatever it was, it was no longer *interest*.

Slowly he raised his fist, gulped in a series of deep, shuddering breaths. Drew back for the killing blow as Jim stood dully waiting for it.

And then Elwood froze, a pause as fraught as the interval between lightning and the roll of thunder that always follows. His gray gaze searched Jim's ruined features as a searchlight probes for meaning in the rubble of some mindless, meaningless disaster. And finally fell away, defeated.

He breathed slowly out and let his fist fall.

"You win," he said.

He lowered his head, an involuntary, perhaps unconscious obeisance, and stepped away from the captain's chair. He walked carefully around Jim, as if he feared even the slightest physical contact with him. He moved out onto the ramp, then walked slowly down until he reached the level that held the weapons complex. He turned toward this, then paused, and looked back up the ramp to where Jim still stood, watching him through one slitted eye.

"Cowboys are gone," Elwood said softly. Slowly, his back straightened and he brought his hand to his brow. "What are your orders, Captain?"

Jim raised his own, left-handed salute in reply. "Take your station, crewman," he managed. Then he toppled straight backward into the captain's chair, sprawling as bonelessly as a puppet bereft not only of strings, but of the guiding hand above the strings.

"Jeezus Keerist!" Ferrick bellowed. "Somebody get that autodoc back up here!"

He stared at raw, oozing meat of Jim's face, then turned his head to one side and puked.

2

When Jim awakened, he was looking at the blurry shape of his own monitor screens, floating like fuzzy green windows at some indeterminate distance in front of him. Something huge and dark hulked at his side. His face felt as if somebody had ripped off all his skin with a clawhammer, and when he tried to move his jaw, his first impression was that he'd tried to swallow a bowling ball, but it had gotten stuck somewhere to the right of his tongue.

"Gahh . . ."

"Don't try to talk," Ferrick said. "We'll get you out of here in a second."

"Naaahhh . . ." It came out like the sound a worried sheep might make, so he tried to shake his head. Big mistake. Sheets of white stars flashed across his blurry vision. His stomach cramped with nausea.

"I *told* you not to talk. Hold still. The autodoc's trying to hook you up. Once we get you shot full of pain juice, then we can get you out of here."

"Naahhtt. Gunggg."

"Shut up," Ferrick said.

Jim was vaguely aware of slender, shiny, whippy shapes weaving toward him, and that part of his consciousness not concerned with the agony that hammered at every part of his head thought, *The doc's tentacles . . .*

Something slapped gently at one side of his face, and a moment later, that entire side of his skull went numb. A couple of seconds later, the other side did likewise. It was an odd sensation, like having your cranium packed in cotton. But once the pain was gone, his brain was able to unlock from its overwhelming concern with it. He blinked, felt his eyelids as discrete pads sliding slickly over the surface of his eyeballs. He blinked again, and realized that the blurry green rectangles he'd been staring at were his monitor screens.

They still seemed far away, but he could see them clearly now. On the center screen was a miniaturized version of the alien ship pictured on the big screen that dominated the front of the bridge. For a moment he stared at it in confusion; what it *was*, how it concerned *him* seemed to have been knocked clear out of his mind. He played with the laughable image; a man with a bat taking a full, cutting swing—*thwock!*— and a tight, whirling little ball of thought stuff inside his head soaring up, up, vanishing in the starry distance . . .

Get a grip! he told himself grimly. But it took an almost physical effort to corral his scattered thoughts, herd them protesting back into some semblance of order. Suddenly he missed the pain. It had nearly overwhelmed him, but it had sharpened him, the part that could ignore the pain. Now he felt as if he were slowly sinking into white fuzz, everything smoothing out, losing meaning.

He ground his teeth together, trying to work his jaw, and was rewarded with a sharp chromium jab directly to his pain centers that woke him up a little.

"Jesus, don't move," Ferrick said.

The autodoc noticed, too. Another tentacle came snaking in and landed on his swollen jaw, which was not only broken, but also dislocated. He felt the tentacle land, and then something *crunched* beneath the bloated, bruise-purpled mound that had been the side of his face. All the bones there suddenly turned to liquid, felt like they were sliding greasily around. A sharp *pop*! echoed between his ears, and suddenly he could work his mouth again.

"Just shoot the numbjuice . . ."

"What?" Ferrick said.

Jim's tongue, as anesthetized as everything else attached to his head, flopped around like a fish dying on a sandy beach. It took him two tries before he began to get the hang of talking with what felt like a chunk of raw liver wedged between his broken teeth.

"I'm not going anywhere," Jim said. "I'm staying right here. Unless you want to handle *that* all by yourself." Jim tried to nod at the alien vessel on the monitor, but the autodoc's tentacles were clamped to his head as rigidly as a steel cage. There was more liquid, shifting movement in the area of his jaw, and a growing heat there, as well.

The nanotech bugs injected by the autodoc deep into bone and muscle were working hard to weld him back together at the cellular level. That was good, but it would limit his movements to whatever the autodoc thought was proper for a patient in his condition.

Well, at least the doc must not consider him in imminent danger of dying. Or of overriding the nerve blocks it had applied. Otherwise, it would have just knocked him out. And wouldn't that have been a cosmic joke on all of them?

He wondered if Elwood would appreciate the humor, and decided he might. Elwood was, without a doubt, a little bit crazy, in the cosmic sense of the term, and Jim suspected that, beneath the iron layer of Elwood's never-changing *interest*, his craziness was of the laughing variety. Sardonic in the extreme, of course, but laughing.

He gingerly turned his gaze in Elwood's direction, and saw the clear gray eyes in that sallow-gold face staring back at him, blank with waiting. But no fear there, and that was good. Magda's face looked pasty, her eyes dirty finger smudges punched in a wad of dough. She looked like she was screaming inside.

"Jim, are you okay?" Ferrick said doubtfully.

"Take your seat, Mr. Autrey. We may have a battle to fight, and if we do, I'm going to need all the help you can give me. You and everybody else."

Ferrick blinked at the Mr. Autrey stuff (as Jim had expected he might), but he got it quickly enough. He straightened, snapped off a salute, and said, "Aye, aye, Captain."

It's a start, Jim thought.

He leaned forward in his chair, the massive, floating, tentacled bulk of the autodoc moving with him—it was like being attached to a floating elephant—and stared intently at his screens. The alien vessel, still holding its rigid parallel pattern, was staying with them, but once again, it was moving closer.

"Mr. Autrey, I want reports from our shield monitors on a ten-second basis. Are we getting any probes?"

"On your left-hand screen, Captain," Ferrick replied, his voice all business now. "Nothing hitting the shields except for a slight gluon increase."

Jim checked his screen. Yes, the results glimmering there confirmed what Ferrick was saying. A small, but significant increase in the rate of gluon interactions between the force shields of the *Endeavor* and the background scatter of other standard particles.

Gluons, Jim thought. *What the hell?*

These particular quantum particles were the physical representatives of the strong nuclear force, the force that bound quarks together into protons and neutrons. They were in effect the "glue" that held the material universe together, hence the name they'd been given.

Gluon detectors, as well as quark and lepton monitors, were standard equipment on any deep space vessel. The workings between and among these three particles comprised the "weather" of any position in realspace.

It was all standard stuff, and the readings almost never varied, no matter what part of the galaxy one happened to be in—unless, of course, you were in the neighborhood of a great anomaly like a sun, the mouth of a wormhole, or near the event horizon of a black hole—any of which would probably mean you and your ship were about to be yanked into a storm cloud of your own disintegration.

More gluons . . . but no increase in quarks or leptons. What did it mean? Did it even have anything to do with that alien vessel approaching them?

Deep in the back of his mind, in that place where ancient memories are stored in mental scrap heaps, something niggled at him insistently. He dragged it from its midden into the light.

A mustache?

But what did mustaches and gluons have to do with each other? He had no idea, but this particular mustache was insisting that they *did*. And there was something *familiar* about this subnasal cookie catcher . . .

He could see it clearly. It was a thick mustache, no mere dusting or pencil smudge, but wide, luxuriant, waxed at the tips and curling up into gleaming points. It looked just like . . . Dr. Herrena's mustache. In fact, it *was* Dr. Herrena's mustache. Dr. Herrena, who had made his life miserable when he was eight years old and still trying to work his way through the basics of high-energy physics. Dr. Herrena, mustache quivering with irritation, who had drilled him again and again on gluons, quarks, leptons, hadrons, up and down and charm and color and all the other esoterics of the particle dance that made reality what it was.

One of the very few flunking grades Jim had ever received came at the hands of Dr. Herrena. A major test, now nearly forgotten, but it had made his educational life miserable at the time. A midterm, he remembered now, with such awful results he'd tried to hack his own home's computers to prevent his parents from seeing the grade. He remembered *that* failure more vividly than the failed exam that had led to it, since it had resulted in one of the few spankings his father had ever given him.

Quark-gluon plasmas. That was the topic that had ruined him. That and "glueballs," the extremely odd possibility that the binding force represented by gluons might bind to *itself*, creating the quantum equivalent of blobs of glue.

This was all basic stuff, so basic he'd filed and forgotten it long ago. Now he stared at his screens and wondered if somebody else had done more than just remember the weird possibilities of this cosmological glue.

"The gluon rate is still increasing . . ." he said, mostly to himself, but Ferrick overheard.

"Does it mean anything?" Ferrick asked. "I thought gluons and quarks couldn't exist by themselves, only bound together as hadrons—protons, neutrons, like that.

"Yeah," Jim murmured softly. "I thought so, too. You ever hear of something called a glueball?"

Ferrick's basic education had not included the wilder theoretical wanderings of quantum physics, nor had his later efforts at self-education taken him down this particular crooked path. He shook his head. "Nope. Do they have anything to do with what we're seeing hitting our shields?"

Jim rubbed his chin, then stopped, sucking air, as he felt the bones beneath his skin shift like spaghetti in a bag. It didn't really hurt—the autodoc was blocking his pain centers far too effectively for that—but it made him queasy to feel his bones sliding around like that. He took his bones for granted, or at least he always had.

Elwood's face suddenly appeared on one of his screens. "That ship just reached the edge of our red-zone perimeter. Do you want me to shoot it, Captain?"

"Not yet, Mr. Grieger," Jim replied. "But be ready."

"I already am, sir," Elwood replied.

Sir. He called me "sir" . . .

Ferrick said, "The rate is increasing fast, Captain."

It was. Nothing seemed odd but that one thing. As far as he could tell, the alien vessel wasn't actually doing anything. It had even stopped its approach, though it was still matching the *Endeavor*'s trajectory.

Glueballs . . . what the hell was it about glueballs?

Professor Herrena's mustache quivered in his mind. It had quivered the same way when the teacher explained Jim's flunking grade on the exam.

"I know you can do better," Dr. Herrena said. "What were you thinking? Glueballs are *unstable*. They can only exist in the primordial soup, the quark-gluon plasma at the beginning of the Big Bang . . ."

"Contact rate still going up, Jim," Ferrick said, his voice no longer hiding a pronounced quaver.

Jim was trying to watch the figures on one screen as he kept an eye on the alien ship displayed on another. So when he first saw it, he wasn't entirely sure just *what* he'd seen. As he leaned toward the picture of the glowing blue sticks for a closer look, it happened again.

The space between the two vessels seemed to *ripple*!

Glueballs. Unstable. *Big Bang!*

"Oh my God," Jim breathed. He reached forward to take the drive controls, but the autodoc tangled him up, wouldn't let him extend his arms far enough.

"Ferrick! Wormhole Factor Five! Get us the hell out of here!"

"But Jim—Captain—we're in a solar system. If we—"

"Just do it!"

"Aye, aye, sir." Ferrick rattled his fingertips across a pair of touchpads and the *Endeavor lurched.*

The sudden, jarring shake—as if a vast invisible hand had grabbed the vessel by the scruff of its neck and shaken it like a puppy—sent comm pads and hand mikes flying, rolled crewmen from their consoles like eggs from a carton, and scythed those standing along the walls like wheat before a harvester.

Buried deep beneath layers of hardened duramole skin, beneath sheaths of reinforcing cable, the bones of the ship squalled like rusty hinges as stresses and strains they'd never been designed for plucked them like over-stretched violin strings. Then the artificial gravity snapped off.

Ferrick gritted his teeth and held on to the arms of his chair with white-knuckled concentration as scraps of paper, several brightly colored electropens, a miniature teddy bear (it had been sitting serenely on Magda's console a moment before), a flock of bobby pins, one thick leather boot, and two well-used handkerchiefs (rippling like flags) stormed around and past him with soft clicking and flapping sounds.

Jim found himself floating upside down, his feet still rising, when the gravity generators came back on and slammed him back into his seat so hard that his head—with a gruesome sucking sound—was ripped from the autodoc's steel tentacles. These appendages groped blindly for several seconds before finding him again and snuffling across his body until they had his skull safely in their grasp.

He raised his head and stared groggily at the chaos on the bridge, trying to ignore the dull, all-encompassing roar—like hurricane-spawned breakers tumbling onto a rocky beach—that gouged deep into the dark hollows behind his eyes.

Magda had been flung away from her console. She landed hard against an empty control station the next level up, draped over the top of the station, shaking her head, the slow, dogged motion spattering drops of blood from a Zorro-like slash on her forehead.

From the top level, just inside the main bridge entry, somebody said, in a thin, breathy wail, "It's broke. My gawdamned arm's broke."

When the jump had begun, the shields had automatically closed, restoring the front of the bridge to blank gray bulkheads, but the large holoscreen still hung in midair. It had turned an inky, shifting no-color that somehow seemed to be rapidly *flickering*—but that wasn't right, either, Jim thought. It shimmered on some subliminal level, sucking at both the eyes and the mind, and was nearly impossible to turn away from.

Subspace, hyperspace, warpspace, wormholespace, it had a host of names, but they all meant one thing: the Stygian, vastly empty basement beneath the stars, noplace and at the same time everyplace, a gaping maw beneath the glittering flesh of reality.

He understood for the first time a lesson he'd been taught in his early theory of command classes: *It is unwise*, the instructor had said, *to expose untrained and unprepared passengers to the reality of no-space.*

"Oh, God, turn it off," Ferrick moaned.

Jim slapped his touchpad, and the screen mercifully vanished. The bridge looked like some high-tech office that had been systematically trashed by gremlins. Papers, trinkets, hats, odd chunks of plastic and metal, cushions, even, Jim noted with disbelief, a red wig, were scattered everywhere. The flip-flop of the artificial gravity had also flung living bodies in every direction and now, groaning, white-eyed and staring, the kids were rising to their feet, touching themselves with a soft, worried wonder, looking for reassurance that all their parts were still correctly attached.

The boy groaning about his broken arm coughed suddenly and went silent.

"What the hell *was* that?" Ferrick said, sounding bemused.

"I'm not sure," Jim said—and wished he had a few of his old instructors on hand, though he doubted if they would be sure, either, not even Dr. Herrena—"but what I think happened is that we jumped into wormspace just as that other ship hit us with a glueball wave. And it didn't help that we were inside a solar gravity well at the same time."

Ferrick blinked. None of it made any sense to him. "So . . ." he said finally. "Are we okay or not?"

Jim looked around the bridge. Except for the layer of detritus, everything looked okay. And he'd seen with his own eyes that they'd made it into the safety of wormspace.

"Yeah, I think so," Jim said. "I think we made it."

Ferrick sighed. He looked at Jim, an odd grin tugging at his lips. "You know," he said, "I just puked all over my own feet." He glanced at his lap. "And now I see I've pissed my pants, too. That's gotta be a first."

He looked back at Jim. "Nice job, Captain. You are the captain again, right?"

"Yes, I am."

"No more bullshit games?"

"No more," Jim said. "Don't need them now, do we?"

"Huh?"

"Elwood. He got his wish."

"What's that?"

"He got to beat me in. I'm a real Stone Cowboy now."

Ferrick grunted sourly. "Kerry was right. Stone Cowboys are dead."

Jim's jawbone gave a final mercurial twitch and subsided, leaving that side of his face still numb, but feeling *right* again. The autodoc's tentacles withdrew.

He nodded at Ferrick. "Dead now," he agreed.

3

—————

The omnipresent red lights designed for Kolumban eyes gave Kerry's cheeks a spurious glow of healthy pinkness, though the deep hollows that cradled his eyes gave a raccoonlike air of puzzlement to his expression.

His room was much smaller than Jim's. Even with only him, Ferrick, Sam, and Jim, the chamber felt crowded and stuffy. It didn't help that Kolumbans used a different kind of fresher system than humans, and so the smells of their badly washed bodies mingled in an oppressive scent that reminded Jim of a long-opened can of stale tuna fish.

They were all sitting on Kerry's bed except for Ferrick, who leaned against one wall. "Well," Kerry said, "I guess I'm glad I was out during all the fun." He tipped his head at Jim. "Do you plan to solve all your personnel problems with your face, Captain?"

"Not if I can help it," Jim said. "I hope there won't be any more. Did you hear the latest?"

Kerry shook his head. "What? Monkeys fly out of your butt?"

Jim's lips quivered. "Close. After everything calmed down, Elwood came to me and announced that he was appointing himself my champ."

"Ow," Kerry said. "I thought the idea was to get rid of all the Cowboy traditions."

"Yeah, it is. But I think I'm gonna make an exception in this case."

Kerry thought about it. "Uh-huh."

Ferrick said, "Why?"

"There's an old saying," Jim said. "I don't remember who said it first, but it goes something like this: 'Hold your friends close. But hold your enemies closer.' "

Ferrick nodded thoughtfully. "Within easy striking distance, if necessary."

Jim chuckled. Good old Ferrick. The way his mind worked was a fascination, even if it was brutally predictable. "I guess that works both ways, but yes, that's pretty much my thinking on it."

"It's a risk," Kerry said.

At that, Jim laughed out loud. "And we sure as hell don't want to take any *risks*, do we?" He reached out and touched Kerry's bruised face, then brushed his own freshly healed jaw. "I mean, somebody might get *hurt*."

Sam had been sitting silently, eyes downcast, chewing absently at her lower lip. Now she looked up, her black eyes with their disturbing silver traceries flashing dangerously. *"You did get hurt!"*

Her vehemence startled him. "Well, I'm okay now. And so is Kerry. Even Elwood. Thank God for the autodoc."

Her voice was bitter. "And all for what? All the fighting, the blood, the pain? What was it for? You were the captain before it happened, and you're the captain now. What's changed?"

"I think," Jim said softly, "now everybody accepts me as the captain. That was the important part. The rest of it doesn't matter."

"But it *could* have. You could have been killed. Or Kerry. Or even Elwood. Hell, Frank almost *did* die."

"Which would have been not much of a loss," Kerry muttered.

"Any of us would have been a loss! Why can't you understand that?" She looked like she was about to burst into tears.

Jim leaned forward, stroked her shoulder. "You're right," he said. "We can't afford to lose anybody. That was what I was trying to stop, Sam. After Frank got stabbed, I realized how bad it had gotten, and I had to do something. It may not have been the best thing, but in the end, it turned out okay."

"Aw, come on, admit it," Kerry chuckled. "By the end you were just playing it right out your ass. Nobody else could figure out what you were doing because you didn't have a clue, either."

Jim smiled at him. "My faithful exec officer. Seeing through me again." His expression grew serious. "Did I tell you I missed you?"

Kerry didn't seem to hear this. Suddenly brisk and businesslike, he turned to Ferrick. "And you, ship's engineer. What's going on with the *Endeavor*?"

Ferrick raised his massive shoulders, causing his bullet-shaped head to resemble that of a turtle slowly retracting into its shell. "The food still sucks," he said.

Sam snorted. "It's gonna keep right on sucking, too, big boy. At least until we get something in the way of raw materials that didn't come off a Kolumban hay farm."

"How was I to know the Kolumbans were vegetarians?" Jim grumbled. He tried to make it sound like a joke, but somehow it didn't come out that way. It came out sounding like one more failure in a long string of them. The same thing he thought he saw in Sam's gaze as she stared at him silently. And he wondered what had broken between them, and if it could ever be fixed.

He looked down at his hands and remembered calling Frank a coward. But when the chips were down and the alien vessel coming, he'd cut and run.

The retreat didn't bother him so much. It would have been the logical tactical move for any captain faced with a threat of unknown proportions. What did gnaw at him, though, was that it had been the first thing that had popped into his mind. The coward's reflex.

Running.

So what did that make him?

CHAPTER FIVE

1

K erry and Jim, their bruises fading into blurred yellow shadows, entered the bridge together. It was late at night. In the dim umber glow, the three kids watching their stations down below were vague, shadowy blobs, distinguishable from their machines only by their lack of hard-edged lines and angles.

The shields were still closed, but the main holoscreen was up, showing a broad sweep of stars. Jim went down one level to the captain's chair. Kerry slid past him to reach the exec's seat. He seated himself, yawned, stretched, then leaned back and extended his legs.

"How can you look so damned comfortable?" Jim said. "I always feel like I'm sitting in an electric chair when I'm in this damned hot seat."

" 'Cause you are," Kerry replied. "I'm just your humble assistant, massa boss. If I screw up, it's your fault. You da capitano, mano."

Jim strapped himself in—no more unscheduled free-floating experiences for him if the gravity went off again   and poked at the touchpad in front of him. "You know," he said, "I used to think it would be great, having my own ship. I never expected it to happen like this, though."

"Not quite what you wanted, huh?"

Jim grinned at him. "Let's just say it wasn't quite the way all my classes made it out to be."

He fiddled some more with his touchpad. The big holoscreen slipped, jittered, then threw up the recorded holovid of the alien vessel just before the *Endeavor* jumped into wormspace. "There you are," Jim muttered.

Kerry hadn't seen it before. "That's the bugaboo?"

"Yep. Weird-looking, isn't it?"

Down below, somebody belched, the eructation shockingly loud in the velvety crimson quiet. Kerry laughed. "Thanks to the cook!" he called out.

"Fuck the cook!" somebody replied.

"You are the cook!" Kerry snapped back, then turned to Jim and whispered, "It's Hunky. I've got him running ship's ops on the third shift. He said he was tired of trying to find new and creative ways to cook green goop. He's not bad, actually."

Jim nodded absently, absorbed in the image of the alien vessel on the screen. His fingers moved across the touchpad as he manipulated the picture, enlarging it click by click until the glowing blue picket line— spear line?—filled the huge screen from edge to edge. He froze the image and leaned back, staring thoughtfully as he chewed on one knuckle.

"I dunno," he said. "Tell the truth, I can't even be sure it *is* a ship. It sure as hell doesn't look like anything I've ever seen before." He glanced at Kerry. "What about you?"

Kerry shook his head. "Nope." He wondered why Jim would ask *him*—Jim was the expert, after all. Maybe it was just a captain thing, keeping the exec in the loop. He'd done similar things himself, though running a starship was sure as hell different from running a doper gang. Once again he was glad he'd made the decision to refuse the captain's position for himself. "You said it wasn't in the identification database?"

"I didn't find it. I was in kind of a hurry and just used pattern matching. The *Endeavor* is a Hunzza ship; it should be equipped with the standard database for the local galactic region. And Hunzza database search algorithms are as good as anybody's. Besides, that stick thing out there is just too distinctive. If it was in the database, I would have found it."

"Okay. So what do you think? Is it these Communer bastards?"

"No way of knowing. And no way of finding out, I guess."

"What do you mean, no way of finding out?"

"Well, without any confirmed ID from the ship's computers, there's just—"

"Who said anything about the computers? Why do we need them to confirm if it's a Communer ship?"

"Huh?"

"Who told us about these damned Communers in the first place?"

Jim stared at him. "My God. I'd forgotten all about her."

Kerry nodded in satisfaction. "Ur-Barrba." He rattled his own touchpad. "There's a wallscreen in her room. We can pull a picture up there, have her take a look. If she'll talk to us at all."

Jim stood. "So what are we waiting for?"

Kerry was reading something on his screens, a dubious expression on his face. "Frank's on duty right now. Guarding her door. You sure you don't want to wait till the next shift comes on?"

"Why?"

"Well, the last time you ran into him down there, he had a knife. This time he's got a shatterblaster."

"I can't hide from him. Even this tub isn't big enough for that. Tell you what. If he shoots me, you have my permission to arrest him."

Kerry stood. "You're strapped under your jacket, aren't you?"

As soon as he was reminded of it, Jim felt the heavy weight of the Stiron und Ritter .75 caliber rocket pistol nestled beneath his left armpit. "Yeah. Always, these days."

Kerry reached around and patted a lump nestled beneath his shirt at the small of his back. "Me, too."

"So it's two against one."

"I still think you should have let me take care of him."

Jim shook his head. "Sam was right. We can't afford to lose anybody. Not even Frank."

"Okay. Come on, Mr. Nice Guy. Let's go chat with the gorilla."

2

Ur-Barrba lay on her bed and listened to the rough breathing of the guard outside her door. Alone among the inhabitants of the *Endeavor*—which she still thought of as the *Orichoso-durba, Swift Wings*, in her language—she had no complaints about the food. She'd even enjoyed the pleasingly exotic ways Sam and Hunky had dreamed up to prepare her usual staples. Who of her own people, she wondered, would ever have thought of combining chopped, toasted *ichi* roots and boiled *spada*? Yet the result had been delicious. But that was the only thing she'd enjoyed about the events following the disastrous hijacking that had destroyed all of her crew but her.

She had relived those terrible doings a hundred times in the silence of her cabin cage, staring blankly at the ceiling, only the increased *rub-dub-dub* of her dual hearts (which, unlike human hearts, were situated at the base of her massive spine, shielded by a carapace of solid bone) betraying the anguish she felt.

And she had waited. For what, she knew not. She could only hope. She knew what they planned. Before they had taken it, the *Wing* had been her vessel, and she still knew it better than they did. True, she no longer had the captain's cabin, but even here, in this small cubicle that had once housed a dead crewman named Al-Hurrta (she could still smell his comforting odor impregnated into the bed and the blanket on it) she had resources they didn't know of.

The small screen on the wall opposite her bunk, for instance: hidden behind the gleaming metal scrim that surrounded it was a set of emergency controls. All the screens in all the crew cabins had the same setup. It was designed as an emergency backup communications system, a detail she'd requested the Hunzza shipbuilders add to their basic design. She supposed that because it was a nonstandard addition, the Terrans hadn't discovered it yet.

She'd been watching these stunted, disgustingly hairless humans all along, trying to puzzle them out. What they planned, what they wanted, what they *were*. Much of this was still a mystery to her, but she'd learned a few things, and watched more than a few she still didn't understand. She'd seen them fighting, more than once, and though the reasons for that were impenetrable to her, she'd hoped they would kill one another. She'd been disappointed when it hadn't happened.

And she'd watched the Communer ship as it ghosted ever closer, before the *Wing*—what its hijackers now called the *Endeavor*—had jumped into wormspace. That had puzzled her most of all. She recognized the ship, of course, or at least the style of it. The Communer lords had openly visited the Kolumban system three times in her life that she knew about, and, she suspected, many times she *didn't* know about. She hadn't ever been aboard one of their ships—no Kolumban had—but she'd seen them from the bridge of the *Wing* as Hunzzan instructors patiently trained the Kolumban crews to operate their new ship. She'd even met a Communer face to face (well, they didn't exactly have *faces* . . .) though the experience was nothing she was in any hurry to repeat.

Which made it all the more mysterious, why a Communer ship had been lying in wait in her own home system, ready to pounce on the *Wing* when it reappeared there. If the Communer ship *had* been waiting . . .

Ur-Barrba raised her craggy, fur-matted skull, nostrils widening. *Somebody coming!*

She listened a moment, then rolled over and feigned sleep. A few moments later, the door to her cabin slid softly open.

3

Frank sat hunched over, butt on the deck, back against the wall, belly bulging into his lap. Across his knees he balanced the weight of his shatterblaster.

He'd looked in on the giant monkey an hour ago, his nose wrinkling against the eye-watering, cinnamon-rancid dog-food stench that filled the room. As usual, big ugly was sleeping, its hot breath (Frank had no idea of the sex of his Kolumban prisoner, nor did he care) slubbering between thick black lips in a rusty, fetid rasp.

He stood and stared silently at Ur-Barrba, feeling an odd kinship with the slumbering beast. The alien was caged up like an animal, surrounded by circumstances and beings it probably didn't understand. But Frank understood those feelings very well. He felt that way himself most of the time.

He was a surly kid, big and lumbering just like the alien. He wasn't quick like most of the other kids, either in the head or with his bulky, bulging muscles. Sometimes it seemed to him he spent his whole life screaming, "Huh? What? Slow down!" inside his mind. But the quick ones, the small ones, just batted around him like gleaming moths, ignoring his constant state of angry confusion. Or worse, laughing at it.

He had a sort of grudging respect for Kerry Korrigan, because Kerry had been one of the few who ever took time to explain things to him, make sure he understood what was going on. But Kerry had betrayed him to Jim Endicott, who was just another chatterer, just another of the quick ones. For a short time he'd thought Elwood might replace Kerry, but now he knew that Elwood had betrayed him, too. In fact, he was even beginning to wonder about the night he'd been stabbed. Had that really been Endicott turning the knife back into his own belly, or had . . . ?

He sighed heavily, staring at the sleeping alien. Sometimes he wished he could just go to sleep, too. Everything was too complicated for him. But then, it always had been, hadn't it? Even his mother—he'd never known his father, and doubted that his mother had been really certain on the matter—even that good woman had despaired of him. His whole childhood seemed to be nothing more than memories of her shaking her head sadly when she looked at him, or swatting at him with an old wooden mixing spoon when he did something wrong (which was most of the time), or, worst of all, holding his head against her belly and weeping while he listened to the gurgle of her innards and wondered why he was so terrible.

"You're not very quick, and you never will be," she would whisper. "But you're my big strong boy."

God, how he'd hated that spoon. When his mother had finally succumbed to the Pleb Psychosis in his eleventh year (or so he assumed: she'd gone out one day and never come back, a common enough end for byte suckers), he'd broken the ugly thing, still stained with dark smudges of his own dried blood (her swatting had become less ineffectual the older he'd grown) into a hundred bits of kindling. But he'd never forgotten the pain.

Just as he knew he would never forget the silvery, slithering pain of the knife sliding into his gut, the way it had felt like a sudden, heavy blow crushing his chest. How he'd gasped for air and come up dry, his chest heaving but his lungs as flat as the tires he used to slash for fun on the rich folks' ped scooters. His life had always baffled him, but this had been far worse than that, the helplessness as he felt his own body growing cooler, and seen the slow, creeping approach of death in the sticky red slime that dribbled down his chin.

Gah, he thought. *I could have died.* The fact that it had been Endicott himself who had saved him didn't really register. By the time Endicott got the autodoc turned on, Frank had been out, drifting in a yammering coma where his mother, her face a gleaming skull, beat him with a spoon the size of a telephone pole.

When he woke up, there was nothing left but a scarred depression beneath his ribs not much wider than his blunt-tipped thumb.

He blinked, startled, and realized that this same thumb was caressing the shadow of that wound even as he stared blankly at the sleeping monkey.

"It's all bullshit," he said, not sure if he was speaking to himself, or to the gorilla, or to nobody at all. But the shadowy room and the slobbery sounds of the alien's snoring sent the creeps marching up his spinal cord. He turned and left the cabin, and slammed the door hard on his way out.

I'm strong, he thought as he settled his wide ass down on the deck and balanced the shatterblaster across his knees. *It's all I have, but I do have that. I'm* strong.

Momma had been right about that.

4

Shit, look at that ugly lug," Kerry hissed. "Fugger's sound asleep."

"No, I ain't," Frank said, raising his head and staring at them. His eyes narrowed as he made out Jim Endicott standing behind Kerry. "You tell me to guard, that's what I'm gonna do," he said sullenly as he stood up, knees creaking. "What the hell you guys doing down here?"

"None of your—" Kerry began, but Jim put a hand on his shoulder, silencing him, as he stepped past him to face Frank.

Frank was holding the shatterblaster across his broad chest at port arms. Neither boy looked at it, though both were edgily aware that it was there.

"We came to see the prisoner. Is she awake?" he said.

Frank stared into Jim's eyes, then turned his head to the side and spat on the floor. "I checked 'bout an hour ago, I guess. Thing was sleeping then. It's a she, you say?"

"That's right."

"Ugliest damned she I ever saw, then," he replied. "Yah she is." He spat again.

"Clean that up," Jim said.

"What?"

"You spit on the deck," Jim said. "It's our ship. Not a pigsty. We all have to live here. Clean it up."

Frank's big head came up, locked on Jim, froze. Then he nodded. "Sorry."

Suddenly he thrust the shatterblaster forward. Jim caught it just before it would have pushed him backward.

"Hold that a second," Frank rasped. He stripped off his shirt, knelt, and wiped up the spittle. In the dim light, the remnants of the scar on his belly were invisible. He put the shirt back on and stood again. During all this, he never took his eyes off Jim's face.

"That do for you . . . Captain?"

Jim handed back the weapon. "Thank you, crewman."

Frank looked at the blaster as if he'd never expected to hold it again. Finally he shrugged. "You want me to open the door?"

"No, I'll do it. Stay here. And stay alert. Don't let anybody else come in."

Whatever had just passed between the two of them, it was over. The tension drained out of Frank's hulking body. He took a pace back, lifted his weapon to port arms again, then turned to Kerry. "What am I supposed to do now? Do I salute him, or what?"

"No," Jim said. "When you're standing guard with a two-handed weapon, a salute isn't necessary. But I salute you." He paused. "It's a matter of courtesy. And honor."

He did so. Frank blinked. Jim opened the door to Ur-Barrba's cabin, stepped past Frank, and went in. Kerry stared hard at Frank, but found no response. After a moment, he followed Jim.

Frank did nothing at all.

5

Kerry closed the door behind him, then reached behind his back and drew his pistol. It was a nasty little thing, a hand-ripper, and though it was a bit low on power—the chargers aboard the *Endeavor* weren't designed to handle the Terran battery mechanisms—he knew he had enough juice to slice the big Kolumban into hairy, charred flank steaks if he needed to.

"Wait," he said to Jim, who was approaching Ur-Barrba's whuffling, snoring hulk.

"What?"

"She's never seen a possum in her life. Well, neither have I. But I expect we'd both know how to play one if we needed to." He moved to one side so that Jim was no longer in his field of fire, and aimed his pistol at the lumpy, bulging shape beneath the blanket. "Okay. Wake her up. But be careful."

Jim nodded and cleared his throat as he nervously fingered a round disk that dangled from a gold chain around his neck. The disk was a translator similar to the one that Ur-Barrba had used when he'd first spoken to her, what now seemed like a million years ago. Ferrick had found several of them, and Jim had tried to modify a few to make the Kolumban-Terran translations a bit more accurate. He wasn't sure how well he'd succeeded.

"Ur-Barrba?"

Nothing. He tried again, louder, his throat catching on the unfamiliar, twisty alien syllables. "*Ur-Barrba! Wake up!*"

The hulking mound on the bed, vague and formless beneath the root-colored blanket, exploded in a blur of movement so fast, so overwhelming, that it was as if the bunk itself was flying off the wall toward him.

"No!" he shouted. "Don't shoot!"

"Jesus Christ!" Kerry said, his voice choked and shaking, his weapon at full extension in his trembling hand.

Jim stood motionless, eyes straining at the creature who, even though seated, towered over him like a hairy orange cliff. Her chest was as broad as a hogshead (he'd never seen a hogshead, but he knew they were *big*). Her six-fingered hands rested on knob-boulder knees. Her golden eyes burned like smelters.

He'd forgotten what a monster she was. He wondered what else he might have forgotten about her.

"Ur-Barrba . . . ?" It came out sounding weak. He was sweating in the stifling heat of the room, hot salt running into his eyes as he tried not to glance at Kerry, backing him up with his gun.

Those molten eyes glared at him for what felt like an eternity. Then, punctuated by flashes of long, yellow fangs, her cement-mixer voice rumbled softly, a muted thunder in the thick cinnamon air.

"Jim Endicott," his translator squeaked, its tinny exhalation sounding like a frightened metal mouse on his chest. "What do you want of me?"

He swallowed a hock of something that felt like lukewarm snot. If only she wasn't so damned *big*. It was like trying to hold a conversation with a hair-shingled barn.

"You know me?" he asked. He couldn't remember ever telling her his name. Her voice, like a grizzly bear clearing its throat of something painful, suddenly swept him back to their first meeting, the first time he'd seen her, and then he remembered. Kerry *had* introduced them. "Meet Jim. Endicott," Kerry had said. And then he'd said, "We get the shit from her." And that was how it had all started, for all of them, and this was how it had ended, in a small room stinking of cinnamon and tension.

"I remember you," Ur-Barrba agreed, and this time rolled her black lips back and showed him all her teeth in an ivory chimpanzee grin that flashed far too many sharp yellow teeth. "Have you come to give me back my ship?"

"No, I came to show you something, and to ask you some questions."

"Why would I answer your questions?" Ur-Barrba asked. "You stole my ship and murdered all my—"

What she said sounded like *arrach-hai*, but the translator couldn't render it and made a soft, squalling sound instead.

"All your friends," Jim said softly. Somehow he understood that was what she meant, and not "all my crew." The sound the translator made as it rendered the Kolumban version of his words didn't sound like what Ur-Barrba had said, but she nodded slowly. It was odd, Jim thought, that two species separated by time, distance, and evolution should come to similar head gestures. If they *were* similar. That massive head bob might mean agreement, or it might mean some alien version of "bite me." He didn't know. He'd have to keep that in mind. That there was so much he didn't know about her, or her people, or her world.

He was aware of Kerry moving closer to him, and motioned him back. He'd just gotten a demonstration of how fast Ur-Barrba could move when she wanted to, and the thought of Kerry wrestling with her for possession of his gun sent a trickle of ice water slithering down his spine. How in hell could anything that big be so *quick*?

"Why should I help a killer?" Ur-Barrba said.

"Because this killer didn't kill *you*," he told her. "I could have. I could do it now. Lord knows, I have enough reasons. All the people your murderous drug slaughtered on the colony ship. Slaughtered with your full knowledge, by the way. As you've already admitted to both of us."

Ur-Barrba went on as if Jim hadn't spoken. "What do you want to show me? Show it to me, and I will decide if I wish to answer your questions." Her lips rolled back in that gaping, yellow-mawed grin again, and this time she actually rocked back and forth.

She may be alien to me, Jim thought, *but if that isn't laughter, I'll eat my boots.*

He reached into the pocket of his tunic and brought out a tiny comm unit. "Magda? Flash that holovid onto the screen down here, would you?"

"Aye, aye, Captain," Magda's voice whispered from the comm. The screen on the wall behind Jim lit up, its harsh blue glare mixing with the red overhead lights to paint Ur-Barrba's broad, leathery face with purple shadows.

King Kong on a bad hair day, Jim thought.

The screen flickered, then shifted from blue to star-burned black. The enigmatic alien vessel floated in the center of the field, just beginning to shift from its random structure into the rigid picket of glowing blue spears.

Jim turned his back on Ur-Barrba to watch, holding the comm to his lips, almost unbearably conscious of the huge bulk so close to his rear. *She could claw my spine out in a single swipe . . . does she* have *claws?* He fought the urge to turn and look as he watched the alien ship draw closer, closer . . . "There! Freeze that!"

As he spoke, the space between the alien and the *Endeavor* rippled again, the same odd, liquid shifting he'd seen before. He turned abruptly, hoping to find some clue in Ur-Barrba's reaction—*that's stupid, she's an alien, how would I know?*—but Ur-Barrba was only staring at the screen, her eyes like dying amber coals in the black, leathery pit of her face.

"Have you ever seen a ship like that before?" Jim said.

A fat pink tongue—not flesh-pink, bubblegum-pink—slipped between the yellow cage of Ur-Barrba's fangs, slubbered with wormy vitality across her lower lip, then retreated with a soft, whuffling belch the translator did not react to.

A cloud of hot cinnamon enveloped Jim's head. He blinked and said, "Is it a Communer vessel?"

"Yes. Why did it not kill you?"

He felt a surge of excitement. "What do you mean? Was it trying to kill us? That ripple in space, was it using its weapons on us?"

Ur-Barrba cocked her head. "Star hammer," she said. "Space shaker."

"Is that what you call it? Do you know what kind of weapon it is?"

Ur-Barrba shrugged.

He glanced at Kerry, his excitement still rising. Now they were getting somewhere!

"Did the Communers keep a ship in your system? Or did they just visit every once in a while? What—"

The sound cut through his babble like a wet sheet being ripped in half. *What the hell?* Then the stench, a rich, fuming mixture of what smelled like damp hay, methane, and rotten eggs assaulted his nostrils and he understood.

"Oh . . . God . . ." he said, choking on it.

"Oh, man . . ." Kerry moaned.

"Don't light a match or anything," Jim said, backing away.

Ur-Barrba flashed them that fang-ridden, black-gummed monkey grin, lifted her massive legs, and rolled onto her side on the bunk, facing the wall. Her huge body was covered with long burnt-orange hair, except for one spot. Her massive, muscled buttocks were naked skin, pink as her tongue.

"Let's get out of here," Kerry said.

"Yeah," Jim said. "Right behind you. I think this conversation is over, anyway."

Ur-Barrba saluted them once again just as they were closing the door behind them.

They stared at each other.

"Green goop," Jim said.

Kerry guffawed, and slapped him on the shoulder. "That's right, *green goop!*"

"What the hell is wrong with *you* guys?" Frank grumbled. He shook his head as he watched them stumble down the corridor, laughing so hard they had to hold each other up.

6

So where do we stand?" Jim said to nobody in particular, as he, Kerry, Ferrick, and Sam sprawled on puffy brown hillocks of alien furniture in the captain's quarters. Ferrick had done some investigating here, and discovered that one entire wall of the chamber was a concealed holoscreen. It hadn't taken him much longer to find the controls—concealed in a shiny metal rim around the edge of the screen—and so for the past couple of hours, they'd been watching replay after replay of the attack on the *Endeavor*, until finally Sam had said, "God, would you turn it *off*, please? It's like we're sitting sideways next to the well into forever."

And Jim had thought, *What an odd thing to say. But she's totally right. That's what it* is *like.*

And yes, it was sort of unsettling to have one side of the room you were in apparently open to naked space, even if it also sort of resembled some gigantic vireo game, with sticks slowly lining up and scattering, and the starfields rippling like bedsheets flapping on a clothesline as the attack replayed itself over and over again.

Kerry was holding a small remote control for the screen. He aimed it at the screen and said, "You want something a little, um, more confining?" Jim noticed that the corners of his mouth were twitching.

"Anything but starfields, please," Sam said primly.

"Well, sure, darlin', how about this?" He clicked the control and suddenly the screen was filled with a wall-sized close-up of Ur-Barrba's bright pink butt. It was so huge that for a moment Sam didn't understand what she was looking at. Nor did it help any that Kerry, Jim, and Ferrick were all making muffled snorting sounds as she tried to figure out what the hell was going on.

"What *is* that?" she said.

"You ass me," Kerry said, "butt I can't tell."

She glanced at him, then back at the huge, fuzzy picture, and suddenly her face turned the same color as Ur-Barrba's mighty haunches.

"You . . . *assholes!*" she sputtered.

"Assholes . . ." Jim said, his hand over his mouth. "Assholes." He burst out laughing.

She flounced up, hands on hips, and glared at him. He was pounding Ferrick on the shoulder. "Assholes," he said again.

Her lips began to quiver. A moment later, all of them were rolling around on the soft cushions, whacking each other, roaring with laughter.

"Ass . . . ass . . . ass*holes*," she screeched, tears filling her eyes.

It took another five minutes of whoops, chortles, and red-faced snorting giggles before they finally began to run down. Every time one of them would look at the screen and the frozen landscape of Ur-Barrba's gigantic pink buttocks, it would start up again. Finally Sam, lying on the deck, her arms wrapped around her belly as if she were afraid it would explode, gasped, "Turn it off. T-t-turn it *off*!"

Jim thumbed the control module and the screen went dark. Somehow that made things better. In the shadows, they couldn't make out each other's faces. Jim waited until the room was silent, then clicked the screen on again, this time making sure there were no close-ups.

It was the weirdest thing. Somehow, the bout of near-insane hilarity had cleansed him, taken him out of his miseries, left him feeling more like his old self again. He darted a hopeful glace at Sam, found her looking back at him, a quizzical smile on her features, as if she was seeing him for the first time. None of the darkness, the worry and fear that had been in her expression lately whenever she had him in her ken.

Maybe, he thought. *Maybe* . . .

But now was not the time for that. He cleared his throat and said, "Okay. That's Ur-Barrba. She lied to us before, when she said she didn't know that the dope, Heat, she was selling to Kerry was dangerous for humans. We don't know if she's lying now, about that Communer vessel. In fact, we don't know much about anything at all, except that she did try to poison the *Outward Bound*'s colonists. So the big question, I guess, is what do we do now?"

"You said you'd show us how to take over their planet," Ferrick said. "Have you forgotten? Or was that just some bullshit you and Kerry dreamed up to help you get elected captain?"

"There was some of that, maybe," Jim admitted, glancing at Kerry, who was holding a poker face now. "Kerry was gonna get me elected, no matter what."

Ferrick shrugged. "I don't give a crap about that. I understand why he did it—why you both did it. But was it all a lie, about what you knew?"

Jim shook his head. "No, not really. I've had a lot of instruction and training in what they call low-intensity conflict. It was mostly from the angle of defending against it, but in order to defend, you have to know how the other side will attack." He shrugged. "It's pretty basic stuff, but it's effective."

"Low-intensity conflict?" Ferrick said dubiously.

"Guerrilla stuff. Bush revolutions, urban terrorism, stuff like that."

Ferrick grinned at Kerry. "We know a little about what you call your urban terrorism," he said.

"Yeah, I'm sure you do. And all that will help, because we'll mix what you know in practical terms with what I've been taught. One can check the other, and maybe everything will work better. But I've been looking through the ship's library. There isn't much about Kolumba, just basic stuff, but it tells quite a bit. I don't know how much the urban games you guys know how to play will help, though. Kolumba seems to be an agrarian culture, and doesn't have cities in the sense that we understand them."

"Huh?" Sam said. "They've got spaceships. How can they not have cities? I thought space travel was only possible with a certain level of industrial-technological development."

"Probably true," Jim admitted. "But they really don't have space travel. It was given to them. They weren't even close to developing it on their own. Probably several centuries away, in fact. If they got to it at all."

"Why wouldn't they get to it?" Kerry asked. "Doesn't everybody, eventually?"

Jim was surprised at how good he felt, to find something involving real life that Kerry knew less about than he did. He shook his head. "No, not at all. Intelligent species develop cultures based on their environment and their genetic adaptations to it. Adversity drives mutation, you know."

"What does that mean?" Ferrick said. "Speak Terran, okay?"

"I am," Jim said. "A species that evolves in an easy environment may reach an optimal stage of development that isn't very advanced, by our standards, but is perfectly symbiotic with that environment. For instance, we don't really know why the human race, for instance, is driven to travel beyond the next horizon, and always has been. It is undoubtedly some deeply rooted survival trait, but we also know of some species that don't have it, and are perfectly comfortable staying on one home planet." He paused, thinking about it. "Most of them also have some kind of self-limiting factor that controls a tendency toward overpopulation also. That was a big issue back in humanity's pre-interstellar age, when environmentalist movements sought to control human birth rates to so-called sustainable levels—basically, approximately the same rate of births and deaths, so the population level remained stable or even fell a little. But there were some of those movements that proposed drastic solutions, up to and including destroying the human race itself, which they regarded as some kind of cancer that would destroy everything on the planet."

"What?" Sam said, disbelieving. "That's crazy."

"Yes, in a way it was, but they didn't understand what was happening. As Terra gradually extended industry and high technology over the whole planet, birth rates fell anyway, all by themselves. A high birth rate is only rational when it helps offset a high death rate. Better health measures, contraception, and the improvement in the status of women all worked to bring down birth rates. In fact, by the time humans had advanced to true interstellar travel, the population of Terra had begun to shrink a bit. Japan was the first to undergo this change, but it later spread over the entire world."

"Okay, okay," Ferrick said. "You've got a lot of book learning. But what does it have to do with Kolumba and our little problem?"

"Well, as far as I can tell, Kolumba reached a stable population a long time ago. The women have always been able to practice a sort of conscious contraception—that is, they can decide whether they want to give birth or not. Their culture is a weird blend between hunter-gatherer and agrarian—they cultivate several different crops, but they also live off the land to a great extent."

"Hmph. Sounds kind of primitive to me," Sam said.

"Well, I guess primitive is in the eye of the beholder," Jim told her. "The Kolumbans didn't think of themselves that way. They had plenty to eat, their close relationship with all growing things had given them medicines for most of their diseases so they were quite healthy, they weren't warlike, women held equal status to men, they lived in harmony with their own ecology. And while they weren't advanced scientifically, at least as we would define advanced, they were a race of poets, philosophers, writers, artists, dreamers. Because they didn't maintain a high-technology culture, they had a lot of time for things like that. We might say they didn't know what they were missing, and that was true. But since they didn't know, it didn't bother them."

"You keep saying 'were,' " Ferrick said. "What happened to them? If they were so dumb and happy, how come they turned into interstellar dope manufacturers?"

Jim spread his hands. "What do you think? The Communers happened to them, that's what."

Ferrick blinked, opened his mouth, then closed it. After a moment of thought, he said, "Exactly how did the Communers happen to these happy folks, then?"

"It's a little foggy," Jim told him. "The histories I've read are beautifully written—the Kolumbans really are artists—but whoever wrote them didn't have the right vocabulary—a technological vocabulary, I mean. I've tried to puzzle it out, though, and I think—I hope—I've filled in enough holes for it to make sense."

"What happened, then?"

"Apparently the first thing the Communers did was to set up a satellite network around Kolumba. The satellites were designed to do one thing: amplify and rebroadcast any hyperwave transmissions they picked up." He paused. "The Kolumban writers called it 'the bright net of stars.' "

"Pick up and rebroadcast?" Kerry said. "You mean like regular data links? Video, news, holo, vireo and stimeo, like that?"

"Exactly," Jim said. "I guess you'd call it the background radiation of interstellar civilization. In this part of the galaxy the bulk of it is from the older races—the Albans, the Hunzza, and so forth, but a lot from us, the Terrans, too, because we're closer, and we're expanding so fast."

"You say rebroadcast," Sam said. "Rebroadcast where? If the Kolumbans are so primitive, did they have stimeo and vireo and video?"

"This was almost a hundred years ago—Terran years," Jim said. "Evidently these Communers plan for the long term. Anyway, the answer is no. When they finished their satellite network, they spent some time tuning it. They added translator programs, and censor programs as well, so they could control the content of the satellite rebroadcasts, only let through what they wanted. Then they did something very clever. They air-dropped com-receivers all over Kolumba equipped with independent eternal energy sources. Millions of them, lightweight, almost indestructible, all capable of receiving the satellite rebroadcasts—in Kolumban. That was the second part of their plan. The third part was the most devilish of all; they used cyborgs shaped like Kolumbans—not exact copies, but close—to open a trading station on the planet's surface. They set up shop, opened their doors, and waited."

"I don't get it," Ferrick said. "Waited for what? What good would that do them, sitting around twiddling their thumbs?"

"The Kolumbans weren't primitive, not like Terran cavemen or something. They just weren't technologically advanced, mostly because there was no need for them to be. They lived good, happy, fulfilling lives. Until pictures of an entirely different way of life fell out of the sky all over their world. Then things began to change.

"Slowly, at first. Most of them didn't know what to make of these alien worlds they were seeing on the odd picture things that suddenly seemed to be everywhere. Then rumors began to spread that there was a place people could go where strange-looking Kolumbans would give them some of the things they saw in the picture machines. And some people did go there, even making incredibly long journeys to do so.

"After a while, the Kolumbans opened a second station, but this was a trading station. No more freebies. These fake Kolumbans wanted certain kinds of herbs the Kolumbans knew how to find or, better yet, how to grow.

"Over a period of decades, more trading stations appeared, more goods were traded, and Kolumba became a weird, quasi-technological culture. But they still didn't really know how to make any of the things they traded for, and so they became totally dependent on the 'strange' Kolumbans for their high-tech trinkets.

"The worst thing was that the trinkets themselves became a kind of money, so that eventually, if you didn't have them, you were poor. It was the first time in Kolumban history that the concept of poverty had appeared. Before their corruption, Kolumbans didn't even need words for rich or poor. Everybody had all they needed for a peaceful, happy life simply by living in harmony with their planet and what it gave them. But the Communers changed all that. It took them a while, but they did."

"How could a bunch of comm units do all that?" Sam asked.

"They changed the Kolumban worldview," Jim said. "And in the process, changed the expectations of the average Kolumban." He sighed. "The same thing has happened many, many times in Terran history, when a more technologically advanced culture meets a lesser one. And not just on Terra, either. All over the part of the galaxy we know something about—Alba, Hunzza, all the others, it's happened. The Communers did it on purpose, though. They seem quite sophisticated about it, too. But you know what's really scary?"

Kerry shrugged. "What?"

"If what Ur-Barrba told us was true, then the Communers set out to shape, over a hundred years, an entire world's culture in order to get it to provide them with one thing: a drug that could threaten humans. Which means they must have been aware of us back in the dawn of our interstellar expansion, when the Terran Confederacy was only a handful of planets."

"Whoa," Ferrick said. "I didn't even think of that. But you're right. So you mean these Communers saw us coming even before we knew ourselves we were coming?"

"It looks like it," Jim said. "Not only that, it looks like they decided they wanted to kill us way back then, too. Not just kill us, but do it in a such a sneaky, secretive way that we wouldn't even know what was happening."

"Wait a second," Kerry said. "I see where you're going, or at least I think I do. But if these Communers started planning to use the Kolumbans to kill humans with drugs a hundred years ago, how come we haven't seen a lot more of it?" He paused thoughtfully. "Did you check and see what kind of losses the big Terran colony ships have been having?"

"I couldn't do that, because the databanks of the *Endeavor* never tracked that kind of information. The Hunzza didn't see any need for it, and the Kolumbans probably didn't even know it existed."

"You could just access the databases on Terra via hyperwave," Kerry said.

"That kind of traffic is monitored. Do we really want to advertise that there's an unknown, Hunzza-manufactured vessel out here rummaging through databases on Earth, looking for statistics about the destruction of Terran colony ships?"

"Hmm. Okay, so what's Plan B?"

"Plan B is to go with Plan A," Jim said. "What we set out to do in the first place. Stop the Kolumbans from shipping out drugs to Terran colony ships. That's not the whole solution, of course. The Kolumbans are just a weapon the Communers happen to be using. But they're using it. How much, we don't know. What they tried to do with the *Outward Bound* may have been their first try. A sort of proof-of-concept experiment. If it worked, they might have given the Kolumbans several ships, and moved against a lot more of the colony vessels."

Jim shrugged. "It's more interesting to wonder why they hit the *Outward Bound* in the first place, although it still doesn't matter right now, not if our goal is to take the Kolumbans away from the Communers in the first place. Like disarming a would-be killer."

Ferrick said, "Which gets us back to the basic question. How do we do that? One ship with forty kids, how do we take on a whole planet?"

"Well, the *Endeavor is* a warship. We could just blast the hell out of them. We've still got big guns, and according to you, they still work," Kerry told him.

"Oh, they work, all right," Jim broke in. "But I'll never allow them to be used that way. Are you nuts? Murder God knows how many innocents—and as far as I'm concerned, every Kolumban who didn't know that Heat was deadly to humans, and was being used to try to kill the *Outward Bound*—is just that. Innocent."

"Pretty starry-eyed, aren't you, Jim?"

"You already knew that, Kerry. Besides, there's a practical reason, too."

"Which is . . . ?"

"That Communer ship. Do you think it's gone away? Obviously, somehow they know who we are. After all, they were the ones who bought the *Endeavor* in the first place. I'd figured Kolumba might be watched by the Communers—but I'd hoped we might be able to get past them by masquerading as the ship and crew that had gone out. Ur-Barrba's ship. That's why I'd originally wanted to save as many crew members as we could. But we all know how that turned out.

"Then I goofed again, because I wasn't paying attention to the *Endeavor*'s wormspace programming, and we ended up in the Kolumban system before I even knew we were here. Four hours, Magda said. That was plenty of time for the Communers to make a positive ID on our ship, even initiate whatever communications sequences they normally used. But we didn't answer, or our systems didn't answer properly, so that idea is blown all to hell.

"How do you know that?" Sam asked.

"Because," Jim said patiently, "they tried to kill us. Just like they'll try again, as soon as they see us. What do you think they'll be doing while we're setting up to scorch Kolumba. Handing us matches?"

"Okay, okay," Kerry said, raising his hands. "You've made your point. Which still leaves the original problem, only it's worse now. In order to do *anything* about the Kolumbans, don't we somehow have to be in contact with them? And doesn't that mean going back there? If what you say is right, that Communer ship is gonna toast us the second we stick our nose out of wormspace. So how do we get around that?"

Ferrick, whose eyebrows had crawled together like amorous caterpillars as he sank deeper and deeper into thought, finally looked up. "How is it that Ur-Barrba knew so much about the dope setup? How come *she* was in charge, come to think on it?"

He looked at Kerry. "You know, Kerry, you never did tell the rest of us much about that. About how we got set up in the first place with the Kolumbans."

"I know. I figured the less anybody knew about the deal, the more control I had. But I do know the answer to your question. It's simple. Ur-Barrba was in charge because her father is the source of the dope. He's the biggest drug baron on the planet."

"You mean it's really him who is the source?"

"Yeah, him."

"Then the answer's simple," Ferrick said. "We got his daughter. As the man says, that's some heavy leverage."

"Leverage?" Sam asked.

"Sure. We tell him he gets out of the poisonous dope business, or we send his little girl back to him in a box. No, make that a lot of boxes."

"That won't work," Jim said.

"Why not?"

"It's all stick and no carrot. And it's not a big enough stick. The Communers have the biggest stick. Bigger than we do, at least."

"I don't get it," Ferrick said.

"Okay, say it was you who was in charge down there. You were running this big dope enterprise, and somebody came along and said, oh, we got Sam, and if you don't get out of the dope biz right now, she's dog food. And by the way, ignore Kerry Communer over there, who'll probably blow your head off if you agree to our demands."

"Uh. Maybe not."

"But what if we gave you some kind of alternative. Like, say, if you stop the dope dealing, we'll give you Sam, and at the same time we'll take out Kerry Communer so he can't blow your head off, *and* we'll give you something else to do instead of sell dope. Something that makes you at least as much money, if not more."

"Sure, I'd have to think real hard about that deal."

"Well, that's the way we've got to do it."

"Great. How?"

Jim shook his head. "Honest answer? I'm not sure. The first thing we have to figure out is how to get in touch with Ur-Barrba's father in the first place. Without the Communers blowing us into space slag."

"I think," Ferrick said slowly, "I've got a couple of ideas about that . . ."

CHAPTER SIX

1

—

Jim found Ferrick down in one of the fabrication bays off the main engine room, laboring over a steel construction about forty feet long. The bullet-shaped missile's sides were open, and Ferrick's blocky frame was half buried in its glittering metal guts.

"It has to be that big?" Jim asked him.

Ferrick pulled his head out of the innards of the thing and wiped his hands on the seat of his pants. "Most of it is drives," he said. "It can't be just a dumb missile, because it has to dodge, if that Communer ship tries to track it down and destroy it. Plus, it has to function on its own, which means a fair amount of space for the computers. And then there's the transmitters. Hyperwave transmitters aren't exactly miniaturized yet. Even the lighter doesn't carry them."

Jim peered over his shoulder at the missile and sighed. "Man, I hope this works."

"It ought to," Ferrick replied. "I mean, eventually the Communers will knock it out, but we only need to blanket their Kolumban satellite network long enough for Ur-Barrba's father to get the message. I just hope the specs you figured out for those satellites are close enough for my algorithms to override their security. If we can't hijack their rebroadcast capabilities, then we're shit out of luck."

Elwood came loafing around the corner, saw Jim, blinked, then straightened and saluted. "Captain," he said.

Jim returned the salute. "Mr. Grieger," he replied.

Elwood came on in. Jim couldn't detect much emotional energy emanating from Elwood toward him, either positive or negative. He was still not entirely comfortable with Elwood's sudden conversion, but what could he do? Elwood was valuable. He was also good at concealing his feelings when he felt the need. Especially in the newly formal captain and crew relationship that now seemed to hold between them.

"Ferrick," Elwood said, "I don't think those black boxes you've got me programming are gonna work."

"Huh? Why not?"

Elwood shrugged. "I did a traffic analysis of the satellite rebroadcasts. We've been assuming the Communers used their own equipment and programming, especially for the censor programs, and so we were gonna go for brute-force overrides. Just overwhelm their programming and take over the hardware for ourselves." He shrugged again. "The theory being that form follows function, and no matter what kind of hardware they were using, since it had to do certain things, it would also have to operate in certain ways. Well, it doesn't seem to. I don't think those satellites of theirs are using hardware at all."

Jim stared at Elwood, astounded. He'd always known the kid had potential, but this sort of competency was far beyond what he'd expected. Suddenly he wondered what other talents were hidden beneath the "uneducated" facades of other crew members. Maybe even Frank had heretofore unknown abilities.

"I see," he broke in. "So what does your traffic analysis indicate *is* the situation? If the Communers aren't using hardware, what are they using?"

"I don't know how they're doing it," he said, "but if I absolutely had to guess, I'd say wetware. They're using something alive. What that might be, I'm not sure. But it would probably be immune to the hardware override methods we'd planned to use."

Ferrick scratched his head. "Biochips?" he said at last.

"Something more powerful," Elwood replied. "But like I said, I don't know what."

"How can we find out for sure?" Jim asked slowly.

"Well, there's an easy way," Elwood told him. "We grab one of those satellites."

"Huh. Easy," Ferrick grunted.

Elwood grinned. "Easy to figure out," he said. "Maybe not so easy to do the actual grabbing."

"But you're pretty sure what we're planning now won't work?"

"Uh-huh. Pretty sure."

"Crap!" Jim muttered. "Can't anything *ever* be simple?"

The other two boys stared at him, then chuckled in sour unison. He closed his eyes and tried to think it through.

"So we've got to go physically grab one of those sats. But if we do that, we reveal to the Communers that we're still hanging around, and on top of it, we show that we're interested in their satellite network. And if we do that, they may figure out some way to block whatever we try to do to take over those satellites for our own purposes."

Ferrick grinned suddenly. "Sounds like a captain-level problem to me," he said. "Captain."

Jim could feel the challenge—mild though it was—hanging in the air. *You're the captain, you figure it out.*

"All right," he said, "keep on with the rest of it, but hold off, I guess, on the hijack boxes. As soon as I have something, we'll try to grab one of those sats."

"When will that be?" Ferrick asked.

Jim shook his head. "Beats the hell out of me," he said. "But soon. It'll have to be soon."

"Got that right," Ferrick said.

2

The pain was bad. As bad as Ur-Quillam had ever felt it. His body throbbed and ached, muscles grinding against muscles, bones icy with cold fire. The vague red blob of the sun overhead, dim and curtained by the perpetual mists, burned at his eyes like a flame. His skin burned. Even the gentle brush of his long, golden pelt against his skin felt as if something were flaying him alive.

He gasped. One of his minders soothed his forehead with a cool, wet cloth. He'd known her name once, he was sure of it, but now he couldn't remember it in the fog of agony that wrapped him like a shroud. He felt absurdly grateful for the small gesture, and wished he could remember her name so he could thank her.

The world, as it always did when his seizures took him this strongly, had gone vague and shadowy. Sounds boomed and echoed without form in his ears and in his fevered brain. He was dimly aware that he must be showing some evidence of his pain—shouting, perhaps, or groaning, perhaps even weeping—and he felt ashamed that he should lose so much control. But he couldn't help it. And so he was grateful for those who watched over him, who kept and fed and protected him through the long watches of his disease.

If it was a disease. In his lucid moments, he privately suspected it was a curse.

Again the blessedly cool feel of the cloth on his burning skin, and then a trickle of something icy down his broken, rasping throat. The great torturing waves receded a little, and took with them the worst of the shadows, leaving his nerve endings twitching and exhausted.

"My son," a rough, deep voice rumbled near him. "My poor, poor son."

"Kill me," he whispered. "If you love your poor son, Father, kill him."

But the reply was as lovingly implacable as it always was. "Never, Ur-Quillam. Never."

Ur-Quillam, golden-haired son of Ur-Quolla, beloved brother of Ur-Barrba, known to all his people as the Shining One, nodded and closed his eyes. He bore the blame. He must pay, not for his evil, but for all evil.

A curse, indeed. But he would bear it as long as he could. Maybe the gods from beyond the stars would be able to heal him. Maybe.

3

Are you nuts?" Kerry asked him mildly.

"Way I see it, there's two choices," Jim told him. "Either you go, or I do. If I was being heroic, I'd say it has to be me. But I'm a better pilot than you are, and I understand the *Endeavor*'s systems better, too. So I should stay here and run the decoy, while you pilot the lighter and grab the satellite."

"Oh, that's not what I meant," Kerry said, waving his words off. "Of course I have to be the one who goes. The satellite grab is the more dangerous of the two jobs, and we can't afford to risk you anyway." He shook his head. "No, I just mean the whole deal. It's like unraveling a ball of thread. Pull on one strand, and you just get tangled up in a dozen more. That's what this whole escapade is turning into. I know we originally thought it would be difficult, but we presumed we were dealing with a relatively primitive culture, and so we figured that with the power of the *Endeavor* to back us up, we might be able to pull it off. But we didn't count on a Communer ship guarding the Kolumban system, and we didn't know about the satellite rebroadcast network. Everything just keeps getting more complicated, more dangerous. We're grabbing at straws now, and risking everything to do it."

Jim listened quietly, then sighed. "Okay, everything you say is true. But what else can we do? We can't just walk away. Even if we . . . dispose . . . of Ur-Barrba and head out for the wild blue with the *Endeavor*, the original problem will still be here. The Communers will buy another ship—or maybe a dozen other ships—from the Hunzza, and Ur-Barrba's father will still be in business."

"Sure, but why is that our problem specifically? We're a bunch of kids. If the Communers really are going after Terran colony ships, taking them on is a job for Terra and the Confederation, not us. I mean, what's to stop us from setting course for Confederation territory, popping out of wormspace, and sending a message to whom it may concern at the Combined Intelligence Agency about what we know? Let them take it from there."

"One answer. Proof. What proof do we have? Are you gonna stand up and tell the CIA that you and everybody else on this ship—me included—were peddling alien poison to anybody who would buy on the *Outward Bound*?"

"Mm. I could see a couple of problems with that scenario, yes."

"Or maybe we could hand them Ur-Barrba. But that would mean we'd have to *hand* her to somebody. You think the captain of one of the Confederation's starships is just gonna let us go on our merry way after we hand her over? A bunch of kids with a Hunzza starship?"

Kerry rubbed his chin. "They could take a look at what happened to the *Outward Bound*. There are the ship's records. They could verify what we tell them by analyzing the ship's records, the same way we did."

"Yeah, I thought of that. So I started pinging the *Outward Bound*, just a locator sweep. Guess what?"

Kerry closed his eyes. "From the tone of your voice? That's easy. No *Outward Bound*."

"Not a trace," Jim agreed.

"Jesus," Kerry said softly. "You think those bastards took it out? The whole ship? Ten million people?"

"All I know is that I can't find the *Outward Bound*."

Neither of them wanted to think about what that might mean, but the awful possibilities couldn't be ignored.

"My God. Darnell, all the rest of the Cowboys."

"And everybody else," Jim said softly.

"That would mean . . . we're all that's left. Just us." Kerry's face was pale as the skull beneath his skin. He laughed softly, bitterly. "And we thought we were taking on the dangerous part." He looked up. "If they did that, I want to kill them all. If we can."

"Well, we won't be able to do anything if we're sitting in a Confederation jail for peddling killer dope. And maybe setting off a chain of events that resulted in ten million innocent colonists getting killed. Let alone joyriding around in a hijacked starship."

"Jim, I don't know. It would almost be worth it, if we could be sure that Terra would do something. If they *did* decide to take action, they could do a lot more than we can."

"I know. But look at who we are. I'm already on the run from somebody high up in the ConFed government, maybe even the CIA itself. And the rest of us, well . . ." He shrugged.

"Yeah. We're all Plebs, the lowest of the low. Why would they listen to us? Far as they're concerned, we're all dope dealers anyway."

"We need hard proof," Jim said. "Something nobody can ignore. And the place to find that proof is down on Kolumba. If it turns out we can't stop the Kolumbans—and the Communers—then maybe we can find enough to force somebody else to stop them."

"All right. Okay, I'll go along. For the time being. But I want to know that if we screw up, it isn't all over. That somehow we can get a warning to Terra. Even if they ignore the warning."

Jim thought for a second, then said, "How about if we send a couple of the kids out with the lighter after we grab the satellite. Just set the thing on autopilot and aim it at Terra. Have it broadcast a locator beacon once it's far enough away from the Kolumban system. We could program the lighter's databanks with everything we know."

"I dunno, Jim. The lighter doesn't have hyperwave ability, so it could be a thousand years before anybody heard the messages. Besides, it would leave us without any dirtside landing capability."

"You think we're gonna need it?"

"If we end up trading Ur-Barrha, we will."

"Right. God, I'm going nuts. I forgot about her."

"You got a lot to think about. That's why you got me. To think along with you."

Jim nodded, then smiled at Kerry. "You know, we do make a good team."

Kerry slapped him on the shoulder. "The best, buddy. The best."

"Do we get superhero capes when this is over?"

"Nope," Kerry said. "But I'll buy you the biggest tub of green glop Sam can come up with."

"Nothing like incentive," Jim replied.

4

The *Endeavor*'s lighter, normally used for ferrying cargo or personnel dirtside from the orbiting vessel, was a relatively small affair, with chairs for two pilots, seating for a dozen passengers, and enough pressurized space at the rear to handle a few tons of light cargo. It was about a hundred feet long, nestled comfortably in its own launch bay near the outer skin of the larger ship. The bay itself could be sealed against the vacuum of space, so that the lighter could be loaded beforehand, the bay depressurized, and the smaller vessel launched on a moment's notice.

Jim's footsteps echoed hollowly on the steel decking of the bay as he and Kerry walked up to the lighter's passenger hatch, which stood dogged open at the head of a short flight of portable stairs. Kerry stopped at the bottom of the stairs, turned, and stuck out his hand.

"If I don't see you again . . ."

They shook. Kerry's palm felt dry against Jim's skin. He hoped his own grip didn't betray the qualms he felt. It was the captain's duty to send his crew—and himself—into harm's way when necessary, just as it was the captain's duty to keep himself out of harm's way when *that* was necessary. He knew that, and yet it still felt wrong to be sending others to do a dangerous job he was capable of doing himself.

"Don't worry about it, buddy," Kerry said softly, as if reading Jim's mind. "I know it's tearing you up, but this is the right way. Besides, you know the tough part is gonna be when you come back to pick us up. And I'm telling you I'd rather it be you doing that side of it than the other way around."

"Yeah, you're probably right. I can't get over the feeling I should be out there with you instead of safe behind the *Endeavor*'s shields."

"Well, get over it, pal." Kerry checked his nailtale, then mounted the first step. "Jim?"

"Yes?"

"If this doesn't work out, well ... we played a hell of a game, didn't we?"

Jim looked up into Kerry's arctic-blue gaze. Was there something glistening there? He couldn't tell.

"We did," he told him. "Take care of yourself. And don't worry. I'll be back for you."

Kerry nodded, swallowed once, turned, climbed to the top of the stairs, and vanished into the hatch. A moment later, the hydraulics hissed and the hatch slid shut.

Something felt as if it were lodged in Jim's throat, and he swallowed, too. Whatever it was, it didn't go down easily. He turned and headed for the hold's air lock.

Party time.

5

Jim settled into the captain's chair and absently slapped the switch for full restraints. As he did so, he spoke aloud into his command microphone, a tiny silver bead floating at the end of a spidery wire extending from his control helmet.

"Full restraints, please, everybody. This ride could get a little rough before it's over."

He placed his vireo helmet on his head, then closed his eyes as he felt the net of monomolecular probes sliding past his hair and penetrating his skull. He couldn't really *feel* the probes as they sought out thousands of bundles of axons and insinuated themselves into the tangled nexi of nerve impulse conductors, but he could imagine them. Sometimes this mind picture of his own brain criss-crossed by a web of tiny, shimmering wires gave him the willies.

On his main console, a message appeared on one of his screens: "Vireo control network in place. Initiate?"

"Initiate vireo network," he said softly.

As soon as he finished speaking, the virtual-reality audio-video network created by the direct connects between his brain and the *Endeavor*'s main computer banks slid seamlessly into existence, linking his own mind and that of the ship's into a single functional entity.

Good pilots—and all ship's captains had to be good pilots—were initiated into the vireo process as early as possible. Jim had experienced his first vireo connection shortly after his fifth birthday. That had been a narrowband hookup, only a few dozen probes, but in its own way it had been as stunning a revelation as the first time he'd used the socket beneath his right ear to jack into the Universal WorldNet. It had . . . what *had* it felt like? Like being in two places at once . . . no, that wasn't quite it. More like being two *people* at once, though one of those people was more a feeling—like having a stranger staring constantly over your shoulder. This was disconcerting enough for a five-year-old, but it was mild compared to the full-blown linkage that he was a part of now.

This really did feel like being two people at once—even to the moment of slightly blurred vision, as if two sets of eyes were looking out of his eye sockets—as the linkage overrode his own internal vision centers.

The blurred double-vision effect passed within a couple of seconds, leaving his eyes seeing sharp and clear again. But there was a difference. He could choose to see what his physical eyes saw, or he could see anything the *Endeavor*'s computer sensors saw. If he wished, he could use one eye to view the real world, and the other to view the vireo world, just as he could split his ears in the same way. Or any of his other senses.

This schizophrenic way of approaching virtual reality and actual reality at the same time could be profoundly disorienting for the uninitiated, but all space captains learned to multitask their own brains, and Jim had mastered the feat well. He found nothing unusual about seeing, through his right eye, the rank of monitor screens on his control console, and, through his left eye, a complicated, computer-generated schematic of the electron flows coursing across the shields of his own ship. Nor did he find it odd to listen through his left ear to a conversation between his crewmen at their consoles, while the computer droned a stream of cargo-shifting statistics into his right—sometimes the mix of sounds blended pleasantly, and he thought of the hum of bees in a soft green meadow.

Some people couldn't tolerate it at all. Others actually became addicted to the multiplicity of input, and would suffer withdrawal symptoms without regular doses of it.

He blinked once. People used different cues to control some aspects of vireo, and a rapid eye flutter was his own personal choice. Immediately the input from the computers receded, and he took a final look around the bridge.

Ferrick was in Kerry's seat, with Timmy, looking seriously grim, standing in for him in the chief engineer's chair. Elwood was manning the weapons console, and Sam—

No, Sam wasn't. Jim glanced at Ferrick. "Is that Hunky in the operations console?"

Ferrick looked. "Yep."

"Where the hell's Sam?"

"I dunno."

Jim patched into the ops console. "Hunky!"

The chubby boy's voice sounded sharp and clear in Jim's right ear. "Yeah? I mean, yessir?"

"Where's Sam? Isn't this her shift?" As Jim spoke, he called up the crew schedule, and examined it through one eye, while he watched the back of Hunky's head through the other. Yes, Sam *was* scheduled to be in the ops chair. Hunky wasn't due on for another four hours.

"She asked me to sit in," Hunky said. "I owed her a shift, so I said sure."

"Why? Where is she? Is she sick or something?"

"No, she said she was going with Kerry."

"What!" He glared at Ferrick. "Did you know about this?"

Ferrick shrugged. "Not a clue. You know Sam, though. She gets a wild hair . . ." He shrugged again.

"God*damn* it!" Jim hissed. "Doesn't anybody around here understand the concept of following orders?"

Viciously, he swiped at a switch on his console. He wanted to do this in the real world, not by vireo. Kerry's face popped up on his central screen.

Kerry looked surprised. "Sir?"

"Is Sam with you?"

"Yes. Why?"

"She's supposed to be up here on the bridge."

"But she told me—" Kerry's head bobbed offscreen. Jim could hear him speaking, his voice low and intense, but he couldn't make out the words. He blinked, and suddenly a conversation between Kerry and Sam was clear as a bell in his left ear, picked up by the computer aboard the lighter.

"—you told me Jim had reassigned you to me!" Kerry was saying. He didn't sound happy at all.

"Maybe I made a mistake. Maybe it was somebody else," Sam replied. She sounded as angry as Kerry did.

Jim overrode both of them. "Sam!"

"What?"

"Get the hell out of there. You aren't going. It's too—" He stopped then, but the damage had already been done.

"Dangerous?" Sam said. "Is that what you were going to say, Captain? That this mission is too dangerous for a silly, weak *girl*?" She almost cooed the words. Sweetly. Far too sweetly.

How the hell did I get into this*?* he wondered as he stared blankly out over the bridge, feeling the heat rush into his cheeks as he gritted his teeth. He saw heads down below turning, and then faces staring at him, felt his own flush deepening as he realized she'd patched their conversation onto the ship's intercom so everybody could get an earful.

"Turn that off!" he grated, and switched one of his eyes to the interior of the lighter.

"I thought it was off, Captain," she replied. Now he could see her smiling triumphantly. Her voice echoed doubly in his ears. She hadn't switched off. Likely she had no intention of switching off.

He opened his mouth to give her a piece of his mind—a *house*-sized piece—and saw her smile widen. Her eyes were sparking with the flare of battle. He could almost imagine a wind streaming through her hair.

"Ms. Hamilton," he said.

"Yes, Captain?"

"After the completion of the mission, you will report immediately to the captain's cabin. Understood?"

"Aye, aye, sir."

And wipe that shit-eating grin off your face, he wanted to say, but fortunately did not. Instead, he slammed the comm switch on his console harder than necessary, bruised a knuckle, sucked on it, and saw Ferrick regarding him with great sympathy.

"What are *you* staring at?"

"Nothing, Captain. Sorry." Ferrick sketched a hasty salute, all the more ridiculous because he was sitting down.

Jim took a deep breath.

"Okay, people. Here we go," he said. "Kerry? Count down to begin atmosphere evac of the launch bay, on my mark."

"Aye, aye, sir. Ready for your mark."

"Ten, nine, eight . . ."

Some part of his mind—or maybe it was the ship's mind; at this point he didn't really make the distinction—was aware of powerful pumps hissing softly as they sucked all the air out of the bay containing the lighter. But he wasn't really paying attention. He was sinking deeper and deeper into the main control systems of the *Endeavor* herself, losing his own physical awareness as that of the ship's reality extended from his brain out through the countless paths of his own nervous system, as if his veins were filling with fizzing foam and his skin were becoming an exquisitely sensitive metal hide.

Now Jim was looking directly on the slick, shimmering oil-steel visage of wormspace itself, that vast and gripping disorientation. It sucked at him, a negative hungry blot that tore at his consciousness.

His voice rumbled from some distant place, an iron throat he no longer recognized as his own: "Eject wormspace on five and four and three and two and one and . . ."

All hell broke loose.

In wormspace there was no such thing as motion. Nor was there acceleration or deceleration, mass, any of the usual physical signposts that let you know you were in a universe that made sense. Wormspace was a place where time ran backward, or reeled crazily forward, or didn't run at all. The human brain, though a wonder of quantum effects itself, did not understand, could barely even perceive, wormspace. As soon as you entered it, reality, for all intents and purposes, stopped happening. And when you exited it, it was as much an act of creation—or re-creation—as of transportation.

Jim yanked the *Endeavor* out of wormspace with her huge nuclear engines bellowing as much thrust as they were capable of generating. It was like riding the biggest blowtorch in the universe.

And he was in charge.

It felt to him as if his own body were burning, blazing with power, his skin melting with the force of the thrust, a long, screaming dive across the plane of the Kolumban solar elliptic, a fire arrow aimed at the heart of the sun.

As he flew and fell and screamed, other parts of him, of his metal body and cybernetic mind, looked and listened for the Communer ship, for the deadly pattern of glowing blue pickup sticks.

Part of him rode the fire and laughed, and part of him watched the world with icy concentration.

"Mr. Grieger?" he said. "Anything?"

"No targets, Captain," Elwood replied, his face pasty beneath its almond veneer, his gray eyes frozen as chunks of dirty, windswept ice.

Jim had every probe the *Endeavor* owned stretched in the widest web he could imagine, a vast pseudo nervous system spread quivering across the entire Kolumban solar system, waiting for the tingle, the tight, hot, burning point that would mean the Communer ship was there.

Nothing.

The *Endeavor*, still under full thrust, roared and howled deeper into the gauzy necklace of the twelve planets that made up the system. He was aware of the two outermost ice planets, stunted snowballs forever frozen in the outer darkness, flashing past.

Now a huge purple gas giant was coming up. Through one of his eyes he saw it as a vast, stately ball of swirling color, bejeweled with bright moons and polished iron rings. Through his other eye he saw the same gigantic world as a vast nexus of force, of swirling energy and the dark, beckoning undertone of its gravity well, its moons as tiny tinkling sounds, its rings hissing like rushing swords, and beneath it all, the rich, chocolate hum of the gases themselves rubbing against the superheated core.

It was half planet, half sun aborning. Twenty million years from now, the Kolumban system would have *two* suns, as the gas giant collapsed into nuclear fusion and became a secondary star orbiting the larger star at the center of the system. Seeing it that way—*sensing* it that way—made him feel like a god; wave after wave of crazed exhilaration thundered up his spinal cord, bubbled in his skull, made the hair on his head lift slowly away from his scalp.

And still the power of what he was trying to do kept on building. There were ways of exiting wormspace that were much harder to detect than the raving horn of power he was riding now. But that was the point: by returning to the Kolumban system as the spacefaring equivalent of a marching brass band, he hoped to draw all attention to the *Endeavor*. Enough, at least, to mask what he was really trying to do.

"Flash the shields, Mr. Autrey," he told Ferrick.

"Aye," Ferrick grunted, busy with his own problems, most of which involved keeping the structural integrity of the *Endeavor* stable under the abnormal strains of a high-speed exit from wormspace so close to a star. But he was good; he followed Jim's orders cleanly, with no perceptible pause, and in Jim's vireo input, the *Endeavor* suddenly began flashing like a humongous lighted Christmas tree ornament.

"Mr. Korrigan, prepare to eject. Matching trajectories . . . now."

Kerry's voice was loud in his ear, harsh and rasping with barely concealed tension.

"Opening bay door," Kerry said. A moment later, he said, "Launch bay open. Ready to eject on your mark, Captain."

"Hold for my mark," Jim replied.

He took a final scan of local space, extending his machine perceptions to the edges of his vast, trembling web. The gas giant was far behind now, and they were entering the wreckage of some other gigantic world, torn apart by ancient forces that left a system-wide ring of rocky debris, a kind of orbiting gravel pit—except that some of these chunks of gravel were a hundred miles across!

It made for some tricky piloting, trying to snake the *Endeavor*'s huge bulk through this spinning, whirling minefield, where the slightest miscalculation would slam them all into subatomic gas in a nanosecond.

His human reflexes weren't up to that task, of course. Only in combination with the eerie speed of the *Endeavor*'s banks of computers was he able to zigzag his way through those looming, deadly rocks.

Beyond the immediate dangers, the rest of the Kolumban system moved through space in awesome silence, like a vast and ancient clock ticking to a rhythm set three billion years before. There was Kolumba itself, swathed in perpetual clouds, like an old gray dowager lit by the ruby light of the sun. Closer in, a trio of bright, tiny planets danced in an interlocking orbit, so close to that sun they brushed its corona, like glittering fireflies dancing far too close to the fire.

He saw nothing of the Communer ship. Unless it had masking capabilities far beyond anything he'd ever heard of, it wasn't in the Kolumban system.

He checked all the readings one last time, then took a deep breath.

"Ready for my mark, lighter?" he said.

"Ready," Kerry replied.

"Three, two, one, mark!"

A long moment of silence. Then, "Ejection successful, Captain," Kerry said. "Lighter under way. Thrusters off, running cold. Check trajectory."

The inner edge of the belt of rubble was coming up. Jim consulted his instruments and picked out the silent shape of the lighter, coasting along the trajectory they had set for it. Without knowing that trajectory, even he, with his superhuman, computer-boosted senses, would not have been able to distinguish the tiny vessel from the other bits of orbiting debris.

"Trajectory optimal, lighter."

"Optimal," Kerry acknowledged. "Initiating comm silence now."

"Good luck," Jim said softly.

"Luck," Kerry replied. Then the comm link went silent.

Jim glanced at Ferrick. "Well, they're off."

Ferrick nodded. "You want me to keep flashing, Captain?"

"Yes. If those bastards are hiding somewhere, I want them looking for us. Not for Kerry and the lighter."

Ferrick nodded. He knew the plan as well as Jim did.

Jim leaned back in his seat, feeling his spine creak in protest as the big muscles at its base suddenly relaxed. "Setting course to exit system," Jim said.

Ferrick acknowledged, but Jim had shifted his attention to the weapons station, which had its own web of specialized detectors probing the reaches of the Kolumban system.

"Anything at all, Mr. Grieger?" he asked.

"No, Captain, I—wait a minute!" Elwood's normally cool tones suddenly sounded breathy, as if he'd been punched. "I've got . . . *do you see it?*"

Jim more than saw it, he *felt* it. It was like a clutch of white-hot needles pricking his skin as the Communer vessel came boiling out of wormspace from behind the gas giant.

"Arm photon lasers!" he barked.

"Armed," Elwood replied, his voice no longer shaky, but calm as moonlight on a wintry pond.

Good man! Jim thought.

"Primary target lock?"

"Locked," Elwood replied laconically.

"Fire all batteries," Jim said.

He was almost entirely in vireo mode now, his fleshy body subsumed by the cybernetic digital fire that ran through him ten thousand, a million times faster than his own human brain could manage. In the real world, he knew that firing all ten of the *Endeavor*'s photon lasers had had no effect on the people inside the ship. There had been no roar, no shuddering recoil, nothing but a few lights on some of the consoles rapidly flickering from green to red and back to green again.

But in the vireo universe, things were popping right along. He felt the electron lattices of the *Endeavor*'s shields creak with precisely the sensation that had resettled his spine into his chair. He smelled the stink of overcooked eggs as long, twitching lines of perfectly aligned photons reached out like clawing fingers toward the burning nexus of the Communer ship, which was *still* boring a smoking hole in what felt like the skin of his forearm.

The gas giant from behind which the Communer vessel was still emerging was a broad, swirling hole of flickering darkness that emitted a chorus of low, humming groans, like the bass section of the biggest barbershop quartet in the universe booming away at the top of their lungs.

And over the top of all of it, like a crazy relative—a *huge* crazy relative standing in the middle of the room shouting, the great red sun at the center of the system snapped, crackled, popped, smelled of dust and sweat-rank socks, masking everything else with a hissing fog of shifting energy.

Jim's pseudo-nervous system, jumped up to incredible levels by the cybernetic boost the *Endeavor*'s machine minds supplied, slowed everything down, so that he could examine any single part of this hellish symphony, or all of it at once. He could see the charges from his own photon lasers approach and finally, like slow-motion lightning bolts, strike the shields of the Communer vessel, which had by this time moved once again into the familiar picket-fence arrangement.

There was a momentary bluish flash—the smell of burning rubber filled his nose—and then one of the pickets was gone, and another slowly dulling from eye-searing blue to dim, pulsing black.

In the back of his mind he heard distant cheering, and realized the people on the bridge were celebrating.

"No—" he said, but then the Communer ship was firing back, and he had everything he could handle. More than he could handle. The alien ship's response was overwhelming. Space began to ripple, as he had seen it do before, but with the magnification given his senses by the vireo, it was like watching a tidal wave of molten lava lurch across space toward him. Space itself rotted and disintegrated in the face of that awesome rush, leaving behind patches of empty, writhing worm-space, pseudo black holes in the naked fabric of spacetime.

Something *whipped* past the gas giant and sheared off the top of its turgid, boiling atmosphere as neatly as a baker leveling a crème pie.

Then the rocks of the Kolumban asteroid belt began to explode like kernels in God's own popcorn popper.

"Repeat fire! Photon laser, *repeat fire!*" Jim ordered, his breath caught in his throat as he watched that wall of death and chaos spreading from the Communer vessel toward his own. His vireo ears roared with the sounds of a billion bedsheets flapping in some hellish wind. He felt the atomic structure of the *Endeavor* straining as Elwood fired another salvo.

"Here we go, Ferrick. Button her up!"

He wrenched the Endeavor into wormspace, letting the computers control the jump, which he had preprogrammed to take them to a spot half a light-year out from the Kolumban system. He felt a moment of slick, oily darkness, and then they were out again, floating silently in empty space, Kolumba's sun receded to one of a trillion colored sparks chipped into the cold velvet of the universe.

He leaned back in the captain's chair and realized his forehead was drenched with sweat. "Jesus," he breathed. "That was close."

"Did we get them?" Ferrick asked.

"Hell," Jim told him. "They almost got us."

"What about Kerry and the lighter?"

Jim did a quick scan of vireo space. "I don't know," he said. "I think we covered them. But with what the Communers threw at us . . ." His voice trailed off.

"They could have gotten them by accident."

"So what do we do now?"

"All we can do," Jim said. "We follow the plan, and we wait."

6

T he cramped interior of the lighter's pilot cabin stank of fear and sweat and—something else. The hatch to the cabin had popped its lock and was flapping back and forth like a window shutter in a storm. Somebody back in the passenger cabin had lost control of his bladder. Kerry wrinkled his nose, wincing at the lance of pain the tiny motion sent arrowing through his forehead. He'd wiped the blood out of his left eye, but he could feel the lump growing above his eyebrow. Bad frigging headache coming, no doubt about that—

A grim chuckle, as involuntary as a burp, passed his lips. "My God," he said, grinding his teeth as he yanked at the rudimentary controls of the *Endeavor*'s lighter. His face gleamed red as a furnace as he fought to hold the tiny ship steady against the waves of turbulence batting it around like a helium-filled Ping-Pong ball.

"Kerry, you're bleeding," Sam said from the copilot's chair next to his. He spared her a glance, saw that her emergency auto-restraints were still jammed, and she was still pinned as tightly as any straitjacketed loony against the seat.

"I know," he said.

Another thunderous blow swatted the lighter sideways, and his own restraints—unjammed, thank God, or *nobody* would be trying to control this tin can—cut cruelly into his chest. At least his arms and legs were free, and he could reach most of the controls.

Somebody began to weep, loudly, in the passenger cabin.

"What happened?" Sam said. Her voice sounded distant and tiny, like a querulous child's.

"I don't know," Kerry said. "Did you just wake up?"

"A minute ago," she said.

"You were out. Speaking of bleeding, you've got a pretty bad slice on the side of your face."

"Don't worry about *me*."

"I'm not," he told her.

She began to struggle against the busted restraints. "If I could . . . damn it, this damned thing . . ."

"In my pocket," he said. "Your side. I've got a knife, if you can reach it. Maybe you can cut them."

Doggedly, she began to try to work her left arm free. The restraints fought her, but inch by inch she managed to slide her arm further out until her fingers brushed against his pants pocket.

"If you could scrunch your butt a couple of inches . . ."

He did, and felt her fingers slide into his pocket, groping for the knife. "Careful," he said. "You don't want to run into anything you can't handle down there," he told her.

"Asshole. I've handled it before."

"I think I can—whoops, *hold on!*"

A chunk of molten rock the approximate size and shape of Mount Everest came roaring out of nowhere directly toward their forward shields.

Kerry let out a choked screech and yanked hard on the control stick, feeling the lighter's engines—such as they were—give him a soft boot in the ass. Sam, her fingers gripping the knife in his pocket, was flung hard away from him. He felt his pocket and half that pants leg rip away, but he didn't have time to worry about his modesty, which he didn't have anyway. He felt a cool breeze down there, though.

He stared, transfixed, at the huge, flaming boulder spinning larger and larger on his main screen. Slowly, it began to slide off toward the right . . .

"Come on, baby, come *on*," he gritted, as he continued to yank hard on the control stick. At the last possible moment there was a flare of white that washed the monitor screen clean. Something in that light banged hard against the hull of the lighter, and Kerry's heart leaped into his throat. Then they were clear.

"Jesus . . ." Kerry breathed. "You know what that white flare was?"

He heard a scratchy, ripping sound from Sam's direction, and turned as she said, "No, what?"

She'd managed to saw halfway through one of the belts holding her down.

"Vaporized rock. We were that close. A half mile one way or the other, and we'd . . ." Kerry shivered. "Damn, woman, you think you could have at least left me my pants?"

The first strap gave way, and Sam went to work on the second.

"I don't want to be a backseat driver," she told him, "but don't you think you'd better keep an eye on the road?"

But the road was clear. That last burning mountain had been on the inner edge of the rubble belt, and once past it, they were coasting in open space. Behind them, the battle between the *Endeavor* and the Communer ship raged on, but as Kerry watched, the telltale flare on his instruments showed that the *Endeavor* had vanished into wormspace.

The Communer vessel, still rushing toward the point of the *Endeavor*'s vanishment, looked different. It took him a moment before he realized that two of the distinctive pickup sticks were gone.

"Way to go, Jimbo," he murmured. "Hurt that mofrucker."

"What happened?" Sam said, as she finished cutting through the final strap. "Score one for the good guys?"

"Yeah, but I dunno how big the score was. Jim ran, just like we planned, but he did knock out a couple of those stick things." He leaned forward, peering intently at his screen. "All right! The Communers are still out there, but they're heading for where Jim took off. Don't seem to be paying any attention to us at all, even with us having to light the engines. Maybe we *did* manage to pull this off."

Sam peeled off her helmet and fluffed her hair, succeeding in doing nothing but further disarranging the wild explosion of curls and beads that covered the top of her head like some sort of glitter-collecting bird's nest: a magpie, perhaps.

She brushed her fingers across the cut on her cheek and winced. "Ow. That hurts."

"I'll take a look at it in a second," Kerry told her. "Let me make sure we're still on course first."

The lighter had limited vireo capability, which he was using—he was far less skilled than Jim, though—but it didn't take him long to make a basic course analysis.

"Shit," he muttered.

"What's wrong?"

"All that bouncing around knocked us off the trajectory. Not bad, but we'll have to fire jets to correct."

"Right away?"

"No, but we can't wait too long. I hope that damned pile of sticks keeps heading out-system. We won't make a big torch, but if they happen to be looking when I light us up, it'll be pretty obvious we aren't just a chunk of random space rock. And we don't have the option of ducking into worm-space if they decide to come hunting. Which they undoubtedly would."

He turned back to his controls. "Let me run one more check on the engines, and then—"

His eyes suddenly narrowed. He hunched forward in his seat, looking as if someone had laid a cane across his shoulders. His fingers skittered like crazed spiders across his touchpad.

"What?" Sam said. "What?"

"Shut up."

"Well, excuse me!" The jibe came out halfhearted, though. She could see that something was wrong, but she couldn't see what it was, not looking at Kerry. She slid around in her seat, stripping away the last of the broken restraints that still festooned her like Christmas ribbons, and began to tap her own touchpad.

A moment later she let out a soft gasp. "Is this right?" she said. "About the engines?"

Kerry was still muttering to himself. He ran his forearm across his brow, wiping away a layer of sweat. "Yeah. Looks like it."

"But . . . what happened?"

He sighed. "I don't know, but it looks as if that last slam we took when we were going by that big chunk wasn't just concussion. We must have hit something. Something pretty small, or we wouldn't be talking about it now. But it was big enough."

"My diagnostics say one of our two engines is gone, and the other one may be damaged."

"Yeah, that's what I'm getting, too."

"My God, Kerry. What does it mean? Can we fly this thing, get it back on trajectory?"

"I doubt it," he said.

"Then what?"

"Then we stick with what we've got."

She was frantically shifting from screen to screen, looking for an answer, looking for a way out. "Kerry, the way we're heading now, we won't make an orbit around Kolumba."

"Nope. Doesn't look like it."

"Damn this thing! I can't get it—"

"Don't bother," he told her, his voice flat. "I've already run it. We're not gonna orbit the damned planet. We're gonna hit it right smack in the middle."

She gave up messing with the controls and wheeled around, her eyes wide and terrified. "We can use the remaining engine! We can miss the planet!"

"Sure," he said. "If the engine will still work at all. But say it does. We can miss, but we don't have enough power to pull an orbit. So we go right on out of the system. And when Jim comes back looking for us, he finds . . . what? Nothing, that's what. We're gone. And I don't think the Communers are gonna give him a lot of time to spend looking for us anyway."

"The radio . . ." she sputtered.

"Speed of light only. We don't carry hyperwave, remember?"

She shook her head. "This can't be happening."

"Hey, babe, you invited yourself along for the ride."

"That's not what I mean, and you know it!"

He grinned at her, but there was no humor in it. "Only thing I know is I wish you hadn't. If we're all gonna die, I wish you weren't gonna be a part of it."

She didn't know what to say to that. Once upon a time she had loved him, and it was obvious he still loved her. She could see it in his face, in his eyes. And in her own heart, she could see she still loved him at least a little. Maybe that would never change.

"Are we all gonna die?" she asked softly.

He shrugged. "I'll do everything I can to keep it from happening," he told her. "But no guarantees." He leaned back in his chair, shoulders slumping, and knuckled both eyes hard. "Right now my best guess is we don't make it at all."

CHAPTER SEVEN

1

We follow the plan, and we wait," Jim said.

"How far out are we?" Ferrick asked.

Jim checked his console. He was deliberately lowering the power of the vireo hookup, gently disengaging himself from the real-unreal world of swirling atomic structures and chattering machine languages, bringing himself back to the physical world. Though sometimes he wondered if it wasn't the machines that saw the truth of "physical" reality, which was nothing more than the human perception of patterns and arrangements of atoms, and the mostly empty space in which they existed.

"Right where we're supposed to be. Half a light beyond the Kolumban system."

"Any sign of the Communers?"

"Nope. What I programmed was a half-light jump to any random point on the sphere. If we didn't know where we were going, I don't see how they could, either." A thought struck him. He still didn't know what that Communer ship was really capable of. "What about the shields? Are we running black?"

"Black as I know how to run."

Jim glanced over the top of his own console, looked down toward where Elwood was fiddling with the controls of the weapons systems. "Mr. Grieger, anything?"

"Not a peep, Captain," Elwood replied.

Jim tilted his head back and stared blankly up at the ceiling. Faint shadows flickered in his left eye: the vireo was scanning through its many shipboard cameras, an automated survey it did every five minutes. Jim was so used to it he barely noticed it anymore.

So now comes the ugly part, he thought. *Where I sit on my butt and wait to find out if my best friend and the girl I love are dead or alive. And while I wait I can look at the stars and wonder if a malevolent game of pickup sticks is going to come boiling out of wormspace and blow the rest of us into kingdom come . . .*

He closed his eyes. His right eye went dark, but his left eye continued to show the vague vireo shadow parade throughout the ship, a flicker of empty corridor, a glimpse of the main engine room, a lightning pan of the galley, a peek at the door to Ur-Barrba's guarded cabin . . .

"Whoa!" Jim sat up straight in his seat, fingers already working his touchpad. The main holoscreen suddenly appeared across the front of the bridge, focused on the corridor in front of Ur-Barrba's cabin. The view enlarged, spilling rapidly off the side of the screen as he brought the camera's point of view closer, closer—

Rushing up the empty corridor.

Empty.

"Ferrick," Jim said. "Who's guarding Ur-Barrba?"

Ferrick's eyes slid quickly to his screen, then back again. "Frank."

Jim blinked. Immediately he was inside Ur-Barrba's cabin, looking at the alien's bed from a viewpoint equivalent to the holoscreen inset in the wall across from it. The room was dim, shadowy, burnished with a faint, red glow. In the glow, a large, shapeless lump filled the top of the bed—the blanket, and whatever was under it.

"Get somebody down there right away," Jim barked. "No, wait a sec. I'm going. You come with me."

Ferrick didn't argue, just released his restraints and stood up. He read the tone of Jim's voice perfectly. "Got a gun?" he said.

"Yep."

"Me, too," Ferrick replied.

Two minutes later they stood, guns in their hands, flanking the door to Ur-Barrba's quarters. Carefully, Jim leaned down and checked the tiny telltale screen above the door handle.

"It's unlocked," he said. "No card in the slot."

Ferrick nodded, then moved to face the door, grasping his own weapon in a two-handed grip. "I'll go first," he whispered.

Jim hesitated, then nodded. "Okay."

Ferrick took a deep breath, raised one thickly muscled leg, and booted the door wide. He lunged inside. Jim followed a split-second later, his heart pumping, the snout of his S&R .75 questing out before him.

The room was dim, silent except for the sound of their hoarse breathing. Ferrick glanced at Jim. Jim nodded. Ferrick moved one way, Jim the other, both of their weapons aimed at the shapeless, hairy brown lump on the bed.

Something wrong with that lump, Jim thought, that ungainly form beneath the scratchy blanket. A picture of Ur-Barrba's bubblegum-pink butt flashed across his mind, and he repressed a nervous giggle. But something *was* wrong. This lump was big. But was it big *enough*?

He licked his lips. "Ur-Barrba?" He braced for the lightning move he'd seen before, felt Ferrick also tensing.

"*Ur-Barrba! Wake up!*"

Nothing.

Then he realized that something else was wrong, too. He could hear Ferrick's hushed breathing, and his own. But nothing else. None of the stentorian rumble of alien snores.

He switched his pistol to his left hand and crept closer to the bed. The air was thick and rank with a cinnamonny dog-food stench, but not thick *enough*.

He reached down, grabbed one corner of the blanket, and hauled it as hard as he could. It caught on something, then pulled away with a liquid, sucking sound, as if it had been glued down, and the glue not quite dry yet.

Another smell smote their nostrils, thin, coppery, bitter.

"Oh, Jesus," Ferrick moaned, turning away.

At first Jim wasn't sure what he was looking at. In the hellish red light, the blood looked black. And the shapes the blood coated—oozed from, dripped from—at first didn't look human. One of the pieces had stuck to the blanket and now clunked to the deck at his feet as he let go of the scratchy alien cloth.

He stared down at it, feeling his gorge leap into his throat. At the end of the lumpy cylinder bumping against the toe of his boot were fingers. Four of them. And a bloody thumb.

Fighting the urge to puke, he lifted his head and looked at the jumble of body parts piled on the bed. On top of the grisly heap, Frank's battered head grinned at him, lips stretched back in agony, his teeth streaked with blood that gleamed like thick, black ink smears.

"Oh . . . aaahh . . ." Jim mumbled, turning away, the fingers of his right hand, delicately spread, rising to cover his mouth. Then he dropped to his knees and curled over, his back heaving as he sprayed stringy green vomit through his fingers onto the deck. Off to his left, he could hear the wet, gagging, ruptured sounds of Ferrick doing the same thing.

"Uh . . . uh . . ." Ferrick gasped. "What *did* this to him?"

Jim wiped his mouth with the back of his trembling hand. "Pretty obvious, wouldn't you say? Can you think of anything else on this tub big and strong enough—and *mean* enough—to pull a guy Frank's size apart at the joints like a roasting chicken?"

Ferrick climbed shakily to his feet. In the dim inferno glow, his normally dark features were painted the pale, wavering color of a surrender flag. He stared at the bed, then pointed with one shaking finger.

"What don't you see?" he said.

At first Jim didn't get it. Then he did. "Oh, God," he whispered. "She's got Frank's shatterblaster."

2

Kerry knuckled his sweat-slick eyelids but it didn't help, only pushed the sting deeper into his tired, aching eyes. He glanced over at

Sam. She was slumped in her seat, the raggedly chopped straps of the broken restraint system sticking out from the edges of her seat like twisted fangs, so that it looked as if she'd fallen asleep in some yawning, hungry mouth. The tiny cabin reeked of their mixed odors, a stink that was somehow greasy and dusty at the same time, and beneath that stink a sharper, bitterer odor he recognized perfectly well. It was the smell of fear.

He was scared shitless.

He hadn't passed the word back to the other two kids in the passenger compartment about what had happened, that they were down to one engine, maybe even *less* than one engine, and he hadn't let Sam tell them, either, though she'd argued heatedly that they had a right to know.

"Is that so?" he'd snarled at her. "Either of them back there know anything about piloting? About engine systems or jury-rigged hyperwave units? About *anything* that might help us here? Or will they just panic, and get in the way of whatever we might try to do? Go on, Sam, you tell *me*."

And of course she hadn't told him, but she hadn't liked *that* very much, either.

Exhaustion seeped from his bones. His muscles felt weak, flaccid, and seemed to be remembering on their own the multiple beatings he'd taken of late. An exquisitely precise point of pain throbbed above his right eye, as if somebody was probing there with an icepick.

So how deep in the warm and brown *were* they? He chewed his lower lip as he tried to add up all the bad news. One of the two engines was definitely gone. The diagnostics reports he was getting were so screwed up he couldn't make sense of them at all. His vireo capabilities were much more limited than those aboard the *Endeavor*, but he could still get a kind of half-assed view of the outside of the lighter. A check of the hull in the vicinity of the engine area showed streaks of bright, scraped metal and a single smoking hole about twice as long as he was, but the view of this ended near the rear of the lighter, before the cargo hatch. Beyond that was a completely blank. Sensors probably gone back there, he guessed. The other engine looked untouched from the outside, but his tests indicated it was only functioning at half power, maybe even less. And no guarantees that it would keep on functioning if he *did* fire it up.

Just to complicate matters further—thank you, God—he had no hyperwave capability, only standard radio and laser communications, both limited to the speed of light. In other words, if Jim had taken the *Endeavor* where he said he was going to take her, any SOS messages he sent would take a half year to arrive.

By then, even if the remaining engine functioned well enough to divert them from their collision course with Kolumba and send them drifting out of the system, they would have died in any number of grisly ways— with dehydration or starvation sitting at the top of that suicidal hit parade. Luckily, they did have an atmosphere recycler, so they wouldn't strangle.

This all presumed that the Communer ship didn't return, find them, and grind them all up for Communer food, whatever it might be.

And that's the bad news for the day, Kerry thought. He found a shred of comfort in the knowledge that he couldn't think of anything else immediately dangerous.

"Well, at least it can't get any *worse*," he murmured as he turned in his seat to see what the commotion was back in the passenger compartment.

He couldn't see anything back there, though. The door to the pilot's cabin was completely blocked by what looked like a wall of shaggy orange hair.

At first he didn't get it. It was so weird, so outlandish, that he didn't understand what was standing there, plugging the hole. Not until Ur-Barrba's face poked into the cabin, along with the glittering snout of a shatterblaster, and enough grinning yellow fangs and blood-streaked yellow claws to furnish any nightmare from one screaming end to the other.

Yep, he thought. And she still smells like rotten dog food with a cinnamon topping.

He tried to raise his hands against the butt of the shatterblaster rising over the back of his seat. A light as bright and soundless as a nuclear explosion flared in his eyes, and then he saw no more.

3

Man, we were lucky to get out with our butts in one piece the first time," Ferrick said. "And you were doing the piloting. You're nuts to try it again, Jim. You're risking everything—all of us—just to try and save four people."

"I can't just let them die," Jim said. "Just abandon them?" He took a deep breath, scrubbed his fingers through his tousled hair. "No way."

"You're our best pilot. And you'll be in this tin fish. Kerry's second best, but he ain't here, either."

"You'll do fine," Jim soothed him. "We know what we're dealing with now. And we did hurt that sonofabitch the last time. Knocked out two of its segments. You might not see it at all."

Ferrick sighed heavily. "I'm not gonna be able to talk you out of this, am I?"

Jim shook his head. "Help me with this suit," he said.

They were standing in the lighter's launch bay, next to the long missile shape that Ferrick had been working on earlier. It was up on jacks, its needle nose pointed toward the launch bay hatch.

The center part of it had been refitted into a tiny compartment barely large enough to hold two people in a horizontal position. Small thrusters, no larger than basketballs, ringed the rear of the vessel. One of the sardine-sized compartments contained a rudimentary control panel for the jets, so crude it looked as if it had been wired together by a demented child genius. Two of Ferrick's engineers-in-training were still working on the jury-rigged contraption, their tools making soft, ringing sounds in the echoing vastness of the launch bay—like wind chiming across winter icicles.

Ferrick stared in disgust at the huge space suit reclining like a half-deflated corpse on the deck. "And that's another thing," he muttered.

"Well, if we'd brought suits of our own when we hijacked this barge—which we didn't, because we couldn't—then I wouldn't have to use a modified Kolumban rig," Jim said reasonably. He thought he sounded reasonable. As reasonable as anybody could sound, given the utter insanity of the course he'd decided upon.

"You're gonna rattle around in that thing like a baseball in a bowling alley," Ferrick said.

The only noticeable modification to the suit was that the long, thick arms and legs had been roughly chopped down, then glued back together with thick layers of shiny red glop.

"All I need is to be able to work the controls," Jim said. "For the suit, and for the ship."

"Ship, huh," Ferrick said. "That's a fancy name for what's really nothing more than a torpedo without the high explosive. Although," he said darkly, "knowing you, you'd find some way to make it blow up anyway."

The sound of an inner hatch sliding open with a dull, metallic *thud* drew their attention. Elwood was there, dragging in another modified suit by its heels, like a villain in a bad holovid dragging a body toward a hasty grave. But that image was much too close to the reality of the situation, and Jim resolutely shoved it to the back of his mind. Too bad that the images—corpse, grave—didn't fade away quite as fast as he would have liked them to.

"Here comes your good buddy," Ferrick said, the sneer in his voice only partly concealed.

"I tried to make him stay," Jim said. "He wasn't having any. He still keeps saying he's my champ, and where I go, he goes, too. Like a shadow."

"Or a curse," Ferrick said. "You ever consider that if old Elwood there wants another crack at you, taking it in that sardine can about half a light-year away from the *Endeavor* would be as good a place as any?"

"Yeah, I thought about it," Jim said. And he had. Especially after he wondered if anybody—like, say, Elwood—might hold a grudge against anybody—like, say, his captain—over what had happened to his former buddy Frank down in Ur-Barrba's cabin. But there was something changed about Elwood. He couldn't really put his finger on it, but he was sure it was there. Elwood's *interest* might shift, the focus of it, at least, but when he got interested, he tended to stay interested. Jim thought Elwood's interests now sort of paralleled his own. He was into the crew thing, the ship thing, the comforting feel of a quasi-military social structure. Sort of like what the Stone Cowboys had once been.

Or maybe it was all bullshit and Ferrick's misgivings were more to the point. He didn't know. What he did know was that he didn't look forward to wedging his space-suited bod into a jury-rigged guided missile all by himself. Did that make him a coward?

He thought maybe not. Maybe it only made him human.

He slapped Ferrick on one beefy shoulder and tried a grin that, from the expression on Ferrick's blunt, dark features, probably didn't look as cheerful or self-confident as he'd hoped.

"Let's get going," he said. "Sooner started, sooner done." He remembered, with a twinge, that this saying had been one of his father's favorites. The man he'd thought was his father, anyway.

"Yeah," Ferrick replied, his tone bleak. "Soonest blown to kingdom come."

4

Waking up was like coming back from some far, dark place full of grinding, roaring silences and sudden dry flashes of white lightning that lit up the arid interior of his skull like hell's own photo opportunity.

Kerry tried to groan, but something filled his mouth, something that was wedged between his teeth that pressed down on his tongue, a tongue that felt very much like an overcooked sausage.

"Aaugh," was the best he could do. His right eye popped open with a faint ripping sound, as if his eyelashes had been glued together. Everything through that eye was red. His other eye didn't seem to want to open at all.

Somehow he'd gotten his hands twisted behind him, but when he tried to lift them, bracelets of pain whipped jagged lines around his wrists. The sudden anguish slapped him fully awake and left him gasping, but the red haze in his good eye seemed to clear a bit. Sam was looking back at him through the crimson haze. Her lips moved slowly; the sound hissed in his ears. It took him a second or so before he realized what she was saying.

"Shhh . . ." she whispered again, and this time she shook her head.

His skull still felt like a cracked china bowl in danger of spilling his brains out onto the deck (*I'm a little teapot, short and stout*, a tiny voice blurted madly in the background), but enough of his wits seemed still to be functioning for him to realize he was no longer in the pilot's cabin of the lighter.

He tried to answer her, but that thing in his mouth still had his jaws wedged painfully wide, and all he could manage was a gargle or two. Sam leaned toward him as if she meant to kiss him, which seemed the nuttiest thing of all.

A dream, he thought. *Must be some kind of weird dream.* He closed his eye as her face loomed into his, and then he felt her lips at his cheek, and then at his mouth. Her teeth nibbling, working—*what the hell*?

The knot between his jaws suddenly slipped, moved, and then slimy roughness was sliding out between his lips. He opened his eyes and stared. Sam was pulling back, what looked like a spit-soaked sock dangling from her teeth.

It *was* a spit-soaked sock.

I ought to recognize it, he thought. *That last time I looked, I was wearing it.*

"Ptui!" he said.

She let the sock drop. "Maybe that sort of thing works for a gag with the Kolumbans," she whispered. "Those big fangs of theirs slant inward, probably hold it tight once they get a big enough wad jammed in there."

He licked his lips, tasted salt over a crust of scabs at the corners of his mouth where his jaws had been most distended by the makeshift gag.

"How long have I been out?" His tongue really did feel like a squashed dried salami or something.

"I can't see my nailtale, but I'd guess a couple of hours. You had me worried."

It was all he could do to keep from laughing out loud at her. "And now that I'm awake, you're *not* worried?"

"We'll think of something. In fact, I've already thought of something."

"Huh?"

The passenger cabin was a narrow affair, a single aisle with six rows consisting of one crude seat on either side. She wiggled in her chair, lifted her legs, and slid her hands, which were bound behind her back at the wrists, underneath her butt. A couple of wriggles, a soft grunt, and suddenly, like a magical gymnastics trick, her wrists were in front of her. He saw they'd been crudely but thickly taped together. She extended them across the aisle toward him.

"You always did have those nice teeth, Kerry," she whispered. "See if you can't gnaw your way through this."

When he tried to move his head spun dizzily, and with the dizziness came a sudden wave of nausea fluttering up from his belly into the back of his throat. He opened his mouth, gagging, but nothing came out, and after a moment that filled his one good eye with whirling white spots, he was able to lift his head again.

He began to gnaw.

5

Elwood's voice was tinny in his suit speakers. Just after he started speaking, he broke up in a hissing shower of static. It sounded as if they were communicating by cans and a string, which, Jim reflected, wasn't all that far from the truth. Everything about this little jaunt—the equipment, the transportation, even the plans—was jury-rigged, slapped together under high pressure and low time limits. It would be a miracle if nothing blew up on them out of sheer sloppiness, no matter what else happened.

But the miracle, so far, still seemed to be in good shape. He said to Elwood, "Sorry, repeat that, please?"

". . . can't see a . . . thing. My faceplate's . . . fogged . . . we there yet?"

Jim's own faceplate was as blurry as a rain-swept window, but he could see a little bit. The tiny screen in front of his helmet was focused on a large dark blob occulting the stars about six miles in front of him. They were slowly closing on the shape from the rear, but he recognized it easily enough. It was the *Endeavor*'s lighter, and it was right where it was supposed to be. Well, not exactly. Its trajectory was supposed to take it into orbit around Kolumba, where Kerry and his crew could scoop up one of the Communer satellites, but by Jim's horseback calculations, for some reason the lighter was heading dead-on into the center of the planet. If he didn't know what the lighter's mission was supposed to be, he would assume that Kerry planned to make a landing on Kolumba. Which wouldn't be all that hard, since the lighter was designed to do exactly that, with its retractable wings and exterior jets. But a landing wasn't supposed to be on the menu, so this weird trajectory was all the more worrisome.

He could think of one very good reason *somebody* might be trying to land the lighter, though. If Ur-Barrba was aboard and in control, it would make perfect sense.

And he was very much afraid that was exactly what was going on. After discovering Frank's mutilated corpse, he and Ferrick had turned the *Endeavor* upside down, but had found no trace of their murderous alien prisoner. No trace but one; in the lighter's bay, one of the kids had found a greasy patch of hair. Orange hair.

"We're here," he told Elwood. "I'm gonna use our jets to maneuver toward the rear of the lighter."

"Why . . . the back?"

"Because I want to try to enter the lighter through the cargo door, and it's in the back, below the engines."

"Okay."

Jim fiddled with the screen, trying for a better view of the lighter. It was coming clearer now, partly because they had both finally moved out of the shadow of Kolumba, and partly because Jim had managed to close the distance between the two craft considerably.

Like creeping up on someone tippy-toe, he thought, amused at the strange image the thought conjured. The lighter obviously wasn't under power, and now he began to see why. There were two large engines positioned on the outer hull of the ship, and where one of those engines should have been was only scraped and curling metal. The other one looked undamaged, though.

What the hell happened to them? he wondered. *Is Ur-Barrba there? Did she do that somehow? But why would she?*

Another mystery. He had no time for it. He was working on the assumption that Ur-Barrba *was* on board the lighter, and probably in charge, too. She was three times as big and twice as fast as anybody else aboard, and she had a shatterblaster.

If that was the case, he didn't have much hope of success in a frontal assault. Even damaged, the lighter's engines had to be more powerful than the makeshift thrusters on his own tiny ship. If Ur-Barrba saw him coming, she could simply run away from him. Or if she was really creative, she could maneuver until he was in the flare area of her own jets and fry him like so much country barbecue.

His jets used liquid nitrogen as a propellant. Not very powerful, but silent and without heat. Hard to detect. And they had power enough for what he had to do. At least, he hoped they did. If they didn't, he'd be finding out soon enough, he guessed.

But it was tricky work. He was operating without vireo, without any sort of major computer help, without *any* of the aids and backups he'd been trained to use, to depend on. This was all seat-of-the-pants stuff, a tiny push here, an adjustment there, a faint billow of white steam trailing off behind him as he moved closer, closer . . .

He was sweating heavily inside the confines of the modified Kolumban suit when he finally shut down his own engines. They were floating about a hundred feet from the lighter, directly at its rear. He was staring down the gullet of the lighter's single remaining engine, and he was uncomfortably aware how much that blackened throat looked like the mouth of a gun barrel aimed right between his eyes. All Ur-Barrba would have to do was place her thick finger on the engine controls and push once. That would do it. He'd have no warning. Maybe a sudden flash of white before the intolerable blare of heat crisped the skin from his bones, and then charred his bones.

He pushed the smoking image from his mind. If it was going to happen, there was nothing he could do about it. In fact, at this point, there was only one thing he could do.

"I'm going out there," he said into his intercom.

"I still think you should let me go," Elwood replied. "It's too dangerous."

The static in their comm systems seemed to have diminished. That was a good thing. Over the next few minutes, one hell of a lot might hinge on what they were able to say to each other. Any mistake might be the last one—for both of them, maybe even for the people aboard the lighter as well.

"Elwood, I don't know what we might have to do, and I'm a lot more familiar with the lighter's systems than you are." He was still trying to get used to Elwood's solicitousness about his safety. It hadn't been that long since Elwood was trying to get him killed. And he still wasn't sure he trusted him.

So why did I bring him along, if I don't trust him?

It was a good question. He didn't know the answer. But then, there were a lot of things he didn't know. Like what was going on aboard the lighter, for starters.

"Getting ready to evac," he said.

"Be careful," Elwood told him.

"Yep." The makeshift alterations they'd used to fit a pair of tiny human cargo modules into the probe necessitated that he physically open four latches, which would allow one whole wall of his module to open onto naked space. No fancy airlocks here! Which made sense. You didn't need airlocks when your compartment was as empty of air as the space beyond its walls.

When he finished, the wall popped open with a dull *ting*! He heard the sound through the contact his suit gloves made with the latches. It swung wide, and for a moment vertigo grabbed his stomach and squeezed. He was floating, but his eyes told him he was falling toward the Kolumban surface ten thousand miles below.

He took a deep breath and waited for the feeling to pass. Then he gently pushed himself out of the probe, starfishing his arms and legs until he was facing the rear of the lighter, which now loomed less than fifty feet away. He used his chin to activate the suit's jets. The tiniest of bumps, and then he felt a gentle, ghostly hand press at the base of his spine and move him forward.

6

There, that's got it," Samantha whispered. She twisted her wrists, hard, and the tape that had bound them parted with a soft, ripping sound.

Kerry pulled his head back and spit out bits of half-chewed tape. "Phew. Nice taste." He grinned at her. "Better than your cooking, anyway."

Sam ignored him as she bent down and started to work the tape around her ankles loose. She worked with single-minded intensity, her hair falling forward in her face, the tip of her tongue just barely protruding from one corner of her mouth.

"Hurry up," Kerry said.

"Hold your britches," she muttered. She gave the tape a final yank and it separated with a soft shredding sound. She wadded it up and tossed it down the aisle, then hoisted her legs up on the seat and massaged her ankles. "Oh, man. They went to sleep."

"Come on, come on," Kerry said. "Get me loose."

She continued to work on her ankles for a few more seconds, groaning quietly in pleasure, then turned and flashed her teeth at him. "Okay, baby. Momma fix."

She rose from her chair and went to work on Kerry's restraints. She had to do a bit of gnawing herself, but finally he was free. As soon as he was, he tried to stand, but the sudden movement sent his head whirling and set stars spinning wildly in his vision.

"Whoa!"

"Take it easy," she said. "You've got a lump the size of my fist right above your eye. And blood all over your face, too."

"I'll live," he said. "What happened after the gorilla conked me?"

She shrugged. "I sat there and tried not to pee my pants while she pointed that huge gun at me. She taped me up, then she dragged you out and did the same. Then she hauled us back here and dumped us with these other two guys, went back into the pilot's cabin, and slammed the door. Locked it, too, from the sound of it."

The other two kids—both boys, both no older than fourteen or fifteen, made grunting sounds in the seats behind them. Kerry barely knew either one of them, and mentally named them Frick and Frack.

"Better get them loose, too. Though I dunno what good it's gonna do. I doubt if Ur-Barrba left us anything that might be dangerous, right?"

"Your breath," Sam muttered.

"Hey, I forgot to brush this morning," he told her.

He wrapped his fingers together and cracked all his knuckles at once.

"Don't *do* that," Sam snapped.

"Sorry." Kerry used the arm and back of his seat to lever himself slowly upright. His head gave one solid lurch, but he found he was able to stand okay, as long as he didn't make any sudden movements.

Sam finished undoing the bonds of the other two, but Kerry doubted if they would be much help. They both sat in their seats and stared at him with eyes so wide they seemed to drift off the sides of their faces. He had

no doubt they were probably brave enough under normal conditions—
they were Cowboys, after all, and they'd volunteered to go on this mission in the first place—but it was dubious what they could do against
several hundred pounds of heavily armed and obviously irritated gorilla.

Far as it went, he wondered what *he* would be able to do.

"You oughta sit down before you fall down," Sam said.

"I don't think I've got time for an extended convalescence," he told
her. He glanced at the door to the pilot's cabin. "Has she come out since
she chucked us back here?"

"No. Not a peep."

"Huh. I wonder what she thinks she's gonna do?"

"Can she fly this thing?" Sam asked.

"Don't have a clue. She was never very talkative with us, you know.
And Jim wouldn't let us do anything to encourage her to be more
chatty. Like sticking needles under her fingernails. Said it would be a
violation of the laws of humanity."

"That thing is no more human than a fencepost," Sam said. "I love
Jim dearly, but does he ever strike you as just the teensiest bit . . .
impractical?"

"He's the captain," Kerry said. "Anyway, it doesn't matter what I
think about him one way or the other. He isn't here, and—"

He broke off and turned slowly to stare at the open door to the cargo
bay. Soft sounds issued from the darkened hold. Sounded like rats. Or
like something scratching at the outer cargo hatch . . .

"What the hell?" His glance snagged on Sam's. Her eyes were as
round as those of the two younger kids, who were also turning slowly
toward the rear.

A line of invisible ants began to march up the center of Kerry's back.
He was as hardheaded as anybody, but it was impossible that anybody
could be outside the lighter, scratching on the cargo door. Ghosts?
Ridiculous, he told himself.

But the sound was still there, a faint, rhythmic scraping. "You stay
here," he told Sam, as he tried to slide past her toward the rear door.

That got her attention. "Like hell," she said. "I'm in better shape than
you are right now, Mr. Man, upper body strength or not."

Before he could do anything to stop her, she was through the door, vanished into the empty shadows of the cargo bay. A moment later she was back, milk-faced and shaken. "Kerry, there's somebody *out* there."

"What? That's nuts, there can't be."

"Well, the inner lockwheel is turning. Somebody's activated it."

"Holy shit! Come on, we've got to get this door closed. You guys! Move it, close that door between us and the cargo hold. Make sure it's sealed!"

Frick and Frack stared up at him.

"Goddamn it, I said *move!*"

They both shot out of their seats as if he'd rammed hand grenades beneath their butts.

Sam was looking from the door to Kerry and back again. "Kerry, what—"

"There's no air lock on that cargo door!" he told her. "If it opens, we've got explosive decompression in here. You already came close to sucking vacuum once. Want to try again?"

She shook her head. He could see she was holding her breath now, and she didn't let it out until Frick and Frack had the door to the cargo bay closed, locked, and sealed.

"Will it hold?" she asked slowly as the two boys shuffled down the aisle and took their seats again. Kerry noticed that neither one had yet to speak a single word. Stark terror, he guessed. It had a way of drying up your mouth.

"It should. It was designed to, at least."

She shut up then, and so did he, and all four of them stared at the door. After a minute or so of tension, Kerry suddenly barked a laugh.

"What a bunch of idiots we must look like," he muttered. "Standing here gaping at a closed door."

Her hand had stolen to his wrist. Now she clamped down, so hard he could feel the small bones in there grinding together. "Hush!" she barked hoarsely.

She'd heard it first, somehow, but now they all heard it. A dull, soft cludding sound, barely audible, and all the more frightening for the near silence of it.

Clud . . . clud . . . clud.

Nothing.

Kerry felt the hairs on his forearm come to attention. He licked his lips.

"Are you gonna open it?" she whispered.

"Christ, let go, you're breaking my wrist."

"Sorry."

Clud . . . clud . . . clud.

Frick—or maybe it was Frack—let out a strangled squeak.

Kerry shot him a glance that slid him down in his seat, his chin on his chest.

"All right," he said. "Sam, sit down. I don't know what's back there, but something is. And I guess it wants to come in for a visit. So what do you think? Should I open up?"

Sam shook her head violently back and forth. No, no way.

Frick and Frack just gazed up at him in round-eyed, shivering splendor.

"Big help, guys. Thanks," Kerry said.

Sam stared at him a moment, then took a breath. "I'll open it," she said. "You sit down." And she was past him, heading for the door, before he even thought to grab her. By the time he did, it was too late.

Clud . . . clud . . . clud . . .

7

The shape of the lighter was something like a huge eyedropper, with the bulbous rubbery part at the rear representing the cargo hold, and the sleeker glass dropper comprising the two forward cabins. At this point the lighter's atmosphere wings were still in their hidden cradles, but the larger circumference of the cargo hold hid Jim's approach from any forward eyes. He came ghosting in, a black spider-shadow against snowfields of stars, followed by disintegrating, light-fractured puffs of nitrogen crystals.

It was touchy work. He didn't know what the situation was aboard the lighter, but he had to assume the worst, especially given the amount of damage he'd seen on the outside of the ship. Everybody inside could be dead. Or Ur-Barrba could be holding all the humans hostage, trying to figure out how to get them down to the ground on Kolumba. As he thought this, he flashed for a moment on Sam's face and then, in a sickening lurch, on what the Kolumban had left of Frank.

His stomach did a nasty flip-flop, and he swallowed hard as he drifted the last few feet to a soft landing on the rear of the cargo bay.

Once he was down, he turned on the heavy electromagnets in his boots and stuck himself to the hull, offering a silent blessing that the Hunzzans built space suits pretty much the way everybody did—the magnets were inside the boots and padded, so they didn't clang harshly against the hull with every step he took. The only sound he could hear was a faint scratching noise as he shuffled across the hull.

Around his waist was tied a high-tension cable. He unstrapped it and dogged it down to a massive grommet protruding from the hull. The rest of the cable extended back to the probe, where it was connected to the forward portion that housed the hyperwave transmitter.

He moved clumsily to the wheel lock recessed behind a clear-steel plate set into the hull. He pushed hard on the plate; after a moment of strain it slid aside with a rusty whisper, giving him access to the wheel. And then he stopped.

This whole thing is insane. I don't know what's going on in there. I don't know if they're alive or dead. I don't know if it's just Ur-Barrba, and she's watching me, waiting on the other side of this hatch with the ugly snout of the shatterblaster aimed at the door. Or if she's not there, maybe they are, and when I open this hatch I'll vacuum-dry every single one of them into arid, dusty husks . . .

He took a deep breath of the stale, cinnamon-flavored air in his suit. He didn't know anything, and he was risking everything. Their lives, his own life, Elwood's—

Stop it! Just do it!

Was this what being a captain meant? Flying blind, playing god? No wonder people like Frank and Elwood and even Ferrick distrusted him. And hadn't Frank been right, in the end?

Suddenly Frank's decapitated head was there again, in his mind, perched on a pile of dead meat, leering at him . . .

He took another breath as sweat slipped down his forehead and burned into his eyes. For a moment his vision blurred. He blinked until it came clear again, felt his fingers trembling slightly against the padded metal interior of his gloves. He glanced back at the probe, but found no answers there, either.

At least Elwood hadn't tried to kill him on the trip out.

He took as firm a grip as he could manage on the stubborn wheel and put his back into it. More scratching squeaks as the seal fought him, and then, with a sudden muttering ratchet, finally began to revolve.

He spun it all the way and pulled out. Light appeared in a sudden dim rectangle around the shape of the door, and a gassy outrush of air froze in glittering clouds as it hit the cold vacuum of deep space. He waited until the ice vapor was gone, then opened the hatch wide enough to slip inside. Vacuum in here, too, but there was greasy steel around him, a few dim, shrouded shapes, and on the far side of the cargo bay, beneath a glowing danger light (nope, no atmosphere in there now, danger, danger, he thought) was another blank door.

He closed the outer hatch, then trudged slowly across the bay, keeping a watchful eye on that warning light. When it went off, the lighter's atmosphere system should have replenished the air there. He hoped.

He had to do it that way. He couldn't stay in his suit, because he couldn't fire his weapon from inside the suit. And he thought he might have to do some shooting.

After a while the warning light flickered, then went out. He stood in darkness, then stripped off the suit, left it like a deflated balloon on the deck behind him. He tried the handle on the inner hatch.

Locked.

He took out his S&R .75 and tapped the butt of the grip three times, softly, on the metal door.

Clud . . . clud . . . clud.

Waiting to see who—or what—would open it.

Clud . . . clud . . . clud.

Waiting to see who was faster, if it came to it. Like a gunslinger.

Clud . . . clud . . . clud.

Waiting . . .

8

U r-Barrba was not a pilot, at least not a pilot familiar with the crude controls of the lighter. The humans had modified the vireo setup somehow, and she couldn't make much sense of it now. It took her quite a while to figure out that one engine was gone and the other damaged.

For the past hour or so, she'd been trying to decide what options she had left. The escape from her jail aboard the *Endeavor* hadn't been difficult, nor had she expected it to be. The humans had badly underestimated her resources. What had they been thinking, to leave one stupid boy to guard her, no matter if he did have one of their killer weapons? After she'd lured him inside the room, she'd plucked the shatterblaster from his stunned hands as easily as she had twisted his head off a moment later. The rest of the carnage was just the anger she'd been repressing at such great cost ever since the humans had captured her ship, killed all her crew, and imprisoned her.

She knew they had intended to hold her hostage against her father's submission. She had spied on them from her own cabin, listened to their arguments, watched as they made their plans. That had been the final goad that led her to try to escape, risky though it had been. But what did the risk matter? She had every intention of killing herself if she couldn't escape. Better that than let herself be used against her own family, her own people.

These humans are terribly shortsighted, she thought. *They didn't even think of what I might do. An arrogant, and arrogantly stupid, race indeed.*

But now she had different goals. She *had* escaped, and even better, now possessed hostages of her own. But there was still the problem of what to do with them. She was not at all confident of her ability to pilot the lighter down to the surface of her own planet, not as damaged as the lighter seemed to be.

After much thought, she had finally narrowed her options to three: First, remain in orbit and hope the Communer vessel returned and found her before the humans did. Second, try to make a landing on Kolumba, with her and her cargo alive. Third, return to her original fallback plan and kill herself. It wouldn't be that hard. All she would need to do was allow the lighter to continue on its present course, but make no attempt to control it. The small vessel would burn in Kolumba's upper atmosphere long before it touched the ground. And a part of her was drawn to this final solution. She had disgraced herself by allowing her ship to be captured. A final blazing fall, her ashes the long, glowing tail of a shooting star, seemed a fitting way to atone. Nor was there anything in her culture that prohibited suicide as an honorable way of redressing shame. In fact, it was just the opposite.

The first option, simply waiting and hoping for the Communers to show up and rescue her, did have its appeal. She wouldn't have to do anything but maintain the status quo, and she had no doubt of her ability to do that. Her human prisoners were trussed up in the passenger compartment; they could go nowhere, and she was safe from anything they might try to do, behind the locked door to the pilot's cabin. Not to mention that she had the only gun, and even barehanded, probably outweighed all four of her captives together. But the problem with this option was also simple: the lighter was bound on a crash course with the planet's surface. She had a fair amount of time yet, but if she waited too long, then her options would reduce to suicide, or . . .

Option number two. This one was best of all. To get lucky and actually land the craft intact, and triumphantly bring her hostages to her father. Short of not having stupidly lost her ship in the first place, this would be the best of all possible outcomes. Then, if her father ordered her to commit suicide for her original shame, at least she could do so with honor.

She mused over all this for quite some time, but when she finally reached a decision, it was a combination of all three possibilities, and this seemed fair enough to her. She decided to wait, to give the Communers a chance to return and find her. But she would wait no longer than necessary. Before she was irrevocably committed to a crash, she would try to fire up the remaining engine and make a safe landing. And if she failed? Well, there would still be that glorious star burning across Kolumba's crimson sky to mark her passing.

Yes, that would do. She was very tired, and the struggle had made her even more exhausted. Everything was shipshape. She could afford to rest awhile.

Her massive head nodded forward. Yes, rest awhile . . .

She slept.

Much later, Samantha's shriek of joy awakened her.

9

Samantha took the door handle in both hands and rammed it down. The lock emitted a sharp double click as the bolts around the edge of the door slid back. She didn't hesitate, just pulled hard at the handle.

Behind her, Kerry tensed reflexively, knowing he didn't have enough left to make a difference in a fight, but ready to try anyway.

The door swung open. Jim Endicott stepped through, the big pistol in his hand swerving back and forth, seeking targets.

"*Jim!*" Samantha shrieked, as Endicott aimed the pistol at her.

She faltered, the joy melting from her face like icing on a cake left out in the rain.

"No, wait—" she screamed, throwing up her hands like a referee signaling a touchdown.

He pulled the trigger. The bell-like tones of the pistol filled the small chamber, hammering at their ears, the backwash from the blast blinding in the confined space. Jim, who blinked reflexively whenever he fired the S&R, was the only one whose vision wasn't full of painful white blobs, so he was the only one to see the huge figure at the far end of the cabin stagger back, shatterblaster rising in her clawed hands.

His second shot, joggled slightly by Sam leaping blindly toward him, only grazed the side of Ur-Barrba's skull. The blow sent the shatterblaster flying, and knocked her back into the pilot's cabin. Jim tried to leap over Sam, who had fallen to her knees, but ran straight into Kerry.

He shoved him aside, but was too late. The door to the pilot's cabin clicked shut in his face. He yanked at the door.

Nothing.

He stepped back, aimed his weapon at the lock plate, and then a choking groan froze him. He turned. One of the two kids Kerry had thought of as Frick and Frack was standing, a look of horror on his face, most of his left arm below the elbow gone.

Ricochet! Jim thought.

He lowered his pistol, rammed it into the top of his pants. Then he leaped for the kid, who toppled forward to meet him in a fountain of blood.

CHAPTER EIGHT

1

Help me . . ." The kid—was it Frick? Or Frack? Kerry couldn't remember—kept repeating the two words over and over as he toppled, staring in pale, horrified disbelief at the enormous quantities of blood spraying from the stump of his left arm. It sprayed across Jim's face like water from a hose.

Kerry fumbled for his belt and ripped it off as Jim grabbed the kid in a bear hug and lowered him quickly to the floor. "Stay down, don't move!" Jim said urgently, trying to grab the butchered arm, which flopped around like a beached fish.

"Grab him, hold him!" Kerry yelled as he knelt in the aisle. Jim made a stab for it, but his fingers, slimed with blood, slipped away. He tried again, this time managed to snag the kid's elbow. He looked across the boy at Kerry.

"Do it now!"

Kerry whipped the belt around the end of the stump, threaded the tongue of the belt through the buckle, and savagely yanked it tight. The kid's heels began to spasm hard against the deck. Sam, her face as drained of blood as the wounded kid's, squatted and held his legs down.

The astonishing, terrifying geyser of blood stopped as if somebody had turned off a faucet. The boy raised his head, stared at the wad of shredded, purplish flesh protruding beyond the constricting band of the belt—a single jagged white finger of bone in the center of the malign blossom—and then his eyes rolled back in his skull. The back of his head hit the deck with a soft thump, and he lay still.

"Oh my God, oh my God . . ." Sam said. There were sticky streaks of red in her hair. Jim looked as if somebody had attacked him with a sprayer full of red paint. He stared across the boy's silent body at Kerry, his gore-splashed expression shaken.

"A ricochet," he managed at last. "I didn't mean . . ."

"It's not your fault," Kerry said bluntly. "If you hadn't shot that monkey when you did, we'd all look like—" He glanced down at the kid, licked his lips, shook his head. "We would."

Jim sucked in a gout of air. "Ur-Barrba!" He turned and peered over his shoulder. The door to the pilot's cabin was still closed, but nothing seemed to be happening. He set down the kid's arm carefully, glanced at Sam, and said, "You take care of him." Then he stood, spraddle-legged, and clambered clumsily across Kerry's kneeling form.

"What—where are you going?" Kerry said.

"Elwood's with me. I've got to get him in here. And we brought a hyperwave transmitter."

"Huh?"

"Close the cabin door behind me and don't open it till I tap on it again. I've got to get back in my suit and depressurize the cargo hold."

Kerry's head was still swimming—from the blow Ur-Barrba had slammed into his skull, from the surprise at Jim's amazing appearance, from the gun battle, from . . . "What?" he said. "What?"

"Just *do* it!" Jim snarled. He reached the cargo bay door, stepped through, began to close it. He paused. "It'll be okay, guys. But I have to hurry."

He closed the door.

Kerry and Sam and the other kid stared at one another. "Oh, my God," Sam said a third time, in the barest of whispers.

"Kid?" Kerry said.

Frack looked at him. "Huh?"

"What's your name?" He glanced at the still, pale, blood-streaked body on the floor. "And what's his?"

They both looked at him like he was crazy. *Hell*, he thought. *Maybe I am.*

2

As the door to the cargo bay swung shut, Jim watched the insane tableau—all that *blood*—narrow and then vanish. The last thing he saw was their eyes, big as coffee mugs, staring at him. When the door was finally closed, it was as if some invisible chain connecting him to them snapped, and he was able to think again.

Hurry!

The word began to toll in his mind with a harsh, brutal cadence, a cold brass sound that might have signaled a funeral.

Hurry!

His muscles felt sludgy and tight at the same time. He had to think about each individual movement he wanted to make, though his thoughts were tumbling as if a hurricane had set up housekeeping inside his skull.

Hurry!

He finally got himself moving, clambered into the suit, made as sure as he could that all the seals were functioning properly, then inflated it. Stood for a moment as it popped out, turning him into a bloated sausage shape, and filled his nostrils with the stench of cinnamon and dog food.

He moved toward the outer cargo hatch and shoved at the handle. He felt rather than heard the sudden explosive *whoosh*—a spectral wind that tried to push him out into space—but he was ready for it, his grip on the door handle firm as the outward air pressure swung it aside.

Then he was on the hull of the ship, feeling the magnets in his boots grip the hull with that odd sticky but not sticky adhesion of magnetism.

The probe was where he'd left it, maybe drifted a few feet closer, but still tethered at the end of the line that he'd dogged to the big grommet next to the hatch.

His helmet earphones crackled. Elwood's voice, thin and worried: "Jim? Is that you?"

"It's me. We don't have much time. Come on across."

"Aye, Captain." Elwood's tone was stronger now, more assured. "Be right with you."

Jim watched as the outer wall of Elwood's pod popped open and tumbled away. Elwood snagged his end of the cable, then hand-over-handed his way across to the lighter. When he was standing next to Jim, his own boots firmly planted on the hull, he tipped his helmet forward to touch Jim's. When he spoke, his voice, carried by the contact instead of the weak radio system, was much stronger.

"What next?"

"You got the remote?"

"Yep."

"Okay. Go ahead and blow it apart."

A pause. Elwood said, "You sure? That thing out there ain't much, but at least it's a ride."

"We've got a bigger one," Jim told him. "I hope. Go ahead, just do it."

"Aye." Elwood stepped away from him, turned to face the probe floating like a needle stitching rhinestone-crusted velvet. Jim could see no movement until, suddenly, sharp puffs of white, like rapidly expanding snowballs, appeared at various places on the probe's hull. They drifted away quickly, leaving the probe seemingly unchanged. But a moment later, it became plain that what had been a long, pointed cigar shape was now several pieces spinning slowly apart from one another. After a minute or so, only one chunk remained—the one tethered at the end of the cable. This was about the size of a pair of refrigerators welded together, and approximately the same blunt, rectangular shape.

Jim reached down and wrapped both hands around his end of the cable. "Okay," he said. "Let's haul it in."

3

What did he mean? What's he doing?" Sam said. She'd tried to wipe some of the blood from her hair, and had only succeeded in smearing it across her face.

"I don't know," Kerry said. He felt as if somebody had punched a hole in his chest, and used his own head to do it with.

Sam's eyes had begun to *dart*. He found it disconcerting. She would look at Frick (whose name turned out to be Bobby Turner), lying unconscious on the floor, what remained of his left arm beginning to swell and turn a stomach-wrenching purplish-yellow, and then her gaze would *dart* away. Or she would look at his own face—he had no idea what he looked like at that point, probably as much a gory finger-painting as Jim, and then her eyes would *dart* again. It seemed that whatever she looked at repulsed her or terrified her so greatly she couldn't look at it for more than an instant before she had to look some-where else. A sniggering, horrified little voice in the back of his mind wondered what would happen to her; would her eyeballs eventually get to moving so fast they'd explode right out of her head, like grape-sized blood bombs?

"Come on, Sam, help me get him out of the aisle. There's enough space at the back of the seats to lay him on the deck. And we need to find something to cover him with. I think he's going into shock."

Privately, he thought young Bobby Turner was already deep in shock, and he wouldn't be coming out of it. But whether Bobby made it or not, Sam going into paralyzing panic mode would help neither him nor her. Which was why he hadn't said anything about the problem that was really worrying him.

"Okay, Sam?" he soothed her. "You take his feet, I'll take his shoulders."

Her mouth opened, closed, and Kerry thought of fish. When she finally moved, she reminded him of the puppets his little sister used to make, out of socks and cotton stuffing, and he wondered if she was really gone, or if he could snap her out of it long enough for her to be of some use.

Use for what? he asked himself. Hell, he didn't even know if *he* could be of any use.

"Lift," he told her, as he gently raised Bobby's shoulders. Bobby's shirt felt as wet and cold as the skin beneath the cloth, and though he was a small kid, he had that peculiarly slack, weighty feel that dead people—or nearly dead people—possessed. He looked down to see which it was—dead, or nearly dead—and saw that Bobby's lips were moving slowly, as if he were trying to say something from the depths of a dream.

One hell of a bad dream, he thought, as they gently wrestled the kid to the back of the compartment and got him settled as well as they could on the hard steel deck.

"Maybe we could take some of the cushions from the seats . . ." Sam said uncertainly. "Make him a bed or something. Are they bolted down?"

"That's a *good* idea," Kerry told her, trying to put as much sincerity and encouragement into his words as he could. They sounded sickeningly fake in his own ears, but she seemed to brighten a little. "Have Nikita help you." Right, that was Frack's name, Nikita Chudov.

Jesus, what a mess.

For a moment everything inside his head went swimmy and vague. He put out one shaky hand and took a good hard hold on the back of one of the seats and just stood there, taking long, slow breaths, trying to get his yammering heart to slow down, run in harness with his consciously slowed breathing.

After a little while—he never, even later, could remember how long—the sheer, swirling madness of everything seemed to subside a little, and out of the maelstrom, like a few discrete hailstones, dropped some nuggets of fact and memory.

Jim was here. How he'd gotten here, or why he'd come in the first place, Kerry had no idea. But he was here, at least he had been for a few minutes, and now he was gone again.

Ur-Barrba was also here, locked up behind the pilot cabin door, whether dead or alive he didn't know. But that thought was the one that actually got him moving again. He hoped the huge alien was dead, but if she wasn't . . .

His gaze tracked up and down the cabin until he saw what he thought he'd remembered. Yes, there it was, wedged between two of the seats where it had fallen: the shatterblaster, its sleek, gleaming surfaces spattered with congealing drops of blood.

He moved quickly down the aisle toward it, his heartbeat ratcheting up again as he realized the horrible danger they were in. If Ur-Barrba had come out of the pilot's cabin while they were lugging poor Bobby back to what was likely going to be his final resting place, she could have had the thunderstick in her clawed hands in an instant, and if that had happened, poor Bobby's blood loss would be about as significant as a scraped knuckle in a slaughterhouse.

He breathed out, a long, relieved sigh, when he finally got his fingers wrapped around it. He picked it up and quickly aimed it toward the pilot's door and started backing down the aisle again—he knew how fast Ur-Barrba was—as his fingers automatically checked the safety, the magazine, the power module—

"Shit."

The power module was a snap-in affair more or less in the middle of the bulbous stock. Or at least that was where it should have been. But there was only a heavy dent and some black, powdery streaks there. Now he knew why Jim's first shot hadn't taken Ur-Barrba down. It had caromed harmlessly off the stock of the blaster, and turned it into a gleaming, high-tech baseball bat. Not even that. At least a baseball bat was easy to swing in a confined space.

His butt hit the cargo bay door at the end of the aisle. Sam and Nikita were both kneeling with a load of cushions to his right, tending to Bobby. Kerry straightened his shoulders against the door and stood, facing the pilot's cabin at the far end of the aisle, hefting the useless blaster, wondering what his chances were of using it to beat Ur-Barrba to death if she did come storming through the door and down the aisle toward him.

Not very good, he suspected.

4

The darkness had layers. Somehow it reminded her of home, of those magical springtime moments in the foothills north of her father's hacienda, long enough before dawn that the sun was only the vaguest of pink hints beyond the western horizon, and above that delicate tincture, darkness piled on darkness all the way up to the stars.

She watched the darkness for a while before she realized what a change that was, that she was actually aware it *was* dark, that her mind was functioning, at least a little. That she was still *alive*.

The damnable humans!

She'd recognized the one called Endicott as soon as she saw him, of course, although by all the Kirellian gods, she couldn't imagine how he'd appeared in the passenger cabin of the lighter. Which hadn't stopped her from doing her best to kill him, but he had the reflexes of a *monja* cat, and his gun was already out. She'd lost that one, all right.

Without opening her eyes, she lifted one hand to her head, feeling for the part of it that didn't seem to be there. Or at least, all she could sense from the right side of her skull was an aching, icy blankness.

She was afraid that when she touched it, her fingers would find only a mushy, soft hole, and go right through into her brain. Instead, her skull seemed to be intact, although when she did probe a little, the pressure sent a thundercloud of agony screaming to the base of her spine, where it kicked both of her hearts into a pounding drumroll that crushed the breath from her massive chest.

She lay on the deck, panting, waiting for the pain to subside, her huge frame heaving and shuddering. She heard somebody whimpering, a pathetic, mewling sound almost lost in the howling distance. It took her a few moments to realize she was making the sounds.

Time went drifty on her then, as wave after wave of shame pounded a bloody surf on the beach of her humiliation.

First a fool, and now a whimpering babe!

How could she face her father? How could she face her *brother*?

Her father would spit in her face and banish her from his house, but her brother would *forgive* her, and she couldn't bear that.

She opened her eyes and found herself looking at a single large rivet in the deck. It seemed an enormous task to lift her head far enough off the deck to see a second rivet, but she would try, oh yes she would.

The humans had their guns, and they had *her* gun as well. Because of that, she couldn't do what she really wanted to do, which was smash shrieking through the door into the cabin and rip their flimsy carcasses into quivering, blood-drenched rags.

But there was something she *could* do, something that would pay for all. If she could only hold everything together long enough to reach the controls.

Shooting star, she thought.

Fire across the sky!

5

The red light above the door from the cargo bay into the passenger compartment flickered, then went out. Jim twisted off his helmet, set it down, and climbed out of his suit, watching Elwood do likewise.

Elwood's dusky golden features were streaked with grease and sweat, his almond eyes mapped with scrawling red veins. He ran long fingers through his plastered-down hair and exhaled heavily.

"Oh, man. These suits *stink*." He looked down, grimaced, and kicked his suit aside. It floated clumsily across the cargo hold and came to rest in a deflated lump against the bulky metal shape of the hyperwave transmitter. "What's going on here, Captain?"

"Trouble," Jim said shortly. He drew his pistol, turned to the passenger cabin door, and rapped on it three times. Immediately, the door locks clicked, and then the door opened, revealing Sam's bleached, blood-smeared face and huge, shadowed eyes.

"Sam!"

"Oh, God, Jimmy, hurry. I don't—" She was reaching for him as the lighter lurched slightly, then lurched again. She uttered a short, muffled shriek and turned away. "Kerry, what is it?"

Jim took her by the shoulders, moved her gently aside, and stepped into the cabin. Kerry spun around, the shatterblaster cradled in his arms, a huge lump on the side of his skull. There was a strange wild glint in his blue fractured-glass eyes, a sharp flickering light Jim had never seen before, and he realized with a kind of horror that Kerry was very close to his limits. Jim had never thought Kerry *had* a limit, and it was frightening to know that he did.

"Don't shoot me with that, okay?" Jim said, forcing a soothing mildness into his tone. Kerry's answering grin was a quick white twitch, a rictus, and did nothing to make Jim feel any better about the whole situation.

"She just did something, that alien bitch," Kerry ground out. "It feels like she's trying to fire up the engines."

"Can she?" Jim asked. "You said one's gone. Is the other one working?"

"I dunno," Kerry replied, stepping aside to let him pass. "The vireo says it's screwed up, but for all I know, the vireo's the one that's screwed."

The cabin lurched again. Kerry staggered slightly, right into Elwood's arms. "Easy, man," Elwood said. "I got you."

Jim lifted his head. The deck under his feet was vibrating very faintly. "She's got something going," he said. "And it doesn't feel right. If it was okay, there wouldn't be any vibes, just a steady push."

Sam's voice was a tremulous whisper from the end of the cabin. "Why's she using the engine?"

Jim and Kerry looked at each other. Neither said anything.

"God damn you!" Sam yelled suddenly. "Don't you play your bull-shit macho games with me!" Tears were streaming down her face, carving sharp, clean tracks in the rust-brown smears of dried blood. "I'm a girl, but I don't break! *Damn you, I don't break!*"

"She's trying to kill herself. And us with her, I guess," Jim said simply.

Nikita's face rose from behind the seats, where he was cradling Bobby's head in his lap. To Jim, he looked about eight years old, and scared out of his mind.

"What are you talking about?" he squeaked. "How can she do that?"

"By diving full tilt into Kolumba's atmosphere," Kerry told him, his voice so rasped with exhaustion it was barely audible. "And she can do it, too."

"How's Bobby? Can we move him?" Jim asked.

"Move him?" Sam said. "Move him where? Why?"

"Back into the cargo hold," Jim said. "And the rest of you, too. Because it'll be safer there."

She stared at him blankly. "I don't get it. Safer how? You mean if we crash?"

He shook his head, feeling as tired as Kerry looked. "We won't crash," he said. "I told you. We'll burn long before we hit the ground."

"Then why? What difference will it make, whether we're in the cargo hold or right here?"

"Remember how Bobby lost his arm?" Jim said. "Ricochets. Our only chance is if we can get through that pilot door. And the only way I can think to do it is to blow it down. But that will mean a lot of crap flying around the cabin. I don't want another Bobby if I can help it." He looked down, not wanting to say it to her face, but needing to say it anyway. "Don't you understand? I don't want *you* to be another Bobby." He raised his head. "Or any of you. This is all my fault. If I hadn't screwed up so many things, none of us would be here in the first place. So it's up to me to finish it, if I can."

"Bullshit," Elwood said. He stopped, a surprised expression on his face. Then he continued, "It ain't your job, it's mine. And it don't matter none whose fault it is. I got as much claim in that department as anybody."

Before Jim could say anything, Elwood moved up to Kerry and put his hands on the shatterblaster. "Come on, give it to me."

"Sure, but it won't do you no good," he said.

"Huh?"

"It's busted. Don't work."

"What?" Jim said. "You mean you were standing here waiting for that monster to come out of the pilot's cabin with nothing but a club?"

Kerry shrugged, a rueful grin flickering on his tired features. "It's not like I had a choice, you know?"

Elwood stepped around him and approached Jim. "Come on, Captain. Hand over that hand cannon of yours." He reached beneath his shirt and hauled out a small, glittering pistol. "Take my ripper. It won't bust down a door, but it'll slow that monkey down pretty good if she gets past me somehow."

"Elwood, I appreciate it, but this is my responsibility."

"Like I said, bullshit. Uh, sir. It may be your responsibility, but it's my *job*. And I'm good at it. So why don't you cut the crap and let me get on with it?"

"He's right, Jim," Kerry said softly.

"Oh, hell, I know he is. I'm the best pilot here, and if we can pry that ape out of her hidey-hole in time, we're gonna need the best we got. But damn it, how come I never get to take any risks?"

"Jim?" Kerry said. "How did you get here? Somehow I don't think it was in a nice, safe, grav car. How much frackin' risk do you *want*?"

"Well . . ." He smiled sheepishly. "Okay. Enough. Here, Elwood." He handed over the .75. "You know how to use it?"

Elwood handed him his ripper and took the big .75. "I'm guessing the part that goes *bang* comes out of this end, when I pull this little curved part down here."

Jim couldn't help it. He chuckled. "Asshole," he said.

"Yes, sir, Captain," Elwood replied.

After that it was okay, or at least as okay as something like that could ever be. Elwood's grin faded away into a set, serious expression, and he moved on past Jim and set himself near the door to the pilot's cabin without saying another word.

Jim and Kerry went back to help Sam and Nikita move Bobby into the cargo hold. Jim was last through the door. He stopped before he closed it, and looked down the aisle at Elwood. Elwood had climbed behind a seat in the left-hand third row, and was crouched down, the .75's chunky barrel resting on the back of the seat, so he was protected from ricochets by all the rows in front of him. He sensed Jim watching him and turned.

"I figured I'd take a pop from this angle." He shrugged. "Should take any shrapnel off to the other side, over there."

"That's good thinking," Jim said.

They stared at each other. "Be careful," Jim said. Then, without realizing he'd intended to do so, he brought his right hand to his forehead in a stiff, quivering salute.

Elwood straightened up and returned the salute. They both held for a moment, then dropped.

"Don't worry, Captain," Elwood said. "It'll be a piece of cake."

Jim nodded, turned, and closed the door between them. His last sight was of Elwood's calm, blank features. Elwood looked very young then, and somehow also very old. But what he most looked, Jim thought, was . . . *interested.*

6

Elwood heard the cargo bay door click shut behind him, a sound that for some reason made him think of a bone snapping. He settled himself, took a deep breath, and sighted down the barrel of Jim's .75.

A strange moment came to him then, a stretchiness that made it seem as if he had all the time in the world. His thoughts began to skitter like drops of hot grease on a griddle. One part of him remembered his childhood, something he hadn't thought about in years. He knew why. Those memories weren't pleasant ones. They were things that, as his dad had sometimes said, in his lucid moments when he wasn't using his own son for batting practice or as a handy, squirming substitute for masturbation, "You better forget this, boy. Won't do you no good to remember. Or talk about, either."

Then another voice spoke up, a mean, scornful voice, that damned him for a fool. *Why are you doing this? Why are you risking your life for that asshole Endicott? You hate him!*

And yet another voice chimed in, a calmer, surer voice, that whispered, *He trusts you. Nobody ever trusted you before. Nobody ever cared enough to trust you . . .*

Regular damned chorus in here, he thought. But he couldn't deny, even to himself, that something had changed for him. And Jim Endicott had been the catalyst. No, he wasn't turning overnight into some kind of soppy, sentimental idiot—at least he didn't *think* he was—but his future, which until recently he'd perceived as a dim and changeless vista that led inexorably to some kind of nameless, violent death—now seemed, if only in occasional moments, a bit clearer. Ferrick had helped, but it had been mostly Endicott's doing. And he found this weird new future he was almost able to see very interesting. As interesting, in fact, as the death dreams that had filled him like cold, dirty water as long as he could remember.

He wondered if this was making him weaker. When you don't give a shit, he'd always thought, you got nothing to lose, and that makes you strong. Now he actually *wanted* something, and he could see just how easily he might lose *that*. Would it make him cautious? Would it make him scared? Would he hesitate, be one instant too slow when he needed to be fast? He didn't know.

What he was about to do was as big a test for him as it was for the rest of them. Maybe Endicott had even understood that, when he'd given him the .75 and put *all* their futures on his own back.

Does giving a shit make you weak? he wondered suddenly. *I hope to God not, but I guess we're gonna find out.*

He licked his lips, steadied his arm across the back of the seat, took another deep breath, squinted, and pulled the trigger twice.

In the confined space the two explosions sledged his ears into jelly and made his head feel as if it had just been slammed in a door. The multitoned crash was so overwhelming that for an instant he just froze, wondering if he was dead or not.

His gaze slid to the right, toward the hull across the aisle from him. Above the tops of the chairs was a single bright streak about six feet long—as if somebody had swiped a silver paintbrush along there.

That one didn't get me, one of the voices from the chorus in his mind snickered uneasily.

His eyes moved back toward the front of the cabin, and now he saw that the first two seats on that side—the backs of them, at least—looked like somebody had set off good-sized bombs in them: a haze of dirty gray stuffing was still rising from their ruined frames.

And with a final, almost audible click his gaze moved on, to the very front, to the door half off its hinges, bent in the middle as if some giant had kicked it as hard as he could.

Wisps of smoke rose from the scorched steel. Beyond, he could see a portion of the pilot's cabin, the two oversized seatbacks like shark fins in a drifting gunmetal haze.

But no orange monkey.

Don't do it! The chorus, in full agreement this time, hit bass, alto, and soprano tones of terror inside his skull.

He put one hand on the back of the seat before him, vaulted out into the aisle, charged into the pilot's cabin, tripped over the rug, and went flying headfirst into the control console.

Crangg!

Everything went a sharp, chrome-edged black that slowly faded into a blood-purple field of whirling white stars. He shook his head, winced, and understood for the first time what that weird phrase *really got your bell rung* meant. In fact, his bell was *still* ringing, and shaking his head didn't help that one little bit, friends and neighbors.

"Uh." He tried to sit up, but this was complicated by the fact that he was spread-eagled across both pilots' chairs, with the edge of one digging painfully into his crotch.

"Goddamn frickin' *rug*," he groaned as he tried to pull himself out of that ringing purple haze.

Rug? *What* fricking rug? Rugs weren't standard operating equipment in pilot cabins. They weren't—

He came awake in a horror-charged rush, phantom electricity crackling up his spine as if somebody had hooked his gonads up to a battery charger. Yanked himself over the top of one seat and looked down, expecting to see a claw-studded paw the size of a Christmas ham rushing toward his face.

And instead he saw the rug, and burst out laughing. Well, *burst* was too strong a word. Leaked out laughing, more like, a weak, thready sound of utter relief, like a little kid after Mommy shows him there really is nothing under the bed but dust bunnies.

He stood, wincing as his bruised balls sent a couple of quick telegrams of protest to his still-ringing skull, and stared down at the huge orange ape stretched on the floor, snoring like a runaway steam engine, a pair of bloody vireo phones half hooked to her huge (and oddly misshapen, wasn't it?) skull.

It was that pink baboon butt, thrust into the air like a double mound of strawberry ice cream carefully dipped onto a pile of dirty-orange fur, that finally brought him to his knees, laughing so hysterically he thought his eyeballs would explode.

7

The biggest problem was moving her back to the cargo hold. Ur-Barrba was too wide to fit in the aisle. It took all of them, and far too long a time, to lift her deadweight carcass over the top of the chair backs and move her, a few feet at a time (and then stop until the fires in their lungs abated a little) until they finally got her wedged through the cargo door and down onto the deck.

"Find something to tie her up with," Jim said. "There's probably more of that tape she used on you guys around here somewhere."

Kerry glanced at him, then at Elwood, who was staring silently at Ur-Barrba, though the corners of his lips quirked every once in a while, as if he were trying to keep from laughing about something. "Frick that," Kerry said. "One of you hand me a gun. I'll tie her up, all right. I'll tie her up so she don't *ever* get loose."

Jim ignored him. He pulled the ripper from his belt, handed it to Elwood, and Elwood returned the .75.

"Elwood, give me your ripper," Kerry said. His voice was as cold and empty as the hiss of a rattlesnake.

"No," Jim said. "I won't let you do it."

"She's gonna die anyway. Look at that hole in her head. But she's caused enough trouble. I say let's end it."

"She may die, but we won't murder her," Jim said, his gaze now locked on Kerry's. "We aren't murderers."

"Don't give me that crap, Jim, you know I'm right, and just because—"

"Captain," Jim said. "Not Jim, Mr. Korrigan. Captain."

Kerry opened his mouth, closed it, opened it again. Elwood still held the ripper loosely in his hand. But Kerry noticed that Elwood was now facing him, that the ripper, while not *exactly* pointing at him, would require only an inch or two to be aimed right between his eyes. Most unsettling of all, Elwood's chilly gray eyes were now sparking with *interest*. Interest in *him*.

"Damn it, Jim—"

"I gave you an order, Mr. Korrigan. Tie up the prisoner. We aren't savages. We won't behave like savages. No matter what the provocation. Am I clear?"

Kerry's pale features began to throb pink beneath their smears of dried blood. He spoke in a low, choked voice that trembled slightly despite his efforts to keep it steady. A vein ticked like a bomb timer at the side of his high forehead.

"It's just us chickens, here, Jim. You can't pull that rank bullshit with *me*. Remember how you got to be captain in the first place."

Jim did not so much as blink. He shoved the snout of his .75 into his waistband. "Mr. Grieger?"

"Aye, Captain?"

"I have given Mr. Korrigan a lawful order. If he refuses to obey it, he is under arrest and will have to be restrained along with the other prisoner until he can be tried before the *Endeavor*'s executive council."

He nodded at Elwood and turned toward the door, ignoring Kerry completely.

Kerry looked up at Elwood. He noted that Elwood's ripper *had* moved that final two inches. It wasn't a big weapon, but the brassy electrode nestled in the center of the barrel looked about the size of a basketball.

Elwood smiled at him. "You heard the captain, Mr. Korrigan," he said.

"Oh, put it away, Elwood," Kerry said, his voice suddenly tired. "I'll follow the *captain's* damned order." He looked across Ur-Barrba's prone body. "Jim? I was afraid of this. I made a mistake. You're too soft to be in charge."

Jim paused, his back hunching slightly as if he'd been punched between his shoulder blades. He didn't turn, though. He said, "But I *am* in charge. I'm still the captain. Do your duty, Mr. Korrigan."

Then he opened the door, stepped through it, and was gone.

8

Jim was shaking with his own anger as he made his way down the aisle toward the lighter's pilot cabin, a nasty witch's brew of humiliation, betrayal, rage, and fear bubbling in his stomach and boiling over into his brain.

Goddamn it, what do they want *from me? I'm too hard, I'm too weak, I'm too smart for my own good, I'm too stupid. . . .* The torrent of outrage wailed and hammered at him, a vicious spew of frustration and disillusionment and downright loathing. *If I'd known this was what being captain meant, having my own ship, I'd never have—*

Bullshit, another voice said, and oddly enough, he recognized it. It was his father's voice. *Did you think it would be some kind of game, that everybody would kiss your butt because you've got some bright gold stars on your shoulder? A captain* earns *the rank, and then keeps on earning it all over again, every single day. Oh, sure, when they give you that star, it's yours unless they take it away, but if they* have *to take it away, you've lost it long before. So stop your whining and do what you know is right. That's how you* earn *your rank, how it always was, how it always will be.*

His father had never said anything like this to him in his whole life, but he could *imagine* him saying it. In fact, he just had. He realized that he'd stopped walking to listen to this voice, had even closed his eyes. Now he opened them, stung by the tone of his father's words. Dry, brusque, devoid of charm or care, as if pointing out a few home truths to an especially stupid child. But truths about what? Jim wondered suddenly.

About being a man, the voice said, and then fell silent, with a finality that Jim suspected meant Carl Endicott had said all he intended to say on the subject.

An uneasy little sound escaped his lips. He looked around the cabin as if seeing it for the first time; the bright silver streak marking the wall on his right, the exploded chair backs, the film of stuffing coating everything with a dull gray pelt, the shattered door to the pilot cabin still barely hanging by one twisted hinge, the odd pink glow leaking from behind it . . .

His heart gave a double thud and then leaped out of its starting blocks on a hundred-yard dash.

Pink glow! Pink glow!

The ominous drum of those two words pounded a dreadful backbeat in his mind as he leaped the last few feet down the aisle, slammed the twisted door aside with one shoulder (ow! that *hurt!*) and did a full belly slam against the back of the left-hand pilot's chair.

In the small cabin, the pink glow was much brighter. As he dragged in breath, he saw that Ur-Barrba had opened the outer shields that covered the forward windows. These windows were for use during atmospheric flight, when the lighter became, essentially, a high-powered rocket plane. Well, not so high-powered *now*, not missing one, and maybe even two engines . . .

He slid quickly into the seat, his eyes still focused on the source of that malign pink glow that was now flaming even more brightly beyond the forward windows. It came from the needle tip of the lighter, a ceramic-armored point designed to withstand the extremely high temperatures caused by friction with the atmosphere upon reentry. Extremely high temperatures, but not impossibly high ones, he thought, as he saw how the sharpest section of the point was no longer glowing pink, but white, and the pink part, shading off into orange and then dull red, was almost imperceptibly sliding farther and farther up the nose of the craft toward him.

He fumbled the vireo-phones out of the console and slapped them onto his head. While he waited for the implants to penetrate his skull into his brain, he yanked the touchpad out across his knees and began to tap furiously. There were two small digital screens in front of him. As he worked, figures began to scroll down both of them, a running tabulation of all the processes currently under way in the ship's main computer banks. It wasn't as interactive as the vireo was, not by a long shot, but it told him what he needed to know.

The lighter's wings weren't extended. Which made the ship, in effect, nothing more than a missile aimed right at the center of Kolumba. And not a guided missile, either.

He was trying to get a full report on the one remaining engine when the vireo kicked in, slapping away half his normal vision and hearing with an overwhelming rush of pure machine sensation, like a spectral hand sweeping the table of perception clean.

With his cybernetically expanded senses, he was able to piece the whole picture together in split-seconds. The lighter's vireo certainly wasn't the awesomely powerful setup he was used to aboard the *Endeavor*, not even the standard training equipment on which he'd first learned in school, but it was sufficient to the task at hand.

The hole where the missing engine should have been gaped like a scraped wound on one side of the lighter. It wasn't just dead, it was *gone*, leaving only a terrifying blankness. Which he knew already. The other engine, however, was still there. Hanging on by a thread, you might say. Or you might not, he thought, as he plunged deeper into the digital representation of it, checking out stress lines, welds and seals, switches, nozzles, and microfilament monocables a hundred times as thin as a human eyelash.

Vireo could show you a lot—in fact, it could show you everything— but you had to be able to interpret what it showed you to understand those ghostly, flickering pictures, those odd bursts of sounds (like unnamed animals howling and squawking across snow-sere fields), those sudden bursts of scents and stinks and vinegary machine perfumes, even the tastes it sent: cherry and tobacco and varnish-slicked wood, vanilla ice cream and rotten tomato and charred Thanksgiving turkey and kisses. Kerry was getting good at it, even had a natural talent for doing the necessary interpretations, but he was no way in Jim's class. And given that Ferrick had modified this vireo to accommodate human needs, Ur-Barrba might as well have been trying to shove her naked eyeballs through a concrete wall as figure out what the alien sensations pummeling her mind really meant.

But it wasn't easy. It took him nearly three seconds before he felt he had an accurate picture of the damage the remaining engine had sustained. There were at least two minor control breaks, one whole system shorted out, and a valve that he wasn't sure would work, though it looked like it ought to: in short, the engine would work. Not at a hundred percent, but not as bad as fifty percent, either. He thought that if he was careful and patient, he could coax between eighty and ninety percent of its rated power out of it. Which wasn't bad at all. That last ten percent was really emergency override, and with luck, he wouldn't need it.

Quickly, he reviewed what he knew of these types of landers. Everything was designed to be fail-safe. It carried two complete pilot consoles, though only one pilot was needed to fly it under standard conditions. Two engines, but one was sufficient to power it with perfect ease, even under JATO landing and launching conditions. It carried a pair of retractable wings, and it did need both of those, although in absolute extremity, he would be willing to chance a single-wing landing.

He glanced out the forward windows. The glare arcing off the nose, now bright as an acetylene torch viewed with unshielded eyes, was blinding. Most of the rest of the tapering front was pink, and the outer ring of dull, molten red had crept almost to the windows themselves.

He stuck his tongue into the side of his mouth, leaned forward over his touchpad, and murmured, "Well, here goes nothing . . ." and began to fire up the one remaining engine.

It was ticklish business, because there was some damage there, and it was always possible that the mere act of ignition would somehow cascade into something catastrophic. Which meant he had to watch *everything*, and perform the usual steps not in an automatic, unthinking series, the kind of near-physical reflexes he sometimes felt when running a perfectly functioning machine, but instead do everything step by baby step, making sure each single thing was functioning properly before he went on to the next. It was like being a stranger in a strange land. Everything might look normal, but nothing could be trusted.

The whole process was ticklish, irritating, not a little frightening, and incredibly complex. Nonetheless, he felt himself sink into it with a profound sense of relief. Machines were hard and unforgiving, but they had no emotions. They worked or they didn't, and when they worked, they were right, and when they didn't work, they were wrong. No shadings, no hundred hues of gray. Machines were black and white. He could understand them, because all machines, in the end, could be understood.

Unlike humans. Unlike Kerry, and Elwood, and Ferrick. And Sam . . .

He closed both his eyes and let his vision fill with the myriad waterfall surges of numbers and symbols and cryptic, flashing pictures that danced across the interface between his mind and the machine mind. It was a dance he could do. He switched off the human part of his brain and proceeded to do it.

9

Ur-Barrba's snoring had grown rougher, more liquid, and more erratic. The grinding, mucus-filled sounds would shudder to a crescendo, then stop entirely, then like a balky shifter, lurch once or twice, and repeat the process again.

"She don't sound good, Kerry," Sam said. She was sitting on the deck next to the hyperwave transmitter, back against the wall, arms clasped about her shins, chin on the tops of her knees. Her hair was limp, greasy, and plastered with dusty gray fuzz from the passenger compartment. Even the tiny sparkling ornaments with which she brightened her multitude of braids and curls looked dull and tarnished. Her eyes were pits in skin that had once blended chocolate and honey, but now looked jaundiced and sick.

Elwood was still standing next to the door, but the ship had begun to jump a bit, like a boat crossing a patch of rough water, and he'd spread his legs for balance. Gravity was returning as well, real gravity, not the weak artificial fields produced by the lighter's puny generator. Not far from him, Nikita still watched over Bobby, who lay on his makeshift bed of cushions, silent, ghostlike.

Kerry sat cross-legged on the third wall, elbows on knees, chin on fists; he looked glum and exhausted. The blue fire had leaked from his eyes, leaving them empty as marbles, and as cold.

"Good," he replied. "Let her die. Couldn't happen soon enough for me." He glanced up at Elwood. "What the frack you looking at, bud?" he snarled.

Elwood shrugged. "You."

"Well, cut it out. And sit down. Our fearless leader will be angry if you break an arm or something."

Elwood cocked his head, thought about it. "Okay," he said, and slid bonelessly to the deck. He leaned his head back and closed his eyes.

"If you're gonna take a nap," Kerry muttered, "give me your damned gun."

Elwood shook his head. "Not taking a nap," he said.

"Huh," Kerry grunted.

"Kerry, he can't help it. You know how he is," Sam said.

Kerry stared at her. "I know how Elwood is? Yeah. Elwood's an asshole. Jim said so."

Elwood lifted one finger in a lazy salute.

"You know who I mean."

"Mr. Bleeding Heart, our captain? Our don't-hurt-a-flea buddy? Officer Softy?"

"You're just pissed because he won't do what you tell him to. But why should he? He's the captain. And don't forget who made him captain. I was there, remember? When you and Ferrick and the rest of us made the decision. He didn't want it. You made him take it, forced it on him, so if you've got a problem with it now, blame yourself."

"How come you're all of a sudden his big defender? I thought you two were on the outs."

Her troubled gaze shifted a bit. "Maybe we had a couple of problems. But he's so busy, and so tired all the time, and he worries so much . . ." Her voice trailed off. "You know he depends on you more than anybody else, Kerry. Even more than me." There was genuine hurt in her voice as she said the last.

"Then why the hell doesn't he listen to me?" Kerry said.

"He does listen. I know he does. But that doesn't mean he has to agree with you all the time. You know how he feels. The buck stops with him. In the end, everything's his responsibility. He tries, Kerry, you know he does. He tries so hard."

"He tries hard, Sam, but he has to *be* hard sometimes, too. Sometimes being hard is necessary."

"How can you say he isn't!" she flared, color flooding her cheeks, her eyes suddenly sparking. "You saw him! I wasn't there, but you were! You and"— she turned, glanced at Elwood, glanced away— "and him. He stood there and let himself be half killed. How fracking hard does he *have* to be, damn you?"

"Not just hard on himself, Sam," Kerry said gently. "Hard on other people, too. If it's necessary. If it needs to be done. That's part of it, too." He sighed, now speaking almost to himself: "It's a hard old world out there. You have to be as hard as it is, or it will kill you. Sometimes you have to listen to your head, not your heart."

Sam started to reply, but before she could speak, the red light over the door suddenly flared on. The ship took a crazy, lunging hop, tossing them about like sacks of grain. A warning horn began to bleat in the passenger compartment, muffled by the closed door, but still loud. A speaker in the ceiling emitted a rusty burp, and then Jim's voice, sounding as cold and inhuman as the machine that carried it, rasped out.

"Grab hold of something and hang on tight. We're going in rough, and it isn't going to be pretty."

CHAPTER NINE

1

The world was red above, and green below, and in the center, stone.

Bakka of the family Ir of the clan Lud sweated beneath his thick, dark brown pelt. He farmed as his fathers had farmed, and their fathers before them, an unending war against the great trees with their light-eating canopies; against the weeds that grew fast enough for a man to see their dumb, writhing progress; against the myriads of tiny bugs that burrowed or crawled or flew but ate anything that grew; against the sullen, fiery upheavals of the mountains; against the storms that rolled across the face of the world like great gray boulders, crushing everything in their path. The life of a farmer was, as it had always been, a struggle. Only recently had the nature of the struggle changed. In fact, Ir-Bakka-Lud could still recall the day it had changed.

He had been only a pup then, barely six full turns old, his head rising to the height of his father's great belly. He had loved to stand with his head pressed against the muscled, laughing drum of that gut, feeling its warmth, humming with pleasure at the touch of his father's strong fingers in his hair.

They'd been standing like that on the night the change—or at least the leading edge of the change—had appeared. Now, forty years later, he trudged to the edge of the field where he'd stood then and turned his face up at the sky and let the evening wind slip through his hair like fading memories. The fields had been his for a long time, and his father was gone. Now his own sons were grown, and there was no one to stand with him on the edge of the field and look up at the blood-dusk sky and remember how things once had been, before the change, when he was young.

He wasn't quite sure why he'd wandered out to the edge of this particular field, except that it was the same place where he'd first seen the fire across the sky on that long-ago night, safe in his father's warm embrace. Even the field was different now. Then, it had been given over to the cultivation of the *oranja* fruit, low, rambling bushes that, over the course of the growing season, twice yielded crops of shimmering, clear-skinned yellow globes. His family had grown that crop for generations, had even become famous beyond their village for the tart, sweet taste they'd developed in their fruits. His sons still cultivated the family treasure, and so did he, but not as much as before. This field, for instance: where it had once shimmered with golden fire in the setting sun, it now gleamed a dark, woody green, as dusk touched the thick, curled leaves of two acres of *gir* trees. The *gir* could be harvested only once in a growing season, not twice, like the *oranja*, but the price that harvest brought in faraway Ald, home of the Ur, was *forty times* what even the best *oranja* brought.

Of course, back when this field was filled with *oranja* bushes, nobody shipped anything to Ur. But now the great metal birds fell from the sky in flocks during harvest season as everybody, even the youngest of the pups, labored night and day to fill the endless, gaping maws of those ships. Ir-Bakka himself had never seen the city of Ald, but he heard it was a wondrous place, full of buildings that scratched the sky, some of them almost as mighty as those he saw in the picture machines that also had not existed when he was a pup.

There was a sharp edge to the breeze wafting out from beneath the eaves of the tall trees, back in the dense, secretive woodlands that surrounded his fields, a breeze scented deeply with the sticky cinnamon sap exuded by the bark of those forest giants. His black, pug nose wrinkled happily at the comfortable familiarity of that smell; it was the smell of home, of his world, of everything that was right, and proper, and predictable.

Not like things were now. Only the sweet smell remained, but the rightness, the propriety, and the predictability were gone. Maybe forever, he thought. For one thing, now he knew he was poor.

He had not known that before the change. In fact, he sometimes thought that *was* the change, that before he'd stood with his father at the edge of the *oranja* field and seen a fire spill across the sky, he hadn't known he was poor. Now he believed that everything that had happened since, much of which he thought was evil, had come from the new knowledge that followed the long-ago fire in the night sky.

He sighed. The forests, which were all he really knew, them and their endless war with his fields, were especially lovely tonight. He knew them, at least the local part of them, as well as he knew the hair on the backs of his well-seamed hands. He knew that in them right now was a soft, drifting blanket of shadow, pierced by the last few crimson rays of sunset. It was a quiet time, as the birds and small, quick beasts of the daylight scurried for shelter and rest, and the larger animals of the dark awoke and made their first tentative appearances, nostrils wide, sniffing for the night.

So strange. He hadn't *felt* poor, before he discovered that he was. In fact, he hadn't even had a *word* for poor. Oh, yes, there were words that meant something like it, words having to do with loss and less, but never a word that meant *none*. Never a word that contained poverty and humiliation and shame all wrapped up in a deadly package that sapped the will, broke the strength, and filled the heart with a sick lust for all the things you didn't have.

Of course, back then, he hadn't known he didn't have these things, because he didn't know they existed. Sometimes, he thought that the picture machines that had rained from the skies, falling and bouncing like a sudden squall of hail, had been a curse sent by the Bad Gods to punish the people and anger the Kirellians, the Good Gods. Unfortunately, not many agreed with him, only a few among the silvertips like himself, and even fewer of the younger ones.

He sighed heavily as he watched the last of the sun, a dull round furnace, sink behind the peaks to the west, leaving behind a gauzy veil of clouds whose bellies throbbed with fire. The breeze was growing colder now, lifting his fur, chilling his bones as he raised his great, grizzled head and stared up at the stars just beginning to twinkle in the night high above.

His twin hearts gave a sudden lurch, and for a moment confusion draped a fog across his thoughts; he couldn't remember if he was standing at the edge of the field now, or then. For across the sky came a light just as it had come before, a bright line etched in the darkness like the slash of a sudden wound, and with it, the dry mutter of distant thunder.

As he watched, he came back to himself, to his sagging, aged body and his fading, aged memories, and he realized he was firmly in the *now*, not in the past time when things had changed.

There were no sweetly transparent golden globes in the field behind him now, and now he knew he was poor (and old, and tired, and more than ready to let go his grip on a life that had turned sour and unforgiving), but still he stared raptly at the burning scribble across the night and wondered: *Is this a change? Is this the beginning of something new?*

2

The last step down was a killer.

At least, that was what it felt like to Jim as he embraced vireo space and battled on the man-machine interface for the life of his ship, his crew, and himself.

In the end, it was luck as much as his own skill that saved them. Ur-Barrba hadn't made any effort to control the ship when she'd started it on her death dive, merely locked in the autopilot and then, evidently, passed out. But by the time they were able to blast her out of the pilot's cabin, much damage had already been done. The lighter was deep into

Kolumba's atmosphere and moving fast enough that there was an immediate danger of friction melting the forward ceramic heat armoring. It had taken Jim only a couple of minutes to fix the problem, but it had been a rough and ready hundred-twenty seconds.

He'd used the one remaining engine to tilt the lighter back and up, so that instead of arrowing point-first straight down toward Kolumba, the ship was now falling belly-first. This had the effect of slowing its rate of descent at least a little bit.

He began to adjust the flight path itself, smoothing it out, making it more circular, almost orbital in nature. He didn't trust the engine enough to try to blast up and out of Kolumba's gravity well; Ur-Barrba's efforts had brought them close enough to the surface that, one way or another, they were going to make a landing. At least this way he had enough control to make sure the landing wasn't nose-first at ten thousand miles per hour.

Over the next hectic minutes he whipped the lighter in long, sloping arcs across the face of the planet below, much as a stone skips across water, gradually cutting deeper and deeper. At the end, shedding a long trail of fire, he managed to kill almost all his velocity (barely missing the highest peaks of a great mountain range as he skimmed over them) and saw where he would have to land: a broad, flat plain that ran right up to the foothills of those mountains. A sharp, bright river traced a silvery vein through the center of the plain. Along the river, the trees faded away, leaving a strip of grass about a mile wide.

He thought it would do for a makeshift landing strip. He switched on the lighter's comm system and said, "Grab hold of something and hang on tight. We're going in rough, and it isn't going to be pretty."

Three minutes later, after carving a fiery scar across the last treetops and then the grasses of the plain, they were down.

Jim sat and listened to the creak of the lighter's hull as it shed heat into the night. He switched off the virco, waited for the probes to withdraw, then tugged the phones away from his head.

He took a long, shuddering breath, wiped his lips, looked around. Beyond the front ports the river gleamed dully in the starlight, wavering in and out of the smoky clouds from the grass burning around the lighter's superheated hull.

"Okay," he whispered, "we're down."

3

I can smell cinnamon," Sam said, "but no dog food."

They moved Bobby back into the passenger cabin and left Ur-Barrba bound and locked inside the cargo hold, with Nikita standing watch over both of them. Then Jim undogged the passenger hatch, and for the first time (in years, for all of them but Jim) they left the lighter, went down the short flight of metal steps, and stood on the living, breathing surface of a planet.

But it wasn't their planet. The stars overhead were alien. The cool, almost chilly winds sweeping down from the forested foothills that rose just beyond the grassy plain were scented with cinnamon, and the trees, what little could be seen of them in the dark, looked oddly misshapen. Even the dusty, bitter smell of the smoke rising from the charred grasses held a tang both familiar and at the same time strange.

The fires were dying now, leaving only a swath of glowing ashes that stretched out from the lighter in a long, slightly curving tail that lay along the edge of the river. The only thing that sounded really familiar was the sound of the river as it slid inside its banks with a long, sighing hiss and the muted roar of a lot of water in steady motion.

They walked out past the strips of char into the grass, which whispered gently all about them, a breeze-ruffled carpet as high as their knees, silvered with starlight all the way to the hills.

"Wow," Kerry murmured, his thin features soft, almost stunned with wonder. Even Elwood seemed affected; he stood off to the side, by himself, staring at the vague shadows of the distant peaks, sucking in one long breath after another. "Man," he murmured to nobody in particular. "I'd forgotten what it was like."

"Let's build a fire," Sam said suddenly. "You know, like a campfire or something." She took Jim's hand. "Did you do that when you were a kid, Jim?"

He heard the sharp sound of longing in her voice, and wondered if she'd ever enjoyed the simple pleasures of a camp fire out in the open. Maybe not. She'd been a city kid all her life, but not the kind of city kid who went to expensive summer camps and toasted marshmallows over glowing coals. Pleb kids didn't do that kind of thing.

"Don't forget," he told her, "we're strangers here. And not friendly strangers, either. Worst of all, we didn't exactly sneak in. Anybody within fifty miles of this spot has to know that something's going on."

Kerry walked up to them, Elwood trailing along behind. Kerry's expression was hard to read in the shadows. Jim faced him, wondering if his executive officer was about to indulge in another outburst. But Kerry surprised him.

"I've been thinking," Kerry said. His voice was soft, hesitant. "I want to apologize to you, Captain."

"Forget it," Jim said.

"No, I don't want to forget it. You need to hear this. You know why I wanted you to be captain, Jim. And when you accepted, even though you didn't want to, I signed on for the whole trip. I thought I knew what that meant, but I guess I didn't. What it really means is that I'm not the captain anymore. Maybe . . . I got too used to being in charge when I ran the Cowboys. But we aren't the Cowboys anymore, and I'm not in charge. You are." He grinned and stuck out his hand. "It may take me a while, but I'll learn. Eventually."

Jim took his hand and shook it, feeling his shoulders straighten a bit, as if he'd been carrying more freight than he understood, or realized. But he still had a question.

"Kerry, is this your heart or your head talking?"

Kerry paused. "I think it's mostly my head. That's the problem, you know. It's my heart that causes the trouble. But you know what they say." He grinned again.

"What?"

"Grab 'em by the balls. Their hearts and minds will follow. Well, my mind's in step. A few more squeezes, and maybe my heart will start marching, too."

Jim dropped his hand and hugged him hard. "I hope so," he whispered. "I need you, my friend. I really do. I need you as much as a friend—more!—than I need you as an exec."

Kerry nodded. "Well, you got me. Count on it." He stepped away. "Okay. So what do we do next, Captain? Now that we're really here?" He looked around and shook his head. "And I got to say, I still hardly believe we *are* here. You know how long it's been since I had my boots on good, honest dirt?"

"Good, honest alien dirt," Jim said. "I don't really like where we are. I had to put that crate down where I could, but I'd really like to move her. We're way too exposed out here."

He paused, turned, stared at the river. His gaze followed the gleaming line it made toward the mountains. "Maybe up to where that river spills out of the foothills. Back in the forest."

"Can we do that?" Sam asked.

"Sure. She'll do a vertical takeoff, even with one engine. Gotta be careful, that's all."

"What about Bobby?" Elwood broke in. "Shouldn't we try to do something about him before we start moving all over the place? He's not in real good shape."

Jim shook his head. It was an issue he'd been trying to avoid. "I don't know if we can, Elwood. We don't have an autodoc—"

"Huh?" Elwood said. "What do you mean? Of course we do. I mean, it's not a big rig like the one on the *Endeavor*, but it's a field version. It ought to be able to give him some help."

"What? But I didn't see anything about medical equipment in the vireo."

"Because it's freestanding. It's just a tiny unit, stored in one of the bulkheads in the passenger compartment. You have to unpack it and power it up first."

"Well, *hell*!" Jim said. "How come you know about it?"

"Hey. Besides you, I work for Ferrick, too. If he taught me just one thing, he taught me to read the frackin' manual. So I did."

Kerry winced. "Huh. Some executive officer I am."

"I didn't read it either," Jim told him. "You know, in the end, that's what being a crew is all about. Even the captain can't know everything, do everything. We all depend on each other."

Elwood nodded. "In the end, who else do we have to depend on?"

There seemed nothing to say to that. Almost as one, they silently turned and began to walk back to the lighter. Many miles away, at the edge of a field clinging to the foothills, a tough old man named Ir-Bakka stared out across the plains beyond his perch. There was no fire, no light he could see, not from this distance, but . . .

Down there, he thought. *It fell somewhere down there.*

4

So what have we got?" Kerry said.

They were out of the lighter, which was snugged up beneath the overhanging branches of the tallest trees any of them had ever seen. Elwood, Nikita, and Kerry had constructed a rough lean-to of scrub brush, which sheltered Bobby, who was still recovering from his wounds. The autodoc, as Elwood had said, was a very basic model. It had been unable to regrow Bobby's missing limb, but it had repaired the damage to what remained. Bobby had a stump, but he would recover in time.

Meanwhile, he mostly slept, and ate ravenously from the lighter's stores when he was awake. The rest of them were sitting in front of the lean-to, on a couple of chunks of deadwood they'd dragged over to the fire now crackling cheerfully in a ring of stones. The red sun overhead cast ruby shadows from a painted crimson sky. It was neither hot nor cold, but the breezes were bracing as they tumbled from the higher mountains down into the foothills where they'd set up camp. The fire felt good on their faces, its slow heat as friendly and comforting as a kitten.

Jim stretched out his hands toward the flames. "Well, what we've got isn't much. We're here, and we're mostly in one piece. That's number one. Number two is we've got a ship that's not really in one piece, but it works. Number three, we've got a hyperwave transmitter, so we can get in touch with the *Endeavor*, even talk to the ConFederation if we want to. We've got some food, plenty of water, and we've got guns."

Elwood spoke up. "Which reminds me. I took a look at the shatterblaster. I think I can fix it."

"All *right*," Kerry said, turning to slap a high-five with him. "Score one for the good guys!"

"That's great, Elwood. Good job," Jim told him. He raised his left hand, on which he'd been ticking down the things they did have. Only his little finger was sticking up. He wriggled it. "And this baby is for nada. It's what we've got as far as what we set out to do in the first place. We've got enough to stay alive here—maybe. I want to do some repair work on the ship, and if that goes okay, we can probably get back into orbit, maybe get picked up by the *Endeavor*, assuming the Communers don't get one of us first. We can communicate. My problem is that I can't quite figure out how to use that to stop the Kolumbans from growing dope and selling it to the Communers. So I'm open to suggestions. Really open, you know?"

"You left out one other asset," Kerry said. "A big hairy asset tied up in the cargo hold."

"I thought we already decided she might not be worth too much. In a trade, I mean. As a hostage."

"Well, when all you got is eggs, all you can make is omelets," Kerry observed.

Jim considered it. "Okay, you may be right. I don't like it much, but if it's all we got, then we have to go with it. But before we do, I'd like to do some scouting around. From what I read and remember, this part of Kolumba is still pretty backward. Even by their standards. It's a mountainous region, remote from their cities and the Communer trading stations. But they grow a lot of dope here, evidently. I'd kinda like to try to get to know them, learn the lay of the land. Maybe I can get a few more ideas—even better ones—on the best way to play the Ur-Barrba card."

"Jim," Kerry said, "how much time do we have? Tell the truth, I'm fairly surprised we haven't had an attack boat full of Kolumbans—or Communers—landing on top of us already. Besides, exactly how do you plan to get to know the locals better? Just waltz into one of their villages—if they have villages—introduce yourself, and ask for directions to the nearest local witch doctor and oral tradition specialist? I mean, you said these yokels are pretty rural. How do you think they're gonna react to a bunch of weird humans showing up just in time for Sunday dinner? Hell, from what I saw of what Ur-Barrba left of Frank, they just might turn *us* into the main course."

"Well, we do have some translation necklaces." He touched the one dangling from a chain around his neck. "Part of the emergency packs. So we can talk to them, at least. Beyond that—"

Jim shrugged. "Play it by ear, I guess."

Elwood stirred. Jim noted he now suddenly had his ripper in his hand, the small hand weapon resting casually on his right knee. Elwood said, "You want to chat with the locals?"

"Uh . . . yeah."

"How about that one right there?" He gestured toward the edge of the clearing.

They turned and stared. Beneath the trees, in utter silence, a great, silver-streaked Kolumban male stood watching them.

5

Ir-Bakka had been quietly studying the strange alien visitors for several minutes when they all suddenly turned and stared at him. He wasn't sure what to make of it; he wasn't even positive whether the ones who jumped to their feet, jabbering strange, high-pitched noises, were male or female. But he didn't feel—or smell—much danger coming from them. There were not, for instance, any gestures he interpreted as threatening, though he thought one of the skinniest of the group might be holding a weapon of some sort, a shiny metal thing he lifted and pointed at him.

Best not do anything to startle them, Ir-Bakka thought. *They look excitable.*

The other reason he wasn't particularly frightened was that, although he'd never seen people like this in the flesh, he *had* seen their kind before. The picture machines showed many different races, lizardlike things, wolfish people, some he couldn't really describe at all, but also this particular kind of species—like and yet so unlike his own. Sometimes he imagined them as short, thin, hairless versions of his own kind, alien, but still somehow familiar. Other times when he saw them in their cities, which were so crowded they looked like knots of worms beneath an overturned stump, he thought them wholly strange, and repulsive. How did they live with no trees, no flowers, no crops, no animals, no birds, nothing but themselves and clattering metal and great piles of stone? *What had they done with their world, anyway? Had they killed* everything *but themselves?*

They looked harmless, though. He guessed that, even as old as he was, he could crush them all in a fight. If they didn't use their weapons. He was certain they had weapons, though he saw no spears or knives in evidence. But he'd seen the sticks the guards who protected the harvest ships used: they were like black, shiny clubs, but they didn't use them like clubs. If some farmer wandered too close to the ships, the lightest touch of one of those clubs would send the hapless victim crashing to the ground, to lie twitching and jerking for as long as an hour. He knew of two who had even died from those fits.

So he wasn't stupid about these strangers. The way they stared at him, every line and stance of their bodies betraying their tension, made him feel wary, too. But he didn't sense murderous intentions emanating from them. He didn't think they intended to kill him, at least not right this moment.

You're an old fool, he thought. *They are* alien. *How can you guess what they're thinking?*

Nonetheless, he remembered the thought that had burst in his mind as their long, falling star had burst across his sky: *Is this a change?*

He hoped it was. He stretched out his huge arms, palms up and open, and said "My name is Ir-Bakka. I mean you no harm. Welcome, strangers from far away."

One of the males (he thought) wore a thin chain around his neck that was weighted down across his chest by a round pendant. To Ir-Bakka's astonishment, the pendant began to make sharp, indecipherable chattering noises. The male paused, his head cocked, listening to them. As he did so, he visibly relaxed. He turned and spoke to the one with the small metal (weapon?) thing in his hand. That one lowered his arm, though Ir-Bakka noticed he didn't put the thing away entirely, nor did he take his sharp gray gaze off Ir-Bakka's face.

The male with the pendant—the pelt on the top of his head was dark brown, almost black—then did an odd thing: he took the chain from around his neck and held it toward Ir-Bakka, as if offering a gift. The pendant dangled, catching the sunlight on its golden face in crimson shimmers—and began to speak.

Ir-Bakka froze. As the stranger chattered—his voice was high and quick; it *sounded* like the busy mutter of some small animal—Ir-Bakka was astonished to hear his own language (though in an equally high, strange tone) issue from the pendant.

"Thank you, Ir-Bakka," the pendant said. "My name is Jim Endicott." The male pointed at his own chest with his free hand. "We mean you no harm. Welcome to our camp. Will you join us and speak with us?"

Ir-Bakka found this wondrous. He had never seen such a thing on the picture machines. He wondered if a pendant like that could be purchased in one of the strange people's trading stations, the places where the ones who looked like his own people, but somehow were not, kept the stores of goods that were like those seen on the picture machines, and that could be purchased in trade for the plants the strange people desired.

He had never himself gone to one of these stations, but his sons had, many times. His village, and those in nearby regions, grew many different crops, some in large quantities, and some less. The big harvests were picked up by the sky wagons, but the smaller ones had to be lugged, sometimes a bag or bale at a time, to the nearest station. His sons had made the journey often, and had returned with many wonderful things. In his village, his family was considered rich.

But not rich enough, evidently, to possess one of these alien-speaking machines. Ir-Bakka stared at the pendant and said, "Are you speaking to me through that thing? Am I speaking to you?"

The one who called himself Jim Endicott smiled. "Yes, it's called a translator."

Ir-Bakka kept on going until he was almost to their circle. He thought they smelled as if they were still a little afraid of him, but that was all right. He knew his scent would waft his own uneasiness to them.

How do you know they smell the same way we do? he thought. *Maybe it's like speaking, like words. They mean different things. Maybe what I smell as fear is the scent of their happiness.*

At least they could talk to each other. Maybe it would be enough. He wondered if they knew about the strange people, who were and yet somehow were not true Kolumbans. He wondered if they knew the source of the picture machines, or why the strange people would only trade their goods for new kinds of crops. But most of all, he wondered if they were the harbingers of yet a newer change, and, perhaps, a better one.

But he didn't know quite how to ask them all this, or maybe just wasn't ready to do so, and so he merely said, "May I sit with you?" and gestured at one of the stumps they'd arranged around their fire.

Jim Endicott smiled again and waved him in. As Ir-Bakka seated himself, his sensitive nostrils wrinkled. Somewhere around here was another Kolumban. One who was sick or injured, and terrified.

6

That rank, raw scent, so disturbingly obvious to Ir-Bakka, stayed with him as he led the aliens through the forest toward his own fields and village.

He thought the smell had come from their sky wagon, but he had not been able to think of a way to look inside. In fact, when he'd wandered too close to it, he noticed that the golden-skinned one with the gray eyes and the weapon just happened to be wandering in the same direction, but a bit closer, so that he stayed between Ir-Bakka and the ship. He had the weapon in his hand again, too.

Ir-Bakka was not ignorant. He might think of these visitors' vessel as a sky wagon, but he knew it was something far different than a wagon dragged by invisible *oklaks* across the sky. He, who had been alive since the beginning of the change, had watched all the other changes with a sharp and intelligent eye. He knew that there were other worlds, countless numbers of them, and that Kolumba itself, which he'd once been taught was the center of everything, was only a single planet in a great sweeping arm of the starry galactic spiral. The lights in the sky had turned out to be not lamps, but stars.

These strange beings came from one such distant world, and he had seen their world on the picture machines that were now everywhere on *his* world. He had never expected to see, let alone meet, any of the beings he'd watched on the picture machines, but now that he had, he felt neither shock nor terror. They were human, he supposed, as human as he was. Well, uglier and weaker, perhaps, but still.

His hearts beat with a brisk double pump as he tramped along, and a kind of singing joy seemed to hum in his veins. It was a beautiful day, not yet noon, and the well-worn paths through the trees were as familiar and comfortable to him as the trails of his own village.

He was excited by the possibilities these strangers might represent. As far as he knew, they were the first *aliens* to visit his world. Excepting the strange people, who *looked* like Kolumbans, but who were not; Ir-Bakka was quite certain about that. For one thing, the strange people had no odor. For another, there was nothing in their eyes but a flat, glassy gleam, like looking in a mirror. Now that he had finally met these visitors from another planet, he thought that the strange people might be far more alien than this Jim Endicott was.

"Call me Jim," the boy had said. He sensed that Endicott was still in his youth, or what passed for it among his people. And he knew Jim—and all but one of the rest—was male. He'd pulled Endicott aside and politely whispered his question about that, which had caused a red flush to rise in the boy's cheeks—Ir-Bakka wondered what *that* meant—and made him laugh as well.

Hard work, trying to not offend them, and not be offended by their own errors. They were strangers of the most distant sort. One couldn't blame them for not knowing the local ways. He made a mental note for himself, though; there were some in the village who might not be so forgiving. He would have to stay close to his newfound friends, make sure they didn't step too far over the line in their ignorance.

It never crossed Ir-Bakka's mind that there were also some in the village who would be interested in these visitors for different reasons, and who would report their presence to places Ir-Bakka had not yet even considered.

Jim Endicott was trying to match him stride for stride, but the way was steep, and now Ir-Bakka noticed with dismay the boy was breathing hard, and seemed to have trouble keeping up. He stopped, faintly disconcerted by the way all the others also instantly paused, as if he were some kind of puppet master leading them by invisible strings. He could feel all of them staring at him as he pointed at the translator dangling from Jim's neck. Jim lifted it toward him.

"Is something wrong?" the translator squeaked, a high, tinny sound that Ir-Bakka still found hilarious—it sounded the way he imagined a weedhopper would if that tiny red insect tried to talk to him.

"I wanted to ask you that," he said. "You look like you're having a hard go of it. Are you?"

"Uh, well, you're a lot bigger than we are," Jim said, as Ir-Bakka listened in delight to the translated words chattering from his chest, and odd but pleasing counterpoint to the unintelligible sounds coming from the boy's mouth. All of a sudden, an idea for a song that used such contrapuntal rhythms sprang into Ir-Bakka's mind. He wanted to sit right down and work it out, but decided such behavior might offend his guests. They would probably not know of the Kolumban affinity for all things musical.

"I see," Ir-Bakka replied gravely. "Longer legs, is that it?"

"We can keep up," Jim replied stoutly. But he was still breathing rapidly, almost panting. So were the rest of them.

"I'm sorry," Ir-Bakka said. "I wasn't thinking. Forgive me, I guess it's the excitement of meeting you. And I love strolling in the forest. Sometimes I forget myself. I'll walk slower, how will that do?"

Jim grinned at him. That was another thing. He would have to mention it to the boy. Among his own people, bared teeth were not a friendly gesture. Of course, he wouldn't know that, but it might cause trouble in certain quarters.

So much to think of.

"That would be great, Ir-Bakka," Jim said.

"Would you like to rest a few moments before we continue?" Ir-Bakka asked politely. "There's a pretty spring just off the path, right over there. We could share water. It's quite cool beneath the trees."

Behind him, the girl—her name was Sam, Jim had told him, such strange names—said something in her own tongue. Jim glanced at her but didn't reply. "That sounds wonderful."

"Right this way," Ir-Bakka said, and led them off the trail into the red-washed green shadows of the great trees. He decided he'd done the right thing when he saw how gratefully they all slumped to the ground next to the small, spring-fed pool held cupped like a bowl of liquid crystal beneath an outcropping of blue-veined sandstone. They settled on the mossy rocks, and some of them took off their footgear and trailed their feet in the water, sputtering shocked laughter at the iciness of it. Ir-Bakka felt their pleasure as a warm glow across his chest, and was pleased; they liked his world. Well, why not? He did, too.

He tried to imagine the strange people taking pleasure in something so simple, and couldn't quite manage it.

Why can't I stop thinking about them? Why are the strange people tangled in my thoughts like burrs in an unbrushed pelt all of a sudden?

Without warning, his nostrils were full of the memory of the fear-stink he'd smelled near the alien ship. He narrowed his eyes, leaned back against the bole of a thick-leaved tree, and watched the aliens dabble their naked toes in the water.

What kind of changes are coming? he wondered, suddenly uneasy in the brightness of the day.

7

Jim put down his comm unit. "Nikita says that Bobby is doing better, and our guest isn't doing anything."

"Well, at least that part's going okay. So far," Kerry said.

"Smell that air. Isn't it great?" Sam said. She had a happy, dazed look on her face. Jim reached over and patted her on the knee.

"I didn't know you were such an outdoorswoman," he told her.

She grinned. "Neither did I."

They spent the day wandering with Ir-Bakka through his farming village, being jostled by huge, hairy bodies, and being stared at, in some cases suspiciously, by those same cinnamon-scented residents.

They toured fields and orchards of astonishingly great fecundity. The Kolumbans seemed to be a race born with green thumbs on *each* hand.

They saw much that was beautiful. But they also saw an ugly side to village life, a side that, on the surface, didn't seem to make much sense. Jim tried to talk to Ir-Bakka about some of that, but the old man brushed him off. It was plain the whole subject made him uneasy.

The oddest thing about the daily lives of the Kolumbans here was the mixture of high tech and low. Many homes had a plethora of shiny gadgets. All the homes they saw had at least one, an item Ir-Bakka called a picture machine. It was the comm unit Jim had read about. Although of obviously alien manufacture, its purpose was as straightforward as such things always are in any technologically advanced culture—although all these units had been hardwired for one-way communication only. They could receive, but they couldn't send. Something like the ancient "television sets" his ancestors had once watched on Terra. In other words, perfectly tailored propaganda machines, a direct conduit into the Kolumban gestalt, a perfect way to manipulate the naïve and technologically unsophisticated populace.

Ir-Bakka took them to his spacious family compound and showed them his own picture machine. Jim noted that he kept it buried deep in the bottom of a chest, and when he dug it out, he had to blow the dust off its sturdy metal case. This was in contrast to some of the other villagers, who apparently carried their units with them everywhere they went.

Every home they visited had a comm unit, even the poorest hovels. Jim was surprised to see the extent of the poverty in the village. His readings of human history had taught him that small freeholding farmers were usually at least well fed, but there was a clear stratification evident in the social lives of the Kolumbans here. Yet everywhere he looked, he saw crops in abundance. His research on Kolumba had prepared him to expect poverty, but it still didn't make sense.

Ir-Bakka's family seemed quite well off. There were many of them, and they lived in a large, well-kept compound. Large enough, in fact, that Ir-Bakka had given them a small structure for their own. He'd told them they could use it as long as they wished. It was a small building, square, with low brick walls from which beautifully carved hardwood beams extended up to support a room made of dark red fired-clay tiles.

There were no glass windows between walls and roof, but blinds made of soft leather served equally well in the mild climate, and provided excellent ventilation. The floor was made of well-fitted planks of some light-colored wood, polished to a glowing sheen. The furnishings were simple and comfortable: big, puffy pillows; thick, scratchy blankets; a few low, sturdy tables covered with intricately incised patterns.

Ir-Bakka left them with several bowls of goop, amazingly enough, none of it green. And some of it turned out to be almost edible, certainly better than anything they'd been able to come up with aboard the *Endeavor*.

"So what's next, Captain?" Kerry said, as he wiped his hands on a colorfully patterned piece of fabric the size of a small tablecloth that the Kolumbans evidently considered perfect for a napkin.

"I don't know. There's a lot of poverty in this village. If the others are like this . . . maybe that's a chink, a way in," Jim said.

Sam said, "But why? Why are these people poor? They have farms, fields, orchards. Yet some actually seem to be starving. How can that be?"

Jim thought a moment. "I think that what the Communers did with their comm units was to alter the distribution system. They pay for the crops they want with the gadgets the Kolumbans see—and want—on the picture machines. So, in order to get these gadgets, the Kolumbans start growing these crops instead of what they used to grow. Ir-Bakka said he used to grow fruits, but now his family mostly grows *gir*, a crop for the Communers—or as he calls them, the 'strange Kolumbans.' My guess is that the 'strange Kolumbans' are androids wholly controlled by the Communers. Anyway, *gir* isn't a food crop. It isn't valuable to the Kolumbans at all, except that it buys them gadgets, which have become wealth. Then they trade the gadgets to other Kolumbans who *do* grow food."

"But why does that mean poverty?"

"Simple," Kerry broke in. "Farmers who can't grow foodstuffs, and who also can't grow sufficient *gir* for the Communers, end up with only a few gadgets for trade. So they starve, because they can't be self-sufficient, and they can't obtain enough gadget 'money' to properly feed themselves, either."

Sam thought about it. "So it's the new system that impoverishes them?"

"Yes," Jim said. "And I suspect it was designed by the Communers to do exactly that. Now the Communers control an economy they themselves created."

"So what's the answer?" Sam asked.

"One answer would be to change the equation," Jim told her.

"And how could we do that?"

"Well . . . the Communers have created a trading monopoly, and a highly artificial one, at that. Now if we could break that monopoly . . ."

"Break it? How?"

Jim winked at her. "The way you break any monopoly. Bring in some competition."

"Competition? Like who?" Kerry said.

"Elwood?" Jim said.

"Yeah?"

"You know what stuff's aboard the lighter. Is there anything we could rework into some analysis machines? Like for plant genetics?"

Elwood considered. "There's the various atmospheric analyzers, toxin counters, like that. I could probably come up with something. Ferrick would be better at it, though."

"Well, Ferrick isn't here. So I guess it's you."

Elwood nodded. "I'll take a shot."

"That's all well and good," Kerry said. "But you sound like you plan to settle down, spend a lot of time in Friendly Village here. And I don't think that's very practical. The Communers have to be looking for us, and if not already, soon the Kolumbans working with the Communers will be, too. On top of that, our ship is a four-hour hike away. We can't exactly bring it here, because we're holding Ur-Barrba captive inside. Well, maybe we could, but it would draw even more attention to us. We can't keep the word of our presence from going out. Somebody's got to twig on us being here pretty quick."

"I don't know," Jim said. "Ir-Bakka told me the next harvest pickup won't be for several weeks yet. This village is pretty isolated, and the comm units only work one way—they can't send out with them. We might have a window of opportunity." He shrugged. "Anyway, do you have a better suggestion?"

"Sure," Kerry told him. "We've got the lighter, and we can fly it. We've got guns. We know about this Ald place, and about Ur-Barrba's brother. The one everybody thinks is a saint. Now *he* would make a pretty good hostage, don't you think?"

"Oh, man, I don't know," Jim said. "Ur-Quillam is like a symbol to these people. For the really poor ones, he's all they have, their only source of hope. You really want to mess with that? It could blow up in our faces. Besides, it seems kind of immoral. Like kidnapping Jesus or something."

Kerry's gaze hardened. "Survival is moral, too, Jim. This is a huge operation here on Kolumba. How many more colony ships might die because of what your pal Ir-Bakka's family is growing?"

"It's a short-term solution," Jim said. "Even if it worked, even if we could use his kids as hostage to force Ur-Quolla to break his agreements to supply dope to the Communers, what would keep him from going back on his word as soon as we were gone—or as soon as he had his kids back?"

"Nothing says we *have* to give them back," Kerry said softly.

"Break our own word? That would make us as bad as the Communers."

"Do we care?" Kerry asked.

"I do," Jim told him.

8

Two weeks later, their borrowed house was heaped high with strange bundles; weeds, leaves, roots, dried and fresh blossoms, baskets of berries, sheaves of grass. Kerry and Elwood had hiked back to the ship and returned with an odd-looking contraption Elwood had rigged up from several of the analyzers he'd ripped out of their housings. Jim sat in front of the thing now, with Sam behind him, taking notes.

He shoveled a handful of copper-colored blossoms into a hopper on the side of the machine, watched as various beams and rays played over the mulch, then noted the results.

"Sample Four One Seven A," he said. "Odd polysaccharides, three novel glycoproteins." He paused, waiting. "Possible applications include dopamine regulation and/or tailored stem cell stimulations."

He turned off the machine, scooped out the now smoldering test sample, and sighed.

"You get it?"

Sam nodded. "We've tested almost a thousand samples, but we really haven't gotten what we need, have we?"

Jim shook his head. "There's some interesting stuff here, but nothing truly revolutionary. No silver bullet for anything still not curable." He grinned wanly. "That's the problem with first world medicine. It already does so much, it's hard to find something really new. Most diseases are already conquered."

"But we're not looking for just diseases, right? Anything with a major pharmacological effect would do. An immortality drug. An intelligence enhancer. Anything like that."

"Or a cure for the Pleb Psychosis," Jim said. "That would be a winner."

An uneasy expression washed across Sam's face. "Yes, that would be wonderful. But unlikely. They've been working on that one for years, and they're no closer now than they were when they started looking."

Jim nodded, wondering why she looked so upset. Maybe she'd lost friends or family to the dreadful affliction. Many Plebs had.

"Well, we aren't likely to find anything, either. The disease is so rigidly human-centric. Although you never know . . ."

He stood up and stretched. His spinal cord yielded a couple of satisfying pops, and he yawned. "Where'd Elwood and Kerry get off to?"

"Wandering around, poking their noses into stuff where they probably don't belong."

"Quite a few people in this place don't seem to like us much. We're lucky old Ir-Bakka sort of took us under his wing. He seems to have a lot of clout here."

"How long can it last, though? How long can we stay here, fiddling around looking for something that may not even exist?"

"As long as it takes?" he said.

"You know we can't do that. Kerry does have a point. Eventually, one way or another, word about us is going to get to somebody who doesn't like us. Like the Communers. Then what?"

He eyed her glumly. "I don't know."

"Huh. Some all-knowing captain you are."

"Aw, come on, Sam. Don't start. I get enough of that crap from Kerry."

"Maybe Kerry's right," she said slowly. "About grabbing another hostage."

"He's wrong," Jim said.

She gestured at the piles of samples. "Well, *this* doesn't seem to be getting us anywhere."

He didn't reply. He didn't have an answer to that. He was beginning to think he didn't have any answers at all.

CHAPTER TEN

1

The uneasy look that Jim had seen on Sam's face when he mentioned finding a cure for the Pleb Psychosis was explained two days later, in the middle of the night, when a piercing shriek wakened him from his own bad dreams of a dark man striding across a field of stars.

At first he didn't realize what had awakened him. The thin, shrill cries—more like painful gasps, really—blended seamlessly with the sounds that had accompanied the dark man—in his nightmare, Jim had thought the stars were screaming.

He woke confused, shaking his head, to see shadows moving quickly about the cottage. "What?" he blurted. "What is it?"

He sat up, feeling the rough scratchy blanket fall away from his bare shoulders. Somebody struck a light. It was a locally made candle, casting a flickering, uncertain glow, in which Jim could see Kerry wrestling with somebody on the far side of the room. Elwood, holding the candle, stood over him.

"What's going on?" Jim said, as he threw the blanket aside and clambered to his feet.

"Not your problem," Elwood said. "Go back to sleep."

"Bullshit," Jim replied, moving toward the scene. His gorge leaped into his throat when he finally saw what was going on. "Oh my God, what's wrong with her?"

The shape Kerry wrestled with was Sam. Jim tried to get closer, but Elwood stuck one long, skinny arm out like a railroad crossing guard, and barred his path.

"Damn it—"

"You *can't help her*, Endicott!" Elwood hissed. Then, in a somewhat more kindly tone—though he didn't lower his arm— "Leave us alone. We know what to do."

But what Kerry was doing, it looked like to Jim, was trying to strangle Sam to death. His long, strong body was clamped around the heaving, bucking girl like an octopus. His legs encircled her hips. His right forearm was across her throat.

Every muscle in Sam's body stood out as if swollen in stone. Her lips were drawn so far back the lower part of her face looked like a grinning, toothy skull.

She snapped and growled and screeched. Her eyes bulged sightlessly, pupils shrunk to tiny points. Jim stared at her in dry-mouthed horror.

"Is that . . . is it . . . ?" he whispered.

"Yeah. The psychosis. Our own little Pleb cross to bear."

For some reason, that picture of the dark man jumped back into Jim's mind, the dark man and his screaming stars.

He could *hear* Sam's tendons creaking as Kerry squeezed her tighter, his own face drawn and haggard from the enormous effort he was expending to restrain a slender girl who weighed fifty pounds less than he did.

"He'll kill her," Jim said.

Elwood's voice was flat. "If she gets loose, she'll try to kill us—or herself. Is that what you want?"

Jim was amazed. Elwood—hard, tough Elwood—sounded close to tears.

Sam let loose with a single, ear-piercing shriek that felt as if somebody had driven a silver spike into the back of her skull, and then went as limp as a strand of soaked spaghetti.

Elwood dropped his arm. "It's okay now," he said softly. "She'll be out for a while."

Kerry untangled himself as Jim dropped to his knees beside her. "Is she . . . ?" He reached for her, the gesture tentative, frightened.

"Go ahead. She won't break," Kerry said. There was a darkening bruise beneath his right eye, and deep scratches slashed across the opposite cheek. He shuddered at the sudden release, and rocked back on his haunches, gasping for breath, sweat gleaming on his face like molten silver.

Jim smoothed Sam's hair away from her forehead. Her skin felt dry and burning hot. Her eyes were closed, but her eyelids twitched with galvanic regularity, as if, even in unconsciousness, she still was suffering a series of electrical shocks.

Jim licked his lips. They felt as rough and dry as his throat. He glanced across Sam's body at Kerry, who was wincing as he massaged some feeling back into his biceps.

"Pleb Psychosis?"

Kerry nodded.

"Will she be okay?"

"Who the hell knows?"

"Hey, I didn't mean . . ."

Kerry shook his head. "I know you didn't, Jim. I'm sorry, I shouldn't yell at you. It's not your fault."

He dusted his hands on the seat of his pants and stood. "You can watch her for a while if you want. Like Elwood told you, she'll be out for a while."

Jim stared up at him. "How long?"

"I don't know. Maybe a couple of hours. Maybe forever."

He turned and walked out of the room.

2

Two days later, Sam was still out. There were deep bags under her eyes. Her skin looked as if it had been shrink-wrapped around the bones of her skull. Elwood had hiked down to the lighter and returned with Nikita, carrying the portable autodoc. Nikita went back, to help Bobby guard Ur-Barrba, but the doc remained, now hooked up to Sam's wasted body. It was keeping her alive, but barely.

She'd kept on having convulsions, though not as strong as the first one, and she didn't waken when they occurred.

"Sometimes it happens that way," Kerry told him. "Sometimes there's just one, sometimes a whole series. Be glad she's staying knocked out. If she was awake, they'd be a lot stronger. Eventually, we'd probably hurt her trying to hold her down. Break bones or something."

She was having one now, the weakest yet, as if the terrible strain had worn all her strength away. Even so, it was awful to watch. Her back would arch, so that for a moment she was supported entirely on her drumming heels and the back of her twitching, bouncing head.

Ir-Bakka crouched over her, a mountain in hair, watching her intently. After a while the spasms ceased, and he stood. "The shaking disease," he said.

Jim stared at him. "The shaking disease? You've seen something like this before? Among your own people?"

"Something similar, yes. The strange Kolumbans suffer from it."

"The strange Kolumbans have this?"

"Yes, the ones who trade their gifts with us for our crops. The ones who tell us what we must grow. The ones who made us poor." Ir-Bakka turned his head and spat. "We grow the *ilka* bush for them. Not one of our plants, they gave it to us. It's said that it cures the shaking, but I don't know. Nobody knows."

Sam uttered a series of soft snorts, then subsided. In a shaft of pinkish light from the window, she looked like a corpse smeared with dried blood. It sounded crazy, the notion that an alien plant, grown by other aliens on a different world, might help her, but what else did he have? She was dying.

"Can you get me some of this *ilka* bush?" he asked.

3

Jim had moved his makeshift analyzer out of the hut to the front, by the door. He couldn't stand to watch what was happening to Sam. Despite the best efforts of the autodoc, she was wasting away. She still had convulsions, but now they were so weak that Kerry could hold her down simply by pressing gently on her shoulders.

The smell of cinnamon drifted down from the great trees. Birds flew like chattering jewels overhead. The dust beneath his bare feet was warm and soft. Every once in a while, some member of Ir-Bakka's extended family would wander by, staring, but Jim didn't notice.

A pile of *ilka* bushes, their glossy brown leaves withering, blood-colored sap oozing from where the branches had been chopped, was mounded next to him. Ir-Bakka told him the crop was nearing harvest, and pointed out the bruise-purpled berries dangling beneath the leaves.

He'd tested them all, sap, branches, leaves, berries. Now he was running a fresh series of analyses on various combinations: leaves and sap, berries and branches. The *ilka* was an odd plant: loaded with exotic molecular structures, huge sugar molecules, strange linkages to carbon rings that shouldn't exist. But so far, he'd found nothing that looked as if it might help Sam.

He leaned back, felt his spine pop, and uttered a sigh. He'd been hunched over the machine for almost twenty hours straight, and his muscles were grateful for release.

Kerry came out of the hut and stood next to him, looking pale as a cave fish. He'd barely left Sam's side since the psychosis struck her.

"Anything?" he asked.

Jim shook his head. "This thing is alien. I can't find anything that could act as a receptor for human proteins on the large molecules."

"How much testing have you done?"

Jim sighed. "Enough. I'm running combo analyses now, but I'm afraid I'm just spinning my wheels." He looked up at Kerry. "She's gonna die, isn't she?"

Kerry's gaze was shadowed. "Yeah. Probably."

Jim lowered his head, so that Kerry wouldn't see whatever it was that was causing his eyes to sting. But Kerry evidently sensed it, because he let his hand fall gently to Jim's shoulder. He squeezed, once.

"It's part of being a Pleb, Jim," he said. "It could happen to any of us, any time. We all know it. We all live with it. And some of us die with it."

Jim looked up, and now his tears were plainly visible, tinged with red by the sun, like tiny blood drops. "It's *wrong*! Doesn't anybody *care*?"

Kerry just stared at him. After a moment he shook his head. "We're Plebs, Jim. Anybody who matters quit caring a long time ago. That's how Plebs came to exist in the first place. Didn't you know?"

Jim pawed one hand across his damp cheeks. He sniffled, then turned back to his work. After a while, Kerry went back inside the hut.

"Do you need more *ilka*?" Ir-Bakka asked.

The old man startled him. He'd been working half asleep, and hadn't seen him come up.

"Uh? No, I guess not."

"Did it help?"

"No."

"I was afraid it wouldn't," Ir-Bakka rumbled. "*Ilka* is for the strange ones, not for the little hairless ones."

Despite his despair, Jim had to grin at that. "Is that what you call us? The little hairless ones?"

"Well, you are. To us, at least." He looked down at Jim. "Come with me."

His big hand wrapped around Jim's arm, tugged him upright. "You smell of sorrow."

Jim nodded. He knew what he smelled like, he just hadn't yet put a name to it.

Ir-Bakka led him out of the compound, through the village, and out into the fields. Dusk was coming on, a few stars beginning to show. They found a place where the fields met the forest.

"I stood here when I saw your light in the sky," Ir-Bakka said. "I watched it fall across the stars."

Jim nodded.

"I saw the same kind of light a long time ago, with my father," Ir-Bakka continued. "That light brought change to my world. Not good change, either. I hoped that your light would be different."

"I'd hoped it would be, too," Jim said. But in the extremity of his grief and desperation, even the cause for which he'd come here now seemed a pale and hopeless thing. Who was he to imagine shifting an entire world? He couldn't even save the girl he loved.

They stood in silence for several moments, as the night rustled softly around them. The huge field of *gir* gleamed like a sea of dark emeralds before them in the wan starlight.

"What do you use it for?" Ir-Bakka said at last.

"What do you mean?"

Ir-Bakka gestured with one huge hand. "The *gir*. We grow it for you. Do you eat it?"

Jim stared at him. "You grow this for us? You mean humans? How do you know that?"

"One of my sons heard it in Ald, home of the Ur." He glanced at Jim. "*Gir* is not one of our crops, you know. The strange Kolumbans gave it to us, just as they did the *ilka*."

Jim's eyes widened slowly as he realized what lay before him, thick green leaves whispering beneath the stars. It was from this that the drug that killed humans was distilled.

"How do you replant it?" he asked suddenly. "Does it generate seeds that you save after the harvest?"

"No. When we trade it, the strange ones give us more seed." Ir-Bakka squinted. "I don't think it grows as normal plants do. We've had many crops, and some of the fields have been left fallow to regenerate.

But the *gir* never grew in those fields until we planted it again. None of our own plants do this."

Sterile seeds, Jim thought. *A genetically tailored plant.*

"Tailored for humans," he murmured.

Like a man moving through a dream, he stepped out into the field, felt the leaves scrape gently against him, smelled the bitter-lemon aroma of their oils. He took one of the leaves, pulled it loose from a thick, woody stalk.

"Can you help me?" he asked Ir-Bakka.

4

Once he realized that there were not one, but two alien plants being farmed on Kolumba (and who knew how many more, though it didn't matter; two were enough), Jim thought he might have what he'd been searching so desperately for all along, but hadn't been able to find: a handle. A way in. He was no longer trying to turn apples into oranges. He had a pair of apples to play with now. To be sure, they were very *different* apples, but they were apples nonetheless. One poisonous to humans, one engineered for things entirely inhuman. But both engineered by the same race.

As he walked back to the hut with his arms full of *gir* leaves, he thought that he might—just *might*—be able to take those apples apart and put them back together again, into something entirely new and different. Maybe not even an apple anymore. Maybe an orange.

It took him two days, and by the time he finished, Kerry had come out of the hut to tell him that he thought Sam was dying.

Kerry led him into the hut. Though it was shortly after noon, the interior was dim and gloomy. Elwood had put all the shades down, because when they were open and the light struck Sam's face, sometimes she would start to twitch. That was all, though; she'd grown too weak to muster anything resembling a convulsion.

Now Jim stood over her, aghast. Sam had always had a kind of wiry slenderness to her, but what was lying before him, mouth open, lips drawn back, a rough cascade of gluey snoring sounds belching from her constricted throat, was as close to a corpse as a living being could get. The bones of her face glowed beneath her fevered skin, as if the fire inside her brain was illuminating her from the inside out. Her arms were wrinkles wrapped around pipe stems. Her breasts had disappeared. Her hair was tangled and lank as a sodden bird's nest.

The autodoc was still hooked up to her; it crouched over her with a sinister, insectile grace, like a praying mantis feasting on its mate. Various critical readouts scattered about the machine flashed red, adding to the effect: a myriad of demonic bug eyes.

In his hand, Jim held a small vial of crystalline green powder. "Elwood, turn everything off," he said.

"She'll die," Elwood said.

"She will anyway. I don't want anything to interfere with this." He raised the vial.

Elwood nodded and shut down the monitoring and maintenance programs. The machine quit blinking.

"Okay, now code in a full override. I want this blended with distilled water and infused over a two-hour period."

He handed the vial to Elwood.

"It's a long shot," Kerry said.

"Of course it is," Jim replied. "But have you got a better shot to take?"

Kerry shrugged.

Elwood fiddled with the autodoc, then stepped back. A pair of green lights began to glow. "Infusing," Elwood said laconically.

Two hours and three minutes later, Sam opened her eyes. She stared at the rest of them, puzzled. She couldn't understand why they were all jumping around and screaming like maniacs. But when Jim fell to his knees next to her, raised her up gently and pressed his lips against hers . . . *that* she could understand.

* * *

"Is it a cure?" Kerry asked later.

"Yes," Jim said. "It prevents certain saccharides from bonding. I don't know what causes the psychosis, but I could see the results. Probably anybody could, who looked. But there was no way to reverse the process after the bonds. This does."

Kerry still seemed stunned. "You found the answer," he murmured. "A cure for the Pleb Psychosis."

"Which," Jim told him, "is the answer to our other problems, too."

Kerry wasn't stupid. He only had to think about it for a couple of seconds. Then he smiled. "Yep, it sure is," he said. "How do you want to do it?"

Jim shrugged. "We've already got Ur-Barrba. I guess we might as well use her."

Jim sent Kerry down to fly the lighter back to the village, while he stayed with Sam. She recovered slowly; her mind was clear again, but her body had suffered terrible damage while she was locked in the deadly coma. Ir-Bakka brought her soups made from local vegetables, rich and thick with exotic oils. They tasted wholly unlike anything they'd eaten before, and were delicious. Jim wondered what else might be in them, because Sam began to noticeably recover after he started spoonfeeding them to her every couple of hours.

Kerry arrived and landed the lighter a quarter-mile beyond the outskirts of the village, on a broad shelf of weathered stone protruding from the flank of the mountain. That night, he and Jim went to the ship, passing through a strip of forested land before reaching the landing site.

"Pretty out here," Kerry remarked.

"You're a city guy," Jim said. "I've seen big trees before."

"Yeah, on that podunk planet you hail from," Kerry agreed.

Jim recalled his last trek in the woods, and the mountain cabin where armored assassins had come to kill him and his family.

"It could get pretty up-to-date every once in a while." For a moment, an ache so real it was like a punch in the sternum filled him, as he remembered Carl and Tabitha as he'd last seen them. In the dim but revealing illumination of memory, he saw things now he hadn't seen then: fear, loss, heartbreak. They had loved him then. *So why did you let me go?* he asked those departed faces.

"I dumped the lighter just up here, at the top of the ridge," Kerry said. "We have to get off the path here." He led Jim through a stand of hardwood giants, and then into a rising patch of scrub trees, dense with flowering thickets and thick-leaved brush.

They were both breathing hard when they crested the ridge and saw the darker shape of the lighter outlined against the hulking flank of the mountain rising behind it.

"Hold it," Kerry said softly, putting out his hand to stop Jim. "Nikki?"

"Hey, Kerry," Nikki said, rising from behind a clump of crumbling rock thirty yards in front of the lighter. He cradled the shatterblaster. "So you brought the boss this time, huh?" He waved. "Hiya, Captain."

"Good to see you, Nikki," Jim said as they moved toward the younger boy. "It's been a while. Everything okay here?"

"Sure. The gorilla says we ain't feeding her right, but I dunno what we can do about that. Bobby's come back strong. He's inside keeping an eye on the cargo bay. We did what you said. Never untied the ape, never let her out of the bay." He paused, grinned. "But man, you never told us vegetarians shit so much. Keeping her cage clean is just about a full-time job. Stinky one, too."

The mental picture brought a grin to Jim's face. "Well, I think your days of hauling crap are just about over."

"Man, that would be good."

As they approached the entry hatch, Nikki said, "You want me to stay on watch out here?"

"No, better come with us. I'm gonna have a talk with our prisoner. I'll feel a little safer if with all of our guns aimed at her. Just try not to shoot me by accident if something goes wrong, okay?"

The passenger cabin still showed signs of the battle that had taken place there, the scorch marks, the door to the pilot's cabin blasted and dangling from its hinges. Jim glanced at it all and thought how long ago it seemed—as if it had happened to a different person than he was now.

Somebody more certain. He wasn't certain of much of anything any longer.

Bobby sat bolt upright in his seat at the rear, next to the locked cargo bay door. From his puffy face and rapidly blinking eyes, Jim guessed he'd been grabbing a snooze.

"Uh . . . Jim! Sir! I'm sorry, I didn't see you . . ." Bobby stood and sketched a rough salute.

"At ease, Bobby. How's the prisoner?"

"I checked about an hour ago. She was sleeping. Well, snoring, at least. With her, you never know what's really going on."

"I know," Jim said. "I'm gonna open the door and have a little talk with her. Kerry will come with me. Nikki, give him your shatterblaster."

Nikki handed it over. "What do you want us to do?"

"Stay right here at the door as backup. At some point, I'm probably gonna let her loose. That will be the critical moment. If she goes for us, if she gets by Kerry some way, just start blasting. We'll both try to hit the deck, give you a clear field of fire." He stopped. "Although if she really gets going, she'll probably just throw one of us at you."

Nikki nodded as Kerry handed him his own ripper.

"Okay, Bobby," Jim said. "Open her up."

Bobby unlocked the door and slid it aside. It was very dim inside the cargo bay, only a single emergency light glowing redly. "How come so dark?" Jim asked.

"She wanted it that way. Said she likes the red light, the brighter one hurts her eyes."

Jim nodded. He'd gotten used to the perpetual dimness of the red Kolumban sun.

"Well, crank it up a little. I want everybody to be able to see."

Bobby headed back down the aisle to the pilot's cabin. A moment later, the illumination in the cargo bay dialed up, and Ur-Barrba's bound, hulking form became visible, hunched against the far wall. If she had been sleeping, she wasn't anymore. She was sitting up, her eyes blazing like hot yellow coals.

As Jim stepped into the bay, she growled at him: "You brought me home alive, and in shame, Jim Endicott. What do you want now?"

Jim moved toward her, and squatted down just out of reach. Although Ur-Barrba was tightly bound, he was taking no chances. He remembered what Ur-Barrba had done to Frank. Pulled his head off like yanking a grape from its stem.

Ur-Barrba's odor was overwhelming, a mixture of cinnamon, stale sweat, dung. Her once-beautiful pelt was matted, and in places rubbed away, so that she looked like a huge piece of rotting furniture.

"What I want is to let you go," Jim told her. "What would you say to that?"

She stared at him a long moment, fangs glinting behind black lips, eyes burning like watch fires.

"I'd say you want something from me," she rumbled finally. "Some treachery that would help you, not me or my people."

"Depends on what you call treachery," Jim said. "I want you to carry a message to your father."

Silence. Then, "What kind of message?"

"A message of peace. Between your people and mine."

"Why should there be peace between us? We don't know you."

"Why should you try to kill us?" Jim asked. "Because a bunch of aliens neither one of us really knows *wants* you to kill us? So the strange Kolumbans can give you worthless trinkets while they change everything about the way you've always lived? While they make you *poor?*"

Ur-Barrba shifted slightly, and Jim felt an impression of great muscles suddenly bunching. He was abruptly glad he hadn't untied her before beginning their conversation.

"What do you know of the strange ones?" Ur-Barrba said finally. And was it his imagination, or did she sound uneasy?

"I know they aren't Kolumbans, and I'm pretty sure they aren't living at all. Not living the way you and I are, at least."

"I don't understand. They are different from us, but the walk and talk. They think."

Jim stared at her. "Do you know what a clone is? Or an android?"

Ur-Barrba didn't answer.

"They are things that are . . . well, made. Built, constructed, whatever. In some ways they are alive—especially the clones. But some clones are like . . . do you have puppets?"

Evidently he'd strained the translator's capabilities a bit, because Ur-Barrba said, "What are puppets?"

"Little figures that dance on the end of strings."

"Ah. Children's toys."

"Yes, like that. But clones can be made to dance on invisible strings. Somebody else controls them. They don't control themselves. That's what your strange Kolumbans are, I think."

More silence. "It could be true, I guess. But what does this have to do with us?"

"You grow poison to kill humans with, because the strangers tell you to, and pay you for it. They even make you deliver it."

"Yes? So? Why should we care about that, as long as they do pay us?"

"They pay *you*, your family, a few others. The people in charge. But can't you see what they've done—what they're still *doing*—to the rest of your planet? Your people no longer grow for themselves, grow what they need. Now they grow for you and the strangers, and if they can't grow enough to trade for the trinkets, they become poor. Some of them even starve."

"The strangers say that in the long run, everybody will be rich. They say that soon they will bring new crops for us to grow."

"I'm sure they do. Do they tell you also that someday you will live like the people you see in your picture machines, that you will all be rich and powerful like they are?"

"They have promised."

"I see. And have they kept their promises? They've been here a long time. Have your lives changed for the better? Do your people have the things you see on the picture machines?"

"Some of them."

"Yes, I've seen them. Little things, bright, shiny things that don't do anything much, that change your lives not at all. The ship you fly to the stars—you didn't build it, did you? You can't even make the picture machines. All you can do is grow what the strangers ask, and take the useless things they give you in return. Tell me, Ur-Barrba. Since the strangers came to you the first time, has Kolumba grown richer, or poorer?"

Again, Ur-Barrba made no reply.

"Well, I'll tell you. You didn't even *have* a word for poor before they came. Nobody starved here then. Everybody had enough to eat, and shelter for themselves and their families. They had friends, and songs, and the art they made. What have the strangers brought you to replace what they've taken away from you?"

Ur-Barrba remained so silent he thought she wasn't going to answer again, but finally she spoke. "What you say may have some truth in it, Jim Endicott. But what do you propose to change any of it? You are only a few, and the Communers hunt you even now, if I don't miss my guess. Why should I listen to what you say? No matter what I do now, or what *you* do now, you will all soon be dead."

Jim stared at her. "That may be true. But before that happens, I will use the hyperwave transmitter sitting right over there"—he gestured toward the large piece of equipment he'd brought with the probe—"and get in touch with my home planet. I'll tell them what is going on here. What you have done to our colony ships. Can you guess what will happen then?"

"Nothing will happen. Your people are very far away. The Communers are right here, and they are strong. They will defend us."

"Will they? Think about it, Ur-Barrba. If the Communers are so strong, why do they need you? Why do they have you make their poison and deliver it? Why not just send their ships out to attack the human colony vessels?" Jim paused, thinking. "We tried to contact the *Outward Bound*, you know. After we hijacked your ship. There was no reply. And the *Outward Bound* isn't the only ship you visited, is it?"

Ur-Barrba turned her huge head away from him.

"If you look at it right," Jim went on, "the whole thing feels like a setup to me. Even if Terra figured out that something was destroying their colony ships, who would they blame? I think they'd blame you. Which doesn't sound to me like the Communers have a whole lot of confidence in what you call their 'strength.' In fact, they sound a lot like cowards to me, getting somebody else to do their dirty work for them, while they lurk in the background."

"We are not pawns," Ur-Barrba said. "We do nobody's bidding blindly."

"Then you can change your minds. Is that what you're saying? If you wanted to, you could tell the Communers you aren't going to grow crops for them anymore."

"Yes. We could do that. But why should we?"

Time for the trump cards, Jim thought. *I hope they're trump cards, anyway.*

"Because if you don't at least listen to my proposals, and carry them to your father, Ur-Barrba, then I will do what I said, and tell Terra about you. Perhaps the Communers might try to defend you. But they cannot defend your sun. Do not judge Earth by the ships you've seen so far. The Terran ConFederation is far greater than you imagine. Earth does not even need to enter your system in order to put its finger on your sun. And should it do that—should Terra reach out its armored hand to grasp your star—then your sun will explode as easily as a squeezed *oranja* fruit. And there will be nothing the Communers—or anybody else— can do to stop this from happening."

Ur-Barrba's eyes seemed to flare. "Then why have you not done so already, human? Why haven't you sent your damned message?"

Jim bowed his head. "Because I don't want to kill you all. I don't want your deaths on my conscience. You are pawns. But have no doubts—if you don't take my offer to your father, then I *will* send the message. And then, pawns or not, you will die." He paused, leaned forward slightly, his gaze boring into Ur-Barrba's own. "That's what pawns do, you know," he said softly. "Pawns die."

He held Ur-Barrba's eyes, refusing to look away. In the end, it was the Kolumban who flinched. "Tell me what you want me to say," she said at last. "I will think about it."

"Think hard," Jim agreed, "but not too long."

Then he told her.

5

I wondered when you would tell me you were holding one of my people prisoner," Ir-Bakka said.

Jim was leading him toward the lighter. He stopped, stared. "You knew?"

"I could smell her. From the very beginning, when I first saw your ship." He tilted his grizzled head. "I think we smell better than you little ones do."

Jim had to grin at the inadvertent double meaning. "Yes, you do smell better than we do," he agreed.

"Are you taking me to meet the prisoner now?" Ir-Bakka asked.

Just as he spoke, Kerry and Elwood emerged from the lighter with Ur-Barrba shambling between them. They had unbound her legs, but her arms were still securely tied. Elwood immediately stepped away from her, holding the shatterblaster, which he aimed at her broad chest.

Ur-Barrba stood blinking in the sunlight. Her flanks rippled. She raised her head and let out a low moan. Then she saw Jim and Ir-Bakka coming toward her. Her eyes widened as her gaze focused on the old Kolumban. She rumbled a series of imprecations the translator didn't quite catch, but Ir-Bakka certainly did.

He froze. "Do you know who your prisoner is?" he said.

"Yes, I think so."

"This is one of the Ur, the rulers of Ald!"

Jim nodded. "Yes. She is the daughter of Ur-Quolla, the sister of Ur-Quillam."

"Blessed be his Name," Ir-Bakka muttered softly. "You must release her at once!" he continued. He seemed terrified. "If I'd known who you held . . ." He shook his head. Then he stepped away from Jim and raised his hands in a warding motion. "You've betrayed me and my family! I should never have helped you!"

He continued to back away from Jim, his head swiveling back and forth as if he were looking for a place to run.

"Ir-Bakka, stop! Wait! *I am releasing her!*"

He gestured at Kerry. "Cut her loose," he said.

Kerry didn't hesitate. His knife flashed crimson in the sun, and suddenly Ur-Barrba raised her arms, strips of tape still dangling from her wrists. Ur-Barrba's massive arms and watermelon-sized fists kept going up and up in a long, stretching move that bent her backward as she moaned softly, joyously, at the first physical freedom she'd felt in almost a moon. And maybe it was a psychic freedom as well, for she stood on the soil of her own world, unfettered, and of all the crew she'd commanded when the *Endeavor* had first embarked, the only one still left alive.

Jim wondered what was going through her mind. He thought he could guess at least part of it, and it looked as if Elwood could, too. He saw Elwood's grip tighten on the shatterblaster and his eyes narrow to slits.

For God's sake, don't shoot her! And for one wild instant he thought Elwood might do exactly that. Then Ur-Barrba dropped her arms, which made her look decidedly less fearsome. Elwood relaxed, and Jim started to breathe again.

Ir-Bakka still wouldn't move. He seemed afraid to do anything as long as Ur-Barrba was watching him.

"What's wrong?" Jim said. "Are you frightened of her?"

"You don't *know*," Ir-Bakka said. At least, that was what came out of the translator. But his own voice was a long, low moan.

"Don't worry about him," Ur-Barrba said, moving toward them. "You! Farmer! Leave us!"

Ir-Bakka's head snapped up. He scuttled backward, bobbing his head.

"Hey, wait a minute," Jim said.

Ur-Barrba glanced at him. "He is not necessary. He's nothing more than a peasant, and he knows it. Look at him."

Ir-Bakka was now crouched so low he was almost crawling. He looked terrified. Jim started to say something, but Ur-Barrba cut him off.

"It doesn't matter. What matters is that I will take your proposal to my father." She looked down at her body, at the matted hair, the scabby abrasions. "But first, I want a bath." She looked up. "And some decent food." She paused. "I almost sympathize with what you must have endured, eating from the larders aboard my ship." Her fangs appeared. She might have been grinning, but Jim doubted it.

"Almost," she added.

Not a friend. No, not a friend at all.

Ur-Barrba, her coat combed and brushed to shining splendor, stood at the head of the small company that would accompany her back to Ald. They were at the edge of the village, near the mouth of a wide, hard-packed trail.

"How long will it take you to get home?" Jim asked.

"This is the beginning of the rains," Ur-Barrba replied. "Once we get down out of the mountains, the going will become easier. But the way is long, and unless I can find better transportation than my own two feet, it will take many days."

Jim wished he could read her better, but that was impossible. Ur-Barrba was *alien*. Her facial expressions were indecipherable, and he was never absolutely certain that the translations he heard were accurate in his own language. In the end, all he could hope for was that the proposal he was sending to her father would appeal to his self-interest strongly enough to override any other considerations—like decades of Communer domination and continuous propaganda.

And he was risking everything on that slender hope.

This captain stuff sure as hell isn't everything it's cracked up to be, Jim thought. *How come none of this kind of stuff ever makes it onto the vid-net shows?*

He raised one hand in farewell. "Have a good journey, Ur-Barrba. I'm . . . sorry that things have turned out . . ."

Whatever he was going to say became moot. Ur-Barrba uttered a soft snort—which the translator ignored—then turned on her heel and stalked away. A moment later, her entire party vanished into the forest.

"Do you trust her?" Kerry asked.

"Of course not," Jim replied. "She hates us. And I think she's lying to us."

"So what do we do?"

"If you were in my position, what would *you* suggest?"

"Huh. Thank God I'm *not* in your position, but since you asked, I'd load all our butts on the lighter, get back to the *Endeavor*, and get the hell out of here. Send a message back to Terra and let *them* handle it."

Jim remembered his dreams, a dark man, striding across the stars. "You know what Terra would do, don't you?"

"Yeah. Blow this place to hell."

"And with it, any chance of a cure for the Pleb Psychosis?"

"We've got a sample. They could duplicate it."

Jim shook his head. "I've had a chance to do a deeper analysis. There are mutations in the plants. They'll only grow here. The drug can't be duplicated. Kolumba is the only source."

Kerry blinked. "Well, we could tell them that. It might stop the sun bombs."

"Do you really think so? Terra has lived with Plebs and the psychosis for centuries. But the Communers are using this planet to wage war against our colony ships *now*. What do you really think the decision would be?"

Kerry shook his head. "Like I said, I'm glad I'm not you." He paused. "So what do we *do* now, my captain?"

"We wait," Jim said.

6

Ur-Barrba trekked steadily downhill until the sun was just past its zenith, then called a halt. One of Ir-Bakka's sons was in charge of the villagers who accompanied her. He was feeling nervous, and not just because Ur-Barrba had not spoken a single word during their march so far. And he had never been close to a Great One, not this way. He'd seen them in Ald, on the few occasions he'd traveled to that great city, but there they traveled behind a screen of armed guards that kept the common people away. Now he was close enough to smell the rage on her.

"Farmer's son!" Ur-Barrba barked.

"Yes, Great One?"

"I judge we are far enough away from your dung pit of a village and the monsters you sheltered there. Did you do what I told your father to have you do?"

For a moment, his mind went blank. He could feel Ur-Barrba's anger ratcheting up another notch, and feared the Great One might kill him then and there. He stared dumbly at Ur-Barrba, until she snarled, "The picture machine, you idiot. Did you bring one?"

He scrabbled in his pack, found the flat panel, and handed it over with trembling fingers. Ur-Barrba's mobile, rubbery black lips stretched in a wide, horizontal line, teeth carefully hidden. He smelled her rage begin to abate.

Ur-Barrba took the alien communicator, fumbled with a catch on its back, and flipped open the case. She poked around inside for a moment, then closed the case and walked several paces away from the rest of the party. No need to let these peasants know the communicators could be rigged to broadcast, as well as receive.

She brought the unit close to her face and spoke in low, rapid tones.

Two hours later, a black, needlelike shape settled out of the sky. Before Ur-Barrba boarded, she repeated her orders to the terrified villagers.

"Do not return to your homes for a week. The invaders must not know what I did. Do you understand?"

Ir-Bakka's son nodded. "See that you do. If I return and find you there before me, your entire village is forfeit. You have already committed criminal acts. If you disobey me now, everybody in that filthy hole of yours will die."

"Yes, Great One," Ir-Bakka's son mumbled. "We understand, and obey."

Ur-Barrba cast a final glowering glance over all of them, then turned and boarded the vessel. After a few moments the ship lifted off as silently as it had come, and vanished into the afternoon sky.

Inside, Ur-Barrba settled into the copilot's chair. The ship was even smaller than the lighter she'd returned to Kolumba in, but there was more room. Two of her father's guards sat in the passenger seats, and a single pilot conned the ship next to her.

She switched on a viewscreen and watched the little party of farmers dwindle below. Their faces were all turned upward. In a way, she felt pity for them. They were ignorant peasants, and had no idea of the issues they'd accidentally gotten themselves involved in. Nonetheless, it had been necessary to frighten them. She had learned a grudging respect for Jim Endicott, and the yellow-skinned, gray-eyed one was downright scary—at least as long as he had a shatterblaster in his hands.

But Endicott was a fool. He had, against all odds, set her free on her own planet. She'd never expected such an outcome, not when she was contemplating her own suicide as she aimed the lighter toward the surface of Kolumba.

Strange how things turned out.

She didn't know how her father, Ur-Quolla, would respond to Endicott's proposal, but she had her hopes. And her shame. There was only one way to erase that shame. It was a way she hoped she could show Endicott personally.

Sooner, rather than later.

Her black lips stretched wide as she thought about it. On Kolumba, that was a smile.

CHAPTER ELEVEN

1

Ur-Barrba's ship landed on a broad concrete promenade situated at the rear of her father's vast compound in the center of Ald.

Ur-Barrba disembarked quickly, but paused at the bottom of the ramp, her nostrils wide, her heart at ease for the first time since things had begun to go wrong aboard her vessel so many moons ago.

The city skyline rose around her, towers gleaming in the red sun, forty, fifty stories high. The air was rich with cinnamon, and the deep, thunderous scents of thousands of Kolumbans going about their daily business. Her broad chest slowly rose and fell as she sucked in the sights, sounds, and smells of a home she'd feared she would never see.

The pilot ambled down the ramp behind her. "Was your flight satisfactory, Great One?" he asked obsequiously.

"It was fine," she replied. "But the best part was the end. Right here."

She'd been badly weakened by her captivity, but now, in the heart of her family's power, she could feel strength flowing in her muscles, coursing in her veins. The endless days trussed up in the lighter's dim cargo hold like a *zoart* about to be slaughtered for its leather had dulled her mind. She knew it, and hoped she'd not revealed anything important to the Endicott alien. But she could feel herself growing sharper.

Still, something was wrong with her homecoming. She stood at the bottom of the ramp, waiting for her guards to join her, and saw that nobody had come to meet her. She had sent messages to her father, but had received no reply, just acknowledgments that the messages had reached their destination. And she'd also sent a message to her brother, though she hadn't expected much from him. His illness was growing worse, and even before she'd left Kolumba on her mission to the *Outward Bound*, he'd been spending much of his time in seclusion.

Still—nobody here to meet her *at all*?

It didn't bode well. Perhaps her shame was even greater than she'd supposed. Ur-Quolla was a stern man, harsh and unforgiving. If he thought her sins great enough, he might easily see her presence here— her *living* presence—as a stain on his honor and hers. A stain that could only be eradicated in one way. One *fatal* way.

She sighed. If that was how things were, then that was how they were. But she wouldn't find out standing here, no matter how pleasant it was to luxuriate in all the sensations of home.

She glanced at her guards. "Let's go," she said, and led the way across the plaza toward the rear gates of her family's compound.

Just before she reached the gates an ancient Kolumban tottered out to greet her. He was even older than the farmer Ir-Bakka. His entire pelt was the color of winter ice. One of his eyes was the same milky hue, filmed over with cataracts. He walked—hobbled, rather—with the aid of a pair of thick, sturdy canes grasped in his desiccated hands. Ur-Barrba recognized him immediately, and hurried to him.

"Ur-Molla!" she cried. Carefully, she swept the old man into a gentle hug. His bones felt like dry twigs beneath his dry, rough coat, but the gleam in his one good eye, as he peered up at her, was as sharp and lively as ever.

"It is good to see you again, daughter," he said in a whispery voice. "When you didn't return on schedule, I worried for you." His lips stretched. "But you're too tough to kill, eh? Like your father." He paused, then slowly shook his head. "I wish I could say the same for your brother."

For a moment she misunderstood him, and a bolt of terror sent Ur-Barrba's hearts thrumming like a struck gong. "You don't—" she began. Then she realized that if her fears were true, this man, above all others, could not bring her such devastating news without weeping. "He still lives? My brother still lives?"

Ur-Molla tottered away from her embrace, which had become crushing. "Oh, yes, Ur-Quillam still lives. But not for long, I fear. And much as I'm saddened to say it, that may be for the best."

That the old man should utter such words at all told her that, while her brother might not yet be dead, the news was only slightly better. "He's dying, then?" she asked.

"Daughter, he's been dying for many years. The process has not been an easy one, and it's harder than ever now. I think the only thing that allows him to bear it at all is the knowledge that soon it will come to an end."

"How . . . bad is he?"

The old man shrugged. "The fits hit him harder, and more often. The respites between them are painful; he doesn't recover as quickly as he used to. You can see the path he walks. One day a fit will begin, but it won't stop. Not until it kills him."

"But what about the aliens? The Communer drugs, their treatments? Don't they help?"

Ur-Molla sighed heavily. "They keep him alive. But that is all. They claim that they will find a cure. One day. Soon, they say. In the meantime, thanks to their magic, he lives. But as I told you, that is no mercy. When he is in pain, he begs your father for death. Even on his few good days, when he is as he was when he was a child, doom is plain on his face. He's shadowed by death, daughter, and the shadow grows ever more dark."

"He begs for death, you say?" She found it hard to imagine. Ur-Quillam had always been the strongest one. Stronger even than their father, she secretly believed. For him to beg? It was almost impossible to believe.

"In vain," Ur-Molla said. "He begs in vain. These Communers . . . and their strangers . . ." The old man lowered his head, turned away.

"What about them? They keep him alive!"

"And so they are evil, daughter. If your father loved him as I do, as I love the both of you like my own son and daughter, he would let him go. He would *make* the strangers release him from this life. But your father does not, and so I cannot."

He shook his head. "Forgive me. I've said too much." He planted his canes and, groaning softly, lurched away from her.

She followed, caught him, tugged him to a halt. Took him in her arms again, and lowered her great head to his frail shoulder. "You have been more a father to me than my own father, Ur-Molla. I owe him honor . . . but I owe you love. Will you take me to my brother now?"

Slowly, the old man nodded. He took her hand. Next to her, his shrunken frame looked like that of a child. But it was he who led her through the gates, into the ancient seat of her fathers.

2

—

After what Ur-Molla told her, Ur-Barrba was prepared for almost anything, but even so, her first sight of her brother was a shock.

Ur-Quillam had his own set of rooms in a wing of the main compound. He needed a lot of space for his entourage of doctors and attendants, because he was never left alone. His disease had robbed him of all privacy a long time ago. That alone was enough to make Ur-Barrba, a solitary person by nature, wonder how he was able to stand it.

As she'd expected, Ur-Molla led Ur-Barrba to the largest room of the suite, a broad pavilion open along three sides to the light and the air.

Just before they entered, Ur-Molla motioned Ur-Barrba closer and whispered, "He's better today. The last seizure ended three days ago. But don't strain him. He's still very tired."

"How bad was the last seizure?"

Ur-Molla glanced at her, his gaze hooded and sorrowful. "It lasted for two days. At the worst of it, he broke his left arm."

"What? Why wasn't he restrained, so he couldn't hurt himself?"

"He was," Ur-Molla replied. "His own muscles did the damage. I heard the bone snap myself, during the worst of the fit."

Ur-Barrba shook her head. "All right," she said.

They entered the room together, through a wide pair of double doors. A large bed dominated the center of the room. A pair of attendants stood nearby, talking quietly, but Ur-Barrba noticed they never took their eyes from the figure lying on the bed, propped up against a shoal of soft, fluffy pillows.

Ur-Barrba walked to the bed and looked down. She uttered a soft gasp. Despite Ur-Molla's dire news, she still wasn't prepared for the sight of her brother, and what the disease had done to him.

He was sleeping. A light coverlet lay across him, but he was naked from the waist up. Most of his once-beautiful pelt was gone. His exposed skin looked dry, somehow overheated. His bones showed through everywhere, like a sack of ungainly, twisted sticks. In a race where healthy males outweighed their female counterparts by a third, Ur-Quillam weighed less than half what his sister did.

She closed her eyes for a moment, but the sight of him didn't vanish, just hung in the darkness behind her eyes like a curse. She sighed, bent over him, and kissed his high, wide brow.

He stirred, smiled (as if his dreams were pleasant), and then opened his eyes. "Sister!"

She smiled down on him. "My brother. I missed you."

He slowly extended one arm, and she took his hand in hers. His fingers felt as frail and brittle as Ur-Molla's.

"They told me you were dead."

She seated herself carefully on the edge of the bed, noting the way he winced as her weight shifted the balance of the mattress. "I'm harder to kill then they expected."

He nodded. "I always knew that. You are the strong one of the two of us."

She thought differently, but now was not the time to talk about it. She squeezed his fingers lightly. "How are you feeling?"

"Oh, much better." He glanced at Ur-Molla, who was hovering at the foot of the bed. "The doctors say I should be able to get out of the damned bed in a day or two."

"Perhaps, my son," Ur-Molla said. "Perhaps. If you continue to recover."

"I will," Ur-Quillam replied. "I can usually tell. And the strangers brought a new treatment this last time. I feel stronger."

Ur-Barrba nodded, though she'd heard similar things before. They never worked out.

"Enough about me," Ur-Quillam said. "Tell me about you. Who are these 'they' that didn't kill you? Is it true, sister? That some of the people from the picture machines have actually come to our world?"

Ur-Barrba turned to the old man. "Ur-Molla, forgive me, but I would speak with my brother in private, if you don't mind."

Ur-Molla looked startled, but recovered quickly. "Of course, of course." He hobbled away from the bed, spoke a few words to the nearby attendants, and then all of them retreated to the far side of the room.

It wasn't that Ur-Barrba didn't trust the old man. She did, but she also understood him. He had watched over them, far more than their own father, since the days of their birth. He knew them too well to fully understand that neither of them were children anymore, and because of that, he was capable of relaying things to their father "for their own good."

He meant well, but that sort of love could be dangerous. When she was sure he was out of earshot, she leaned forward and spoke in low tones: "Yes, it is true."

A light gleamed suddenly in her brother's eyes. "Oh, wonderful! Did you bring them to see me? Are they here now?"

For a moment, he reminded her of the boy he'd once been, curious as a *bedah* bird, fearless as a *racth*, and it was all she could do not to weep.

She took a breath and said, "No, I didn't bring them. In fact, it was they who brought *me* back. After they hijacked my ship and killed my entire crew."

The light in Ur-Quillam's eyes changed to something less brilliant, but more sharp. "You'd better tell me everything, then," he said.

She did, leaving nothing out. He was the only person in the universe she would speak to with such unflinching honesty, and once again, her trust was not unrewarded.

When she finished, he closed his eyes briefly, then opened them and stared at her for a long moment. "Do you think it's true, what these humans said? That the drug we sold them was a poison?"

She thought before replying. "Yes, I think so." She paused again. "I've had my suspicions before."

"But why?"

"Because it makes sense, brother. The plant from which the drug is made was given us by the strangers. It is they who charge us with growing and selling it. They've never told us why, though, just that we must. If we want to be paid with the things they bring us." She let her gaze slide down his wasted body. "With the treatments they give to you to keep you alive."

Now it was his turn to fall silent. "Then we are pawns," he said finally. "Tools they use to war against these humans. And now we are caught between two grindstones."

She nodded. He had not disappointed her. It had taken her long hours of thought to reach the conclusion he found in only a few moments. He'd always been a hopeful, trusting youth, but his illness had ground the stars from his eyes, and now, with clearer vision, he saw reality naked. Nor did he fool himself about what he saw. Sometimes all choices were bad. Sometimes there really was no hope.

She started to speak, but he held up a hand. "What about this Jim Endicott? What about the humans? Could they protect us from the strangers?"

She shrugged. "Perhaps. But we don't know. I don't think even Jim Endicott knows. I told you I watched the humans for a long time, while I was captive. They didn't know I could tap into the ship's systems from my room."

"What did you conclude?"

"They're a brutal race," she said. "They'd certainly have no qualms about crushing the Communers. And I'm sure they would feel that a Communer attempt to destroy their colony ships would be cause enough. But can they do it? Your guess is as good as mine. Anyway, that's not the real question, is it?"

"No." He sighed. "The real question is not can they, but would they?" He shook his head. "I did say grindstones, didn't I? Well, if I were a brutal race, and I were in their shoes, the simplest answer would also be the easiest, for them. Destroy us. That would solve the immediate problem, and buy them time to worry about the Communers later, when they knew more about what they were facing."

"Yes, that was my analysis, too. I'd hoped you wouldn't agree."

"You knew better, though, didn't you?"

"Yes. I knew better."

They regarded each other in silence. "You go to see our father next?" She nodded.

"What are you going to say to him?"

"What I said to you. Pretty much," she added.

"He's changed since you saw him last."

"Oh? How so?"

"He's harder. More abrupt. Less forgiving."

"He was never very forgiving."

"And he's less so now. Sometimes I think that what's happening to me . . ." He gestured at his wasted body. "It's been hard for him."

"Hard for you, too."

"I can accept, sister. He can't. He never could."

"I know." She sighed.

They chatted about a few more things, and then she rose to take her leave. He stared up at her. "I'd still like to meet them," he said wistfully. "Talk to this Jim Endicott."

"Maybe you will," she told him. But as she walked away, she knew that neither of them believed that. They both had lived in hard schools. They both knew the difference between hope and reality.

3

Ur-Molla met her outside Ur-Quillam's room. "Are you my escort to my father also?" she asked him. "You're a guide, now, in addition to all your other duties?"

"He asked me to bring you," the old man replied. "He still listens to me, you know."

They walked in silence for a while, down gleaming, polished halls, past bright, intricately woven hangings, the scent of cinnamon drifting in the warm air. As they drew closer to the central compound, the corridors grew more crowded with rapidly striding clerks and more languid functionaries. Everybody had a nod for Ur-Molla, or a cheerful greeting, but Ur-Barrba noticed that those who spoke directly to her did so in noncommittal monosyllables, perhaps an indicator of the temperature awaiting her in her father's chambers?

No point in wondering. She would find out soon enough.

My shame, she thought. She had not even discussed *that* with her brother, though she was certain he was aware of it. After all, he knew her better than anybody, better even than the iron-willed man she was going to meet now did.

Not that it mattered. Her father would no doubt make his decisions with scant consideration for whatever she might think, feel, or do. Once, he'd regarded his children as simply extensions of himself. Now, who knew what he felt about Ur Quillam? But she doubted his estimation of her had changed much. "Take a club and beat them," was one of the ancient mottoes he valued.

She was his club. And she had let him down. She had shamed herself, but in his view, that might mean nothing more than that she had shamed *him*.

"My brother says our father has grown harder, more abrupt. He was always a hard man. But abrupt? What does that mean? Has he grown hotheaded to the point of rashness?"

Ur-Molla shook his head. "He is still your father. Hotheaded will never describe him. Perhaps it would be more accurate to say he's grown more . . . ah . . . *coldly* . . . rash."

"That makes no sense."

"Then wait, and judge for yourself."

A pair of guards flanked the huge carved door that gave entrance into Ur-Quolla's chambers. One of them saw her and, instead of his usual subservience, raised one burly arm. For a moment she thought he would attempt to block her passage, but Ur-Molla gestured and he stepped back. The door swung wide, and she entered a huge room with high, open windows across the back, overlooking the city of Ald. A cinnamon-drenched breeze ruffled through the room, which was empty of people except for one burly figure seated behind a broad table that was heaped with books, papers, and several bundles of dried plant samples.

She squared her shoulders and marched up to face the man sitting behind the desk.

"Father," she said. "I've returned."

He was reading a report of some kind and didn't look up. He let her stand there until he finished. He put down the paper. "Yes, returned," he rumbled. "In shame, after losing your ship and crew to a mob of hair-less midgets. I'm surprised you dare show your face to me. Perhaps you have more courage in the safety of your home than you do on the field of battle. Or is it that you simply fear me less than you do them? If so, you are wrong to do so."

She bowed her head. "Father, I—"

"Silence!"

He let her hang, miserably suspended, for the space of several rasp-ing breaths. "Have you brought me anything but your own wretched, dishonorable self?"

She knew better than to protest this harshness. It was too close to her own feelings, anyway. All she could hope for was that he might give her an opportunity to redeem herself. What shape such an opportunity might take, though, she had no idea.

"The humans are here. Six of them and the lighter from my ship landed close to one of the farming villages. A village of the Ir."

He waved one huge hand irritably. "Didn't I send the ship that brought you back from there? Why are you telling me what I already know? And leaving out that the lighter you landed in—with these *humans*—was one that held you captive. Again."

His disgust was palpable. She wanted to hide her face, to simply crawl away and, in solitude, rip out her own veins. But that would be shameful, too, now. She had sunk so low that even the remedy of honorable suicide was denied to her.

There was only one role left for her to play, as a conduit, as the lowest sort of messenger, as a faceless, mindless relay of the words of Jim Endicott. Let her father hear them, and then he could decide what her role—if any—might be.

Penance? Shame? Death? Only vaguely did she think of the possibility of redemption. Not from this hard, cold, iron-willed man before her.

She told him everything. It took nearly two hours, because she left nothing out, nothing of what she'd seen, thought, or endured, no matter how shameful—and so much of it was shameful—it might be. He listened in stony silence, and when she was done, he gestured at a pillow-piled carved wooden chair next to his desk.

"Sit," he said gruffly.

That was when she began to hope. Not much, but a little.

As he told her what she would have to do now, she began to hope a little more. This was so unexpected that she hardly noticed when three of the strangers, so like her and yet so unlike, their eyes like dry, dusty stones, entered the room.

After they had spoken, in their harsh, metallic voices, her hope grew even stronger. Vengeance would obviously not be hers, but it would be vengeance. It was a cold dish, but it would fill her.

Jim Endicott wouldn't like the taste of it, though. That was the best thing; one poisonous taste of it would pay for all.

"When do I leave?" she asked when everything had been decided.

"Soon," Ur-Quolla replied, "but not right away. Let them relax, let them lose their wariness. No one can stay at high alert forever. Especially when nothing appears to happen. Are you sure they keep a watch on the hyperwave transmitter?"

"Yes, I watched carefully. It is their one true weapon against us."

"We'll see about that," he rumbled.

The strangers didn't say anything, but that was fine. They didn't have to.

As she ran the plan through her mind one more time, Ur-Barrba watched her father's face. It was stony as the mountains she'd just departed. She knew that if he were asked, he would say he was rejecting Endicott's offer in order to protect his people from the wrath of the strangers and their Communer masters. But she knew the truth. He protected only one. His son, who lived because the Communers brought the medicines that kept him alive.

Well, that was all right. If Endicott triumphed, Ur-Quillam would die. That was enough for her.

She hoped that, in the end, her honor would be restored enough that her father would grant *her* the privilege of tearing Jim Endicott's head from his shoulders, and washing her fur in his blood.

4

There was a heavy fog about the ship, like a gathering of blood-tinged ghosts. Nikki stood in the open port, his fingers idly scratching his scalp through his tangled hair. This was boring duty. Nothing ever happened, and now with the prisoner gone, they'd called Bobby down to the village with the rest of them. That left him with his own company, and since Nikki was naturally outgoing and gregarious, this was something of a trial.

But it was important. He knew that. Back in the cargo hold, the hyperwave transmitter was always fully warmed up, ready to go, a long, encoded message prepared and ready to send to Earth at the touch of a single key.

That was the real reason he was there, Nikki knew. Jim had explained it to him. If worse came to worst, if he—or the rest of them— was attacked, he was to flip that key and send the message. The message contained everything the captain knew about the Communers and the Kolumbans, and what they were trying to do to the human colony ships. The captain called the message a "death warrant" for the entire Kolumban planet. Nikki wasn't entirely certain of the technical meaning of that phrase—since he'd left the *Outward Bound*, he'd started reading ancient Terran history, and knew that some phrases had deeper meanings than were first apparent, but the basic meaning was plain enough. Twenty feet away from where he now stood, scratching and staring out at the morning, was a key that was basically a trigger on an enormous gun. If he pulled the trigger, the gun—which was the massed military might of the ConFed fleets—would fire, and destroy the planet whose cinnamon tang filled his nose right now.

It seemed like a big responsibility, but he was glad Jim had given it to him. He would carry out his duty, if it became necessary. So far, though, there had been no reason to do so. Nothing happened, nothing at all, except for the occasional wandering Kolumban farmer passing by, pausing a moment or two to stare.

He wore a translator on a chain around his neck, but none of the farmers ever tried to speak to him, though he hailed them cheerfully enough whenever they came close. Usually the sound of his voice alone was enough to send them scuttling off the rocky scarp, vanishing back into the forest.

Boring duty, indeed.

He yawned and gave some thought—though not too much—to the notion of breakfast. Sam—bless her warm heart!—while not recovered fully from her bout with the Pleb Psychosis, was well enough to think about what even a nobody like Nikki was eating, and she'd walked up here with some dried strips of something that didn't taste half bad. She said it was a recipe she'd gotten from some of the village women, modified to make it more palatable to humans. It still smelled like cinnamon-flavored shoe leather, and chewed about as easily, but at least he didn't feel like puking it up after he was done eating.

He heard the Kolumban before he saw her. Branches rattled, then snapped off to his left. He turned in that direction, automatically reaching for the pistol Kerry had left with him. A moment later the huge figure lurched from the underbrush and staggered toward him. He thought it was female; it was smaller than the males he'd seen.

Hideous groans issued from her distended mouth. She clutched wildly at her chest, and as she grew closer, he saw why: her pelt was matted with blood, her great hands dripping with it.

"What—wait!" he cried, and heard his translator chuckle tinnily in response.

The Kolumban didn't seem to hear, just kept on coming, until about ten feet away from the hatch, she gurgled softly—blood spurted from her mouth and hung in long, viscous strings from her chin—and collapsed with a heavy thud to the ground.

"Oh my *Jesus*," Nikki breathed, ramming his pistol back into his belt.

He looked around but saw no help. He took a deep breath and rushed toward the writhing alien, and skidded to a halt a step away. But he quickly saw there was nothing to fear. The woman was subsiding, her groans trailing off into a harsh, liquid death rattle as her fists beat a weak tattoo against the stone on which she lay before returning to the terrible wound in her chest.

He moved to her, fell to his knees, tried to tug her hands away from her body, thinking that maybe he could help, maybe he could do *something* . . .

When her eyes shot open he found himself looking down into molten pools of yellow rage. Before he could move, those bloody fingers found his neck.

He felt a sudden wrenching *yank*, and then he was spinning high into the air. He felt light, as if he were floating through the fog without his body. Around his neck burned a necklace of ice (as if an icy wind caressed him just below his Adam's apple), and below that, nothing.

5

"Come on, one more snort," Jim said.

The interior of their cottage was dim in the foggy morning light. The compound was just beginning to stir—he could hear Ir-Bakka's extended family moving about, the women calling softly to one another.

He raised Sam's head a bit and pressed a fingertip closer to her nostrils. She was half asleep, but it was time for her dose. On the fingertip a smear of white, crystalline powder remained.

"Burns . . ." she said muzzily.

"Go on, snort it down like a good girl," he urged. They had discovered it wasn't necessary to use the autodoc to administer the antipsychotic drug. It was absorbed readily through the nasal membranes, a much easier method of administration than hooking up the machine.

"Not a good girl," Sam said, grinning. She inhaled sharply, and the last of the powder vanished from Jim's finger.

"Hug me," Sam said, reaching for him.

"Huh. Don't start something you can't finish," Jim said.

Her lips shaped a soft kiss. "I can finish anything you want to start," she murmured.

He pulled her to him, half wrapped in blankets, kissed the vein throbbing in her neck . . .

The sudden ratcheting bark of a shatterblaster just beyond the front door blasted them apart. Jim came to his feet, wearing only his underpants and socks, his .75 in his hand.

"That's Bobby!"

"Damn straight," Kerry said, running past him. Jim grabbed his pants, tugged them on, then his boots. He'd learned about boots in his military training vireos. "Never go to a firefight barefoot," he recalled an old, grizzled sergeant in the space marines growling over and over.

"Stay here," he snapped at Sam, who was fumbling into her own clothes.

"Like hell," she snapped back, color flaring in her cheeks. But the distinctive, focused inferno-burp of the blaster outside drowned out his reply as he rushed through the door.

Outside, the morning was full of drifting, fog-shrouded shadows, all moving with the speed of panic. Something *large* shot by overhead, then dropped like a stone somewhere beyond the village.

The farm folks were running for their lives. As Jim skidded up next to Bobby, he saw that not all the fog was fog: some of the growing murk was smoke, acrid and bitter. Off to the west he saw a dull, flickering glow: burning cottages.

And now new shapes began to drop from the sky, smaller than the dark ship that had just landed. These forms hit the ground rolling and came up firing beam weapons blazing with coherent energies that gouged and seared whatever they touched.

Elwood came streaking around the corner of their cottage, roared up to Bobby, and grabbed the shatterblaster from him just as Bobby screamed, threw up his hands, and fell over, his face a sudden mush of blood and bone. A moment later Elwood began to blast the incoming storm troopers while they were still falling from the sky. Jim saw two figures explode in flames as the shatterblaster's bolts pulled them apart.

Kerry was standing as calmly as if he were shooting ducks, firing steadily with his pistol. His less-powerful weapon wasn't doing as much damage, but Jim saw that the enemy was keeping their heads down, and the plaza on which their cottage fronted was still empty of attackers.

Kerry turned, saw Jim, and shouted, "We got to get back to the ship. Ur-Barrba screwed us over."

"She screwed herself over, too. Damn it! Nikki's probably already sent the message to Terra. Kolumba's doomed. Doesn't she realize what she's done?"

Kerry ducked as an enemy bolt sizzled over his head, then snapped off a pair of quick shots in the direction from which it had come.

"They've got us located! If we don't get out of here in the next couple of minutes, we're gonna be pinned down!"

"All right, let's get moving!"

Jim grabbed Sam's hand and yanked her toward the fringe of nearby woods. Elwood and Kerry backed in the same direction, still providing covering fire. Suddenly a squad of attackers darted between a pair of distant huts. A shape like a small ball arced from them toward Jim. He pulled Sam down as the ball landed with a soft thud a few feet away.

No explosion. Nothing happened. Jim peered at the ball. "Oh my God!"

It was Nikki's head, eyes staring blankly back at him.

"Let's go!" he cried, scrambling to his feet. Tears of rage streaked his cheeks. He wanted to kill all of them, the murdering, treacherous bastards. The thought of Terra popping Kolumba's sun no longer bothered him. And that was exactly what would happen, if Nikki had gotten off his message.

But Nikki's severed head told a different story. There would be no message. Not unless they were able to fight their way back to the lighter and send it themselves.

"Let's go, let's go," Jim yelled. A moment later they were all under the canopy of the trees, running for their lives through drifts of morning fog.

"I only see four of them," Jim whispered.

"Let's wait a couple of minutes, see if any more are inside," Kerry replied.

They were crouched behind a screen of low brush at the edge of the rocky outcropping on which the lighter rested. Muffled by the intervening forest, they could still hear the sounds of devastation continuing in the village; thin, wavering screams, the dull crump of explosions, the scratchy hiss of energy weapons.

But it was quiet around the ship. A pair of Kolumbans in battle harness, carrying bulky energy weapons, flanked the open hatch. Another duo, similarly garbed, worked the perimeter of the ship, keeping an eye on the forest beyond.

About halfway between their own position and the ship was a formless bundle. At first glance, it looked like a pile of discarded rags smeared with red paint. Only when Jim looked more closely did he realize it was what was left of Nikki's body.

He tapped Kerry on the shoulder and pointed silently. Kerry nodded. "They must have got to him outside," he whispered. "See all the blood? But there's no trail back to the ship, which there would have been if they'd dragged his body out."

"Maybe they got him inside after he sent the message, then took him outside to kill him."

Kerry glanced at him. "You want to bet everything on that?"

Jim shook his head.

"So we have to get inside the lighter," Kerry added.

"Yeah. If they haven't already disabled the hyperwave transmitter," Jim said gloomily.

"It's the only chance we've got."

But some of Jim's heat had cooled, even though the memory of Nikki's brutal death was fresh in his mind—doubly so, because of the pathetically torn corpse right in front of his eyes.

But he remembered old Ir-Bakka's kindness, his love and dreams for his people, and the way the Communers had so terribly misled and exploited them. Were Ir-Bakka and his people to blame for what the Communers, and their native henchmen, the Ur, had done to the Terran colony ships? And not only them, but all the other Kolumban "little people," the farmers and craftsmen and small traders, the artists, singers, sculptors, composers who would also be destroyed if Terra reacted to his warning as he suspected it would?

An exploding sun doesn't discriminate in who it kills. Kolumba itself, and everything on it, would vanish. Not just the guilty, but the vastly greater number of innocent as well.

Not to mention the possibility of a cure for the Pleb Psychosis, and the billions of *human* lives that might rescue. Would Terra respond so violently to his message?

Not right away, perhaps. It would only be a single message. Surely the ConFed fleet would send a ship to investigate, perhaps even a squadron. But they would find what he said they would; an agrarian, pastoral world full of incredibly talented farmers—but infested by another group of technologically advanced aliens. Would the Communers fight if the ConFed discovered them? He didn't know the answer to *that*, either. But unless the Communers themselves were vastly more powerful than he guessed, they would be unable to defend a sitting duck like a planet—and by even trying, they would almost certainly guarantee the planet's destruction.

Then an even worse thought struck him. Everything about the Communers was hidden, secretive, even the way they'd attacked the human colony ships. And they never showed their true faces on Kolumba, preferring to hide behind the strangers, cyborged or cloned masks that hid their true existence. In fact, the Communers seemed almost pathologically opposed to revealing their true selves. Might not they themselves destroy Kolumba to erase any traces that could lead to knowledge about them?

So many possibilities, so many outcomes, so much potential evil. And all of it now his responsibility.

Abruptly he realized just how mad he'd been, to think that he and a handful of scruffy kids could solve a problem of the scope and complexity that the Kolumbans and the Communers represented.

I wanted to be a hero, he thought. *But I ended up a fool.* And it wasn't just him. Right there in front of his eyes was the mutilated corpse of one of his victims. And there were others—maybe including everybody aboard the *Outward Bound*, with its ominous, suspicious silence.

And now here he was, crouched behind some bushes, trying to make a decision that correctly weighed the lives of an entire *planet*.

This wasn't just *hubris*. It was insanity, and he had caused it with his own stupid, overweening pride.

Enough!

Terra had to know. It was beyond his own power now. If it had *ever* been within the grasp of a sixteen-year-old kid with delusions of competence.

Suddenly the face of his father filled his mind, and he thought, with a dismay so total it shattered him, *I destroy everything I touch.*

And maybe I will destroy this, too. But if I do, at least it will be somebody else pulling the trigger. Not me. Not anymore.

He took a deep breath. "Kerry, you and me. Work your way around the woods to the other side. We'll take them from different directions. Elwood, you provide covering fire with your blaster. Try to take down the two in front first thing. Kerry and I will get the others. Then we all head for the hatch. If there's nobody on board, I'll take us up as quick as I can while you send the message, Kerry."

For once, nobody argued with his plan. For once, everybody seemed perfectly happy to let him make the decisions.

How could they be so stupid, with the evidence of his own stupidity so plain everywhere they looked?

Maybe that's part of being a captain, too. Just making a decision, any decision, as long as you do something.

Still, it seemed an idiotic way to run a spaceship.

"Get going," he whispered to Kerry. "Three minutes."

They checked their watches and took off.

Elwood lifted the shatterblaster to his shoulder and aimed at the two motionless strangers guarding the lighter's hatch. He kept an eye on his watch, soundlessly counting down the seconds. Sam rummaged in the dirt, found a pair of stones, lifted them, saw the digits clicking slowly on Elwood's watch.

Three . . . two . . . one . . .

Elwood stood up.

Zero!

Jim rose from the brush at the rear of the lighter and saw Kerry rising opposite him. They had the two stranger guards sandwiched between them.

Jim pulled the trigger on his S&R .75, wincing as the shattering, bell-like tone of the rocket slug hammered his ears. The nearest stranger guard vanished in a misty cloud of blood. Kerry's ripper flashed, and the other guard staggered, then collapsed.

Both boys turned and rushed toward the front of the lighter as the hell-belch of the shatterblaster filled the rocky clearing.

They arrived in time to see Elwood, the blaster balanced against his right hip, finish cutting the second of the two front guards in half.

Everybody started running for the hatch, Jim sweeping the snout of his .75 back and forth across the dark opening. Nothing appeared there, and for a fleeting instant, Jim allowed himself to hope.

He was still ten feet away when a huge, egg-shaped craft dropped from the sky so quickly it was like a magic trick. The bottom of the craft split open, and a rain of strangers hatched from the egg.

"It's a trap! Run!" Kerry cried, but there was no place to run. Jim planted his feet and blasted the troopers one by one, until his magazine ran out. He clicked the trigger twice, uselessly, then flung himself toward the lighter's still-open hatch.

Off to his right and closing fast, Elwood scrambled toward him, swinging the shatterblaster back and forth like a man wielding a hose. Strangers fell before him like wheat before a scythe, and for one instant, Jim thought he might make it.

"Elwood!" he screamed.

A bolt of lightning reached down from the sky and touched the tall, skinny boy. The shatterblaster exploded in his hands. He danced in a burning nimbus for what seemed an eternity, as Jim watched pieces of burning flesh fly away from his blackening body.

"Noooo!"

A familiar, grinning, fang-filled face rose before him.

"Jim Endicott!" Ur-Barrba rumbled.

He saw a fist the size of a ham rushing toward his face. He felt a crushing impact.

Then he didn't feel anything at all.

CHAPTER TWELVE

1

——

Somewhere during the long passage up from darkness to light, Jim traversed the hidden land of his dreams. It was a jumbled, terrifying place, full of distant, echoing sounds, and sudden flashing scraps of vision. He saw a man in a dark, hooded robe striding across an endless field of stars. The man turned, began to pull aside his hood, but before Jim could see his face (*No! Don't let me see!*), both man and stars vanished. He saw Elwood run toward him, screaming, and then he saw Elwood explode—again, and again, and again. He saw black-gummed fangs opening wider, wider, and smelled hot, rotten cinnamon blasting against his face.

Somebody was talking nearby, but he couldn't make out the words; they were a continuous hushed buzz that almost meant something, but not quite. Something cool drifted across his forehead.

He blinked, and stared up into Sam's face, through the screen of her fingers on his forehead.

She blinked back, startled. "Oh, good. You're awake."

He wasn't sure about that. "I am?"

"You took a couple of knocks. Good thing your skull is as thick as it is." She smiled.

He closed his eyes. The dreams had vanished, but the nightmares remained. Except they weren't nightmares, they were memories. They were real.

"Elwood . . ." he murmured.

"He's dead," Kerry's voice said.

Jim's eyes popped open. Kerry's features swam blurrily above Sam's shoulder. "Thank God . . ." Jim said.

"What? That I'm not dead? Or that you aren't? Or that Elwood *is*?" Kerry shrugged. "I can't see that it makes a hell of a lot of difference. It's only a matter of time till we all join him. If anything, I think he got the easy way out."

"What happened?"

"You saw most of it, before Ur-Barrba took you down. They dropped me a few seconds later, and they caught Sam trying to run away through the woods. Then they brought us here."

Jim winced. He hadn't just let himself down, he'd let everybody down. And they'd paid a far greater price than he.

Kerry's voice was flat, dead. He seemed neither angry nor sad. He reported his grim news with all the emotion of an accountant relaying sums.

"How come we're still alive?" Jim asked him.

" 'Cause they didn't kill us," Kerry said.

Jim sighed.

"Actually, I think our old pal Ur-Barrba will be along to give you her reasons face-to-face. She said she was looking forward to it. But I guess there's no reason to make it a big secret, since she's already gloated to us about it. We're gonna be guinea pigs."

"Huh?"

"That's right," Sam said. "The Communers get us. For their experiments. Evidently they've got some hot new ideas about how to kill humans, but they used up all their old stock, so we get to be the new stock."

"Ur-Barrba promised us it would be a long and painful death. She seemed to enjoy that part. Repeated herself a couple of times." Kerry paused. "I wish we'd killed that bitch when we had a chance."

"Just the three of us? That won't make for much of an experiment."

"Oh, that's right," Kerry said. For the first time, emotion colored his tone, sarcastic and bitter. "You've been resting. You don't know. The Communers captured the *Endeavor*, too. With all hands on board. They'll have *plenty* of meat for their manglers."

"Jesus, she told you that?"

"With whatever passes for great glee among Kolumbans, I guess, though it didn't come through the translator very well. But she seemed happy enough."

Jim hitched himself up, propped his back against the cell wall. The cell wasn't large: a cube about ten feet on a side, high-ceilinged, with a blank steel door in the front. No windows, though he could feel the soft pressure of the ventilation system against his face.

Movement awakened jagged shards of pain inside his muscles. He groaned softly.

"Be careful," Sam said, trying to help him get settled. "There's something wrong with your left arm. The shoulder socket is all swollen."

Jim tried that arm. It felt as if somebody had filled the joint with broken glass.

"I think Ur-Barrba's original intention was to rip that arm from the socket and beat you to death with it," Kerry said helpfully.

"You seem awfully calm about this," Jim told him. He glanced about the cell. "Where are we, anyway?"

"Take a deep breath, see if you can figure it out."

"Huh?" But Kerry only stared at him, so Jim inhaled deeply. The conditioned air smelled faintly bitter, with a metallic tang that was somehow familiar. It made him think of . . . what? He rummaged in his memories and for some reason saw an ant farm he'd had when he was a little kid.

"Formic acid," he blurted. "Ants."

"What don't you smell?"

Jim sniffed again. "Uh . . . cinnamon?"

"You got it, Captain. No dog-fracking cinnamon."

He worked his mind around the knot of the problem, finally unraveled it. "Fully conditioned air, separate from the Kolumban atmosphere. Different smells." He paused, horrified at his own deductions. "Are we on a Commuuner ship?"

Kerry shook his head. "Good deduction, Sherlock, but not quite. We're in the strangers' compound in Ald. Still down on the Kolumban surface, but unless I miss my guess, not for long. The test tubes await!" He paused. "Though I doubt they'll use a lot of test tubes. Needles full of poison, more likely."

Kerry suddenly raised one hand. "Shut up! Somebody's coming."

Jim at first felt, rather than heard, the thud of heavy boots beyond the cell door, but a moment later, with a harsh scrape, the door slid open, and Ur-Barrba tramped inside, immediately followed by another Kolumban, even larger than she. This one carried a weapon Jim recognized, if not by specific type, at least by function: a stun club. The second Kolumban took up a stance by the door, massive arms folded across his chest, stun club dangling like a toothpick from fingers the size of bananas. He stared at them blankly with eyes the color and expression of dust-caked stones.

Jim's flesh crawled. The thing might *look* like a Kolumban, but he realized he was getting his first up-close-and-personal look at a stranger, one of the Communers' cloned golems.

If it was a clone at all. This close, he felt no sense of life emanating from the thing, only a sort of mechanical vacuum, cold and soulless.

"How does it feel, Jim Endicott?" Ur-Barrba rumbled. Her black lips were stretched in a wide, tight grin, no fangs showing.

"My arm, you mean?" He tried to lift his left arm, winced, and gave up the effort.

Ur-Barrba's happy expression vanished, and her fangs suddenly appeared. She loomed over him, glaring down. "Being my prisoner." She made a deep hacking sound the translator didn't—or couldn't— handle. "You should have killed me when you had the chance."

"Yeah," Jim said. "We were just talking about that."

Ur-Barrba snorted. "Perhaps you are wondering why you are still alive, Jim Endicott?"

Jim peered up at her. "The thought had crossed my mind. I suppose you like the idea of me ending up in some Communer lab."

"The idea is appealing, but that's not the reason why. I had promised myself I would personally rip your head from your shoulders, but I stayed my hand." She paused, waiting.

"Okay," Jim said, "I'll bite, pardon the pun. Why *didn't* you turn me into discrete body parts? Somehow, I bet it wasn't because of your warm and forgiving nature."

"You think you joke with me, but you speak more truth than you know. It is because of love alone that you are alive to talk to me now."

"You love me?" Jim said blankly.

"I love my brother," Ur-Barrba replied. "And for some reason known only to him, he wishes to speak with you. Since he couldn't do that if you were dead, I altered my plans for you. Perhaps after he is finished, I might revert to my original intentions."

"That's an incentive," Jim said.

"Incentive enough," Ur-Barrba replied. "Be polite to my brother. Answer his questions, do as he asks. Who knows? You may find him, unlike me, to be what you would call a good person. Make no such mistake about me, though. By your standards, I'm not good. Though in your position, your standards don't make much difference to anybody, even to yourself."

A soft scuffling sound filled the hall beyond the cell doorway. Jim saw several Kolumbans milling around. Ur-Barrba turned, then moved away from the door to allow another figure inside.

Jim stared. This was the strangest native he'd seen yet. If this was Ur-Barrba's brother, there was very little familial resemblance. The new visitor was immensely tall, but built like a rickety pile of matchsticks. Much of his pelt was gone, and the exposed skin looked dry and raw at the same time. He edged past Ur-Barrba and stared at them silently.

"This is my brother, Ur-Quillam," Ur-Barrba said softly. "Remember what I said."

She nodded curtly, stepped out into the hall, and closed the door behind her. The stranger guard, however, didn't budge. If anything, he looked even more alert, although his strange, blank gaze didn't change at all. The sensation of depthless chill that radiated from him seemed to somehow grow stronger, though.

"Are you Jim Endicott?" the new Kolumban said. He, too, wore a translator around his neck, but his natural voice was low, soft, diffident, totally unlike the stentorian tones of his sister.

Jim pushed himself further up the wall, so he didn't have to crane his rapidly stiffening neck to see the Kolumban's drawn, emaciated features. Sam helped him, then settled her head on his shoulder.

"Yes, that's me. And you are Ur-Barrba's brother?"

"Yes. My name is Ur-Quillam."

For a moment they stared at each other in silence. Finally Jim swallowed and said, "Well, you've got a good look at us. Was there anything else you wanted?"

Slowly, Ur-Quillam lowered himself to his haunches. He moved carefully, gingerly, as if even this small effort cost him a great deal.

I think he's dying, Jim thought suddenly. *And well along the way, too.*

"Are you okay?" he asked.

"No, I'm not. But that's no concern for you. I'm not even sure it's a concern for me any longer."

"Your sister said you wanted to talk to me. So I guess I owe my life to you, at least for a while." He shrugged. "What do you want to talk about?"

Ur-Quillam leaned forward, and now Jim noticed the way his eyes sparkled as they bored intently into his own. "Everything," Ur-Quillam said.

"Everything?"

"You, your world, your friends, your life, everything."

"That could take quite a while," Jim said, visions of the *Tales of 1001 Nights* rearing hopefully at the back of his mind.

Ur-Quillam nodded. "I'm not going anywhere," he said.

2

Ur-Quillam was as good as his word. He *didn't* go anywhere. In fact, after a while he lowered himself further and sat cross-legged on the floor, facing them like a schoolteacher before a circle of pupils. He listened, and he talked. His brilliant, golden gaze captured each of them in turn: when he listened, he *listened*, somehow with his whole body, his entire *soul*. Nobody had ever listened to Jim Endicott that way, and he found it oddly compelling. He found himself speaking at length, sometimes ridiculous length. And when Ur-Quillam spoke, he tried to listen as intently as the alien did to him.

And over the space of hours, they became friends. No, different from friends, Jim thought. Almost like . . . brothers. He had always known the phrase "a kindred spirit," but he'd never actually met anybody who summoned up the meaning of that phrase. Yet, somehow, in this wasted, freakish alien he'd never met before, he found a spirit he recognized, respected, even, in some strange way, loved.

It was one of the weirdest experiences of his life. They talked about Jim and his past, growing up on a recent Terran colony planet, and they talked about Terra itself. About the ConFed, and the colonization efforts, the brute size of the colony world ships, and what the drugs Ur-Quillam's sister had sold on the *Outward Bound* had done.

Nor was Ur-Quillam silent. He talked as well, about his own world, about his people, about the way things had once been and the way they were now, and how he felt about all that. He spoke of his illness and his despair, not for himself, but for his people, whom he still hoped to help. And as Jim listened, he changed his mind about a few things. He realized that when he'd thought about them becoming friends, even soul mates, he'd been wrong. Those sorts of bonds would never hold between them; the iron laws of heredity, of alien genetics, would not allow that kind of identity. But there was an even closer bond, one that in some circumstances could be stronger than any of them: the weld of shared experience.

This resonance became most compelling when Ur-Quillam talked of his father. Not much, and not often, because it was obvious that the subject was painful for him. But he didn't need to say much. For every word he spoke, Jim heard a story that tore and gouged at him just as deeply as it did at Ur-Quillam.

He heard tales of love and rejection, of fear and effort, of a continual striving to please, to *live up to*, of small success and great failure. And in his own replies he spoke of similar things in a similar way, a sort of emotional shorthand that, cryptic though it was, still somehow managed to span the vast gulf of heritage and inheritance and genetics and nature and nurture that lay between the two of them. He didn't know how it might be with other alien races, but evidently humans and Kolumbans both had fathers and sons, and both suffered the eternal loving struggle that fathers and sons waged with each other.

Kerry and Sam said very little, as if sensing that whatever hope they still had lay in the bonding that was happening between the Kolumban and their captain. Still, the hours passed, and suddenly, though Ur-Quillam was indeed alien, and Jim couldn't be sure he was interpreting the cues correctly, he got the idea that Ur-Quillam was a lot sicker than he looked. That somehow this conversation itself was draining him, weakening him beyond some critical point.

He reached forward and touched the back of Ur-Quillam's great, bony hand. "We've been talking a long time. Would you like to take a break?"

"No, I'm all right. We don't have a lot of time. My sister and my father give me a lot of leeway, but they are agreed: the Communers want you, and they will have you. That they let me talk to you at all is a sign of how much they are willing to allow me, but their patience won't last forever."

So much for the 1001 Nights, Jim thought.

"I will try . . ." Ur-Quillam said softly. "I'll try . . ." He began to sway.

Jim reached for his hand again, suddenly frightened, but the hand twitched away, as if jerked at the end of some spastic string.

"What's wrong with him?" Kerry blurted, leaning forward.

"I don't—"

Ur-Quillam's jaw yawned wide, exposing his rigid tongue. He twitched again, and let out a long, agonized groan.

"No . . ." he managed.

Then his golden eyes rolled back into his skull. His frail, stringy body went completely stiff, but only for a moment. Then, like a box full of tightly coiled springs suddenly dumped on the floor, he began to thrash wildly about. Spit flew from his lips in long, ropy strings. His heels drummed on the steel floor of the cell, and his clenched fists slammed wildly against the walls. Blood spurted suddenly from his knuckles.

"Oh God, oh God," Sam moaned, as Jim threw himself across Ur-Quillam's bucking, heaving frame. *"What's the matter with him?"* she shrieked.

He's having a fit, just like you, Jim thought, too busy to reply, and that was when he made the connection that changed everything.

"Help me!" he snapped at Kerry. Kerry waded in, tried to grab Ur-Quillam's flailing arms. Even the stranger had moved from his silent position near the door. But Ur-Quillam's seizure was too much for any of them to handle. Though emaciated, he still had a portion of the natural Kolumban strength, only jumped up by a factor of ten. One glancing blow knocked Kerry away, and a whipping, convulsive scissoring of legs toppled the stranger. Jim tried to hang on one-handed as he fumbled in the pocket of his pants with the other.

His fingertips brushed against the slick smoothness of plastic, and then he managed to finger out the glassine envelope full of white crystalline powder. But no sooner did he have the packet out of his pocket than Ur-Quillam's seizure escalated to new heights of frenzy. Jim felt himself fly through the air, and then his head smacked hard into the wall. He collapsed, stunned, shaking his head, everything before him a screaming, howling blur of motion.

But he still held the envelope in his hand. The blow to his skull had nauseated and disoriented him, but somehow his shaking fingers found the seal of the packet and ripped it open. Still blinking hard, trying to see, Jim staggered away from the wall and knee-walked toward the scrambled tangle in the center of the cell.

"Here," he croaked, blindly extending the packet. "Try this—"

But before he could finish, Ur-Quillam shuddered and starfished, and one of his knobby, bony heels caught Jim square in the forehead and sent him flying again. The packet slipped from his fingers. He grabbed for it, but only caught enough to send it winging into the air, turning over and over, spraying out a fine cloud of white dust.

"Jim, you're bleeding!" Sam cried, reaching for him. He tried to push her away, but she held on. "It's okay," she said over and over.

Then other, stronger hands were on him, and Kerry's voice husked roughly in his ear.

"Hang in there, Jim. It's cool. It's over. Just cool off, hang on."

The brief, frenzied wrestling match had taken its toll, reawakening all of Jim's earlier cuts, scrapes, and sprains. His entire body, inside and out, felt like a single, throbbing bruise. His chest burned from the effort of breathing, let alone trying to talk, but eventually he managed to get enough air into his lungs to gasp out a few words.

"Let me go."

"You okay?"

"Ur-Quillam!" he barked.

"Hey, okay. Here you go." Kerry pushed him into a sitting position. He blinked a cascade of flashing white pinpoints out of his vision. A few feet away, Ur-Quillam's form sprawled in limp silence. Just beyond him, like a low cliff of quivering fur, the stranger guard was convulsing instead. But there was a different quality to the guard's twitches and shudders. They were somehow regular, the sort of dying motion a mechanical clock might make, running down. And even as he watched, the stranger gave a final jerking shiver and then stopped moving entirely. Jim stared at the guard's eyes. Before, they'd been like muddy stones. Now they were a bright, bloody red, as if the surfaces were painted with crimson nail polish.

For several moments, the only sound in the cell was a chorus of exhausted breathing.

"Jesus," Kerry whispered finally. "Would somebody tell me what the frack just happened?"

Jim wasn't sure. He wasn't sure at all. But he had a suspicion.

Slowly, he disentangled himself from their grasp, then crawled on hands and knees to Ur-Quillam's side. The alien seemed to be resting peacefully. He looked asleep, nothing more, his muscles relaxed, big fingers slightly curled. The stranger was a different story. His muscular frame was stiff as a board, and Jim had the vague idea that wouldn't change until whatever passed for death and disintegration inside that strange body had progressed a good bit further in its work.

Maybe if we bury the motherfracker for a couple of years . . . he thought, a spring of dark, wild humor bubbling crazily in his mind.

He pried the stun club from the stranger's death grip and tossed it to Kerry, then methodically searched the pouches and flapped pockets attached to the guard's harness. Standard prison guard practice seemed to mitigate against him finding what he sought, but then, as he lifted a dark blue plastic card from one of the pouches, he realized he had no idea what standard Communer procedures were. Evidently, if his luck was in, the Communers didn't consider it dangerous to send a guard into a locked cell with the key that opened the cell.

"Is that. . . ?" Kerry asked as he stood and hefted the stun club experimentally.

"We'll see," Jim said. He moved to the door, examined the region around the frame, and finally located an inset of metal that seemed slightly different from the surrounding steel. He pressed the card against the inset and held his breath.

The cell door slid open.

Cautiously, Jim stuck his head out and peered up and down the corridor. On either side of the cell lay two more crumpled, stiffening forms. About thirty feet down the corridor, a clump of three more.

Ur-Barrba was nowhere in sight. In fact, there was nothing in sight but dead strangers. Kerry moved up beside him, looked out, then stepped into the hall.

"I repeat," he said softly, gesturing with the stun club. "What the frack just happened?"

Jim said, "Wait a minute," and turned back to the cell. He found his plastic envelope on the floor, partly covered by one of Ur-Quillam's massive, stringy thighs. He folded it closed and stuck it back in his pocket, then looked up to see Sam staring at him.

"Did that powder . . . ?"

"Yep, I think so," Jim told her.

"But it's for the Pleb Psychosis."

Jim shook his head. "No, we don't know what it's for. We know it seems to cure the Pleb Psychosis. Evidently it also cures whatever was wrong with Ur-Quillam."

Sam stared at him some more, then shook her head slowly. "And . . . him?" She pointed at the stranger.

Once again that wild wellspring of crazed humor hissed inside his brain. "Well, it looks as if it *kills* them." He laughed softly, if a bit. "So what do you think about *that*?"

3

The stranger compound was very large—chamber after chamber filled with slumped bodies that had been engaged in indecipherable tasks before death interrupted them. As the three of them crept like anxious mice down long, curving corridors (they're like hives, Jim thought uneasily) they saw no living things other than themselves.

"Where are the Kolumbans?" Sam wondered.

"Maybe there aren't any. Somehow I doubt that the Communers give Kolumbans—even higher-ups like Ur-Barrba—free run of their private quarters."

"She said she'd be coming back," Kerry noted.

"Not till Ur-Quillam is finished. And he'll have to send a message out. But there's nobody here to send that message for him."

"You mean we've got this place to ourselves?"

"Looks like it. At least for a while," Jim said.

They came to the end of the long, curving corridor they'd been traversing and found themselves in a high anteroom. This debouched into a huge circular control center. There were hundreds of individual workstations, most of them occupied by dead strangers. Near the center, on a broad, raised platform, was another circle of stations, but only one—the largest—was occupied. Jim led them quickly to it.

"If I were designing this thing, here would be the main access ports to their computers," Jim said. "Since I didn't design it, this might be the control center for their toilet facilities." He shrugged. "We'll find out."

Kerry helped him push the deceased operator out of his seat, and Jim settled into the oversized chair. He ran his fingertips experimentally across one of the touchpads in front of him. Immediately three holographic screens sprang out of nowhere, filled with indecipherable graphics and symbols. Jim cracked his knuckles, sighed, and leaned back.

"Kerry, why don't you scout around and see if you can find something with a little more oomph than that stun club. A couple of those focused beam blasters would be nice. This might take a while."

"What are you trying to do?"

"I'm not sure," Jim said. "But I'll know it when I see it."

Kerry nodded and turned to go. "Hey, wait," Jim said.

"Yeah?"

"Better go back and collect Ur-Quillam, if he's awake," Jim said. "If he's still asleep, see if you can find a way to make sure he doesn't go anywhere."

"You still got that chip that controls the door? We could just lock him in."

"Right," Jim said. He reached into his pocket, found the chip, flipped it across. He rummaged some more, and brought out the plastic envelope with the remaining white powder. "Take this, too. If he goes into convulsions again, just use a little. It won't take much, I think."

"What is that shit?" Kerry said.

"Unless I'm completely wrong, it's the answer to all our problems."

"Ah. Magic powder, then?"

"You could say that."

"I doubt if Elwood or the others would think so."

A shroud of sorrow slipped across Jim's thoughts. "No," he replied softly, "I doubt that they would."

4

Ur-Barrba strode briskly into her brother's chambers and approached the door to his main quarters. Ur-Molla met her there.

"Isn't he back yet?" she asked the old man.

"No. We've received no message from him."

"He's been in that damned compound a long time. What can he be doing?"

"You know your brother," Ur-Molla told her.

"Does he have his minders with him?"

"No, he sent them away. He said they could come back for him when he summoned them."

Ur-Barrba stared uneasily up and down the corridor. In the distance, obvious to her by the faint *wrongness* of their gaits, a pair of strangers were heading toward her. As she watched, both figures suddenly slumped to the ground.

Ur-Molla stared. "What . . . ?"

But Ur-Barrba was already running full-tilt toward the writhing shapes.

5

Ur-Quillam looked a bit shaky, but he seemed otherwise all right. He didn't remember his seizure. For him, it was as if he had suddenly gone to sleep. He told them later that the fits often took him that way.

Jim stood up and let the Kolumban take his seat at the Communer command console. The view of the three screens Jim had running was better there, and he wanted Ur-Quillam to see what he'd discovered with his own eyes, so there could be no mistake.

"Do I look at—?"

"Just the screens. I'll run them from here," Jim said, sitting down at an adjacent workstation. "Just let me know when you're done with one batch, and I'll key up the next."

He'd jury-rigged the stranger translation system to handle Kolumban symbols. At least he thought he had. "Can you understand that okay?" he asked.

Ur-Quillam glanced at the screens, glanced again, then sucked in a deep breath and leaned forward, his attention riveted. "I can read it," he said.

Does he sound a touch grim? Jim wondered. *Let's hope so . . .*

Ur-Quillam turned out to be a methodical reader. He scanned each screen carefully before going onto the next one, and he frequently asked Jim to show him something he'd already seen, whenever some bit of data in a new screen seemed to have a connection.

Jim found himself fidgeting as Ur-Quillam plodded on. How much time did they have? Surely the Kolumbans must have noticed that every stranger on their planet had suddenly fallen dead—not to mention the Communers themselves.

His own research had revealed a new Communer vessel in orbit above Kolumba. Some of the traffic between that ship and the stranger outposts had been encrypted, and he hadn't yet found the keys to break the codes, so he didn't know for sure if this ship was the one that had captured the *Endeavor*. But the mere fact that traffic existed between the planet and the orbiting vessel meant that the Communers must be aware of the disaster that had befallen their outposts. What would *they* do?

And as for that disaster . . . he was *still* not sure precisely what had happened. He knew it had to do with the powder that had filled his cell and brought down the stranger guard. But how could that have also killed *every* stranger?

It was a mystery. His own time on the command console had given him a few hints, but they were flimsy things on which to hang what had happened. He needed to know more. But he didn't know if he would be granted enough time to *learn* more.

And Ur-Quillam looked perfectly capable of spending all the time Jim had while he examined, word by damning word, the tale of what the Communers and their tools, the strangers, had done to him, his family, and his world.

Kerry and Sam had been scouting around the vacant stranger compound, reporting as they went. Kerry messaged back that some unknown stranger security system had closed and locked all the entrances to the compound, which might buy them even more time. And then Kerry sent some unexpectedly good news: he'd located Jim's S&R .75. Now it was tucked into Jim's belt, fully loaded, an uncomfortable yet comforting weight. The only thing he had left from his father, the only reminder of times that had been simple, straightforward, and good.

What a fool I was, Jim mused. *I thought I was miserable, but I was happier than I've ever been since.*

Ur-Quillam shifted in his seat. "Is that all of it?"

Jim straightened. "Yes, all that pertains directly to you. There's a lot more about Kolumba itself, projections, political analyses, anthropology, but it all ties together."

Ur-Quillam sighed. "So it was all a lie?"

"Most of it. About your disease, at least," Jim said.

"Those monsters they sent to help me were actually making sure I stayed sick. It was their disease, not mine."

"Yes, that's what these records say."

Ur-Quillam turned to face him. "You know the most important thing I've learned? And, for me at least, the most surprising?"

"No. What?"

"My father loves me far more than I knew."

"I don't understand."

Ur-Quillam's massive, bony shoulders moved. "The strangers' own analyses were very thorough. They determined that my father was too strong-willed to fully control. But they found his weak spot, the chink in his armor. The place they could strike directly at his heart." He paused. "Me. My father's love for me."

Jim hadn't thought of that, but it was true. And that understanding made him think of Carl Endicott, and wonder whether he hadn't been terribly wrong about his beliefs concerning his own father—if he *was* his father—as well. But he didn't know what to say to Ur-Quillam's epiphany. Maybe there was nothing to say. It was his epiphany, after all.

"What will you do?" he asked.

Ur-Quillam stared at him. "I will stop it. All of it."

"Can you do that?" Jim asked.

Ur-Quillam waved one big hand at a still-glowing screen. "These monsters seem to think I can. I think they are right."

"Let's hope so," Jim said.

"Tell me again about your plan. About Terra, and the drug for this Plcb Psychosis."

"I don't know how much time we have. Somebody is sure to notice what's happened. No doubt your sister and your father have, although the gates to the stranger compound are closed." He paused, thinking. "Can they break in?"

"Not easily, but they do have weapons. Explosives. Things the strangers gave them . . . because my father was so trustworthy. Because he would do their bidding. Because of *me*."

The translation of all this was issuing in truncated metallic tones from the unit hanging on Ur-Quillam's chest, and Jim didn't know enough to tell what the alien's deep, rumbling tones actually signified. The translators never handled emotional overtones very well. But he *thought* Ur-Quillam sounded disgusted. With himself? With his father?

"Ur-Quillam, it wasn't your fault."

"No, I know it wasn't. The fault lies with the strangers, and with the monsters behind them. How could I have known? They offered me the most valuable coin they could. How could I refuse? How could I say that coin was without value?"

"What coin was that?"

"Hope," Ur-Quillam said. "Hope for myself, my family, my people. Don't you think I *wanted* what we saw on those picture machines? How could I look at all the star-spanning races—even your own—and not feel both envy and need? I wanted us to go to the stars, and the only way to do that was to accept what the strangers were willing to give us. So I helped to fool myself. I made their task easier, because I wanted to believe in their tricks." He shook his head. "You're a hard man, Jim Endicott. You've broken my hope. Worse, you showed me that it never existed in the first place. My life has been a greedy sham. I should have let it go a long time ago."

"No, Ur-Quillam, you are wrong."

"How so?"

"Hope kept you alive. False hope, perhaps, but you are here, now, today, and you have learned the truth. And because you still live, you can take up a new hope, one that might fulfill every one of your dreams. If you had died, if you had let go, then there would be no hope for your people."

"Are you sure that you can convince Terra to forgive us our mistakes? To treat us well, teach us and help us to learn? And protect us from the Communers while they do it?"

"No," Jim said slowly. "I'm not sure." Then he looked up and smiled. "But we can hope, can't we?"

Ur-Quillam rose from his chair, came to Jim, and placed one huge hand gently on his shoulder. He looked down, his golden eyes glowing in his hollowed sockets.

"Yes, Jim Endicott, we can do that. We can hope. Together, we can hope."

Kerry came loping into the big chamber, breathing hard, a stranger beam weapon slung over his shoulder. "Jim!"

"What?"

"There's a small army attacking the main gate of the compound. I think Ur-Barrba is leading them."

Jim rose from his seat. "Okay, let's go."

But Ur-Quillam was even faster. "Take me there," he said. "And when we get there, let me handle it."

Kerry said, "Jim. I don't know if—"

But Jim ignored him. He stared into Ur-Quillam's eyes for a long moment, then nodded. "Okay. It's your show."

"Jim . . ."

"It's okay, Kerry. This is the way it has to be."

"You're sure about that? It's a risk."

For some reason, after all that had happened, this struck Jim as hilarious, and he burst out laughing. When he finally ran down, he slapped Kerry on the back and said, "A risk. Yes, it's a risk. So I guess we'd better not do it, huh? I mean, since it's so risky and all." He started laughing all over again.

Kerry finally got it. His lips twitched. He nodded his head rapidly. "Oh God, yes, a risk. And we never take risks, do we, Captain Wild Man." And he started laughing, too, while Ur-Quillam stared at them in blank puzzlement, as he wondered if real understanding between alien races was even possible.

6

Jim's first glimpse of the outside of the stranger compound came from the inside. He'd been unconscious when he passed through those gates originally.

His first impression was how flimsy the security arrangements seemed to be. There was a wall around the compound, of course, but it was only ten feet high or so. He guessed the average Kolumban could have jumped over it without raising a sweat. And even if that wasn't possible, the construction of the wall itself, which consisted of a brick-and-mortar foundation a yard or so high, topped with a wooden wall made of vertical stakes set into holes in the bricks, looked as if even a weakling Kolumban could batter it down with a punch or two.

The gates were beam-and-board affairs, crudely bolted together, and secured by the simplest of locks.

Of course, it wasn't that easy, as he discovered when he reached a rickety observation tower overlooking the main gates, where Sam had set up a sniper's nest.

As he scrambled up the ladder to the small shack swaying at the top of the tower, he realized that the makeshift wooden ladder didn't have the give he would expect from dried, peeled tree limbs—which is what those steps appeared to be, but weren't.

This became more obvious when he entered the room at the top of the observation tower and saw state-of-the-art (well, Communer art, whatever that was) screens and control panels everywhere, surrounding a pair of swivel seats. From what he saw, it looked as if the strangers expected only two technicians to control their entire perimeter defensive system. And when he got a bit deeper into the systems themselves, he saw why his guess had been exactly right.

Everything was a sham, a camouflage, whether designed to avoid offending Kolumban sensibilities or, more likely, to conceal the true extent of the power arrayed here, and mislead the Kolumbans into a false sense of security that the strangers' compounds could be easily captured if it became necessary.

As he quickly familiarized himself with the details of the perimeter systems, Jim realized that unless the Kolumbans had access to modern military siege weapons, they could send their entire population against these compounds with no effect whatsoever.

Inside the low brick foundations were force generators, and the vertical stakes masked cores of monomolecular wire webbing that would, when fully charged, present the equivalent of ten inches of hardened steel alloy. Further, the tops of those stakes housed tiny spray field generators that wove an invisible net of instant death for another twenty feet above the fence itself, a kind of high-tech barbed wire.

Worst of all, at least for any would-be attackers, was the network of "observation towers" marching in ordered, hundred-yard ranks behind the fence. These overlooked the top of the wall, and at first glance seemed nothing more than empty observation platforms, open to the air beneath clay-tile roofs designed only to keep off the worst of the weather.

Only somebody with a suspicious mind—or somebody who understood just how compactly major particle beam weapons could be manufactured—would notice that the floors of these enclosures seemed just a bit too thick for the weight they were designed to support.

Small wonder, he quickly discovered. In these floors were hidden full-traverse field artillery, capable of sweeping not just the areas before the walls, but the entire city of Ald beyond. Should the strangers have wished it, they could have reduced all of the Ir hometown to smoking rubble in less than a minute.

"You haven't been shooting at them?" he asked Sam.

"No. What's the point? It didn't take me long to figure out they weren't coming in here unless we *let* them come in." She looked faintly disgusted. Wanton, needless slaughter had never been one of her favorite activities—although Jim doubted that Elwood, finding himself in the same situation, would have held back. Which was maybe the only good thing he could think of that had resulted from Elwood's death.

A dull *crump* thudded in the air. He settled in the other chair and checked the largest screen, which gave a clear view of the action in front of the main gate.

A large body of Kolumbans, most armed with stun clubs, but some sporadically firing portable beam weapons at the gate (which showed no effect at all except for sudden white-hot bursts of energy backwash), milled in the open area beyond the walls. *Free fire zone*, Jim thought. And in fact another screen was continually updating itself with firing coordinates as the little mob milled furiously about, its bafflement at its inability to pierce the flimsy fortifications becoming more and more evident.

A small white cloud drifted in front of the gate. "They're trying explosives," Jim muttered.

"This is the second or third time," Sam said. "Fat lot of good it'll do them. They'll need pocket nukes to crack that gate."

The crowd had pulled back to let the bomb explode, but they hadn't counted on the energy-focusing capabilities of the screens they couldn't see. Some built-in machine reflex had caught the energy of the bomb and sprayed it back out in a hard fist of energy. Jim saw that two of the attackers were down. Then a large form leaped from the crowd, grabbed each of the wounded by their hair, and dragged them back from the fence.

"There's our buddy Ur-Barrba," he said. "Bet she's pissed off now."

"Who cares?" Sam said, a touch of grim glee coloring her tone. "She can squat out there forever. Be good for her, the impulsive bitch."

"Yeah, that's true. But I doubt if this stuff will keep out the Communers, if they decide to come knocking."

Sam's face went pale. "I'd forgotten . . ."

"Well, I haven't. But we don't have all the time in the world. Listen, you figure out how to run those gun towers?"

"Yeah, it's pretty straightforward. Point and click, mostly."

"Okay. Here's what I want you to do." He told her. When he finished, she stared at him in horror.

"You aren't going out there by yourself? And unarmed, to boot? Jim Endicott, that's the craziest thing—"

He leaned over and silenced her with a kiss. Her lips felt warm and dry, and her natural scent—a dusty blend of clean sweat and something that was almost like lilacs—filled his nose.

"It has to be done," he told her.

"That damned ape is likely to rip your head off before she stops to think."

"Then you'll have to be very fast, won't you?"

She shivered. "You're putting all the responsibility on my shoulders? I don't know if—"

"I can have Kerry do it. But you know you can handle it."

She looked away, then looked back. "Yeah, I can handle it."

"Okay, then. Wish me luck."

She grinned shakily at him. "Wish me a steady point-and-click finger."

He laughed softly, and kissed her again. "I'll be back," he promised.

She stared at him. "I hope so. If she kills you, I don't . . . I don't know what I'll do."

"Even if she does, it won't be her fault. Not really."

"I'll still blame her! I'll still . . ." Her voice trailed off. "I won't be able to help myself."

"Then we'd both better make sure it all goes okay. Hadn't we?"

She nodded slowly.

He kissed her a final time, then turned and walked out of the small, deceptive room. He climbed back down the ladder to where Kerry and Ur-Quillam awaited him silently.

"Everything set up?" Kerry asked.

"Yep."

"I still wish I was up there instead of Sam."

"As you're so fond of telling me, Sam is perfectly capable of handling it. Besides, you have to be out there with me. If Ur-Barrba thinks she's in control of the situation, she might not go off half-cocked."

"Out there with you. Unarmed," Kerry noted sourly.

"Looking unarmed. It won't work, otherwise."

"I won't let her hurt either of you," Ur-Quillam broke in.

"Do you really think you could stop her if she goes nuts?"

Ur-Quillam stared at him, but made no reply.

"Okay," Jim said. "Let's go."

They walked to the gate. Jim waved at the tower. The gate swung out. Several hundred armed, enraged Kolumbans focused on them at the same time.

"Ur-Barrba! Sister!" Ur Quillam shouted.

But the rest of whatever he was about to say was lost in the thunderous rumble of the charging Kolumbans, Ur-Barrba in the lead, bellowing at the top of her lungs.

CHAPTER THIRTEEN

1

J im raised his right hand.

A ravening blast of energy scorched a deep trench across the front of the Kolumban charge. Ur-Barrba, well in the lead of the others, just missed getting her toes fried off as she lunged backward, eyes rolling. She ended up on her huge butt, as the charge toward the gates reversed itself with startling speed.

Thank you, Sam, Jim thought fervently.

Ur-Barrba blinked, momentarily stunned, then began to grope for the beamer she'd dropped. Jim yanked his S&R .75 from beneath his shirt, leaped across the smoking trench, and planted the snout of the ugly weapon right between Ur-Barrba's eyes.

"Naughty, naughty," he murmured.

Ur-Barrba froze.

"Don't shoot her!" Ur-Quillam cried. Jim didn't move. He grinned down at Ur-Barrba's face, showing as much of his teeth as he possibly could.

"Oh, I won't," he said, as much for her benefit as for her brother's. "Unless she gives me a reason. Like twitching even once . . ."

Ur-Barrba didn't twitch.

Ur-Quillam came up, breathing hard, Kerry only a step behind. Kerry scooped up Ur-Barrba's beamer and pointed it at her.

"Got her," he said succinctly.

Jim lowered his pistol and stepped aside, letting Ur-Quillam approach his glowering sister.

"You're on," Jim murmured. "Do your stuff."

Ur-Quillam did his stuff.

2

———

Three hours later, surrounded by the screens of the stranger control center, Ur-Quillam was still doing his stuff, while his sister grew more enraged with his explanation, till it looked to Jim as if she might start spurting steam from her ears at any second.

When Ur-Quillam finished showing her the true story of the Communer treachery, nobody said anything for several moments. Ur-Barrba heaved a huge sigh, then another. She raised her hands and made huge fists, then slammed them down on her thighs.

She looked at Jim. "I still don't like you," she said. "I probably never will. You were responsible for the death of my entire crew, and while I guess I can forgive it—eventually—I'll never forget it."

Jim nodded. "I understand. You're never going to be my favorite Kolumban, either. Many of my own friends are dead because of you— I'll never forget watching Elwood die, or Nikki's head rolling past me. But what I need to know now is whether that is too much of a barrier. Can we forgive enough to work together, work *against* the ones who bear the real responsibility?"

She sat rigid for a while, breathing softly, and finally her fists unclenched. She took a deep breath. "Death to the Communers," she said. She glanced up, her eyes like pits of golden fire. "I will kill them all."

Jim let out a shuddery breath he hadn't realized he was holding. "Not all of them," he told her. "The ones holding my ship will do for a start."

3

Do you think they believed it?" Sam asked.

Jim shrugged. "We'll find out soon enough, I guess."

He, Sam, and Kerry were standing in a small group a few feet away from Ur-Barrba, her brother, and her father. They waited in the broad plaza next to Ur-Quolla's compound.

The old man kept glaring at them. He was, like his daughter, never going to be a true friend. But he was a hard man, not much given to fooling himself, as Jim had learned when Ur-Quillam and Ur-Barrba took him into the stranger control center and showed him the truth of the stranger treachery. In fact, he understood it far more quickly than either of his children, and didn't even bother watching the entire presentation.

About halfway through, he waved one hand and said brusquely, "Turn it off. I've seen enough."

"You understand what they did?" Jim asked.

"They played me for a fool. They crippled my son, nearly killed him, and used *that* to twist me into helping them enslave my own people." He made a deep, growling sound at the back of his throat. "If you hadn't managed to kill every stranger on this planet, I would take pleasure in skinning them all and hanging their bleeding carcasses in the trees for all to see."

Jim swallowed. "All of them?" he said. "Every single stranger died?"

"Yes. From the reports I'm getting, they all died at precisely the same time."

"Was that when the one died in Ur-Quillam's cell?"

"I expect so, yes."

Jim had hoped that would be the case, but until that moment he hadn't been sure. Now, standing beneath the crimson sky, a cinnamon-scented breeze ruffling his dark hair, he hoped that the rest of his deductions would hold true as well.

He'd thought he had a couple of other major problems—how the Communers in space would react to the mass death of their puppets, and how to get himself back to his ship—but Ur-Quolla had solved them in a single stroke.

"I have a communicator in my compound," he said. "I will speak to the Communers and tell them all the strangers have died, but we have no idea how or why, and we need their help. And I will also tell them we wish to send the last of the alien invaders"—he showed a mouthful of teeth—"up to the ship with the rest of the captives. Then I will ask them to send a lander down with help for us, maybe replacements for some of the strangers"—another ferociously toothy display—"and to take you three, under the charge of my daughter, back to the ship that once was hers." He paused. "They think I'm a fool. Very well, that will make it more believable when I act like one. Why would a fool know anything about the sudden death of all the strangers?" He paused. "Or the upcoming deaths of the ones they send me in their lander?"

The sun was warm on their shoulders. Too warm, perhaps. Jim realized he was sweating.

Kerry leaned toward him and said softly, "You think the frackin' Communers really bought it?"

"They said they would send a lander," Jim replied, scanning the skies overhead.

Ur-Barrba left her family and came over to them. She carried one of the big stranger beam weapons. "I don't know how close they are watching, but the lander is due shortly. It wouldn't be good for them to see you standing here in freedom."

Jim nodded. "You're right. Okay, here you go." He put his hands behind his back. "Let's do it."

Ur-Barrba nodded curtly. One of her guards trotted over with several lengths of rope. He bound their hands behind them. Ur-Barrba glanced at the bindings, checked them for tightness, then said, "Any minute now . . ."

A thin, high keening suddenly filled the air. It grew louder, turned thunderous, as a long, burning line traced up over the horizon and across the bloody sky.

Jim stared at it, thinking of Ir-Bakka. Was this the fiery sword that would change things again, perhaps forever?

Time would tell, and would tell very shortly. He moved close to Sam, pecked her cheek, and smiled. "It'll be over soon. One way or another."

She nodded, then leaned into him and kissed him hard on the lips.

A few moments later the alien lander screamed overhead, then let itself gently down, balanced on a pillar of flame. As soon as it powered down, the main hatch dropped open, and a company of strangers marched out.

Ur-Quolla immediately strode toward the strangers and began to rumble at the leader. The others fanned out, some heading across the plaza in the general direction of the stranger compound, one squad peeling off toward where Ur-Barrba prodded him in the back with her beamer.

A few moments later, they climbed the stairs toward the hatch. Jim risked a final glance back at the field, just before they all passed into the interior of the lander. Ur-Quolla was still talking to the stranger leader. Jim noticed that a number of Kolumbans—all heavily armed—just happened to be drifting toward the group of strangers.

Then they were inside. Ur-Quolla shoved him forward into a cabin appropriately sized for huge Kolumban bodies. Jim ended up strapped into a seat big enough for three of him. The strangers watched him in silence with their stony, dusty eyes. Ur-Barrba settled in opposite him, carefully arranging her clanking carry-on bag in her lap so it didn't interfere with the beamer she kept aimed at Jim's face.

"Where are you taking us?" Jim asked.

"To your death," she replied.

A few moments after that, they lifted off.

4

The short trip up to the orbiting *Endeavor* seemed, to Jim, to take much longer than it really did. He didn't know what he might find there. Perhaps, by now, *all* his friends were dead, too, just as Ur-Barrba's crew had died aboard that ship. His stomach lurched queasily at the thought. Ferrick gone? Pretty Jenny? Earnest, tubby Hunky?

He supposed it could have happened. Would it be his fault? Yes, he supposed it would. He could have led them somewhere else. Hell, he could have just shut up when he discovered the true nature of the drug they were peddling.

He shook his head. No, he couldn't have. He realized there was too much of Carl Endicott in him, that stern, righteous, unbending man who had inculcated his notions of good and evil into the boy who thought he was his son so early and so strongly that he could no more have evaded them than he could have discarded his own bones.

Ur-Barrba no doubt blamed herself for the death of her crew, but it had been Jim and the Stone Cowboys who had killed them. In the end, the ultimate responsibility was theirs, just as, if his own crew were dead, the ultimate responsibility lay with their killers—the Communers and their minions.

The knowledge was a bleak comfort, but nonetheless, it *was* a comfort. Although he doubted it would warm him much if his worst fears turned out to be true.

He sighed and glanced at Ur-Barrba, who eyed him steadily. No, that one would never like him, just as he would never like her. But they could work together against a common enemy, and that would have to be enough.

Was this part of the terrible balance Terra's starship captains had to deal with? He suspected that it was. In a galaxy crowded with alien races, some so strange and distant that communication wasn't even really possible, there could be no way that all could get along based on such fuzzy conceits and affection or friendship. Mutual interest, he guessed, would be all that might bind many of these relationships. And when mutual interest didn't exist, the remaining possibilities might be no more than two: separation, or war.

If the Communers were what he thought they were, he wondered how humans and Communers might ever find any mutual interest. Perhaps there was no way, and in the end, the armed might of both races would face each other in a contest where planets were chips, and billions of lives were only fuel for the flames.

Once, when he was a child, he knew he would have thought that a glorious prospect. But though he was still young, he was a child no longer. War, especially war as waged by high-technological civilizations, was an abomination. He had felt only its lightest, most glancing touch so far, but the deaths of Elwood, Nikki, Bobby, even Frank, would disfigure him in some basic sense forever. And he knew that Ur-Barrba, in her own way, felt the same kind of pain.

He supposed that the Communers also felt a similar pain, though he wasn't certain. If he was right about them, what they felt about death might be far stronger—or far weaker—than the scarifying emotions he and Ur-Barrba shared.

He closed his eyes. Well, it would be . . .

The sound of the lander's engines changed pitch slightly. A moment later, the ship lurched. A muffled clang filled the passenger compartment, followed by a long, hollow hiss, as the locks equalized pressure between the two vessels.

Ur-Barrba came out of her seat, growled something unintelligible at the two stranger guards, then poked him roughly in the side with the snout of her beamer.

"Move, you," she rumbled.

The two strangers had Kerry and Sam out of their seats as well. Jim took a deep breath. The door to the passenger cabin opened, and they moved on out.

Jim felt an overwhelming, almost frightening rush of weird nostalgia as Ur-Barrba prodded him through the air lock hatch into the *Endeavor*. It was right here they'd first crashed into the ship, and right here that Ferrick and Elwood stood off the security forces of the *Outward Bound*.

So much had begun in this small chamber, he thought as he stared around, and now so much might end.

Ur-Barrba planted one hand between his shoulder blades and shoved him forward so strongly he lost his footing and tumbled hard to the deck, landing on his shoulder. With his hands bound behind him, he was unable to break his fall. A white bolt of agony coursed down his arm, numbing it.

The sound of tramping boot steps sounded from beyond the entry chamber. More strangers coming to take the captives in hand.

Jim squirmed, trying to right himself, as Ur-Barrba growled and reached down to grab him. Framed by the Kolumban's massive legs, Jim could see the other two strangers shoving Kerry and Sam into the entry. The rhythmic thud of the approaching feet grew louder.

As Ur-Barrba leaned over, the shoulder bag she carried swung forward, toward him. Its flap was open. Jim thrashed again, pulling his bound wrists beneath his butt, then bringing his legs through the circle of his arms in a fluid gymnast's movement that sent another wave of pain surfing through his shoulder.

Now his hands were in front of him. Ur-Barrba growled again, her breath hot in his face as she crouched over him. Her right hand swooped close, something bright flashing from her fingers.

Her razor-sharp blade sliced through his bonds in a single stroke. It all happened so fast that the two stranger guards had still not registered what was going on. They were both still turning toward the commotion when Jim's now-free hand snaked into Ur-Barrba's bag and came out holding his S&R .75.

He darted around Ur-Barrba's tree-trunk legs and shot the still-uncomprehending stranger in the chest, as Ur-Barrba twirled, light as a ballet dancer, and raked her beamer across the middle of the other guard.

"Don't kill him!" Jim screamed, as the second guard collapsed, his guts spilling from the smoking wound in his belly.

Ur-Barrba lunged for Kerry, spun him, and slashed through the ropes around his wrists, then turned to Sam as Kerry scrabbled in her bag for his own weapon.

It all happened in a few seconds. Jim was still rising to his feet, sweeping the muzzle of his pistol back and forth, when the thunder of approaching footsteps reached a crescendo and several figures lunged into the entry chamber.

He shot the first one, another stranger, without thought, barely conscious of Kerry's ripper and Ur-Barrba's beamer humming and belching behind him. More figures fell, in silence or shrieking their lungs out.

Then another shape darted from the ruby gloom. Automatically, Jim targeted him, his finger slowly squeezing the trigger of his pistol—

He froze.

Elwood stood there, a deeply *interested* look on his face, grinning slightly.

He was unarmed.

"You aren't gonna shoot me, are you, Captain?" he said.

"Elwood!" Kerry yelled.

"Jim, no!" Sam gasped.

Jim stared at the apparition, his heart suddenly a rolling thunder in his ears. His hand tensed, then relaxed. Slowly, he lowered the pistol.

Elwood nodded, sighed, and stepped forward.

Jim shot him in the right leg. The force of the rocket slug was so enormous it tore Elwood's leg off almost to his thigh. He dropped as if somebody had taken an axe to his ankles and thrashed on the deck, shrieking.

"Jim!" Sam cried again.

He leaped toward Elwood, who was gushing blood like a fire hose. "Kerry, do one of the strangers! It doesn't matter which one, just *do it*!"

He half slipped on the slickly puddled blood that surrounded

Elwood, caught his balance, and came to rest next to the dying boy. He got one arm beneath Elwood's head and lifted him, as he fumbled in his pocket with the other.

Elwood looked up at him wordlessly, his chest heaving as he fought for breath.

"Jim . . ." he managed.

"Breathe," Jim whispered to him. "Breathe deep."

He brought the opened packet of white powder up beneath Elwood's quivering nostrils. A silvery cloud puffed out, settled over Elwood's straining features like an evanescent shroud.

Elwood lurched, heaved—and died.

Ten feet away, two more Elwoods, both of them armed, rushed into the chamber. As Elwood's face went dull and blank beneath its powdering of white dust, they staggered, their own momentum carrying them the rest of the way in. But they fell like sacks of concrete, and they were dead before they hit the floor.

The silence was like a continuous explosion in their ears.

Slowly, Jim put Elwood's head aside, laid him down, and climbed to his feet, that terrible hush screaming inside his brain.

He looked around. Eight corpses littered the stinking chamber. His feet made soft, wet, sucking sounds in the thick layer of warm blood that coated the floor. More blood was streaked down his front—it looked as if some mad painter had gone crazy with a brush.

His knees vibrated with some malign electricity that drained the strength from bone and muscle. He was afraid to move any further. Even a single step might bring him down.

Kerry and Sam's faces seemed very far away, pale, wavering blobs. Even Ur-Barrba looked stunned. All the light had gone from her eyes, and for a moment Jim thought, with a slash of horror, of dusty stones.

All at once, terror and revulsion clogged his throat. Everywhere he turned, nothing but blood. Hot, bitter, coppery, salty, a sea of blood. He saw it, he smelled it, he could even *taste it*.

He raised one shaky hand and wiped the back of it across numb lips, then stared down at the crimson streaks. The burning in his eyes overflowed, carved glimmering trails through the blood mask that covered his face.

This was war, too. Blood and guts and stink and the terrible death of friends.

Sam said, "Jim?"

His lips—his blood-washed lips—moved faintly, but nothing came out. He gestured weakly, gulped, swallowed, and tried again.

"Oh God, Sam . . . I killed him. I killed him *again*."

He leaned over, put his hands on his knees, and vomited. That came out bloody, too, as if his body was trying to physically expel all the sickness and danger and ruinous, bloody death he'd seen, even perhaps caused, since this mad adventure began. Back when he'd thought the finest thing in the world would be to become *captain* of his own ship.

He convulsed as if it were his soul he was heaving up.

Maybe it was.

And even if it wasn't, perhaps it was something almost as precious: his childhood, his youth, his shining dreams.

After this, in some way and some place deep inside himself, he would always be old.

5

They found seventeen more Elwoods and forty strangers, all sprawled where they had fallen and died. They crept through the ship like ghosts haunting a graveyard, and when they found Ferrick and some of the other kids locked in a cabin, it was as if they had somehow raised the dead.

Perhaps they had done that, as well. Or saved them from becoming something far worse; an army of clones, a host of the living dead.

As he stared into Ferrick's face, Jim wondered what he had killed up there in the entry chamber. Had it been Elwood himself? But it couldn't have been. He'd seen Elwood burning beneath a bloody sun. Yet it had been Elwood he'd cradled in his lap, and in the end, he thought that some part of that Elwood had known him.

They held a meeting in the same echoing hold where Jim had once watched Kerry and Frank fight over his captaincy. A fight he'd thought then was the most important event of his life. Now it seemed trivial. Worse than that; useless. Of all the principals and conspirators involved in that combat, only he and Kerry were still alive. And for what?

There was no formality to this gathering. They all hunkered on the deck in a ragged circle. Hunky slumped against Jenny. Ferrick's broad shoulders drooped. Ur-Barrba, who, even seated, towered over the humans like an Everest of fur, looked as if she'd just returned from a visit to a graveyard.

Everybody was exhausted. Terror had leached vivacity from them. They were a choir of hollowed eyes and sagging muscles, and the stench of death hung over them like a greasy, smoky pall.

"What the frack did they do to Elwood?" Ferrick asked at last.

Jim sighed and shook his head. "They didn't do anything to him. By the time the bastards got hold of him, he was dead."

"He came and talked to me, you know," Ferrick said softly.

"It wasn't him," Jim said. "It was them. The Communers. Sort of them, at least."

"But he talked to me, Jim. He knew me."

"Maybe he did. Ur-Barrba, what did you do with the bodies from that firefight? I don't know, because I didn't wake up till you had me in a cell."

"We took them to the stranger compound, as they asked."

"Was anybody still alive, besides me and Sam and Kerry?"

"No. They were all dead. I made sure."

Once again, Jim remembered that he would never like this huge, hulking, murderous alien. Although, in fairness, that was no doubt how Ur-Barrba thought about him. Murderous.

It wasn't much fun thinking about himself that way, but he had to admit she probably wasn't wrong. Not about him, not about humanity in general. He supposed there were other races, meek, mild, pacifistic races, for whom death and destruction weren't historical pastimes. Hell, weren't genetic imperatives. But none of those races, as far as he knew, had achieved greatness on the broad stage of the galaxy. There were the wolves, and the lizards, and now the Communers. And the Kolumbans themselves. They seemed to have all the requisite characteristics for survival, the prime of which seemed to be a willingness, even a lust, for killing.

We are not a pretty people, he thought. *And if I ever do become captain of a real starship, I probably won't be pretty, either.*

He wondered if he could live with that. He supposed he could. All the others seemed to have done so.

A deep, echoing sadness filled him, so sudden that it was shocking, and all the more so because he couldn't at first divine its source. Then he realized: it was the passing of a dream, or at least the tarnishing of it. And if the dream was tarnished, was it still the same dream? Must he find another?

I'm only sixteen, he wanted to shout at them. *I'm too young for this. I'm still a fracking kid, for God's sake!*

But whatever god—or gods—might have been listening to his anguished inner cry, none chose to respond, and he listened for a long moment to the thunderous echoes of his heart—and they told him nothing.

"So what you're saying," Ferrick went on, "is that they cloned him or something?"

It took Jim a moment to realize that Ferrick was talking to him. "Or something," he replied. "I'm not really sure what the Communers are. If they're even a race or species as we think of the terms. It could be they're more like a . . . like *software*. Except they build the machines they run on out of flesh and blood."

He shrugged. "Or maybe they are a kind of group mind, like the way their clones operated. That's why the powder killed them all, by the way. At least I think it is. It's the only explanation that makes sense."

"I still don't really understand that," Sam broke in.

"I think the strangers were all one entity. Made of lots of individual parts, sure, but one whole *thing*. And they turned Elwood into another one. Whether the Communers were actually *inside* those bodies, or just created them and told them what to do doesn't really matter. They were still *connected* somehow, and what the powder did, it acted on them just like a computer virus through their network—only enough distance could stop it. It broke those connections, broke them so violently that the individual machines died instantly, just the way that if you snap the connections in a local area network, the individual machines won't work right anymore. 'Cause it's the *network* that's alive, not the individual components." He paused, wondering if he should tell her the rest. He wasn't sure. He would have to tell her sometime, would have to tell *all* of them. But maybe not yet.

"But the powder didn't kill me," she said. "It saved my life."

He closed his eyes a moment. If he answered that one, he would *have* to tell them. Or maybe not. Once he replied, most of them would probably figure it out on their own. Sam would, he was sure.

Well, the hell with it. In for a penny, in for a pound. Or, in this case, maybe a ton, given what Ur-Quolla was doing with the entire *gir* and *ilka* harvests down on Kolumba while they were sitting around talking up here.

"It did exactly the same thing to you that it did to the strangers and the Elwoods," he said.

"But . . . what? That can't be right. It killed them, but it didn't kill me. Exactly the opposite. What you're saying doesn't make any sense."

"Yes, it does." He reached over, took her hands, stared into her eyes. "I made the stuff that saved you from a blend of *gir* and *ilka*. Both were plants created by the Communers, but for different purposes. The *gir* was designed with the human metabolism in mind. It had to be, if they were gonna turn it into a drug that would kill us. But the human hooks were there, built into it from the beginning. The *ilka* was a different story. It was made for the strangers, or at least that's what they told the Kolumbans. It was supposed to help a disease the strangers were prone to, something the Kolumbans called the shaking disease, which sounded suspiciously like the Pleb Psychosis."

He squeezed her fingers. "So I combined them. Used the human-based hooks to load the *ilka* cure into the human system. It worked on you. It killed the strangers."

"Yes, but it killed Elwood, too. And he was human." She paused, searching his eyes. "Wasn't he?"

"No. He looked like Elwood, and there may even have been a little bit of Elwood left inside those clones. But most of him was alien. And when the alien bio network that controlled him, all of him, was broken, then he died. But the powder *saved* you, by *doing exactly the same thing*."

She thought about it, as he waited for her to get it. Beyond her, Jim could see Kerry's eyes slowly widening. Ferrick's, too.

"Are you saying . . ." Sam said. She shook her head, but she seemed shaken. Uncertain. "I'm not part of any bio network."

"I think you *are*. I think that's all that the Pleb Psychosis *is*. Some kind of vast neural network that doesn't work quite the way it's supposed to work. And the white powder fixes the network, frees you from the deadly side effects."

And for some reason he thought again of the dark hooded man striding across a sea of stars like a god. That man frightened him half to death. But something else about the dark, striding figure, so shrouded in secrecy, called to him, called with a force so strong he was only now beginning to realize the power of that compulsion. He could close his eyes and feel that arcane summons *sucking* at him.

"But that . . . Jim, there are *billions* of Plebs! Surely you don't think that *all* of them are somehow involved in this . . . this *thing* you're talking about?"

"Not all," Jim said grimly. "But most of them."

"That's *insane!*"

"Well, it's maniacal, I'll give you that."

"Do you have anything at all to back this up? Besides your own crazy theories?" Two red blotches burned on her cheeks. He couldn't understand it. She seemed angry with *him*, as if the psychosis was somehow his fault. For a moment he faltered. But then he gathered himself and went on. Maybe once she understood . . .

"Look, Sam. What would you do if you were in charge of ConFed, and somebody came along and told you they had a cure for the Pleb Psychosis. A cure they claim they've been seeking for years?"

"Why, I'd . . . I'd tell you to bring it to me as fast as you could. I'd give you whatever you wanted. I'd make you a . . . a frackin' *prince*, if I had to."

"Well, me and Ur-Barrba and her father have been on a hyperwave conference call most of this afternoon. Ur-Quolla using the hyperwave in the lighter we left downplanet, and me and Ur-Barrba here on the *Endeavor*. We ended up talking to some guy I don't know, but who I think is high up in ConFed. Maybe *very* high up. And we told him about the Communers, and the attempts on the colony ship—by the way, he confirmed the *Outward Bound* has been destroyed."

A chorus of muted gasps greeted this news. Jim looked around the circle and nodded.

"And we told him about a possible cure for the psychosis. You know what he said?"

Slowly, Sam shook her head. She had gone deathly pale, as if expecting to hear a death sentence. Or maybe worse.

"He told us to stop working on it immediately. He said he was sending a fleet as soon as possible. A big fleet, strong enough to defend Kolumba against the Communers. And with enough technicians to 'properly develop' the cure. Those were his words. 'Properly develop.'"

"Well . . . maybe that's exactly what he means. You're no super bio-chemist, Jim."

"We offered to transmit the formulas immediately. He wouldn't let us do that. He said it was a top-secret matter, now. Oh, and one other thing. He demanded—not asked, demanded—that everybody who knew anything at all about the matter do nothing further, and present themselves to the ConFed fleet when it arrived."

"That . . . doesn't sound right, somehow."

"Because it isn't. I think that fleet will never arrive. At least not the way you hope. I think *somebody* will come, maybe even a fleet. A small one, though. You don't need a big fleet if you plan to use a sunbuster."

She goggled at him. "A *sunbuster*? Why would ConFed want to do that?"

"It would be a hell of an efficient way to get rid of all the evidence. And the witnesses, too, if they were stupid enough to hang around and wait for it."

"But this is all . . . you're just guessing."

Jim shook his head. "Ur-Quolla doesn't think so. In fact, he's so scared he's got everybody on Kolumba hauling in the *gir* and *ilka* harvests as fast as he can. And they're using a huge jury-rigged synthesizer based on my own analyzer to distill about a ton of that white powder. Ur-Quillam will be bringing it up here in the next couple of days. Which should be enough time. I hope. If they send the fleet direct from Terra, it'll take them a week to get here."

"My God, Jim, if you think ConFed is planning something like that, why did you tell them where Kolumba is?"

"We already had, before this guy threw in all that stuff about not proceeding any further, and awaiting the arrival. All that bullshit. But at first we wanted that fleet here. We don't know where the Communer ship that captured the *Endeavor* got to. It could still be hanging around somewhere."

She rocked back, her expression shaken. "Jim, I still don't . . . can't . . . *why*? Why would they kill a whole planet?"

"Think about it," Jim said softly. "If I'm right, then somebody has built a bio network out of Plebs—maybe billions of Plebs. You don't do that from a basement in your house. Whoever it is—whoever *they* are—they must be very, very powerful by now. Because they're using that network for *something*, and I doubt if it's for keeping their Christmas card lists up to date."

"How do you know they're using it?"

"Sam," he said. "The Plebs keep going psychotic."

"But . . . I'd *know*, wouldn't I? I'd have to, if I was a part of something like that!"

"Do you think Elwood did?"

She looked away. Her lips thinned. "Who was this guy you talked to, anyway? Why do you think he's so all-frackin powerful?"

"He felt like it," Jim said. "That's all I can say. He just felt like it."

"What was his name?"

"Delta," Jim said. "I don't think it's really a name. A rank, maybe, or a code word. But Delta. That's what he told me."

Kerry stared at him. "Did you say *Delta* . . . ?"

6

———

Jim sat in the captain's chair of the *Endeavor*. He ached, but it was a good ache. He'd brought the ship into the outer reaches of the system. No more risky in-system hyperspace jumps, not if he could help it.

They'd seen no sign of any Communer presence. With any luck, the ConFed fleet would arrive before the Communers realized what had happened. At least before they could do anything about it.

Of course, the ConFed fleet might be no blessing, either, not for Kolumba, at least. But he had done what he could to prevent that disaster, also. In fact, the last part of that was unfolding before him now, down on the huge holoscreen at the front of the bridge.

He stared at the screen and looked at his own face. Strange, it wasn't at all like looking in the mirror. Or maybe that face on the screen was a lot older, more worn, more *experienced* than the face that had looked back at him from his bathroom mirror before he turned sixteen, when the world was a lot simpler, and a lot more full of dreams.

"*The Kolumbans have recalibrated the Communer deep space early warning systems. Should they detect any attempts to interfere with their system, or their star, the hyperwave transmitter I left behind on this ship's lighter will contact me immediately. I have one ton of the crystalline powder that cures the Pleb Psychosis. If I receive the appropriate message from my friends on Kolumba, I will immediately proceed to*

Terra and distribute the cure as widely as possible, by any means possible." The face on the screen paused. It looked to Jim as if that face meant every word it said. He hoped whoever saw that message would think so, because he had meant every word.

Of course, he hadn't said every word he'd meant.

He did have nearly a ton of the cure in his hold. They had started calling it "netcracker," or "crack," for short. And he did plan to use it, though he wasn't exactly sure right this minute how—or where—he would do it.

Kerry had told him what he knew about the mysterious Delta. So there was that. And there was the dark man and his field of stars. But most of all, somewhere back in the ConFed were his mother and father. And one hell of a lot of unfinished business.

Once, he'd thought his next task would be the Communers. But he'd seen enough of war to last him for a while. Let that ConFed fleet, or Delta himself, worry about the Communers.

I've got a few things to take care of myself, he thought. And they're all back home. So let's go home.

On the screen, the face that was his face finished its warning. Jim slapped a switch and the holoscreen vanished in a round of applause from those in the control seats ranged below him. Sam, and Jenny, and Hunky. And Ferrick. And, of course, Kerry.

No Elwood, though. And too many others gone as well.

He settled his shoulders against his seat, and lifted his hands above the main touchpad of his console.

"Mr. Korrigan?"

"Aye, Captain."

"Take her out. Let's go home."

"Aye, aye, Captain."

They jumped.

BIBLIOGRAPHY

Humankind has always been a traveling race, a race of adventurers and colonizers. It is no accident that, come what may, one of the abiding dreams of the human consciousness remains the vast realms of space and our eventual role there. Nobody doubts that we plan to go. The only questions are when, and how.

There is a wealth of books that try to answer both questions. For the best, see:

The High Frontier by Gerard K. O'Neill, 1976, Bantam Books/SSI Press, ISBN: 0-9622379-0-6

Colonies in Space by T.A. Heppenheimer, 1977, Warner Books, ISBN:0-446-81-581-0

Toward Distant Suns by T.A. Heppenheimer, 1979, Stackpole Books, ISBN:0-449-90035-5

The Millennial Project by Marshall T. Savage, 1992, Little, Brown & Company, ISBN:0-316-77163-1 and 0-316-77163-5

Space Colonies edited by Stewart Brand, 1977, Penguin Books, ISBN: 0-140-04805-7

2081: A Hopeful View of the Human Future by Gerard K. O'Neill, 1981, Simon & Schuster. ISBN:0-671-24257-1

Space Trek: The Endless Migration by Jerome Clayon Glenn and

George S. Robinson, 1978, Warner Books, ISBN: 0-446-91122-4

The High Road by Ben Bova, 1981, Pocket Books, ISBN: 0-671-45805-1

A Step Further Out by Jerry Pournelle, 1980, Ace Books, ISBN: 0-441-78583-2

The Illustrated Encyclopedia of Space Technology, 2nd ed. by Kenneth Gatland, 1989, Orion Books, ISBN: 0-517-57427-8

There is also a plethora of information on the World Wide Web. Start with the wonderful Space Settlement FAQ, written and maintained by Mike Combs. The bibliography above is taken in part from that FAQ, as well as the web sites listed below:

Space Studies Institute: Founded by Gerard O'Neill, this nonprofit organization funds research into space manufacturing. Features the SSI slide show and several good articles.

http://www.ssi.org

Space Settlement: Web page maintained by Al Globus, features pictures of space habitats.

http://www.nas.nasa.gov/NAS/SpaceSettlement/

The Living Universe Foundation: Founded by Marshall Savage, author of *The Millennial Project*. Dedicated to expanding life into space.

http://www.luf.org/

The PERMANENT Web Site: PERMANENT is an acronym for Program to Employ Resources of the Moon and Asteroids Near Earth in the Near Term. This web site goes into deeper detail on many of the subjects of this FAQ.

http://www.permanent.com/

Island One Society: Group emphasizing the political freedom that may be possible in space habitats.

http://www.islandone.org/

National Space Settlement Design Competition: Academic contest for students to design their own space habitats.

http://space.bsdi.com/index.html

The Artemis Society: Devoted to a return to the moon with an emphasis on commercial development.

http://www.asi.org/
Moon Miners' Manifesto: Required reading for all lunar prospectors.
http://www.asi.org/mmm/mmmhome.html
The Space Frontier Foundation: Pushing for the opening of the high
frontier to the average citizen and cheap access to space.
http://www.space-frontier.org/

Military history might seem an odd subject to call a science, but that
is exactly what it is, a division of the larger classification military science. In our day and age, where high-tech smart bombs send us video
pictures before slamming into their targets, one could wonder what
value the battles of Julius Caesar might hold for the warriors of the
future.

Quite a bit, actually. As Robert Heinlein and many others noted, for
all the glitz and glitter, one still has to take the ground and hold it. For
that you need battle tactics, and almost nobody has done better at it than
Gaius Julius Caesar, though two thousand years have come and gone
since he conquered the Gauls and noted in a phrase learned by every
school-age Latin scholar that "Omnia Gallia in tres partes divisa est."
(All Gaul is divided into three parts.)

Alesia is generally considered to be Caesar's finest military hour. For
an excellent, though fictionalized account, read:

Caesar: A Novel by Colleen McCullough, 1997, William Morrow &
Company; ISBN: 0-688-09372-8

For another approach, this one delineating six of the greatest gener-
als of history—Caesar, Alexander the Great, Ulysses S. Grant, Horatio
Nelson, Napoléon Bonaparte, and Georgi Zhukov—see:

*The Great Commanders: Alexander, Caesar, Nelson, Napoleon,
Grant and Zhukov* by Phil Grabsky and David G. Chandler, 1995, TV
Books Inc.; ISBN: 1 575 00003-2

Street gangs, even, or especially, those involved in the drug trade, have
highly evolved, complex social structures. For further discussion, see:

Delinquent Boys: The Culture of the Gang by Albert Kircidel Cohen,
1971, Free Press; ISBN: 0-029-05770-1

BIBLIOGRAPHY

Chinatown Gangs: Extortion, Enterprise, and Ethnicity (Studies in Crime and Public Policy) by Ko-Lin Chin, 1996, Oxford University Press; ISBN: 0-195-10238-X

Always Running: La Vida Loca: Gang Days in L.A. by Luis J. Rodriguez, Reprint edition, 1994, Touchstone Books; ISBN: 0-671-88231-7

8 Ball Chicks: A Year in the Violent World of Girl Gangsters by Gini Sikes, Anchor edition, 1998, Doubleday; ISBN: 0-385-47432-6